# Romantic Suspense

## Danger. Passion. Drama.

**Colton Threat Unleashed**
Tara Taylor Quinn

**The Bodyguard's Deadly Mission**
Lisa Dodson

# MILLS & BOON

Tara Taylor Quinn is acknowledged as the author of this work
COLTON THREAT UNLEASHED
© 2024 by Harlequin Enterprises ULC       First Published 2024
Philippine Copyright 2024                 First Australian Paperback Edition 2024
Australian Copyright 2024                 ISBN 978 1 867 29815 1
New Zealand Copyright 2024

THE BODYGUARD'S DEADLY MISSION
© 2024 by Lisa Dodson                     First Published 2024
Philippine Copyright 2024                 First Australian Paperback Edition 2024
Australian Copyright 2024                 ISBN 978 1 867 29815 1
New Zealand Copyright 2024

MIX
Paper | Supporting
responsible forestry
FSC® C001695
www.fsc.org

Published by
Harlequin Mills & Boon
An imprint of Harlequin Enterprises (Australia) Pty Limited
(ABN 47 001 180 918), a subsidiary of HarperCollins
Publishers Australia Pty Limited
(ABN 36 009 913 517)
Level 19, 201 Elizabeth Street
SYDNEY NSW 2000 AUSTRALIA

Cover art used by arrangement with Harlequin Books S.A.. All rights reserved.

Printed and bound in Australia by McPherson's Printing Group

# Colton Threat Unleashed
Tara Taylor Quinn

MILLS & BOON

A *USA TODAY* bestselling author of over one hundred novels in twenty languages, **Tara Taylor Quinn** has sold more than seven million copies. Known for her intense emotional fiction, Ms. Quinn's novels have received critical acclaim in the UK and most recently from Harvard. She is the recipient of the Readers' Choice Award and has appeared often on local and national TV, including *CBS Sunday Morning*.

For TTQ offers, news and contests, visit www.tarataylorquinn.com!

Dear Reader,

Welcome to The Coltons of Owl Creek! We've got family saga galore as the small, close-knit town of Owl Creek is besieged by a danger with no name. The one constant? The Coltons, of course. These brothers and sisters and cousins are there for each other without fail. Questions are asked, they bicker some, but they lay down their lives for each other. Every single time.

In *Colton Threat Unleashed*, book one, we've got the whole family together as the oldest Colton sister, Ruby, a veterinarian, finds out she's pregnant at the same time someone seems to be stalking her. Her sisters think the stalker is the father of her baby. Ruby knows differently, but can't say. The father is her older brother's friend, Sebastian, a war vet whose dogs are his life. They had a one-night stand after one of Sebastian's dogs almost died. And, well, the saga begins...

Please, turn the page and jump in with both feet. Twelve seasoned authors have poured their hearts into these books. Each one has its own complete story, suspense and romance. And together they make an emotionally intense, compelling experience that will keep you hooked all year!

*TTQ*

# DEDICATION

To the Colton readers, who are the most important
and cherished members of the family.

# Chapter 1

He'd had sex with her. What in the hell had he been thinking?

Clearly, he hadn't been thinking. Sitting in his office, Sebastian watched her through his window. Weeks had passed and still he watched with too much interest as the beautiful veterinarian left the kennel where she'd been seeing to a pregnant dog after her regular office hours at her clinic in town and headed toward his house. That messy bun—did she always have to wear it looking so bedroom-like?

The long blond hair had been down by the time she'd left his bed. Had she loosened it? Had he? Things had been so intense that night, with Oscar being injured by shrapnel from gunfire. Him calling Ruby in the middle of the night, afraid the heavily bleeding canine was going to die on him.

As if sensing his current unrest, the golden retriever mix—and Sebastian Cross's personal canine companion—grabbed a stuffed octopus and brought it over to shove it in Sebastian's hand. He and Oscar had started Crosswinds together, training search-and-rescue dogs, like Oscar, for people all over the country.

Oscar didn't seem at all fazed by that night two months before. But Sebastian, thinking he'd lost his only family member—pacing in his home while Dr. Ruby Colton worked on Oscar—had been thrown back a few years. He'd thought he'd left the panic behind. And the vet—she'd finished with Oscar that night and had come upon Sebastian in a particularly low moment.

One no other human had witnessed before.

How it had gone from there to...sex...

Wiping a hand down his face, he turned from the window in his office—chosen because of the view of his property—and headed toward the back door off the kitchen. The door Ruby used every time she came to check on Oscar.

He grabbed another quick glance out the kitchen window. When it was light outside, the vastness of his land, the lake at the edge of it, soothed him.

Anytime of the day or night, sight of the kennels did the same.

Neither was enough that evening as he heard the knock on his door.

In the two months since "the night," as he'd come to think of it, neither he nor Ruby had mentioned what had happened. They'd both pretended nothing had. They had to, right? Owl Creek was a small town. And she not only tended to the search-and-rescue animals that he trained, but she also gave free medical treatment to the PTSD dogs he provided to veterans who needed them.

Still…if nothing else, he had to apologize.

To her. To someone.

She was his best friend's little sister, for God's sake.

Wade Colton was the closest thing he'd ever had to a brother. And he'd gone and…

The knock came a second time.

He hadn't been himself that night. A reminder to never, for any reason, allow himself to be around another human being when he was sinking.

Oscar stood at the door, staring at him. With a nod, Sebastian opened it.

And, while the dog gave his doctor an enthusiastic greeting, Sebastian took the few seconds that Oscar gave him to find an easy smile and paste it on.

Shamelessly using Oscar as a distraction, Ruby spoke with real joy to the boy wagging his tail and licking her chin, avoiding the big mountain man with his shaggy dark blond hair and beard. She related to animals so much better than she did to people. Understood them. Fully accepted and embraced their unconditional love as her top need in life.

Steadying the dog with her tone of voice as she told him, "Good boy, stay," she checked his left hindquarter and left shoulder—both areas from which she'd had to remove shrapnel that fateful night two months before. Thankfully, neither had suffered muscle damage.

"He's healed nicely," she said to Sebastian, still running her fingers lightly over the dog's fur. "You're such a good boy," she told Oscar. "No bad guy's going to slow you down, huh?"

She stood then. The next thing on her agenda not quite as easy as telling the man his dog was well. It had to happen eventually. The longer she put it off, the less chance she'd seem at all natural as she met the blue eyes of the man she'd known most of her life as her older brother's friend.

A boy they'd seen only during the summers he'd spent at his family's cabin in Owl Creek—the home in which he now lived.

She remembered quite clearly how he'd left one year in August as a boy and had returned the following June as a man. He'd grown what had seemed like a foot, had a mustache and shoulders that blocked out the sunlight when he'd stood in front of her, teasing her about her crooked pigtails. She'd developed a bit of a crush on him.

Something that had faded as she, too, had changed, grown, become a woman.

So why had she, how could she have…?

Her gaze met his. Neither said a word.

They had to talk about it, didn't they?

At some point?

If for no other reason than to verify that they weren't telling another soul, ever, what had happened. Most particularly not Wade.

Big-brother hassles, she did not need.

Sebastian's smile wobbled a little. She opened her mouth…

And jumped, clutching Sebastian as a painfully loud crack sounded, followed immediately by a crash, and then a squeal and deep growl from Oscar. The canine was on point, staring at the door.

"Was that a gunshot?" The words burst out of Ruby, followed by a frantic "I'm calling 911."

Sebastian was already at the door.

"Wait, Sebastian! Are you kidding? Don't go alone. Wait for the—"

He was out the door before she'd finished her sentence.

With Ruby and Oscar in the house, and all the dogs on the premises at risk, no way Sebastian could wait the ten minutes it would take the police to get from town to his five acres on the lake. He had a woman—and dogs—to protect. Grabbing his gun from the metal cabinet on his way out, he kept his back to the cabin as he rounded the corner.

The unsolved shooting in the middle of the night two months before still weighed heavily on his mind. He was in full United States Marine Corps mode as he moved with supreme precision, darting his head out for only a second, focusing in that second and pulling back as the second came to a close.

With the sun starting to set, his vision was somewhat compromised, but he got the job done.

As soon as he knew all four sides of the house were secure, he darted behind the small medical building to get closer to the kennel. His biggest concerns were the outside stalls and large, fenced-in, play-and-training area. His four employees—a full-time trainer and three part-time assistants who cared for and cleaned up after the dogs—were gone for the day. But a dozen dogs were there. One pregnant and another with a litter of new puppies.

At the back corner of the medical building, he repeated his earlier process, shot his head out, pulled it back.

And, adrenaline pumping with a dose of anger, he

flattened himself against the wall. Someone had completely shot out Ruby's windshield. A red glare blinked on and off in the glistening mess and Sebastian turned to see flashing lights coming up Cross Road—the private drive leading to his cabin. He wasn't fool enough to go after a shooter on his own with the professionals arriving. He just kept watch over the kennels until several officers spread out around the entire training facility, and then, with his same military precision, made it back into the house with his bad news.

"You had no business going out there alone!" Ruby's tone was sharp, instigated by the fear raging through her, as Sebastian came back inside the house.

Sitting on the floor with an arm around Oscar, who was half in her lap, she flushed as she saw the displeased expression on the man's face. "I'm sorry. I have no business speaking to you like that," she amended, embarrassed.

And scared.

And so thankful that he was standing, unharmed, in front of her.

His shrug made her want to hug him. "You're probably right," he said. "Military training doesn't preclude sitting around and waiting for others to save you." He was still frowning, though.

"What?" she asked, standing, fear returning in full force.

"Your windshield's been shot out."

Hers? But...

Brow creased in a hard line, she stared at him. The shots two months before—she hadn't been anywhere near the place. She'd assumed whoever had been responsible then was attacking again...

"*My* windshield?" she asked.

Even if the shooter wasn't one of Owl Creek's citizens, who all pretty much knew her SUV, both front doors had been painted with the emblem and name of her veterinary clinic.

Did someone have a problem with Colton Veterinary Clinic?

Or with her personally?

Mind spinning, she couldn't come up with any viable explanation.

It's not like she had any exes. There was no one whose heart she'd broken who could want revenge. No new girlfriend who could be jealous.

And at the clinic?

She drew a total blank.

Shivered.

Sebastian, hands in his pockets, was squirming a bit on his feet, as though he was having a hard time keeping his distance.

At least, that's the way her mind was currently translating his actions.

Because she was afraid, she knew. Felt uncharacteristically vulnerable.

"I'll need to have it towed," she said then, unnerved by her unusual reaction to the burly man as well. They'd had sex. She didn't want, or need, any complications from the one-night mistake.

Of that, she was certain.

She was a doctor. Had built a hugely successful practice and was only thirty.

No room in her life for the prepubescent girl who'd once had a crush on the kid Sebastian had been back then—in spite of the fact that as a grown woman, she noticed that the inches and muscles and facial hair he'd sprouted were attention getting.

No room, ever, for any full-time romantic relationship. It just wasn't what she wanted.

"As soon as we get the all-clear from the police, I'll help you clean out any personal stuff and drive you back to town." The man had found his voice.

She nodded. Smiled at him. "Thank you."

And felt a niggle in her lower belly when he smiled back.

As it turned out, Sebastian didn't get a chance to assist Ruby with her vehicle clean-out, or to drive her back to town. As soon as word got out that Ruby Colton had called the police after being present at Crosswinds Training when there'd been gunfire—and, of course, it had gotten out, since she was daughter to the man who owned half the town—her brothers had shown up in full protective mode.

Chase and Wade were at Sebastian's door within half an hour of the police showing up. Fletcher, the middle of her three older brothers, a detective with the Salt Lake City police force, seven hours away, was on the phone, demanding answers.

Chase, the oldest at thirty-six and vice president of Colton Properties, went straight to Ruby. Within seconds, while Wade still had Fletcher on the phone, Chase had her on his cell with their mom and dad, assuring Jenny and Robert that she was absolutely fine. She'd heard a shot was all.

She'd been safe inside the house, checking over Oscar, the entire time.

Sebastian heard it all peripherally. Wade, the youngest brother, fellow marine and as a kid, best friend to Sebastian, made a very determined beeline for Sebastian, demanding to know every detail of what had happened. And when the police came in, saying there was no sign of a shooter anywhere on Crosswinds' five acres, all three men had been ready with questions.

It turned out there was a fresh set of what appeared to be male shoe prints, size ten to eleven, out by the main road. It was likely the shooter used a scope, and never actually set foot on Sebastian's land.

Which set off more conversations between those in the room and those still on the phone. Did that mean Ruby had been targeted?

Or was this more seemingly random violence aimed at Crosswinds? And hitting Ruby's car would be more impactful than the previous shot into brick that had sent shrapnel into Oscar, who'd woken up Sebastian in the middle of the night to go out.

Oscar had heard someone outside that night. Sebastian couldn't prove it but was certain of the fact. And he told Wade so when his friend asked again about the previous shooting event.

The February ground had been clear at that time, but with the wind chill, they'd been looking at below-zero temperatures and everything had been too hard for footprints. By morning, the land had been covered with a couple inches of snow. Investigators had never found a shell casing.

And they hadn't yet in this instance, but they intended to keep looking.

While Sebastian was still answering Wade's questions, in between Wade talking to Fletcher, Chase was escorting Ruby out of the cabin. Wanting her off the property as soon as possible.

Sebastian watched her go, saw her look back at him, or at least at Wade and him, with something like regret in her eyes. He felt it, too. Had wanted to be the one to help her. Since the damage had happened on his land.

But when he glanced over and saw the way his friend, who was ending the call with Fletcher, was watching his older brother and younger sister leave, the look of resignation on his face, Sebastian made a sharp return to reason.

Ruby hadn't been looking at him. She'd been watching over her big brother. The sorrow had been for Wade—not due to some ridiculous desire to have Sebastian be the one to take her home.

He welcomed the return to reality.

"How you doing?" Sebastian asked Wade then, a question that, a few years before, would have been completely in line with their friendship.

In the past few years, after Sebastian had left the Marines—they'd joined together, but Wade had stayed in—they'd naturally grown apart.

"Not you, too," Wade said with disgust, turning so that Sebastian's view was of the left side of Wade's face only.

The move, more than the words, spoke to Sebastian. He'd received his share of pity since he'd been back in Owl Creek. Had hated it every bit as much as Wade must. "You think you're less than you were?" he asked quietly. Wade hadn't been back long, but the man hadn't come to see Sebastian yet, or accepted any invitations to meet for a beer.

Anger filled Wade's one good blue eye with such

intensity that Sebastian took a step back. And heaved an inner sigh of relief.

"Hell no. I can still take your ass. You want to give me a try?" Wade half growled, and Sebastian fully understood the note of real frustration in Wade's half-teasing invitation. Growing up, the two of them had taken on each other more than once. Wrestled. Tried to prove who was stronger.

No one had ever been seriously hurt, but they'd each landed bruises a time or two.

"Lead with both fists, man, just like always," Sebastian said then. "You know what you know. That there's nothing less about the man you are or the power you wield with one seeing eye instead of two. It's up to you to show the rest of the world."

Wade grunted. Clearly not looking for any warm feelings at the moment.

Sebastian got that, too. A hundred percent.

"People only know what you show them," he said, anyway. Because he'd learned the lesson himself after his stint in the Marines had ended so abruptly.

And because Wade Colton had picked him up, out of his insecurities, and set him straight every single summer his parents had deserted him at the cabin. Leaving Sebastian with a nanny to watch over him rather than a family to have fun with.

"You told me once that my value was whatever I thought myself worth," Sebastian murmured, remembering.

The words had been with him ever since.

# *Chapter 2*

Ruby was not happy about her vehicle being shot at. She'd been shaken up by being present during the potentially danger-filled episode.

She wasn't buying in to any theories that the violence had anything to do with her in particular. Simply a matter of wrong place, wrong time.

There'd be vandalism at her clinic, or her home, if she was the target. Threatening notes or texts. Some kind of altercation.

She'd lived in Owl Creek her entire life. Had never been in a long-term relationship. Wasn't involved in anything controversial, anywhere. Nor had she ever lost an otherwise healthy patient on her operating table. She'd had to deliver some sad diagnoses. None of them brought any anger toward her to mind.

Even online, her clinic had only good ratings. Not a single one-star anywhere.

She'd spent the evening going over the facts, multiple times, with her brothers and sisters and parents. She answered texts from her uncle Buck, whose ranch Wade had recently started working and living on, and from her cousins, too.

And had eventually given in to the pressure and agreed to spend the night at her folks' well-secured home.

"You're a Colton," her mother, Jenny, told Ruby as she peeked into the room Ruby had picked for the night, one of the four upstairs guest bedrooms in her parents' newest home. The bed faced a wall of windows overlooking the lake. "Being a Colton makes you prey to anyone who could want to hurt any of us. Your father's built an empire. You don't do that without making enemies. Even if it's just someone who is jealous."

Her mother was right, of course.

But that didn't change the fact that, with the shooting of Ruby's windshield, Crosswinds was the logical target. Which meant that Sebastian and his dogs, out there all alone, could be in danger.

She told herself, as she was lying in bed worrying about him, that having been there, hearing the gunshot, was what was keeping her awake.

That and the fact that his programs—both search-and-rescue, and the pets he trained to help veterans with PTSD—were vastly important to her, too.

Plus…he'd been a peripheral part of her summers growing up.

And she'd had sex with him.

No. That wasn't it. And she wasn't going to think about it.

She just needed to make sure that he agreed that they'd never, ever talk about it or tell anyone. Ever.

Then she wouldn't have to worry, every time she saw him, that he'd bring it up. Or she would. That it would somehow show up and stand there between them.

She needed it done.

She reminded herself of this fact when, three days later, Sebastian called to tell her that Jasmine, the German shepherd she'd been checking on the night of the shooting, was having her babies. With three other veterinarians working full-time at the clinic, she was able to take a break and head out to Crosswinds.

Ruby had counted ten puppies on the X-ray she'd done earlier in the pregnancy. Sebastian said she'd only had seven and was straining. Ruby made the ten-minute drive in eight. Pulled up with her brand-new windshield, parked on the opposite side of the little dark green medical building, her own little Crosswinds mini clinic, and ran inside.

Sebastian stepped aside as soon as he saw her, and she went to work. Saw the sack of fluid blocking the birth canal, a situation made worse by the fact that the eighth puppy Jasmine was trying to push out was a breech. Ruby handled both issues without pause, and half an hour later, she stood over the litter, telling the big mountain man, with his shaggy hair and beard, and who was clearly worried about both Jasmine and her newborns, "You've got ten healthy pups there."

She cleaned up. Grabbed her shoulder bag, intending to leave Sebastian with the newborns he was perfectly capable of looking after. "I'll send the bill over," she told him. The search-and-rescue portion of Crosswinds was funded by the individuals and organizations that needed the dogs and paid for her services. Usually, she took the time to make out the charges on the computer that was set on the counter for that purpose.

For all he knew, she was pressed to get back to the clinic. Truth was, she wasn't feeling like herself around him.

"I'll walk you out."

She nodded, though being alone around him was what she was trying to avoid. At least until the jitters from the gunshot the other night dissipated a bit. But he was probably right. The conversation had to happen.

Since he clearly had a plan in accompanying her to her vehicle, she waited for him to start.

"I want to pay for your windshield."

What? Not at all what she'd been expecting.

"Insurance covered it. And no. It wasn't your fault."

"The police are looking into Crosswinds being targeted," he told her what she'd assumed all along. And yet, her insides tightened uncomfortably at the news. For Sebastian. And the dogs. "I guess there've been a couple of anonymous complaints about the noise. When one dog barks, they all think they have to get their two cents in." He shrugged.

"Anonymous noise complaints?" she asked, slowing her steps as she frowned up at him. "You're on five acres, ten minutes outside of town. Who's close enough to hear anything?"

His nod didn't feel like a good thing. "That's what I said. And what everyone else seems to get. Which apparently points more to the fact that I'm being deliberately targeted for some reason. They're looking into that now. They didn't find a shell casing the other night, either, so right now, all they have to go on is a size-ten shoe print. It's not like there are traffic cams out here.

And we have no way of knowing if the guy came from town or the opposite direction altogether."

The tension in her grew. Sebastian, the dogs, his programs—they helped so many people. And after burning herself out at the clinic, on call 24/7 for years, she'd hired more people and had been finding her own personal energy and joy return as she volunteered for Crosswinds's PTSD dog-placement program.

"Have you had any disgruntled customers?" she asked. "Someone whose dog didn't perform as they thought it would?"

He shook his head. As she'd known he would. Sebastian personally guaranteed the satisfaction of his clients. His dogs served as they were trained, or he took them back and found them good homes as pets. In all the years he'd been in business, it had only happened once that she knew of.

"I've opened my life up to the police," he said then. "We've had multiple interviews and they're following up on everyone I can ever remember knowing…"

"What about back in Boise?" she asked then. Sebastian had grown up in the city, two hours away from Owl Creek, summering at the cabin on the five acres that was now his permanent home. Property that had been in his family for decades. "Your father was a doctor, right? Maybe something to do with one of his patients?" She was grasping, she knew. Just needed him to have the answers that would bring his nightmare to an end.

"Again, the police are investigating every possibility…"

"What about cousins?" She knew he'd been an only child, but… "Is there someone who felt cheated by you getting the family property?"

He shook his head. "I'm it, in terms of family."

The words were like a punch to her solar plexus.

She couldn't imagine…with five siblings and four cousins right there in town, all growing up together—sometimes all ten in the same house—the idea of having no one…

"What do the police say?" she asked, caring much more than she wanted to. He was a friend of her brother. Not her own intimate concern. Peripheral. Not personal. No matter how many times she'd repeated the words in the past two months, her heart was not getting the distinction.

But Ruby knew she had to.

She'd had enough friction in her home growing up. Her parents, while respectful of each other, weren't close. So she'd basically had two different authoritative sources to deal with on her own, going back and forth between the two, to get any sense of what was expected from her. Then, being one of six growing kids, with bright minds and a ton of energy, and add in her aunt and uncle's broken marriage and her mother trying to compensate for her own twin leaving her husband's brother by taking care of his four kids…

She had enough family to last her a lifetime. And an aversion to sharing her home on a permanent basis. Except with the various animals she fostered.

Which meant that any personal feelings she might think she was experiencing for a man with whom she'd had sex were just going to have to go away.

She didn't want them.

Sebastian watched the expressions flit across Ruby's face as he told her the current police theory was that the culprit was exhibiting behavior that was escalating. Going from bogus complaints to random gunshots.

He couldn't read her. She'd always been such a curious mixture of compassion and aloofness…and not just with him. Growing up, Ruby had been the one who didn't join in. Who preferred to make her own entertainment—reading a lot of the time—rather than jumping in a boat with the rest of them and shooting out across the water.

Didn't much matter what she was thinking. His missive was going to be the same.

"You have to stop coming out here until we get this resolved." He put it right out there. The other night…if she'd been in her SUV when the bullet had hit…

No.

"I've got puppies to watch over," she told him, chin high, as she stood up to him. She didn't even give him so much as a shake of her head, to let him know she was disregarding his wishes. "Fletcher told my parents that if this guy was out to hurt someone, he'd have done so," she continued. "Oscar's injury aside," she added. Then just kept talking. "This person had no way of knowing that Oscar was even out there. That was an anomaly."

The police had said the same. And Ruby Colton was acting as though if she just kept on talking, not giving him a chance to get a word in, she'd change his mind.

"This is my property," he butted in when she took a breath. "All that matters here is what I say. And I'm not going to take a risk with your life…" He'd been up all night that first night after her car had been shot. Dealing with cold sweats and a mind filled with images of what could have happened.

"So you're going to let all the people relying on

search-and-rescue dogs miss out? And all the veterans needing dogs to help them live normal lives…they just go without?"

She had spunk. It got his ire up.

And his appreciation, too. In spite of himself.

"Believe it or not, Dr. Colton, we raise a lot of healthy dogs here who will get along just fine without your services for the time it takes the police to find this guy." He was smiling. Crosswinds needed her. She knew how grateful he was for her help—most particularly with the volunteer veteran program. But his gaze bored into hers, as well. Her safety was nonnegotiable.

"Like today?" She upped her chin another notch. "You confident you'd have ten healthy puppies right now?"

"I only called you because I knew you were coming out to check on Jasmine, anyway," he told her. "And the police say that the perp's pattern, based on the shootings and the complaints, is to hit weeks apart. But this is it. Now. Today. No more until whoever is out to get me is in jail."

"My parents still think the shooter could be after me. With all of the public fundraising I've been helping with, everyone knows how much the work out here, the services Crosswinds provides, means to me."

He hadn't thought of that. If the police had, they hadn't said so.

He wanted to fire her on the spot.

And knew it wouldn't do any good if someone was already after her.

"I don't buy it," she told him. "If someone wanted to hurt me, they'd be going after my clinic. Putting up bad reviews. Accusing me of letting an animal die. Flattening my tire while I was at work…"

She stopped as he cocked his head, frowning, but half smiling, too.

"What?" she asked.

"You sure you aren't the perp?" he teased, even knowing it was in no way a joking matter. Just…someone had to ease the tension.

"I've…given this a lot of thought over the past few days. Having my windshield wiped out, and then dealing with each member of my family—every one of them a know-it-all, mind you—I've had to shore up my defenses. My car was shot at while I wasn't in it. And it wasn't even on my property. That does not mean I need to go into hiding."

He opened his mouth to argue with her, but she got the next word in first. "What about you?" she blurted. "You're right here, going on with your life, running your business, and every single one of the occurrences has to do with this place. Yet, you aren't shutting down."

"I can't shut down. Too many people rely on—"

"Exactly," she interrupted. "So what makes my life more valuable than yours?"

He had an answer for that. But the challenge shooting at him from those unrelenting green eyes kept his mouth shut.

For the time being.

She climbed into her SUV. Shut the door on him. Started the engine.

But he and Ruby Colton weren't done talking about the matter.

And when they were, he intended the last words to be his.

# Chapter 3

Ruby had no cause to visit Crosswinds that next week. Sebastian emailed photos of the puppies feeding, telling her that Jasmine and the gang were doing great.

She'd already released Oscar from her care.

He had no new dogs arrive.

And she knew he was deliberately trying not to need her.

There also hadn't been any other signs of unrest in her life, or, according to Wade, Sebastian's, either. Things at Crosswinds had been running smoothly, with no upsets all week.

And yet, she was still feeling…jittery.

Because she needed to talk to him. To get things back on an even keel. Before Wade noticed the tension between them. The last person she'd ever want to know about her fantastical mistake with Sebastian Cross was her overprotective brother. Wade was a strong adversary on a good day. But with having his entire life upended after being blinded in one eye, with his career in the Marines no longer an option, he wasn't in a good place mentally.

Sitting in her office on the second Thursday in April, waiting for her two younger sisters, who'd called to say they were bringing lunch to share with her, she wondered if she should drive out to Crosswinds after work. Just get everything with Sebastian out in the open. It was not her way to let things linger, or fester, unless doing so let them slowly evaporate into the ether.

Having sex with a client, who was also her brother's close friend, didn't seem to be something that would fade away quietly.

She wasn't acting like herself.

Hence, her sisters bringing lunch to share with her in the middle of their busy weekday schedules. Checking up on her. Or just wanting her to know they cared.

Either way, after the shooting ordeal at Crosswinds, she wasn't going to convince her family that she was fine—her usual, untroubled, independent self—until she started to feel that way again.

She had to talk to Sebastian.

Hannah and Frannie, twenty-eight and twenty-six, respectively, came in together. Hannah was carrying a reusable insulated bag bearing the logo of her catering business, and Frannie had a cardboard holder with three cups of coffee from her bookshop café.

Unusually happy to see them both, she stood to help divvy up the goodies they'd brought, taking a foil-wrapped package out of Hannah's bag, hoping for her sister's signature grape-laden chicken-salad wrap, and caught the scent of coffee when Frannie removed the lid and set a cup in front of her.

One whiff, and the jitters she'd been feeling turned into cold sweats. Her head swam.

And she opened her eyes to see both sisters staring at her with panicked gazes.

One on each side of her chair. A hand each on the arms of her chair.

Her chair.

She'd been standing.

"What's going on?" she asked, hearing the weakness in her tone.

"You passed out, that's what!" Hannah, the no-nonsense Colton, stated emphatically. "We need to get you to the ER."

"I'm fine," Ruby said, sitting up. Waiting for the light-headedness to return. "Seriously," she added, when it didn't.

"Come on, Ruby," Frannie, the quiet bookworm, and baby of the family, said, her hazel eyes imploring. "You don't just pass out for no reason."

"You're a doctor," Hannah added, her green-eyed gaze no less impactful. Because looking into Hannah's eyes was like looking in a mirror. Colton eyes. Similar to their dad's eyes, and exact replicas of Uncle Buck's. "You know this isn't normal or fine."

She was a doctor of veterinary medicine. Not a doctor for humans.

But because Hannah's point was valid, she agreed to let them drive her to the clinic in town. Just to get her vitals and fluids checked. It made good sense.

And would reassure her little sisters so that they

didn't go running to their mother with the news of Ruby's little mishap.

"It's the stress," she told them as they waited for results of the urine and basic blood tests, which would, she was sure, show no infection. "I haven't had much of an appetite."

"I knew you weren't fine," Hannah said, sitting on her right, leaving the chair on the left to Frannie. "You could have been in that car for all the shooter knew. If he shot from as far away as the cops said he did. Of course, you're overwrought."

"The stress from everyone watching over me," Ruby said dryly. "I love you all so much, you know that, but eleven of you, twelve including Uncle Buck, texting me at least once a day…"

Hannah glanced at Frannie, across Ruby's perfectly healthy frame. "Yeah," she said. "We should have been better organized about that." Her middle sister's tone held definite I-told-you-so isms.

"Hannah wanted us on a schedule, so there'd be a timeline," Frannie allowed. "Fletcher said it was better, since you live alone, if we each just check in throughout the day."

Her words dropped off. And Ruby didn't know whether to laugh or groan.

As it turned out, she didn't have a chance to do either as the physician's assistant who'd seen her entered the small exam room.

The first thing the woman did was glance at Hannah and Frannie, then her gaze landed on Ruby. "Is it okay to talk in front of your sisters?"

Frannie gasped, clutching Ruby's left hand so tight that she felt her baby sister's nails digging into her skin.

"Of course it is," Hannah said, covering Ruby's other hand with her own.

Just laying her palm there. Warm. Supportive.

She met the medical professional's gaze. "Yes," she said calmly. There was nothing a simple urine or basic blood test was going to show in such a short period of time. Her vitals had been fine. But then she'd been certain of that before she'd come in.

The PA looked only at her and said, "You're pregnant."

She couldn't be.

It had to be a mistake.

As soon as she got to her own transportation, she was going to get a home pregnancy test—out of town, so no one would see her buying it—and prove the PA wrong.

Sitting in the front passenger seat of Hannah's car, Ruby continued to feel the weight of her sister's open-mouthed, disbelieving stares—just as when they'd been in that tiny room at the clinic.

A room that was now forever ingrained in her brain and would probably give her nightmares in the years to come.

Huh. Her, pregnant?

The woman who knew one thing about herself for certain.

She couldn't ever see herself wanting a husband.

Let alone raising a family.

She could not be pregnant.

"Who is he?" Hannah's question came the second she closed her driver's door.

"There is no *he*."

"You had yourself inseminated?" Frannie asked from the seat directly behind Hannah.

"Of course not. Either of you see me as the mothering type?"

"Yes," they answered in unison. Shocking her so much, she turned to stare at each of them in turn.

"You know the last thing I want is to get married and have a family."

"I know that's what you say, but you'll make a great mother, sis." Hannah's tone was unusually soft. Compassionate. The woman was so in love with little Lucy, she figured everyone would feel the same after giving birth. "Now, who's the father?"

No way. Uh-uh.

"No one."

Sebastian Cross wasn't even her lover. He most definitely was not the father of the child. Even the one that only existed in one PA's words and on a chart.

Charts could be corrected.

Words, maybe not forgotten, but the mistake could be forgiven.

Yes, that was it.

There'd been a mistake. Picking up her phone, she dialed the clinic. Asked to speak to the doctor. Insisted on holding, was still holding when Hannah pulled up at Colton Veterinary Clinic, parked and turned off her ignition.

"I didn't even know you were dating anyone," Frannie said, as they all just sat there.

"I'm *not* dating anyone." She didn't even try to keep the exasperation out of her tone. And then, as reality hit her, she filled with total panic.

Her sisters thought she was…

Turning in her seat, phone still to her ear, she stared them both down. Hard. A big-sister, I'm-seriously-going-to-tell-every-secret-you've-ever-had stare. "Do not breathe a word of this to anyone," she said then. "I mean it. Not Mom. Not anyone."

There was no compromise on that one.

She saw the glance Frannie and Hannah shared. It didn't bode well and did nothing to calm Ruby.

"I'm serious," she said. "My medical information is private."

Frannie shook her head. "But, Ruby…a baby…"

Ruby cut her off with a glare. "It's a mistake," she said. "Which is why I'm waiting to speak to the doctor in charge today. And even if it wasn't, this is my business to share or not, to handle how I see fit, not yours."

She was dead serious.

Hannah, the only mother among them, sighed. And Ruby drew her first easy breath since the PA had made her ridiculous announcement. "Just tell me that you weren't…forced, or…"

In light of the recent happenings at Crosswinds—her car being shot at, all the worry her family had shared on her behalf—she felt Hannah's concern to the bone. "I swear to you, sweetie, no one has ever touched me, like that, without my full cooperation."

"So you did sleep with someone," Frannie said softly. "Who is he?"

"No one," she said again, calmer now. "It's a mistake."

Hannah still sat, door closed. She was the one Ruby knew she had to contend with if she wanted her secret kept. Frannie was naturally quiet. Reserved.

"I won't say anything about the baby," Hannah said

then. "You're absolutely right, it's your secret, your business. But if you are pregnant, your secret's going to start showing itself before too long."

Hannah had been there and done that.

Ruby nodded, looked at Frannie. "You'll keep this to yourself?"

"Of course, I won't say anything." Frannie looked as though she wanted to say a lot, though.

"Say it wasn't a mistake…would you have it?" Hannah asked.

Ruby knew what Hannah was really asking. And was fairly certain her sister wouldn't judge. Whether Hannah agreed with Ruby's decisions or not, she would want to be supportive. "I wouldn't *not* have it," she said softly.

And had to escape the car before she threw up all over her sister's upholstery.


A week had gone by since the shooting of Ruby Colton's windshield and her subsequent visit to deliver Jasmine's last three puppies.

A week without seeing her.

Sebastian was still on edge. Someone had shot up his property. Twice. Causing damage both times. First the shrapnel hit Oscar—though, arguably, that had likely been collateral damage, not intentional—and then Ruby's windshield had been shattered.

And the complaints…

Who was out to get him? When would they hit next?

The not knowing was getting to him—maybe that was the perpetrator's goal?

Give him an enemy to fight, and he'd get the job done. Sitting around waiting for an attack from an unknown source that could come without warning?

All the Marine training in the world wasn't going to prepare him for that.

Not well enough to suit him, at any rate.

So he focused on the training he excelled in—search-and-rescue. Each dog generally took two years of weekly training before being ready for a search-and-rescue mission. At Crosswinds, he had canines at every level of training, all the time. Those just starting out. Those almost ready to go to work. Some had handlers who came to Owl Creek, stayed at one of the motels in town that gave Crosswinds a special rate and came out to the facility to work with the dog before taking them home.

Search-and-rescue wasn't an easy business. Or a cheap one. He ran a highly accredited, elite organization. Yet, a lot of handlers were volunteers. Sebastian did what he could to keep his costs down for them. His property, while outfitted as well as the best training facilities, was all basic brick and wood buildings—all painted one color. The military green he preferred.

And he did as much of the training himself as he possibly could.

The second Thursday in April, he'd spent the morning and midafternoon at Buck Colton's ranch. One of the golden retrievers, Elise, a relative of Oscar, was at the tail end of avalanche training. He'd needed to take her to an unfamiliar site, with another dog and avalanche tools—spikes and shovels—lying around.

Malcolm Colton—Wade's cousin—and Malcolm's SAR dog, Pacer, had helped with this particular session many times.

They had ridges dug out for that purpose. Sebastian would bury Malcolm in one, under a couple of inches of dirt with full breathing capability, and give his trainee—that day, Elise—Malcolm's scent, while Pacer was given a different smell to follow and went off for his prey. The idea was for Elise to ignore Pacer and all other distractions to follow Malcom's scent, and then be willing to dig to get to him. For which she'd get a treat.

The girl performed in record time. Every single time they repeated the exercise. Getting to Malcolm, and then racing straight to Sebastian to lead him to her find.

At one point, when the burial point was on a steep incline, she stayed with the uncovered body and barked until Sebastian came to her.

Sebastian was just heading back to his truck, with Elise trotting, head high, at his side, when Wade came out of the barn. He called out to Sebastian.

In jeans, a long-sleeved denim shirt and cowboy boots, Wade walked with the same sense of command he'd displayed in his US Marine Special Forces uniform, black eye patch and all.

"Quick question for you," Wade said, petting Elise's head as he reached them. "My sister Hannah just called. She says that Ruby's been dating someone, has some boyfriend, but won't say who. Hannah thinks this might be the guy who shot out Ruby's windshield. Said she was really odd, to the point of angry, when Hannah asked her about him. None of us had any idea she was dating anyone. Did you?"

Sebastian shook his head immediately.

Ruby had a boyfriend?

A development he'd never even considered.

Relief didn't flood him, as he'd expected it to.

She might have mentioned that detail.

Sleeping with another guy's woman was not his way.

And could cause unforeseen complications—like a guy targeting her at Sebastian's place.

"Anyone who's been at the kennels that she might have had contact with?" Wade continued to grill him. "She's been spending so much more time out there, and with the handlers you have coming in…"

He thought over the people who'd been in and out of Crosswinds, when Ruby might have been there, who might have taken exception to Sebastian's friendship with her, from before Oscar was shot.

That's when the violence had started. With Oscar's injury.

But the complaints had started before then.

And had continued.

She'd slept with Sebastian while she'd been seeing someone else?

Gut clenched tight, he had to admit it made sense. They could have taken offense at how much time Ruby spent with Sebastian's dogs. Maybe not believing she was just seeing the dogs. The jealous boyfriend…shooting up his place in the middle of the night. Complaining about noise. Then still seeing his girlfriend's vehicle there until dawn?

Maybe she'd explained she'd just been there for Oscar. Had sworn that nothing else had happened. She'd sure been eager to pretend that it hadn't.

Maybe the guy had seen her with Sebastian again.

Made sense that the violence would have escalated.

And most definitely fit shooting out Ruby's windshield while she was parked there.

"I can't think of anyone," he told his friend honestly. Sebastian was reeling from the sudden turn of events. Did the guy know Ruby had slept with him?

How could she not have at least told him she had a boyfriend?

If the perp was this violent without knowing the full story, how much further would he go if he found out they had slept together?

"How sure is Hannah that she has one?" Sebastian asked, careful to keep his question completely casual. Curious. But, because of the violence, concerned, too.

"She's positive. She wouldn't say how she knew but she told me that her proof was one hundred percent positive. She's worried sick."

Sebastian didn't blame her. After that news, he was, too.

Worried about the potential for more violence, worried about Ruby's safety. And a bit concerned about the incredible disappointment coursing through him.

He'd never have taken Ruby Colton for one to screw around on her boyfriend.

Or to have sex with Sebastian and not tell him she was in a relationship.

Not that the sex meant anything.

But with the violence, her windshield... They'd talked about possible threats. About any potential enemies.

Why hadn't she at least told him about her secret possibility?

For that matter, why did she have to keep it secret at all?

That question led to an unpalatable, and yet possible answer.

The guy was married.

And Sebastian's day had just gone down the toilet.

# Chapter 4

Ruby talked to the doctor at the clinic.

And after work, she went back to the medical facility on her own for a second urinalysis.

She'd had a period since she'd slept with Sebastian. Granted, it had been light, but that happened occasionally, based on her workload and stress level.

And since making the hellacious mistake of having sex with her older brother's friend, she'd been fairly stressed.

Besides, they'd used a condom.

She hadn't been kidding, or doubting herself, when she'd been so adamant with her sisters regarding her test results.

She'd known they couldn't be right.

And being a doctor, she also knew that sometimes test

results were skewed. A faulty test strip. Or technician. Both happened, even in the best hospitals and clinics.

Then she'd thrown up.

Something she hadn't done since she was a kid.

And she'd gone into full doctor mode. Symptoms. Tests. Results.

When symptoms contradicted each other, test a second time, just to be sure.

And there she was, walking out of the clinic, just after seven, having watched the test being run, and the results appear, right along with the doctor.

She, Dr. Ruby Colton, DVM, was pregnant.

And in two years' time, there was only one man she'd had sex with.

Once.

She had to talk to Sebastian.

Thought about calling him.

A charged conversation like the one they were bound to have…might be better over the phone.

Easier, at least.

In her car, she glanced at the second set of test results. And knew she had to drive out to see Sebastian. He deserved to see the results, both sets of them.

She stopped by her office and made copies of both test forms she'd received that day, put her own in a folder and folded his and put them in her satchel. She lifted the leather bag up to her shoulder, and, with a "have a good evening" to the evening staff, she left.

On a mission.

A distasteful one.

The best way to handle those were to get them done immediately. No overthinking.

Just complete the task.

Keeping her mind on her meeting with Sebastian, trying to find words for the conversation that would result in the least drama, she felt like the ten-minute trip out of town to his place lasted for hours. She found no words.

Every sentence her mind started sent her into panic mode and she had to abort the effort.

Abort.

She wasn't going to do that.

She'd told Hannah she wouldn't even before she'd been pregnant.

Before she'd known she was.

*I've got this paperwork I feel I should show you, Sebastian, out of courtesy, but it doesn't require any involvement from you at all. Not even a name.*

The sentence appeared as she pulled up Cross Drive.

No one knew she'd slept with him.

No one ever had to know.

Yes. That thought worked better than any other one she'd had since throwing up in her own clinic's parking lot.

Drawing up by Sebastian's back door—because coming from the medical building or the kennels, the back entrance was the one she always used, not because she was afraid to leave her car in view of the road—she pulled open the screen door to administer her customary two short knocks.

The mission was underway. Would soon be complete.

"Eeoowooah!" The male holler rent the air, filled with anger. With gut-wrenching pain. Sending shivers up and down her spine. Instinctively pulling the screen to her body, crouching up against the wooden door keeping her from the house, she glanced at the yard around her.

And toward the kennels.

The sound came again. Animalistic.

Clearly coming from the house. Heart pounding, thinking only of the pain inherent in the sound, she turned the doorknob. Felt it give. Hurried inside, already reaching for her phone.

And saw Sebastian sprawled back in a recliner, eyes closed, with an open laptop on its side on the floor.

"Yaawwwah!"

She jumped back as the horrible sound came from his throat, just before he threw a heavy fist at…nothing.

And it hit her.

Sebastian. In the Marines, just like Wade.

Early discharge.

His head was still, his cheeks and lips skewed right, then left, the muscles scrunching one way, then the other, like he was cringing from one side of his face at a time. All of it hiding beneath the light beard.

She'd taken a training class on PTSD before Wade came home. Mostly for herself. She'd needed to know what her adored older brother might be going through.

Sitting at attention, Oscar watched Sebastian. Glanced at her. And back at his owner. The retriever was a search-and-rescue dog, not one trained for the veterans Crosswinds also served.

She couldn't get close or risk being hit. But Oscar could. She'd seen the dogs in training. Had helped train some over the past few months.

Moving behind Sebastian's chair, she motioned for the dog, pointing for him to sit beside the chair. The big mountain man was striking up, out, with the movements he was making. Oscar's head was below the arm of the chair. Oscar knew to nudge Sebastian's hand for a treat. She waited.

And felt tears fill her eyes as, less than a minute later, the dog, hearing Sebastian cry out, nudged his owner's hand.

Sebastian woke up, his eyes glazed at first, and then crystal clear as he focused on Ruby, moving out in front of him.

She'd never felt less welcome anywhere in her life.

"What in the hell are you doing in here?" Sebastian heard the accusation in his tone, wasn't sure he had the wherewithal to withhold it.

Wasn't sure he wanted to try.

"You have no business being here," he said, angry. With her, yes. Because she was there. Because she'd slept with him without telling him she had a boyfriend.

Because, with everyone working so hard to find out who was behind the attacks at and on Crosswinds, she hadn't said a word.

But most of his anger was aimed at himself.

He'd been gone again—had slipped into the hell that was the part of his life no one ever saw. Or knew about.

"I wanted to talk to you," she said, sounding like some doctor, not the compassionate woman, the friend, who'd been offering so much of her time to Crosswinds. "I heard you holler out…"

Seeing his computer lying sideways on the floor, he snatched it up. Closed it. Stood. "How long have you been here?"

"Long enough."

And didn't that just put the plunger on anything good about the day.

"Yeah, well, I'm fine—you can go now." Oscar nudged his hand and Sebastian went to get the dog the treat he'd already asked for once.

Wait. Oscar nudging his hand…had woken him. He looked at Ruby.

"I made him sit by you," she said. "I didn't know what else to do…"

She cared.

That mattered.

Not for any reason he could come up with.

But it did.

And it hit him why he couldn't seem to get by what had happened between them two months before. It wasn't the sex calling to him, although it had been—yeah—but…she knew.

She'd sat with him, held conversation like any other time, making no mention of the panic attack he'd been suffering. She'd just…brought him down. By being herself.

She knew.

And he wasn't sure he was sorry.

He had no idea what to do with that.

"Oscar's a search-and-rescue dog," she said then, as if his dog was the issue at hand.

He nodded.

"Because you don't want anyone to know you need one trained for…"

"I don't need one," he said gruffly. Then leaned on the corner of the wall, one ankle crossed over the other, as if entertaining in the near dark, while standing, was a normal thing.

Ruby turned on the light by his chair.

Sat down in the one just like it a few feet away.

"How often do you have them?"

He sat, too.

Why not. The day couldn't get any worse.

"I hadn't had one in more than a year." He'd told her the truth, was glaring at her again. "Until the night Oscar was shot. Or rather, the night after that."

He'd had the panic attack first, the night of the shooting.

And sex. He'd had sex that night, too.

With a woman who had a boyfriend. Possibly a dangerously jealous one.

How could she not have told him?

Not only because his place was being attacked, but also...to protect herself? Why wasn't she telling anyone? Didn't make sense to him.

But then, he wasn't at his best.

Not even half best.

"But you had them when you first came home?" Her softly uttered question hit him in a weak spot.

He needed to get rid of those.

All done. No more.

"I was called home to deal with the deaths of both of my parents, who'd been killed in a car accident, what do you think?" he asked, not kindly.

He had to get rid of her before he did another thing he'd regret. Like telling her how someone else knowing, having *her* know, seemed to lighten his load some. Even while it made him feel weak.

His anger didn't seem to reach her. She didn't tense. Didn't stand to go.

The woman didn't even frown at him.

He deserved some kind of facial disapproval, at least.

"What memory does the sound of gunfire trigger for you?"

He nodded. Reminded himself that he was not happy with her. The boyfriend, and all. And said, "Wade and I joined the Marines together, but, as you know, we ultimately served separately." What the hell. If he had to get it out, might as well get it done with.

Better that then get into some wimpy-feeling personal conversation about her having sex with him while she was involved with another man.

Or having sex with him at all.

"I ended up in Afghanistan, along with a buddy, Thane, I'd met at boot camp. Like me, he was an only child. Had no other family. One night we were drinking. A lot. Too much. We were shipping out the next day and he asks me what's the single most painful thing I could ever remember dealing with to date. You know, like he was thinking about the pain we might be walking into."

Her eyes aglow with warmth Ruby sat up straight. Like her shoulders weren't going to bow, no matter what he said.

Like she could take it.

Maybe even wanted to take it.

And it struck him… She could be using him to better understand her brother who'd just returned, seemingly broken. He'd like that.

To help Ruby help Wade.

"I told Thane about Jerry."

"That spaniel you had when we were kids?"

"I had him until I was seventeen," he told her. "He was a rescue dog, and sometimes I felt like he'd rescued me, not the other way around. I was home alone a lot growing up. A lot. But when Jerry came, it was

different. I had someone to greet me at the door. Someone who was as happy to see me as I was to see him."

He stopped. Helping Wade was one thing. Becoming a sap…not.

"Jerry had been abused. All he wanted was someone
to be kind to him. He was the most gentle living being
I've ever known." *Move on.* "So I told Thane about the
night Jerry died," he said, finishing.

The End.

"What did Thane say to that?"

Right. The point he'd been getting at. "He told me
about the night his dog, Bear, died. It gave us something in common. An understanding of what we could
be walking into," he explained, completely serious as
he met her gaze. "We never mentioned our dogs, or that
night again, but it was like we knew. And the knowing, the accepting that life could hurt like hell, gave us
strength to get the job done. To do what we had to do to
try to prevent, or stop, others suffering so much worse."

Her gaze was glued to him. He wasn't sorry.

Until he remembered that she had a boyfriend.
That Hannah Colton had irrefutable proof of a man in
Ruby's life.

What was it about the woman that sucked him in?
Made him someone he was not? He didn't want to connect.

Not with her, definitely. But not with any other
human being, either. Not like that.

"You're about to tell me that Thane died over there,
aren't you?" Her words fell like cotton balls around
him. Over him. Soft. Tender. Until there were so many
of them he knew he could suffocate.

"I was about to not tell you that he died lying right

next to me in a dirt-filled cove we'd dug out of the side of a mountain," he said, standing.

Time for her to go.

She didn't take his hint. Didn't get to her feet and head to the door. Instead, looking up at him, she said, "You can cross-train Oscar. I'll help if you'd like. No one has to know…"

Cross-train… Oscar nudging his hand…

"He can help stop the nightmare at its onset," she said, telling him something he knew better than she did. He just hadn't figured himself for needing the help.

He lived alone. There was no one to protect from his very private, very personal struggles. It wasn't like he dozed off on the job.

Or out to eat.

She was getting too close, pushing herself way too far in.

Hands firmly on his hips, Sebastian did what he had to do. Shoved her right back out again with an accusatory tone that left no room for doubt. "Why didn't you tell me you have a boyfriend?"

# Chapter 5

"Excuse me?" Ruby stood straight, completely affronted at first, and then just worried about him. Was he still in the clutches of his nightmare? Thinking she was someone else?

It was the only thing that made sense.

"That night we had sex, you were seeing someone else." His words would have been her worst nightmare if she'd ever gone off the rails far enough to have dreamed it.

Completely shocked, she stood there with her mouth open. Couldn't think of a single thing to say.

"Wade told me," he continued.

*Wade?* It was like she'd walked into the twilight zone.

"My brother Wade?" She'd gotten the words out. That was a start.

"Of course, your brother Wade," Sebastian said, still

standing there, all burly mountain man. His hands, which had been on his hips, had dropped to his side.

She didn't know what that meant, either.

"It's not like what we did meant something," he said then. "It was a reaction, I get that. Something that happened in the moment without thought. And I get that you didn't owe me anything. The anonymous complaints, even the gunshot that caught Oscar... It could have been him, if he's the jealous type and didn't like the time you were spending out here. But still, we hadn't done it yet, so I can even get your silence until that point. But when the shot went directly through your windshield. That night everyone thought it was personal. The way Chase whisked you out of here, insisting you stay at your parents'. And Fletcher was all over the case. Even the police were asking about everyone we knew, or had known. You didn't think to mention this guy? Just in case?"

She had to go. Get out.

He was out of his mind. Slamming her.

She headed for the door.

And... *Wade*?

Sebastian had to be hallucinating.

She got herself outside. Door shut behind her. Was peripherally aware that Sebastian wasn't following her. And slowed her pace long enough to take a full deep breath.

All of the reading she'd done on PTSD, and she hadn't seen a thing about waking hallucinations that were set in real time.

But there was paranoia...

He had to still be in the throes of the demons that ate at him. Lying next to his best friend as he was shot, watching him die. And immediately following, to be called home to the sudden deaths of his parents—his only living relatives.

She couldn't leave. Not until she was sure he'd climbed his way out of the personal hell she'd found him in the night of the first gunshot. She'd thought his panic then had been induced by Oscar's being shot.

She should have known it was more than that.

And Wade.

Did her brother know that Sebastian was struggling with PTSD-like symptoms?

Was that why Wade's name had entered into Sebastian's rant?

Her having a boyfriend was just ludicrous. No way anyone in her family would spread around that claim.

And…the baby.

For a few minutes there, she'd forgotten.

She was pregnant.

From one night that, in Sebastian's own words, meant nothing.

She couldn't even get a one-night stand right, and he thought she had a boyfriend?

She stumbled on the way to her car.

She had to tell Sebastian about the baby. But not right now. Not until his mind was clear.

But she couldn't just leave him like he was, either.

Heading to the only place she felt welcome at the moment, she entered the medical building with the key Sebastian had given her long ago. Was greeted by Jasmine, who, instead of wagging her tail, whined from inside her large, round two-foot-high fencing, and stared up at Ruby.

Her first thought was that the dog knew, too. That

Sebastian had told her canine patients that she had some secret jealous man who was shooting up the place. Jasmine had walked over to the blanket-covered matting where her puppies slept.

Was nudging at a makeshift bed.

All personal thoughts fleeing, Ruby stepped over the fencing and kneeled next to Jasmine. "What's the matter, girl? What are you telling me?" she asked. She'd come in to check on the puppies—or just to play with them for a second, to get her equilibrium back.

And maybe to have a heart-to-heart with the new mama, feeling a bond with Jasmine.

But as she started to check over the puppies, her heart began to pound. Three of them weren't well. At first, she thought it was the last three she'd birthed, but looking at the markings, she knew it wasn't. Which made no sense.

Phone out of her pocket, she dialed Sebastian immediately.

"I'm sorry, Ruby. So sorry. I had no right to come at you like that—"

"Come down to the clinic," she said, breaking in on him. "Three of the puppies have weak heart rates, raised temperatures and they're panting hard. We need to get them into town, where I have everything I need…"

Where she could do blood work. Run urinalysis. Start IVs.

After dropping the phone, she was already gathering up the babies. Grabbing a box filled with supplies, dumping them onto the floor, to use the box as a carrying bed for them. Had them settled, had picked up her phone, her satchel and was at the door, when Sebastian appeared.

Taking the box from her, he didn't speak. Didn't even look at her.

She didn't look at him, either.

At the moment, their drama didn't matter.

There were lives at stake.

Sebastian drove.

Ruby wanted to be able to watch over the puppies, and he was glad to have her do so. Was thankful that she'd been there.

That, even after his supreme rudeness, she'd gone down to check on the puppies.

"You think they're going to make it?" he asked.

"It's too soon to tell. They aren't convulsing. That's a good sign." She hadn't taken her eyes off the puppies since she'd climbed into the back seat of his truck, right after he'd loaded their box there.

None of them were spoken for yet. He didn't even know if they'd have the characteristics necessary to be search-and-rescue trained.

But if they weren't suited to SAR, they could still make great service dogs for the too many veterans who needed them. Or companions to kids who might need an extra friend.

Like himself?

He'd like to blame his harsh words to Ruby on the nightmare she'd helped pull him out of. She'd calmed him, and he couldn't explain that to himself in any way that didn't set him on edge.

He'd been fighting the effect she had on him as much as he'd been reeling from the news that she had some secret guy in the wings.

Whether the guy was the one vandalizing his place or not.

And that's where his defenses flew sky-high. Why on earth—other than as the possible source of the violence—should Ruby not telling him about her boyfriend matter to him at all?

The only thing that needed to matter right now was the health of the puppies she was tending to. He'd called one of his employees, Andy Martin, to head to his place and sit with Jasmine and the other puppies, to watch over them just in case any of the others started exhibiting signs of unconsciousness, rather than mere sleep. If they couldn't be woken up.

He pulled up to the back entrance of the clinic as Ruby instructed, was out of his seat the second he'd turned off the truck, flinging open the back door and reaching for the box, while Ruby climbed out her side.

She hadn't said what she thought was wrong. He didn't ask. Didn't want to distract her.

He just assisted, following all her instructions to the letter, as she checked vitals, drew blood, looked in noses and mouths.

He knew enough about dogs to write a book. About breeding them. Raising them. Training them.

Medically, he only had enough knowledge to be deeply concerned. Three lives… In all his years at Crosswinds, he hadn't lost one.

She'd told him to stay with the puppies while she went to the lab. Was back sooner than he'd expected.

"They've been poisoned," she said, as she worked over all three dogs with an efficiency that left him in the dust. "It's some kind of petroleum-based something," she explained, no longer asking for his help. "Maria, one of my most experienced techs, is on her way in. We need to get IVs started, but first, I'm administering an absorbent demulcent. We don't want them to vomit. Petroleum-based poisons can do permanent damage to the lungs…"

He held up his hand. "Hold that thought," he said, and then, phone in hand, dialed Crosswinds to check on Jasmine and the other puppies, only hanging up after being assured that all were breathing fine, had normal temperatures and heart rates.

As he hung up, he heard the back door open and shut.

"It might be best if you wait in my office," Ruby said then.

She had other help. Didn't want him around.

He got it.

Knew he deserved her rejection.

Headed to the door.

"Sebastian?"

He turned back in time to see her glance up at him. "If we caught it in time, their chances are good. Only one in one hundred healthy dogs die of poisoning that's caught in time. We should know within a couple of hours, at the most…"

Their chances were good, not great. They were dealing with less-than-two-week-old puppies. Not healthy grown dogs.

And petroleum-based poison? Like paint thinner?

The puppies were in a secure crate. No way they could get into anything.

If Ruby hadn't driven out to check on them, if she hadn't continued on to her task after he'd been such a jerk to her, those puppies would have died.

After turning on the light as he entered Ruby's office, he sat on the edge of the desk and called the detective who'd been assigned to his case. He'd been given a number to use, day or night. Glen Steele, the detective who picked up, said he'd send a team out to Crosswinds immediately.

After hanging up, Sebastian called Andy to let him know the police were coming.

And then, with too much pent-up energy coursing through him, he stood again, knocking a folder he hadn't even seen to the floor. He was going to do as she instructed, wait for her in her office. But cooped up in one room when someone had been on his property? Poisoned puppies?

Who did that?

It took a special kind of sickness to attack babies of any kind.

He picked up the folder, telling himself not to let his thoughts venture back to Ruby dating such an individual.

Whether the perp was someone she knew or not, Sebastian's property had been invaded again. Someone had actually been inside a locked building. Purposely attacked innocent puppies.

His employees had all checked out already, as he'd known they would.

Who else had been at Crosswinds since he'd stopped to see the puppies after dropping Elise back at the kennels upon returning from Colton Ranch?

A piece of paper had half slipped out of the folder. Sebastian opened the folder to right it.

The police would once again interview each of the four Crosswinds employees. Get an accounting of anyone they'd seen on the property.

And...

What was that?

*Express Medical Clinic.*

Ruby's name typed clearly on the first line.

He noticed that part last.

After he'd seen the result marked positive.

She was positive for something.

He closed the folder quickly. Put it back on the desk.

Didn't want to process what his one accidental glance had seen first.

*Pregnancy test.*

## Chapter 6

It was almost eleven that night before Ruby walked into her office. She'd called Sebastian earlier. Told him he could go. Maria had offered to drive her out to pick up her SUV when they were through, but she'd declined. She could call any one of her brothers or sisters to take her, yet that night, or, she finally decided, in the morning.

She wasn't eager to have another conversation with Sebastian Cross that night. Whatever he'd been going through, whether it had been real or the result of an episode triggered from his past, she'd felt as though she'd been stabbed by his words.

Hurt beyond one friend speaking harshly to another.

She'd been hurt like a woman got hurt by a man she'd slept with. As though there'd been something romantic between them.

Because she was pregnant?

The knowledge had surfaced to taunt her any time her head hadn't been filled with medical thoughts over the past couple of hours of monitoring puppies. And waiting.

She was pregnant.

Couldn't wrap her mind around the test results, the fact that they said what they did. Let alone get any further along than that.

The doctor at the clinic had told her to make an appointment with her ob-gyn sooner rather than later. At two months, there were many things they could determine already.

And she needed to be on vitamins.

Some of it she'd remembered from going through Hannah's pregnancy with her.

Nothing that felt at all real to her.

Or as if the information was part of her own life.

The three puppies were showing marked signs of improvement. She expected them to be just fine.

And wanted to just go home to bed with that victory the last thing on her mind for the day.

Instead, she was going to her office to sleep on the couch. The pillow and blanket she kept in the closet for that purpose would do just fine. She'd already set the alarm on her phone to wake her every two hours.

She opened her office door, ready to give up her concerns and rest, and stopped. The one person in the world she absolutely did not want to talk to that night was still there. Sitting on what was supposed to be her bed in about five minutes.

"I thought you went home." Over an hour before. She'd told him to go.

He'd never actually said he would. He'd just asked after his puppies.

"You said the little ones would need two-hour checks throughout the night." He didn't stand, or grab keys from wherever he'd stashed them, or make a single move to vacate what was soon to be her bedroom.

"That's right." She stood in the doorway. No way she was going to be in a bedroom with the man. Not ever again. "I've already set my alarm."

"You can't be getting up every two hours. You need your rest."

What was he? The veterinarian police? As well as the dating general?

"You need to go."

"I need to apologize," he said instead, his hands on his jean-clad thighs as he met her gaze straight on. His beard was like a picture frame to the straight line of his mouth.

Drawing attention to his lack of smile.

"I want to tell you why I overreacted as I did tonight, except that I have no idea how to do that. But I know I was one hundred percent wrong and I'm truly sorry."

She wasn't in the mood to be forgiving.

She was tired. Hurt. And apparently pregnant, too.

"I just want you to know, if you need anything… I know your family gets a little overwhelming for you sometimes, and, you can, you know… If you need someone to spout off to…"

What the hell? He couldn't still be hallucinating?

Was she?

She moved into the room far enough to drop down to her chair. With the desk in between them. An office, not a bedroom. "What on earth are you talking about?"

"You were there for me that night Oscar was hurt. And then again tonight. You've seen me at my worst—at least more of it than anyone else has ever seen. And... I'm hoping that... We're friends..."

"Sure. I guess we're friends," she said, truly confused. And too tired to figure things out. "What's going on, Sebastian? Are you sick or something?" Were his struggles more than residue from his past? Was it something physical? Something that was going to get worse?

Her heart pounded and her stomach felt sick.

"I know," he said.

She frowned. Tears of frustration pushed at her. She held them back and asked, "Know what?"

"I was on the phone, leaned on your desk. I accidently knocked the file off, Ruby. I saw the test results."

The file. Results.

Her gaze landed on the only such item on her desk. The one she'd left when she'd folded up Sebastian's copies of the paperwork and put them in her satchel.

Cold, hot, nervous as hell, panicking, she stared at him. He was so calm.

And offering to be there for her?

"You know?" she asked. Was this something he wanted, then? Something he'd welcome?

She hadn't, for one second, considered that possibility.

They'd never even been on a date.

He was Wade's friend.

His nod was slow. Seemed to be filled with compassion. "Does the father know yet?"

She blinked. Shook her head. Wanted to stamp her feet. Or kick something.

"What do you mean 'does the father know?'" she asked, her tone low. Filled with warning.

He shrugged the big strong shoulders she'd run her tongue all over. "About the test results. They're dated today. And you were at my place shortly after you'd have finished here." With a sideways nod of his head, he kept right on talking. "This boyfriend... I figure, since you're keeping him a secret from your family... there might be some challenges, and in spite of my earlier words tonight, I just want you to know that I'm here to support you in..."

"Stop it." She bit out the words. Stood. Everything he'd thrown at her earlier cascaded down on her. Along with the boatloads of hurt his words had generated. "How could you think that of me?" She raised her voice. Didn't care. "Aside from the fact that we owe each other nothing in the dating department, how could you possibly think that I'd have some secret guy and, in the light of ongoing events, not tell anyone?" *Or, in light of the fact that we had sex, not tell you?* The words were there, wanting to be said. She stifled them for all she was worth.

"Hey, I'm just an innocent bystander here. My earlier outburst aside. I still take full responsibility for that."

"Move on, then. Tell me how you've drawn such a demeaning conclusion about my private life."

"I was at Colton Ranch today," he said, looking as weary as she felt. "With Elise."

He'd been avalanche training, she translated, with a definite lack of patience.

"Wade came up to me and asked me if I knew who the guy was. He thought maybe it was someone you'd met through Crosswinds. Like a handler who'd come in for training, or something."

"What?" The scream filled the hallway of the vacant clinic as she sank back down to her chair. "Has the whole world gone mad?" Or was it just her small part in it?

Pregnant? Her brother claiming she had a secret boyfriend? Sebastian accusing her of putting everyone at risk by not exposing the guy to the police investigation?

"Wade said Hannah came to him today. She was apparently really upset. Which, for Hannah…"

Ruby slumped back, every bit of energy draining out of her.

Hannah had promised not to mention the baby.

"According to Wade, Hannah had irrefutable proof that you've got a secret boyfriend, and they both think that he might be the one after you. They're afraid your secret is putting you in danger."

Which was why Sebastian had been so upset earlier.

At least one thing in the world made sense.

Until she thought about telling the man sitting on her couch, who was being so kind to her, that the baby he thought belonged to someone else was his own.

Her stomach jumbling with nerves, she waved toward the lone folder on her desk. "That was her proof," she told him, slowly. Hoping maybe he'd figure things out on his own and need some space as badly as she did.

That he'd just go and leave her alone.

Because alone was how she was going to have to handle the next phase of her life. Even without thinking ahead, she'd known from the instant she'd heard the second results that she was going to be doing it by herself.

Maybe she was hoping they were going to point at folders, then talk around the issue and leave it at that.

When he sat there, looking at her expectantly, she said, "I fainted this afternoon. Hannah was..."

Sebastian sat forward, frowning, his gaze creased with concern. "You fainted? Are you okay? And you've been standing out there all night tending to my dogs? You should have said something."

He was a compassionate man. She'd known that about him...always. The way he was with dogs—he got them, just like she did. Accepted, and gave the unconditional love without reservation.

"I'm fine," she said, looking at the folder then, not at the man across the room. Thankfully, Sebastian was taking his seat again. Him towering over her was not a good thing for her equilibrium, either.

"Apparently the smell of coffee is going to be off my list for a while," she said inanely. Something she'd only just realized. "Hannah and Frannie were here having lunch," she continued, buying herself time because she was too tired to just take charge and get what was coming, over with. "They insisted we head over to Express Medical, and I did so just to quiet their fears."

"You didn't know?" More of that compassion was showing from his eyes. She hadn't realized how much she'd noticed that about him.

Because it was always focused on his dogs. Or people his dogs rescued. Or the veterans who needed his dogs.

She shook her head. "I was sure it a mistake, and told them both so. And forbade them from telling anyone about the false result. I went back for a second test after work. To prove myself right."

Would he piece it together now? She'd had the test and then driven out to his place.

Sitting forward, Sebastian rubbed his hands together, lightly, as though uncomfortable. "So...who is he, Ruby? Why the need for secrecy?"

He still didn't get it.

"It's you, Sebastian."

*It's you, Sebastian.* He couldn't have heard her right.

No way did his name have anything to do with this one. Coming at her with accusation in his tone—yes. But...being a secret boyfriend?

Because he sure as hell couldn't be what she was trying to tell him he was.

No matter what.

He was going to live without human beings in his home for the rest of his life. That decision had been made years ago.

His dogs were his family.

Being a secret boyfriend, one who still lived alone...

He could, perhaps, in the future, wrap his mind around that one, but...

He shook his head.

There was just no way.

"I used a condom," he said quietly. Careful to be respectful of any emotional state her news would have flung her into. "A fresh one. All three times."

Three times in one night.

What a night that had been.

"I know." Ruby nodded, seeming far calmer than the situation warranted. "That's one reason I was so certain the test had produced false results."

One reason. There were others? He waited to hear

them. Needed to hear them. To build his case against what she was trying to make him out to be. It wasn't happening.

When she didn't elaborate, he pushed. "What were the other reasons?"

"My cycle. I've had it."

Oh. Maybe a bit too much information there. For a friend trying to be supportive. That was maybe better left to the secret boyfriend.

If there was one. The thought hit like a brick to the face. He was generally an intelligent man. Quick to grasp what was in front of him. "Hannah was there to hear the test results," he said slowly, piecing it all together. "She couldn't tell anyone about the diagnosis, and so she did the next best thing. She went to find out who the father was."

"That's my guess. It sounds like Hannah. Definitely my no-nonsense little sister."

Ruby looked tired. More than tired. She looked... lost.

He had to go.

*It's you, Sebastian.* Even if he'd heard her right— which he wasn't sure he had, but he wasn't asking—she had to have confused him with someone else.

Maybe if he wasn't there, she'd call the father.

Maybe she couldn't call him. If he was married. Was at home with his wife. Maybe he even had other children. Clearly, if she could tell the father, expose their relationship, she wouldn't be sitting here talking to Sebastian.

She trusted him. The knowledge felt...good.

But no way could he take on this problem. He couldn't be what she was trying to make him out to be.

And trusted that she'd see that. She'd just received the news. Was still in shock.

Remembering both times she'd come upon him when emotional unrest had him at his worst, he leaned forward, elbows on his knees, and said, "Are there any more reasons?" For him, rational talking helped. Focusing on the reality right in front of him, little pieces at a time.

"I've only had sex once in two years. The odds are just too incredulous to believe."

Once. In two years.

She'd meant two months, right? Only once since him?

He stared at her. She was staring right back at him. Gaze clear. Not happy. But clear.

*It's you, Sebastian.*

He stood up and strode out.

# Chapter 7

Ruby hadn't given Sebastian's potential reaction a whole lot of thought. She hadn't even been able to land on one of her own, let alone imagine his.

However, him calmly walking out on her, without a word, was a complete surprise.

Sitting there at her desk, at nearly midnight, with most of the city outside asleep, she'd never felt more alone in her life.

Hannah, damn her, had been worried, trying to watch out for Ruby, to help her deal with a situation she'd clearly not been tending to well herself. And Ruby loved her for it. But her sister had just put the weight of twelve Coltons on her shoulders, when she wasn't even handling the tiny weight of one growing inside her.

Denial was the first stage of grief.

Was it a stage of life, too?

Was she grieving the loss of the life she wanted?

Or just giving herself time to process?

She heard steps in the hallway. Grabbed the gun her father had made her learn how to use and keep in her desk drawer, because she was a Colton and you never knew...

And saw Sebastian standing in her doorway, the box of puppies in his arms.

She didn't say a word. The little ones were his. And out of imminent danger. Being with their mother would be a good thing. And Sebastian would remain with them all night. She didn't have a doubt about that.

Instead of saying whatever goodbye she'd figured he'd come to say, he walked into the office. He glanced at the gun she held, but didn't hesitate as he stood directly in front of her desk.

"These are the babies in my life," he told her. "The only babies I can ever have."

After sliding the gun back into its place, she locked the drawer with the switch on the underside of her desk. "I'm not asking anything from you, Sebastian," she said, feeling steady with the words.

She hadn't consciously thought about it, but there it was. Sitting right with her.

"Like you, I didn't expect or want this, but I knew this afternoon that if the positive result was accurate, I was going to have the baby. My choice. Made completely without you. We—you and I together—don't have to do anything differently, change anything about our relationship. We work well together, and... I hope, as you said tonight, we're friends, too..."

He shook his head. Opened his mouth and, not ready for his rejection, she blurted out more words. "I can do this alone. As we've already established, I have a huge, nosy, caring family who will butt in all the time and help me. Even when I don't need it." She smiled. It hurt her cheeks.

Everything she was saying hurt, too.

She'd drawn a metaphorical picture of the way she'd wanted her life to look. She was in the middle, a spinster. The cacophony of growing up in such a large family, the tension between her parents, her mother's hurt feelings, the distance…and then Aunt Jessie and Uncle Buck… The idea of bringing any chance of any of that into her own home…

In the picture, Hannah's sweet Lucy had been the little love of her life. Being an aunt fulfilled her motherly instincts just fine. And her practice, the animals who consumed her days and a lot of her nights, too, took up most of the rest of the space. With just enough room left over to fit every member of her family and Owl Creek's citizens. The town was her picture frame. The pieces of wood that supported her, kept her together.

Sebastian seemed to shrink as he stood there, silently holding his box. The puppies were sleeping. She'd noticed that immediately. And were breathing normally.

"You deserve a stable, loving husband. Your children, as much or more so." When he finally spoke, the words carried calmness. Truth. "As you witnessed for yourself earlier tonight, I can't provide that. Not because I don't want to, or because I'm not willing to. Not because I wouldn't give my all to try, but because it's out of my control."

If Oscar was PTSD-trained…or Sebastian got a second dog that was…

She stopped the thought short. No wishing for stars in the sky on a sunny day.

"It's okay," she told him. "I don't want a husband, Sebastian. I've never had a long-term relationship because I didn't want one. I'm thirty and single by choice." The words came easily. There was a new catch in her heart as she said them, though.

And a hose filled with panic blowing a gasket inside her. How did a strong-minded, independent woman like herself accept the fact that she'd had no choice in the biggest matter in her life? Keeping the baby was a choice.

But getting pregnant? She'd taken precautions and...

"That night..." Sebastian said, as though reading her thoughts. Her gaze darted to him as he continued, "If it hadn't been for my panic attack, we'd never have..."

No, they wouldn't have. But... "I wanted to." He had to know that she hadn't been completely selfless that night. Sex asked too much from her to just be a distraction.

For a second there, his eyes lit up and he grinned. Her lower belly responded.

Then he sobered. "That panic attack is precisely why I can't offer you..."

"I wouldn't accept it if you did," she told him quietly. She didn't want any marriage. Let alone one born out of pity or obligation—which was what her parents' marriage had been. Or had become, by the time Ruby was old enough to be aware of such things.

Maybe all marriages became that, inside a home's walls. How did anyone really know?

"I'll be that friend I spoke about a little bit ago. When I was thinking there was a boyfriend..."

She nodded. A little smile flowered inside her. "I'd like that."

And now, he should go. Since he was taking the puppies back to Jasmine, she could go home and get some rest.

Except that her car was at his place.

She most definitely was not going back there. Not this late at night. Without an emergency to tend to.

Besides, her little two-bedroom house on the lake was calling to her. It was all hers. And only hers.

Sebastian wasn't leaving. "I should be there when you tell your family I'm the father."

Her family and Sebastian—her father and Wade and Sebastian—in the same room when she announced that she'd gotten knocked up by mistake and was going to be a single mother?

She could feel the tension all the way up to her ears. The pressure...

"Can we leave that thought for another day?" she asked him. "Let's wait at least until after I've had my first appointment before we tell anyone anything..." There could be something that would prevent the pregnancy from continuing. She was still in her first trimester. Could miscarry.

And did not want to.

A strange sense of grief had hit as soon as she'd thought of the possibility of losing the baby. So much so that she issued a quick, silent and very fervent prayer to the fates that her fetus was healthy.

The sensation took over her entire being. That need for the little raspberry-sized being growing inside her to be well.

Not understanding herself, or life in general, she settled for a "thank you" to Sebastian when he agreed to her request.

Him being the father of her baby would be their secret.

For the moment.

"Would you mind giving me a ride home?" she asked him then, thinking his ready acceptance would be a given. After all, she was carrying their mutual result of the choice they'd made together to have sex. He could provide some transportation.

Didn't mean she needed him. Or wanted his help.

It was just the way the math added up.

Sebastian was so far out of his element that he couldn't find himself. He saw the immediate steps in front of him and took them.

He got the box of sleeping puppies settled in his truck, waited for Ruby to climb in and started the engine.

Looking out the windshield, the future hung before him. Drive off the lot and down the mile or so to Ruby's little house on the lake. He'd been by it countless times. Had never been inside.

His child would be living there.

The thought came and he sat with it.

He wasn't going to be a husband, or a live-in father, but he was going to have a biological child in the world.

It didn't compute.

He'd made his decisions. Set his course.

But sometimes, as had happened with the tragic deaths of his parents, life went off course. He was going to have to adjust.

He couldn't change what he couldn't change. His occasional panic attacks. The unpredictable nightmares. His need to live alone.

But he had a lot of rerouting to do.

The child would come first. What was best for the life he and Ruby had created.

And Ruby was his responsibility, too. In part. Since she was housing the child—over the next seven months, but after that, too.

He'd call his banker in the morning. Start the work on a new financial plan.

And someone was out to get him…and possibly her. A vision of the completely shattered windshield—one bullet in the exact right spot—on her vehicle, not his, shot through his mind as he pulled into Ruby's driveway. Saw the dark house with the huge lake right behind it.

Someone could swim ashore…hide in the reeds, then behind the trees in her yard.

He got out when she did. Reached for the box of puppies.

"What are you doing?" she asked, stopping at the front of his truck on her way to the sidewalk leading up to her front door.

"Based on the poison information you provided, and on some evidence found at the scene tonight, Glen Steele determined that the puppies were being poisoned when you pulled up to my house. That it's likely all the puppies, and Jasmine, too, would have died if you hadn't arrived when you did. This guy's for real, Ruby, and he's escalating."

"And you're afraid to go home?"

How could a woman's scrunched-up face look so cute to him in that moment?

"Hell no. I'm uncomfortable leaving you home alone, especially arriving this late, until we know more."

The set of her chin didn't budge. "What on earth does the time matter? If I'd come home earlier, I'd still be here now, this late."

Right. If she'd arrived home alone, and someone had been watching…

He had to get himself together. Focus.

"I'd still like to stay," he said quietly. How could he protect her if he wasn't there?

"I don't want to be rude, Sebastian, but you are not staying here. I'm going inside. Alone. And I'll have someone bring me out in the morning to get my SUV. I appreciate your concern. I know we're both a bit off-kilter. I'm glad we're going to be friends through all of this. And there's no way I'm risking more intimate moments with you right now. Good night."

He stood there and watched as she turned, walked slowly, steadily, up to her door, went inside and shut the door behind her. He watched until he saw lights come on.

And then he drove around a bit and checked back.

Once. Twice.

Thinking about her. About the baby she was carrying.

Needing a battle plan.

Finding no ready answers.

Sometime after one, he caught a glimpse of himself from the outside looking in. A guy in a truck, driving the same roads, watching a house, when he needed to be getting three puppies back to their mother, checking everything over, setting his alarm for two-hour intervals and stretching out on a mat in the medical building that had been invaded by a would-be killer that night.

The police were on the case. Ruby was a Colton, a member of the family that owned half the town—they'd definitely be watching over her. Robert would have already seen to that.

She wasn't telling anyone he was the father of the baby yet. She hadn't even been to the doctor to confirm that things were in place to progress normally.

He had some time to figure it all out.

Ruby called for an obstetrician appointment in Connors as soon as she was up and showered Friday morning. And was lucky enough to grab a canceled appointment. She'd intended to catch a ride out to Crosswinds to get her vehicle, but there'd been a text from Sebastian saying he'd had it delivered. When she checked him on it, she found the SUV locked in her driveway.

She had the keys.

He must have had it towed.

Which couldn't have been cheap.

When she started to wonder how he'd explained the choice to the truck driver, she shook her head and pushed the thought away. Didn't matter to her what someone else had said to another. She had her vehicle.

The forty-five-minute drive to the medical complex where she'd been going since she was a kid calmed her.

She was taking action. Gathering information. From there, she could determine her next step. And the one after that.

She was taking control of her life, rather than letting life control her.

She was getting away from Owl Creek, shrapnel in Oscar, poisoned puppies, a shot-out windshield, the secret-boyfriend drama created by her sisters... and Sebastian Cross. For the morning, she could just breathe.

And she did so fairly well, remaining calm and in charge of her life, right up until she was lying on the table for the ultrasound her doctor had just ordered. The procedure had been part of the canceled appointment Ruby had snagged, and the timing was right.

Wasn't it great how that all worked out? Saved Ruby a trip back.

Except that she wasn't mentally prepared. Not for the procedure—she'd have worn pants that were easier to slide down to her pelvic bone to make room for the Doppler to travel in the gel. And she wasn't ready to be face-to-face with the screen that would make the inconceivable a medical reality to her.

Internally, Dr. Evelyn had said, everything looked perfect. Things that were supposed to be changing inside of her were doing so right on target and as well as she liked to see them.

According to the doctor, she was most definitely pregnant.

Ruby still couldn't grasp the concept in terms of herself. The past twenty-four hours were like an out-of-body experience.

She felt the gel. Heard the technician explain things she already knew. Ultrasound was ultrasound, whether you were using it to diagnose human bodies or animal ones.

Frozen, lying stiffly, her arms tense at her side, her fingers clenched into fists, she stared at the ceiling as the procedure began.

Concentrated on the sensation of cold jelly spreading over her stomach. The there and then. Not the what-would-be.

Tried not to hear the deafening lack of sound as the technician's silence permeated the room.

Find the fetus. Measure. Determine that everything was normal. She listed the woman's duties as far as she could think through them.

A muffled thump sounded in the room. Again and again. Rhythmically. Booming through every wave in Ruby's eardrum. Faster than she normally heard.

But it was undeniable just the same. Her head turned of its own accord. Her gaze landed on the grayscale image on screen and she couldn't look away.

There it was.

She saw it immediately. Analyzed every inch of material on the screen. Knew exactly what she was looking at. And diagnosing.

Her. Alone. By herself.

The uterus looked great. The fetus. Perfectly positioned.

And that sound, muffled and seemingly so loud…

"We have a heartbeat," the technician said, pleasure in her tone.

Stating the obvious.

And Ruby burst into tears.

## Chapter 8

Sebastian checked on the puppies several times that day, finding irony in the fact that he was tending to babies he owned when he'd never be a father to his own child.

The child couldn't know about their biological connection. Sebastian could be a friend to Ruby and nothing more.

But he could assist Ruby in any way possible. He'd already spoken with his financial advisor, who was setting up a trust fund for the child that Ruby was carrying.

In her name.

And by noon, he was convincing himself that it would all be okay. When problems arose—as they always did—he and Ruby would work them out, with her having the final say.

If he didn't take ownership over the situation, he'd be okay.

What he did intend to get to the bottom of was the escalating vandalism on his property.

Three puppies had almost died.

He wasn't going to sit back and wait for more to happen. He needed answers, even if he had to find them himself.

Calling Glen Steele, he asked for a full rundown of what the police had found the night before, what they made of the evidence and what more he could do to assist.

They'd found a partial smudge of a footprint not far outside a window in the medical building. The window facing the kennels had shrubbery beneath it, which made the footprint unusual. They'd also found some freshly fallen greenery. The window had been found unlocked and had been opened recently, with no obvious signs of a break-in.

Which made no sense to him. The windows, most particularly in the medical building, were always kept locked.

The poison had been administered, they believed, through puppy treats. A tainted one was found several feet from the building, on the way down to the lake.

To that end, Sebastian arranged to have surveillance cameras installed along the shore of his land by nightfall. He wasn't sure what good they'd do, since the culprit had managed to avoid all cameras around the kennels and medical building, but it was worth trying. He threw away all the dog food on the premises and ordered new options to be delivered by feeding time that night.

But he didn't figure that that would make any difference, either, as the puppy treat found in the grass was not anything he'd had on site.

Clearly, his place was being targeted. For what reason, no one knew. The police weren't completely ruling out Ruby as a target, either. Though they were less worried that the attacks had anything to do with her, they noted that she'd been present during the last two of them.

They had acknowledged that perhaps her presence, her arrival at his house the evening before, had prevented the rest of the puppies, and possibly Jasmine, from being poisoned as well.

Her arrival. She hadn't been at his house to see to the puppies. She'd seen the puppies only because she'd walked out on him when he'd been such a jerk to her.

She'd been there to tell him about the baby.

It was no mistake that he'd been in the throes of a nightmare. Fate intervening, showing him why he couldn't be a father, before he found out he'd biologically created a human being.

Still didn't explain his emotional overreaction to Wade's news the day before. His friend had questioned him before the nightmare. After his session with Malcolm and Elise, Sebastian had been feeling good.

But because he'd thought Ruby had had a boyfriend when she'd had sex with him, he'd suddenly felt suckerpunched.

Come at her like a pubescent boy.

At a time when she'd needed him to be a support.

It was just more proof to him that he was best with dogs as his family, not people. His parents, a highprofile thoracic surgeon and a well-known philanthropist, had been gone more than they'd been home when he was growing up. That, coupled with the summers he spent away from his school friends in Boise and being made to stay at the remote cabin at Owl Creek with a nanny, meant that he'd pretty much been a loner his whole life. Not unhappy. At all. He'd always been treated with care and respect. He'd loved Owl Creek. And had had every advantage in Boise, too. He'd had Jerry. The spaniel had been his constant. Winter. Summer. Boise. Owl Creek. Always home. In his room every night.

Until the year he'd graduated from high school. And then he'd joined the Marines, where he'd been a member of another family.

Several times that day he thought about calling Ruby. Felt compelled to do so. But knew the desire was driven by his own selfishness, not with her best interests in mind.

Just as his insistence that he was going to stay with her the previous night had been. It would have made him feel better to be there protecting her from whatever boogeyman might appear out of the ether. In making the choice, he hadn't considered how having him there in her space would have made her feel.

Maybe growing up the only child of wealthy parents had made him a spoiled brat.

He didn't give in to any of his instincts to drive into town and check on Ruby, either. He'd texted her Friday night, just asking how she was.

Saw her text back: Fine. And let it go.

And on Saturday, he got back to dedicating himself to work that helped others survive traumatic situations. Jaxon Walker, a new handler, had arrived in Boise the night before, was driving to Owl Creek Saturday morning to check into a hotel in town. He would be heading out to Crosswinds to meet Echo, the two-year-old male search-and-rescue shepherd that Sebastian had been training for him. Jaxon, a detective with the Buffalo, New York, police had been referred to Sebastian, and if all went well, Crosswinds could be training another dozen dogs through Jaxon and his contacts.

As Sebastian headed to the kennel to prepare for the first session between Jaxon and Echo, he got a thrill considering the potential successful searches, with the future lives saved by his dogs. Similar to the way he'd felt the first time he'd put on his Marine uniform, knowing that he was willing to give his life to fight for his country's safety and freedom.

Protecting and saving lives—those were his callings. And they were good ones. He just had to make sure that he didn't let his enthusiasm to care for others overstep onto Ruby's rights to live her own way.

Even while he spent the rest of his life doing what he could to protect her and the child she was carrying.

Not an easy task he'd set for himself, but one he was up to, he was sure. Easy had never been his way.

As it turned out, Jaxon Walker, clearly as eager as Sebastian to get their association started, showed up more than half an hour early. Sebastian hadn't even gone in to spend his usual few minutes with Echo yet.

Energized by the other man's enthusiasm, he invited Jaxon into the kennel with him, and gave the man a general spiel about the work they did, pointing out various training areas. He was still several yards from Echo's kennel when he heard whining and crashing up against a kennel door.

Instantly alarmed, his mind immediately going to Jasmine and her puppies, Sebastian called for help and had everyone on site checking every kennel for signs of a distressed dog.

He headed straight toward Echo, was relieved to see the dog standing and wagging his tail at his door. Still a few feet away, noting the dog's empty water bowl, he made a mental note to talk to Bryony—his youngest employee, at twenty—who'd been in charge of watering that day.

And then, as Echo started to whine and jump up at her door, he frowned.

"Down," he said firmly. "Echo, sit." Basic commands the dog had followed without fail since his eleventh week of life.

When Echo continued to ecstatically greet his approaching visitors, a sense of foreboding came over Sebastian. Something was wrong.

Very, very wrong.

His hunch played out in the worst possible scenario over the next twenty minutes—which was as long as Jaxon Walker hung around Crosswinds.

Echo, once out of his kennel, ran around uncontrollably. Sniffing. Digging. But not on cue, and not at anything that mattered.

The dog wouldn't come. Jumped up on Sebastian for treats. And ran off playing with another dog in training.

Jaxon, obviously disgusted, told Sebastian that he was not only taking Crosswinds off his list, but was also going to spread the word to other law enforcement as well, and strode out.

It was the single most awful moment of Sebastian's career with Crosswinds.

And he did what he had to do.

He called Ruby.

\* \* \*

When she saw Sebastian's number come up on her phone, Ruby almost didn't answer. His text the night before had been…nice.

Welcome, even.

And enough.

Other than her clients and patients and employees, she didn't want to see anyone—most particularly not him.

So much so that she'd done nothing to stop the spread of her sister's secret-boyfriend saga. Or the amateur detective work her family was engaged in to find her out.

Let them spin their wheels, waste their time and fail, she thought.

At least it would keep them off her back for a couple of days. Time for her to come to terms with the fact that her world had been irrevocably changed…forever.

To accept that she wasn't going to be living the life she'd planned.

And to figure out why her heart was so protective of, so incredibly caring about, a tiny floating mass she absolutely hadn't ever wanted.

She was trying to wrap her mind around the fact that she was going to be a mother. That in roughly seven months' time, she'd be dealing with breast feeding every two hours, diaper changes and…

The phone had quit ringing.

But it started up again.

"Hello?" Sitting at her desk, trying to get her breath back from the gulp she'd just taken, Ruby figured it was better to answer a call then have the man on her doorstep.

If indeed, he had any intention of coming anywhere near her once he'd had the time to process her news.

"Ruby?" His voice had an unsettled tone. If he was just making an assuage-the-guilt call, she'd put an end to that immediately.

"What do you need, Sebastian?" she asked in her calmest, most professional voice.

"You."

Her heart leaped. To the ceiling. Stuck there.

"Out here," he said, loosening her emotions from their elated state, crashing them to the ground.

It had to be hormones, she thought briefly, before she sat upright. "What's wrong?"

She should have known, should have sensed...

"It's Echo. He's out of his head. Won't follow commands, won't..."

He'd had Echo's handler, some bigwig cop from Buffalo, coming in that day. "I'm on my way," she told him, her bag already over her shoulder before she dropped her phone into it.

Letting her receptionist know that she was out on a call, she made it to Crosswinds in seven minutes. Pulled up next to the kennels and headed straight for Echo's caged room, before noticing the confusion out on one of the training courses.

Echo, running and playing with another dog, Lucky, who'd been in training for months.

Lucky, bless his heart, was sitting at attention, on command, while Sebastian and his other trainer, Della Winslow, were trying to corral the shepherd.

"Hey, Dr. Colton, I was just in Echo's kennel, filling her water again—it was empty and I'd just filled it a couple of hours ago. She'd thrown up in the back of it, behind her bed, and I found this in it…" Bryony, in jeans and cowboy boots, held up a couple of pieces of dark paper, and Ruby's heart sank.

After thanking the kennel assistant, she grabbed a handful of dog treats and ran out to Sebastian and Della, slowing as she neared the door to the training area, where they had Echo at least semi contained.

Barely glancing at either of the humans, she held out the treats, calling to the wild dog. Whether it was the new voice in her immediate vicinity or the word *treat*, Echo, looking toward Ruby's outstretched hand, stopped long enough for Sebastian to get hold of the dog's collar and Della snapped on a leash.

Within minutes, Ruby had the dog in the medical building, with Sebastian beside her, holding Echo steady while she listened to the dog's heart rate. She administered activated charcoal and waited in the building while Sebastian turned the dog over to Della and the others to watch over her for the next several hours.

As soon as he returned, Ruby held out her hand. "Bryony found this in Echo's kennel," she said, handing him the crumpled and stained pieces of paper she'd brought back with her.

"Dark chocolate?" He looked from the paper to her. "A fifteen-ounce package?"

"We have to assume he ate it all," she told him, finally, for the first time, meeting his eyes. "It could kill him, Sebastian. I don't think it will. He's young. His heartbeat is rapid, but not alarmingly so. He vomited afterward, so that's a good sign. Hopefully the activated charcoal was introduced soon enough to counteract the theobromine and caffeine in his system."

He nodded. Held her gaze. And it was like he was

talking to her. Out loud. She heard his frustration. His worry. His pain.

And his anger, too.

Still watching her, he pulled out his phone and dialed Glen Steele.

"We've got the type of chocolate, the amount purchased—we have to be able to get something off from this, even if we have to go to every store in town ourselves," he said after hanging up with the detective's assertion that he was on his way out.

At first, thinking his *we* meant him and her, Ruby's heart swelled. With him. For him.

And then she realized that he'd been using a generic *we* to encompass everyone working on the case.

"I'm going to stay a while," she told him then. Because she didn't want to leave. Not him. Not Echo.

She didn't want to sit home by herself on a Saturday night, knowing that she was taking on the biggest challenge of her life and would be doing it all alone.

"If he does go into cardiac arrest, the ten minutes it would take me to get here could be a matter of his life or death."

From chocolate.

Sebastian didn't argue. Because he wanted her there? Felt a sense that she should be there, with him, as she did? Or because he was too distracted to argue? She didn't know.

"It could just be one of your employees brought it to work and…"

"No food in the kennels, ever," he said.

She hadn't been sold on the theory, anyway. Who'd drop a fifteen-ounce bar of chocolate and not notice? Or carry one in their pocket while they were working? It wasn't like a bar that size would fit in a normal pocket.

"I'm guessing he got a hold of it, that it was given to him sometime before daylight," Ruby said then, needing to help him. To fill the silence that was growing too deep. "It can take hours for a dog to react..."

"Before anyone got here," Sebastian said. "Every single attack has been in the dark. I just don't get it. What is this guy trying to prove?"

"You said the police think he's trying to sabotage Crosswinds for some reason. To run you out of business."

"It's one theory." He was watching her again. Really watching. Her eyes, her face, down her body and back to her eyes. "And it makes a certain kind of sense. This thing with Echo definitely cost me today—and who knows for how long into the future." He told her about the detective's parting remark regarding spreading the word among other police departments to take Crosswinds off their list. "Who am I hurting out here?"

Her heart lurched at the tone in his voice. And she took a step forward.

"Don't let him get to you, Sebastian. Don't let him win. He made a mistake, giving Echo the whole bar, paper and all. Maybe you're right and the police will be able to find him through its purchase. And even if they can't, he left behind tangible evidence this time."

He nodded. "Thank God for you," he told her then. "He hits and you swoop in and save us, three times now."

Because he'd called her, yes. At least two of the three times. The puppies two nights before—well, that had been...not him calling her.

She'd been there for an entirely different reason.

And she and Sebastian were going to have to talk more about that.

But not yet. Not with Detective Steele on his way.

"I didn't save you today," she said. "You still lost Jaxon, but, if you'll allow me to, I can call him while he's still here in town. I can explain from a medical perspective why the dog was acting as he was."

Shaking his head, Sebastian pulled out his phone. "That's something I can do myself," he told her, and walked out of the building.

Because that's how he worked. Doing everything he could possibly do by himself.

Just like her.

Independent loners. Both of them.

Which didn't bode well for the baby they'd created.

## Chapter 9

Jaxon Walker agreed to another trip out to Crosswinds. He'd already driven back to Boise, hoping to catch an earlier flight out, but said he'd check into a hotel instead and let Sebastian know when he'd be in Owl Creek the next day. While Sebastian had been adamant about keeping the attacks against his business out of the news and away from his clients, he'd told the detective what had been going on, and instead of losing a client, he seemed to have gained another law-enforcement person with a mind to discuss the case and the motive.

All anyone could think of was that someone needed revenge against him. Or, as Jaxon had pointed out in their phone conversation, perhaps against his mom or dad. The property upon which he'd built Crosswinds had been in his family for generations. It was all that was left of his parents' estate. Sebastian had used a chunk of his inheritance to renovate the cabin and build Crosswinds, as well as to support himself until he'd grown the company into the elite training facility it was. The business was lucrative. And he'd invested well himself. Had more money than he'd ever spend. No one but his financial advisor knew that. He didn't care about spending the money. He needed the security.

Maybe, until he'd made a success out of Crosswinds, no one had known there was anything left of Sebastian's parents to go after.

It was the most workable theory Sebastian had heard. And when he'd shared it with Ruby after the police left, she'd agreed with him.

"Your father was a doctor, so maybe there's someone who lost a loved one he couldn't save—a kid who's now grown, who maybe had a hard life after their parent died." It made sense. Better sense than anything else he'd heard to date.

At Jaxon's suggestion, the police were already broadening their search into his parents' lives. For all Sebastian knew, one or the other of them had had an affair and there was some illegitimate child who was jealous that Sebastian had everything. Maybe it was someone who had just, in recent months, discovered their heritage through one of the popular DNA-testing organizations.

The thought was out there. He recognized that.

And yet…the uncertainty lingered.

He stood in the kennel with Ruby, watching Echo, who'd calmed dramatically and whose heart rate Ruby had just pronounced a little high, still, but within normal range. Sebastian felt a twinge of resentment when his phone rang.

Because…what? He wanted a minute alone with the

woman he'd already determined he didn't want to be personally alone with?

The call took all of thirty seconds. Phone still in hand after he hang up, Sebastian told Ruby, "James Greenaway just quit." One of his three part-timers, James had been cleaning out the kennels. "He said that three interviews with the police was enough. He didn't do anything wrong, but they're treating him like a suspect. He wants to be done."

Sebastian could have argued, tried to reason with James, talk him back to work, but he hadn't. He didn't blame the kid. And hoped that James had nothing to do with the attacks. He'd hired him right out of high school. Had had hopes of moving him up to assistant trainer in another year or so.

Still standing there in the dimly lit structure that housed the dogs' separate living quarters, Sebastian called Steele one more time to report James's resignation.

"It's probably going to make the police look at him harder," Ruby said as he disconnected that call. She still didn't seem to be in any great hurry to leave.

He nodded, not liking the feeling of helplessness that had been pervading his life over the past weeks. First Oscar's gunshot injury, then Ruby's windshield, the puppies, and Echo…

A baby.

"How exactly does putting you out of business, if this is what the guy's trying to do, help him any? You still own the land. And five lakefront acres with the newly remodeled, enlarged and updated home…"

"Unless he's just bitter and trying to make me suffer as he has." Before killing him? And filing for a possible inheritance? The only way that worked was if there was another biological child...

He stared at Ruby.

"What?"

"I set up a trust for...the child. It's in your name, so you can use the money however you see fit without having to go through any hoops."

"I don't need your money, Sebastian." In her jeans, tennis shoes and long-sleeved short black shirt, she stood up to him. Didn't back away.

And he said, "It's done, Ruby. You can choose to use it or not, and whatever is there when the child turns eighteen will belong to them." But something else had just occurred to him.

"On Monday, I'm going to be drawing up a will." He'd write it yet that night. Sign it. In case something happened to him over the weekend. "Everything I have will go to the child in the event of my death."

Her frown, the rush of emotion in her gaze, held him captive. "Don't talk like that," she said. "This guy... they're going to stop him."

He nodded. Wasn't fearing for his life.

He was just figuring out how to be a father to a child he couldn't live with or raise.

She had to get out. Get away from Sebastian's magnetism. His conscientious heart.

He wasn't offering to be an active father to her child. She wouldn't accept if he had been.

So why did his distance, and yet his immediate help with money and wills—legal, lawyerly things—hurt?

He was the only person in the world other than herself who knew that he was her baby's father. The only one who could share that with her.

And he was thinking about money and wills.

She understood.

Admired him.

And had to hold back tears because…his actions left her feeling utterly alone. In a building filled with him. And dogs.

How could she possibly feel bereft surrounded by any of her beloved four-legged beings?

"I need to get back," she said, maintaining her calm as she started for the door. She was not going to make a scene. Or give Sebastian any reason to doubt that she could be pregnant with his child while remaining friends and maintaining a healthy working relationship.

At the door, she smiled at Della, who was coming into the kennel, and when the trainer spoke to Sebastian, Ruby just kept on walking.

With all the outside lights still on in the training areas, she could make her way on her own as though the sunshine still lit her way.

One foot in front of other.

To her waiting SUV. Paid for. In her name. Her property. Hers. And, soon to have a car seat in it, would be the baby's main mode of transporation, too.

The little flip-flop in her heart at the thought was… nice.

Realizing that her vehicle looked a little lopsided was not nice, however. Hurrying, wanting to get out of there before Sebastian came to find her—or, maybe worse, didn't—Ruby looked at the back driver-side tire with a sinking sensation that went far beyond having a flat.

The tires were less than a year old. Still under warranty.

Didn't mean she hadn't punctured one. Driven over a nail. It happened.

But that it would go flat right now? Another injury to her vehicle at Sebastian's? After dark?

She knew what he was going to think, even before she called him.

Truth was, she was having a hard time not going there herself.

Their vandal had struck again.

But to what purpose? And how? The lights had been on.

Around the kennels. Not behind her car. And not down by the lake.

"It's just a flat," she told Sebastian when he came jogging over from the kennels.

"Steele has officers coming back out just to check the area," he told her. "And for now, you need to stay away from Crosswinds."

"Don't be ridiculous, Sebastian. This one is probably not even an attack. Why just do one tire?" And only her car?

"I don't know why." His tone held the frustration she could read on his expression as he bent to the tire, shining his phone light all around it, following with his hand. "I don't know why any of this is happening. But I do agree that one flat tire seems to be a bit of a de-escalation. Why risk getting caught for one tire?"

Unless the perpetrator had been interrupted again. Like with the puppies.

From his squatting position, he came back with, "How could anyone have known that Echo was the one dog that would cost me the most, today of all days?" He looked up at her and then added, "I can't find anything. Not a nail, or an obvious cut." Moving around to the back, he opened the hatch and the flooring to access the spare tire.

"You don't have to change that," Ruby said quickly. "I'll call…"

"Are you serious?" The look he gave her was long and hard. "I know how to change a tire. And would do so for anyone who got a flat on my land."

With a nod, she silently acknowledged her overreaction, with a note to keep a better watch on herself.

"You don't think Echo was just a random choice," she said then. Sebastian had a real issue going on. One that involved both of them. One they could actually talk about.

"Do you?"

She didn't. The handler in town, the potential for so many more clients… "But how would anyone know that?"

He hauled out the tire, set it standing up right next to him, holding it with his jean-clad knee. And met her gaze. "I know, right?"

Only someone who knew…

"You think James is doing this? But why?"

"Maybe not doing it, but he could have been passing on information. Even unknowingly. Just talking about work…"

She loved that he was trying to think the best of his young, ex-employee. And wasn't so sure that James couldn't be behind the vandalism. "His dad died in Afghanistan, did you know that?"

He nodded. "We talked it about it once."

"Maybe he's jealous that you came back. That you're building something great here, and helping other veterans better their lives, when he's struggling to make ends meet."

He shook his head, then said, "Maybe, but it doesn't make sense. I've been paying his community college tuition."

She hadn't known that. Flooded with warmth to know that he'd do such a thing. And remembered the baby she was carrying.

One who wouldn't have a father, but would have Sebastian paying college tuition.

"I went to the doctor yesterday." She didn't plan the words. They just fell out. And when she heard them out in the open, she started to panic. She didn't have answers yet. Didn't want to talk to him again until she had herself firmly settled wherever she was going to land with her new life. "There was a cancellation," she said, starting to babble. "A woman who'd also had an ultrasound scheduled, so I was able to get it all over with in one quick visit."

There. It was done. Time to move on. "What do you need me to do there?" she asked, pointing toward the spare tire he was still holding. When he didn't answer, she looked up at him. The struggle in his gaze grabbed her.

"I can just send someone to get the vehicle in the morning," she said inanely. "Catch a ride home with Della."

"Do I ask what you found out? How it went?" He seemed stupefied. Frozen.

"I don't know." She barely got the words out.

"I feel like I need to know."

Her heart soared for the second it took her to get a hold of it. "Then I guess you should ask."

She didn't offer the answer. He had to need it badly enough to seek it.

Instead of asking, he set about changing her tire. Like a madman in a race to save his life. Bolts flew out, tire off, tire on, bolts back in. All without a noticeable breath.

Tool loaded back in her spare-tire compartment. Floorboard replaced.

He finally spoke. "Steele asked that you leave the tire, for now. As possible evidence. Just in case."

She nodded. "Thank you." She didn't look his way as, hugging her satchel to her side, she reached for the driver's-side handle.

"Is everything okay?"

Freezing with one foot on the floor of the car, the other still on the ground, she faced the windshield, not Sebastian, and said, "Yes."

She moved to sit down, but stopped again as he asked, "What did the doctor say?"

She'd told him to ask. Implied that she'd answer. "About what?"

"Everything."

Ruby took her foot back out of the car, but left the door open, leaned herself against the frame and part of the seat. Ready to fall in. To get away.

"I'm eight weeks along, everything looks perfect— her word, not mine. She said I needed to start prenatal vitamins, and that she'd see me in a month." She left out the part where she'd said Ruby might experience some fatigue, and to get enough rest. Those were both on her.

"And the ultrasound?"

Ruby stared at him. "We're really going to do this?"

His expression didn't harden, really, but it grew less tentative. He crossed his arms. "You said to ask."

"Why are you?"

With a shrug, Sebastian met her gaze, his face half-shadowed by the bright lights on one side of him and darkness on the other. "I have no idea," he said, sounding like the words had been wrung out of him.

And once again, her heart relented. "If you're feeling guilty, Sebastian, don't. This isn't on you. My choice. I don't need a man to complete me. I'm as independent as you are. I don't know why this happened. The odds are so completely against it. We only did it one night. It was my first time in years, and we used condoms. The chances are minuscule and yet…"

She heard herself. Grew instantly self-conscious that she was babbling again, and finally said, "I'm okay doing this alone."

"I don't think it's guilt that's pushing me to know."

Oh. She stared at him, her mouth suddenly dry as her heart pounded. Not in any way that felt good. "What then?" she asked.

When he shrugged, shook his head again, she wanted to sit down, shut the door in his face and gun it out of there.

Which made about as much sense as him just shaking his head at the important answers.

"How was the ultrasound?"

A *fine* came to mind first. Succinct. Followed by a dramatic exit. She waited herself out. "It was amazing," she said, finally telling him the truth. "I look at those films all the time, and so seeing, not only a human one, but my own body, with that tiny orb of life in my own uterus…"

Her throat clogged up with tears and she had to stop. Swallowed. Blinked. Took a deep breath. Needed to show him how strong she was. How capable.

And then she looked at his face, the set chin, unsmiling mouth, eyes wide…and glistening.

"I heard the heartbeat," she told him. Felt her own chin trembling and sat down. "That was it," she concluded, all business, a doctor in her own right. Her own field. "Thanks again for changing my tire," she said, then shut the door, started her vehicle, pulled away and…

Left him standing there.

Unmoving.

The first glance in the rearview mirror was a mistake.

The second one, curiosity.

The third, just plain not smart.

If she lived twenty lifetimes, she was never going to forget the sight of that big mountain man, the father of her baby, standing all alone.

# Chapter 10

A razor-thin spike was found in Ruby's tire. A matching piece had been retrieved from the ground nearby. While there was a small chance that she'd brought the spike in with her, the bigger probability was that the shard had been put in her normal parking spot on the chance that she'd drive over it.

Not a life-threatening event. Not even a potentially dangerous one. At most, she'd have had a slow leak, rather than the more rapid one that had transpired.

Sebastian wanted to believe the flat tire on Saturday night was just a fluke. But his gut was telling him otherwise. No one but Ruby parked next to the medical building.

She parked there every single time she was at Crosswinds.

Her windshield being shot out, and a tire flattened,

definitely seemed to him to have both been done on purpose. Aimed at Ruby.

Other things—the puppies, Echo, the complaints, Oscar—were clearly meant to hurt him. Or, at least, Crosswinds.

And on three of those occurrences, Ruby had saved the day.

Her windshield had been shot out after she'd saved Oscar.

Then the tire flattened after the puppies were poisoned. And her unexpected arrival that evening had most likely prevented the rest of the puppies and Jasmine from also being poisoned.

He didn't want to find out what would happen to her if she returned to Crosswinds after saving Echo. Most particularly after Jaxon Walker paid for the dog and made arrangements for a couple of more weekend training sessions before taking Echo back to New York.

Maybe the perpetrator didn't know that yet, but Sebastian had to figure he would.

By the following Thursday, Sebastian had received three calls through Jaxon Walker's referrals, resulting in at least one sale. And every time something good happened for Crosswinds, he got more tense. Wondering if his stalker, as he was beginning to think of the vandal, would somehow find out and make him pay.

Or, God forbid, go after Ruby again.

The police had followed leads and were watching young James and checking out his associates. But so far, nothing had clicked. The chocolate bar that had poisoned Echo, their most concrete lead, was sold in every tourist shop in town, in hotel gift shops and in the local grocery store, too.

The biggest issue on Sebastian's mind was getting the mystery solved, the threats stopped, before word of Ruby's pregnancy got around. They hadn't spoken since she'd driven away Saturday evening, but he'd texted her every day. Asked how she was feeling. If she'd had any more light-headedness. How her work was going. And she'd responded promptly.

Almost as if they'd made an agreement that it would work that way.

He could go about his life knowing that she was working normal hours, eating well and feeling fine.

But he needed to speak with her. He didn't want any mention of the baby or pregnancy in writing that could be seen, hacked, or looked up by law-enforcement officials. Was he paranoid? Hell, yes.

It was all going to come out. She'd start to show. Her family wouldn't rest until they knew who the father was.

And Sebastian wasn't going to hide from his responsibility, either.

But she wasn't showing yet.

And had sworn her sisters to secrecy.

Dialing her on Thursday afternoon, her early day at the clinic, he half expected his call to go to voice mail. Was pleasantly surprised when he heard her pick up.

"I won't keep you long," he began. "I'd just like to suggest that as long as you aren't showing, as long as we can keep the situation under wraps, I'd rest a lot easier if we could do so."

Her pause made his gut clench.

"Ruby?" he asked when no response was forthcoming after several seconds of dead air.

"I don't intend to tell anyone you're the father, Sebastian, so you can rest easy." Her tone was not friendly.

"It's not that," he quickly clarified, while feeling kind of offended at the same time. Though, to be fair to her, he'd made it quite clear that he wasn't going to be a father to the child. "I've been working with Steele, walking every inch of my property, watching cameras, going over names and faces of people I don't even remember having ever met, getting a daily rundown of James's activities, and everyone he speaks to publicly at least, to see if we can put together any pieces. Until we find something, I'd feel a whole lot better if no one knew you were pregnant."

Silence met him again. It occurred to him that maybe they should have had the conversation in person. "So far, there's no definitive sign of my father having an affair, but I allowed Detective Steele to search all my parents' past financial records and there are suspicious local hotel bills. None of them close to any hospital where my dad might have been dealing with an emergency. There'd always been corresponding restaurant bills. And, in many, if not most of the instances, my mother's credit card showed up in use across town. There are hotel bills for her, too. So maybe they just both had meetings, dinners where they might be drinking, and made mutual decisions to get rooms. Could also be that they were both having affairs, but I know for certain she wasn't pregnant because she had to have a hysterectomy after I was born…"

He paused to breathe. And to check his phone to see that there was still an active connection to Ruby's.

"Who was home with you when both of your parents were gone?" The question hit him from left field. Who cared? It was so long ago.

"By the time I was twelve, no one. Not in Boise."

He'd been plenty big enough to take care of himself. "At the cabin they always hired someone, to keep house and cook as much as anything else. And in Boise, when I was younger, I think at least one or the other of them always came home at some point. There was always someone there when I woke up in the morning." It had all seemed normal to him. He'd had Jerry.

Even when his parents had been out, one of them had always phoned at bedtime.

He'd been fine. Blessed, in a lot of ways. He'd learned independence. Self-sufficiency. Responsibility.

He'd also become a loner.

And if he'd had his way, he'd have had parents who wanted to be at home with him, not out living their lives even though it meant leaving him alone.

Now his own kid was going to grow up with an absentee parent.

He was getting way off track.

"We've been lucky that the attacks have either been misses or uneventful up to this point," he told her, rushing to wipe away any images he might have just planted in her brain. Needing to get them out of his mind.

"But this guy has been at this more than two months. And if you take the anonymous complaints into account, it's been closer to four. There's no reason to believe that he's done. Other than your flat tire, Steele and his team believe that the attacks are escalating. If this guy is going to all this trouble to hurt Crosswinds, to get back at me, can you imagine what he'd do if he knew that you were carrying my child?"

He hadn't meant to put it quite that way.

"I just think, due to your association with me, it would be safer if no one knew you were pregnant," he said, finishing with the only thing he'd really needed to say.

"You're afraid that, if this person gets desperate, the baby could be a target."

It sounded fanciful when she spoke his fear aloud. But… "Yes."

"I agree."

At first, he thought he hadn't heard her right. But then she continued, "Hannah and Frannie have been driving me crazy, but I've warned them that they're going to lose me if they say anything before I'm ready. For their silence, I'm having to put up with one or the other of them bringing me at least one meal a day and sharing it with me. They want to see me eat. And, you know, one owns a café and the other a catering business, so there you go."

She sounded as though the love of her siblings was a huge hassle. But he heard other undertones in her voice, too.

"It's nice being spoiled a little bit, huh?" he asked softly.

To which she said, "Good night, Sebastian," and hung up.

Leaving him with a smile on his face.

Ruby was still asleep at 5:30 Friday morning when her phone rang. Recognizing the number as the Crosswinds kennel line, she picked up immediately.

"Ruby? Della, here. Sebastian took Elise out night training last night and isn't back yet. I just arrived to find the kennel flooded. The sprinkler system won't shut off. All the dogs are partially submerged. I have no idea for how long. They're all responding to me, but…"

Already out of bed and throwing off her nightshirt, Ruby said, "Get them to the medical building, cover the floor with cloth, mats, anything. I'm on my way..." Then she dropped the phone and got herself out the door. They'd been having unusually warm weather, in the fifties and sixties, but it still got down below freezing at night.

As soon as she was in the SUV, she voice-dialed Crosswinds, instructing Della to get the blow dryers used for grooming and, on the low, not hot, setting, dry the dogs as quickly as she could, starting with the puppies. Bryony was there, helping, and Sebastian, Della told her, was still out of cell range.

She drove as fast as she felt she could safely drive. That early in the morning, with dawn not even a promise on the horizon yet, she had the road mostly to herself. And when she noticed a car coming up behind her, just leaving town with her, and keeping pace, she allowed herself to put a little more pressure on the gas. While dogs weren't in as much danger of immediate physical distress as people were in such situations, they were still at risk. And the dogs she was on her way to save would go on to save human lives.

The car behind her was gaining on her, so she sped up more. The sooner she got to the dogs, the better. But when the other vehicle still stayed on her tail at twenty miles over the speed limit, she slowed down instead, hating the time lost, but wanting to let whoever it was pass. For all she knew they were on their way to a human medical emergency.

She watched impatiently as the headlights moved to the passing lane, checked out of habit to make sure nothing was coming from the opposite direction that could crash with it and almost didn't see when the vehicle, another SUV, based on its size, started to cross back over the line. Putting on her brakes, she swerved, keeping the wheel turned hard to the right, and managed to do a complete circle in the shoulder, and get herself safely back on the road in time to see the other vehicle's taillights rush off in the distance.

Thankful that everyone was okay, hoping the other party made it safely to their destination, she slowed down to signal her own turn.

Racing up Cross Drive, she had a moment's unease, seeing herself hurrying to the rescue again, after another bad thing happened at Sebastian's training center. Assuring herself—hoping—she was just overreacting to the near miss on the road, she still cautiously parked directly in front of the medical building. In view of all cameras, and anyone out and about at Crosswinds. Once inside, she forgot about her vehicle completely as she quickly looked in enough mouths, saw enough pale gums, to know she had an emergency situation. Instructing Della in how to assist, she prepared, and began to administer, warm intravenous liquids to the dogs from smallest to largest, puppies first. Took temperatures of the ones showing sluggishness, and warmed water bottles to pack around the ones waiting for treatment, with layers between the bottles and the dog's skin.

By the time Sebastian called in, she'd taken the temperatures of every dog on the premises, and Della reported to him that every one of them showed some sign of hypothermia. Echo and a few of the larger dogs were warming just with the water bottles. Ruby was just finishing up the last of the IVs. She'd been monitoring heart rates and felt that every one of the dogs, including the new puppies, was going to be fine.

But only because Della had come in early. And thought to call Ruby immediately.

She couldn't be certain that the faulty sprinkler system was due to what Sebastian now called his stalker. But as she assessed the damage, looking at all the dogs that could easily have been lost, that possibility loomed larger inside her. It gave the early morning emergency an additional sense of dread.

Detective Steele arrived before Sebastian did and quickly drew the same conclusion that Ruby had. He stopped by the kennel briefly to say that the attacker had likely struck again. The locked box controlling the thermostat in the kennel had been cracked. It was possible the unknown subject had turned up the heat high enough to trigger the sprinkler system, but more likely that he held some kind of lighter up to a sprinkler head, and then only used the thermostat to turn off the heat. They'd know more once they got inside the computerized thermostat.

Sebastian, the lines under his eyes making him look worn out, burst into the medical building minutes after Steele headed back to the kennels. "They're okay," she said at his first frantic look around the room. Della had gone with the detective, to give him access to the office attached to the kennel by a bricked hallway.

The big mountain man nodded, but walked from dog to dog, starting with the puppies, squatting down in front of each one, feeling feet and tails, calling all the newborns "little one" and each of the adult dogs by name. Asking how they were doing.

Ruby watched with a lump in her throat.

Hating what was happening to Sebastian.

His animals were his family. His only family. He placed every one of them carefully. Like a parent sending his children off to college. He followed up with them all after they'd found their permanent partners as well.

For a brief second, watching him give his all to his dogs, she was swamped by a wave of jealousy. Because her own child wouldn't get the benefit of Sebastian's undying attention or unconditional love.

The thought passed and by the time she left the medical building late that morning, helping to transition the dogs back to their kennels, she and Sebastian were working seamlessly together again, exactly as they had for the past several years.

Walking out of the kennel with him to get some lunch, she was feeling better than she had since before Oscar was hurt. Seeing a way for her and Sebastian to be friends, to take on challenges, and work through them together.

They were passing her car, on the way up to his house, when he stopped. "What's that?" he asked, pointing to a clod stuck in one of her wheels. And then, walking closer, they could see the dirt stuck in her bumper, too.

"That's from the three-sixty I made in the mud this morning," she told him, hoping again that the party who'd been more in a hurry than she'd been, had made it to wherever they were going safely. As they started walking again, she told him about the incident.

"He was probably drunk," Sebastian said. "You should have called the police."

If she'd had any inkling that the vehicle was out of control, she definitely would have. The person had almost run into her, had effectively run her off the road. Why hadn't she considered alcoholism for the excessive speed?

Filled with panic for a second, she worried that her failure to alert police might have gotten someone killed. But she slowed down her thoughts to go back over the morning's incident more carefully.

"There was no sign of any lack of control," she said aloud. Checking herself. "The vehicle stayed steady in the lane the entire time it was behind me," she recalled slowly. "I kept watching it because I was going so fast and it was clearly coming up on me. Not like someone who was racing, just like…someone—" catching up to her "—in a hurry."

She'd been in a rush. Had she transferred her own tension-inducing motive to the other car?

Before she could answer her own question, Sebastian was on the phone, talking to Glen Steele again, relating what Ruby had just told him.

"He's on his way over here," Sebastian told her, hanging up. "He wants to speak with you, and he wants to see your vehicle before you drive it again."

She nodded. Kind of glad at the moment that the morning's odd event was getting looked at again.

And hating the shadowed look that once again marred Sebastian's face.

# Chapter 11

Leaving Della and Bryony with the dogs, Sebastian insisted on following Ruby back to Owl Creek after Steele was done with her. The detective had not only taken photos of her car, but he'd also taken the dirt clumps, too, in case that could help prove how she was forced off the road.

Ruby thought his following her home was overkill. He'd received the message loud and clear. From the looks she'd sent him, and from her repeated words, too.

He'd just nodded. And climbed back into his truck. He'd been out half the night. Had to get back to the dogs. He felt like a sitting duck, just waiting for the next bullet to hit.

He had to talk to Ruby.

And he'd wanted her off his property the second Steele had said she was free to go.

They'd had grilled-cheese sandwiches at his place while they'd been waiting for the detective. She was going home to shower and change before heading into work for her afternoon and early evening appointments.

He didn't like that, either, but knew that he had no say on that one.

Just like he wasn't packing up and taking his dogs and going into hiding, he couldn't expect Ruby to curl up under her couch and quit living.

Steele had stressed that if the perpetrator wanted Ruby gone, he'd had plenty of opportunities to try to make that happen. Same went for Sebastian. It continued to appear as though someone was out to sabotage his business.

To what end, he had no idea.

He was considering finding other boarding for his dogs until the stalker had been caught. He'd already, at Steele's suggestion, hired three full-time, armed and bonded security officers from Boise to patrol the kennels at night. Two patrolling outside. One inside with the dogs.

The sprinkler system would be reset and ready to go by dinnertime.

The kennel was going to be kept locked, day and night, with only Crosswinds employees and security allowed inside.

And Ruby was to be nowhere on the premises.

She waved at him as she pulled into her driveway, as though she thought he'd just drift off into the wind.

He pulled into her driveway behind her, instead. She'd opened the garage door, and he was standing inside the garage when she got out of her car.

"Sebastian, what are you doing?"

Glancing around, he said, "Can we go inside for a

second? We probably don't want anyone to see us having a fight." He just put it right out there.

And with one look at him over her shoulder, she led him inside.

"What's going on?" she asked, the second her door was shut. The garage led into a laundry room, and she didn't lead him out of it. Instead, with her satchel still on her shoulder, she faced him down right there by the washer.

"You are not to step foot on Crosswinds again," he said, every bit of frustration inside him seeming to roll out with the words. "If you do, I'm going to press charges for trespassing."

Okay, that was more than he'd intended. But the woman and her independence and her refusal to let him help her and the baby inside her...were upending him a little.

"I know I can't dictate your actions and I have no say in where you go or what you do, but I do have a say on my own property."

To his utter astonishment, he saw tears brim her eyes. What the hell?

With a nod, she turned to head into the kitchen, telling him to let himself out.

"Wait," he called behind her, following her to the kitchen door, but going no farther. He wasn't invading her home unless she invited him in. "Ruby..."

She turned then, no sign of the tears, but her gaze was filled with something worse than disappointment. Sadness, maybe. Accompanied by resolution.

"It's okay, Sebastian. You have to do what you have to do. I knew the baby was going to be a problem for you. And you were quite clear that you couldn't be a part of their life. It stands to reason that, since right now the two of us, the baby and I, are one, you can't have me in your life as well."

*What the...?* He took a step. Stopped. "Ruby," he called softly. "I'm doing this so you and the baby will be safe..."

With another nod, she met his gaze, looking sadder than he'd ever seen a woman look. Or that's how it felt to him. "I know. You're afraid you'll have an episode and one of us will get hurt..."

Well, that. But... "That's why I'm never going to marry or have a family, but...you, and the child, will always be welcome to call on me anytime, day or night." He told her something he hadn't yet come to terms with on his own. And yet the words rang with such truth, he accepted them fully. "I hope we'll stay in contact," he continued, working things out as he went along. Feeling...freer for having said them.

And then, before things got rocky, said, "This no-trespassing thing...it's only until whoever is after Crosswinds is caught. This *person*," he growled, "obviously knows who you are, and knows that every time he tries to create a situation that hurts me, you're there, fixing things. You heard Steele say it almost seemed as though the perp lay in wait this morning, watching to see if you'd head out to Crosswinds, and was out on the road, ready to stop you from saving the dogs."

Sebastian had barely been able to remain standing there in calm conversation when the detective had let that piece of information drop.

"We don't know that for sure," Ruby responded, finally speaking, taking a step closer to him. But when he looked her in the eye, she glanced away. As though the theory made sense to her, too.

"You'd already figured that out on your own," he challenged her.

When she glanced up again, she met his gaze and nodded.

He took a step. Stopped. "May I come in?"

"Of course." The tone of voice, like there'd never be a question of his welcome, sent warmth through parts of him that felt like they might just freeze to death.

Walking up to her, he took her hands in his. "I'd die if anything happened to you because of me," he told her, letting honesty guide him. He had nothing else left but raw truth. "And now, with the child, and these attacks…how do I fight the unknown? It's like I'm this tense bundle of potential screwup with no power to do anything about any of it. Except this. I can forbid you from coming to Crosswinds, until we know it's safe."

She smiled then. A wide, slow, warm smile.

And Sebastian figured he'd won the round in a battle that was never going to end.

Ruby had a call from Detective Steele while she was in an appointment that afternoon. And listened to his message as soon as she was free.

Police had found evidence of a large vehicle parked in some brush behind leafy trees, about a mile outside of Owl Creek, on the road to Crosswinds. The vehicle had been facing to pull out toward the dog-training facility. They could tell by tire tread and track depth that the vehicle had to be at least a full-size SUV. Which was exactly what she'd thought it to be.

There was nothing on traffic cams in town to show anyone in an SUV driving from town toward Sebastian's after the bars closed. And no traffic cams a mile out of town.

She hadn't even finished the message when a new call coming in interrupted the voice mail. Seeing Fletcher's name pop up, she answered immediately.

"I'll be in Boise by eight," he announced as soon as he told her hello. "By the time I rent a car, that should put me at your place by around eleven."

"What?" she asked, dropping down to her desk chair, with a glance at her watch. She had two more exam rooms with patients waiting.

"Didn't Steele tell you? I've taken a leave here and I'm heading to town to help Steele figure out what in the hell's going on there. You could have been killed today."

Her heart fluttered with love and gratitude at the same time it tightened with tension. She didn't need her family overreacting. Or thinking she couldn't take care of herself.

In her current circumstances, she needed as much time apart from all of them as she could get.

"I didn't hear his full message," she uttered inanely. "I was listening to it when you called. And you most definitely don't need to fly home for this."

"I'm already at the airport," he said. "Finding criminals is what I do, sis. One of my own is being attacked— no way I'm not going to be there."

The tone of voice, and the words, stopped any other protest she might have made. Because she knew it would be pointless.

"Do Mom and Dad know you're coming?"

"Not yet. I was planning to bunk with you tonight. I'd like to hear everything you can remember, about all of it, in your own words. Tonight. Without anyone else interrupting. That way, I hit the ground running tomorrow. I'll move in with Mom and Dad tomorrow night."

She nodded. Realized he couldn't see her. And said, "I'll have the coffee on," before she remembered that the smell of the stuff made her nauseous.

She'd stop and pick up some beer for him instead. Or fix him some tea.

And then get him the heck out of her house before he figured out that she wasn't drinking alcohol, or caffeine, and threw up if she smelled coffee.

Detective that he was, Fletcher would figure out her secret and then all hell truly would break loose.

Call him over-the-top, but Sebastian was bunking out at the kennels Friday night. He sent the third security officer outside with the other two. One was watching the road frontage. Another patrolling along the lake.

And the third had the buildings.

He was on a cot with a sleeping bag, with Oscar's bed beside him, right in the middle of the kennel building. Or he would be. He'd also brought in lawn furniture, including a small table, and sat, sipping a beer and reading a book about prenatal care on his tablet.

If he was going to protect, support, he had to know the dangers. He'd expected to struggle, had bought the six-pack to relax him through it. But, still on his first beer, he was more fascinated than agitated. There were possible malfunctions, to be sure, but Ruby's age and physical condition allayed most of the concerns.

The birthing process he was familiar with, having birthed many puppies over the years. He wouldn't be there, of course, but…

His phone interrupted the thought.

Ruby.

"Something wrong?" he asked, picking up in the middle of the first ring. She didn't randomly call him. Ever.

"Why would something be wrong?"

He could come up with dozens of reasons, both stalker- and pregnancy-related. "No reason."

"I'm just finishing up here at the clinic and wanted to check in on the dogs." Which he should have figured from the get-go.

"I just did rounds half an hour ago," he told her. "All gums look healthy and pink. Everyone's eating, responding to stimuli, and the puppies' temperatures are all normal." She'd left a thorough list with Della.

"Thank goodness. I'm so glad to hear that." She sounded glad. Genuinely happy, in fact. Which gave him pleasure, too.

"So, what did you have for dinner tonight?" he asked—a personal question that would never have occurred to him to ask until she got pregnant. She'd told him earlier that it was Hannah's turn to provide the daily meal and she was bringing Lucy along to the clinic to share it with her.

"Grilled chicken salad with, I think, every vegetable known to man in it. And pudding for dessert. I need my dairy, after all." He heard the note of sarcasm in her tone—and pictured her smiling.

"I picked up takeout when I went in for some beer."

"I had a juice box. Lucy said she got to share one of hers with me."

Her five-year-old niece. He'd met the little girl several times. She was a cutie. He'd never, ever considered what a child of his own would look like.

Until that second.

"Have you heard from Detective Steele?" she asked then, sounding a whole lot more tentative. In light of their earlier conversation in her kitchen, he suspected.

"About the fresh tire tracks hidden in brush and trees a mile outside of town?" He'd been right to ban her from his property. He was not going to back down on that one.

"Yeah. Did he tell you about Fletcher, too?"

Sebastian's brow raised. "No."

"He took a leave of absence and is flying in to help Steele. He lands later tonight and will be staying at my place until morning, when he's moving to my parents' place."

"He heard about your road incident today."

"Yeah. Steele called him. After the windshield thing, I haven't told my family about any of the stuff at Crosswinds. But apparently Fletcher, one detective to another, had asked to be notified if there were any further actions against me. Steele didn't think the flat tire qualified, but this morning's run off the road did."

"You don't sound happy about his arrival."

"I don't need my big brother disrupting his entire life over something the local police can handle. Something that I dealt with quite fine this morning, I might add."

He'd stopped to look at the tire tracks in the dirt not far from his place. Could retrace her three-sixty. Standing there alone in the dirt, he'd been angry as hell that it had happened, frustrated that he couldn't stop the jerk from getting near her again, and impressed, too, at her driving skills. He'd been thankful she'd kept herself alive.

Not something he wanted her to have to be doing. Ever again.

"Fletcher's a decorated detective, Ruby. Him and Steele working together—they're going to catch this jerk. The sooner that happens, the better."

Her pause gave him pause, until she offered, "As you said, he's a great detective. And... I have secrets I don't want my family to know about yet."

Ahh. Sebastian finally caught up to her. With a screech. Knocking his palm against his head.

"If you feel like you need to tell them—"

"I don't," she interrupted before he'd figured out how to finish the statement.

She had every right to tell her family anything she wanted them to know. He needed a plan to weather the backlash.

Once a Marine, Always a Marine. War in Afghanistan, raising search-and-rescue dogs, a stalker, an unexpected pregnancy. He needed the best training he could get, the ammunition and the battle plan.

"I need some time to myself. To figure out what I want and need, regarding the future, before I have a dozen people telling me what's best."

He couldn't imagine the tension in that particular situation.

"I guess that's where I'm lucky," he told her, glancing around at his own family. Reaching down to pet Oscar, who rose immediately and nudged his hand. "I have listening and support, but no advice givers."

Hearing the words aloud, he didn't feel that lucky, and said, "Advice can be good, you know. Different perspectives sometimes show you something you didn't think of yourself."

"I'm all for advice," she said with a chuckle. "But with five siblings, four cousins and two parents and an uncle all coming at you at once, it's hard to hear any one piece of advice."

For a second, he envied her. *Hard.* "You also have five siblings, four cousins, two parents and an uncle who have your back," he said softly.

Hence, her big-brother detective taking a leave of absence to find whoever was putting his sister's life at risk.

"It's kind of funny," she said, her words coming back softly. "You and me, two totally independent people, who live alone because we want to, who dedicate ourselves to our careers, which both happen to revolve around animals, and yet we come from completely opposite backgrounds."

"I guess it just goes to show you that no matter the upbringing, we are who we are."

"Yeah, as long as we can find ourselves…"

Or until life threw you a curveball you weren't sure you could catch.

"I'm sorry, Ruby. So sorry."

"Sorry?" Her tone stronger. "For what?"

"I'll get backlash, a hell of a lot of it from your family, I imagine, once they know I'm the father of this unplanned pregnancy. I expect there's a good chance I'm going to lose my closest friend over it. But my life is still going to be just me. Independent. Heading up a family of dogs. While your whole future has just changed course. It's not right."

"It's my choice."

"What?" She'd chosen to… Wait, had he…?

"To have the baby is my choice," she told him. "To keep it is my choice. If nature were different and you were the one carrying the embryo we created, the choice would be yours. And you'd make the one that suited you best."

True. "It still doesn't seem right."

"Then maybe you need to do more thinking," she told him. "I've learned that if something doesn't feel right, I'm probably not where I need to be, or doing what I need to do, or with who I need to be with."

"You live a second life as a shrink?" he asked, with a friendly chuckle he hadn't heard in a long while. Hadn't realized he'd lost the ability to just relax and converse.

"No one is preventing you from being a father to this child, Sebastian," she said then, as though he hadn't just lightened the moment. "A lot of fathers don't live with their children, many don't ever have them for overnight stays, but they're still important entities in their children's lives. They're present for the choices, the big events, for some smaller moments. For giving advice…"

Sneaky, the way she'd brought that advice bit back to him.

In new light.

He took a sip of beer. Made note that he wasn't jumping up out of his chair and moving on to whatever he could find that needed to be done.

"I'm not asking, Sebastian. I fully understand if this isn't your choice. I don't blame you. I won't hold it against you. I just…"

"I'm not hating the idea," he said. And then quickly added, "I'm also not seeing it yet. Can we…revisit what this might look like?"

"Anytime you're ready."

He wasn't there yet. But he wanted to be.

Which scared him way more than any stalker ever would.

# Chapter 12

Ruby's late-night interview with her big brother was nice. Really nice. Fletcher's questions, the way he led into them, opened her mind to a little more detail. Nothing that identified a suspect, or a motive, but Fletcher seemed pleased with the result.

More than that, he'd treated her like an equal, someone fully capable of taking care of herself. The relief was palpable.

The validation was more needed than she'd known.

And it all came crashing down the next morning, when Hannah burst into her office even before she'd seen her first patient.

"This is it, Ruby." Her shoulder-length dark blond hair flew around her and her green eyes shot daggers. "I just heard that Fletcher's in town to help the police figure out who ran you off the road yesterday?" When

Hannah's voice rose a notch, Ruby got up and closed her office door.

Her office was secluded, down a hallway from the rest of the clinic, but there was no way she wanted anyone hearing the conversation.

"You shouldn't be here," she told her next younger sister, standing by the door, arms crossed against her white doctor's coat. "I wouldn't burst in on one of your catering events."

"Not even if my life was in danger and you knew I was hiding information that could lead to my intended killer?"

"No one is trying to kill me."

"Fletcher wouldn't be here if he didn't think otherwise."

"I think he's just trying to make certain that it doesn't get to that point," Ruby said, leaning her backside against her desk. "The police are pretty certain that I've only been targeted because I'm at Crosswinds. I'm not going back there until this is cleared up."

Hannah's mouth stayed closed. The fire brimming in her sister's eyes spoke for her. She met her gaze to gaze. Had fought the battle many times over the years. Intended to win.

And then, Hannah said, "The police, and Fletcher, don't know that you're hiding a man for some reason. And that you're carrying his baby." Her sister kept her voice low.

That was the only credit Ruby could give her.

"Let it go, Hannah." The warning was implicit in her tone.

When Hannah looked down, Ruby filled with remorse, but didn't back off from her position. "It's going to be okay," she said.

Hannah's eyes glistened when she looked back up. "I know. Because if you aren't going to tell, I have to, Ruby. I can't shake the idea that some guy might want you gone because he doesn't want it known that you're pregnant with his child. I don't care if he's married, or famous, or whatever reason you have for keeping him secret. It's not worth your life…"

Ruby started to speak, but Hannah cut her off. "I'd never be able to live with myself if I stayed silent and this guy got to you."

Sitting down, Ruby took a deep breath. Hannah's valid claim was changing her tactics. But not her decision. "He's not going to get to me, Hannah." She met her sister's gaze, held on steadily.

"So…" Hannah closed in, perching on the edge of Ruby's desk, closer to her. "You admit that there is a *he*."

"No." Ruby crossed her hands at her waist, needing her calm to be the only thing that showed. "I'm not in any kind of a relationship. I told you that from the beginning."

"You're not still going to try to convince me that you aren't pregnant, are you? Because when I tell the family, you're going to have to lie to them, too, and then when you start showing, everyone's going to know you lied to their faces."

She got the message.

Hannah was hurt that she was lying to *her*.

And she'd made her point.

"I am pregnant," she said aloud, shocked at the fissure that passed through as she heard her own words. Not an entirely unpleasant experience. "But I still need you to keep it a secret for now, Hannah." Her tone was no longer commanding. "Please. Just until we figure out what's going on here. I don't want whoever is behind these attacks to know about the baby. I don't want to give this jerk more bait."

Hannah's head shake put knots in Ruby's stomach, as did her sister's words when she said, "I can't keep that promise anymore. There's something not right about this guy. So you aren't in a relationship anymore. It's clear that two months ago, you were having sex with him. And this is the kind of motive you read in the news all the time."

Always-practical Hannah.

But her sister had known her own share of heartache. Which she'd taken on the chin. And grown up out of the ashes to make a great life for herself and her daughter.

Ruby met Hannah's gaze again. "I know the father is not behind this, Hannah. I am as positive of that as I am that Lucy is your daughter."

She was that serious. Hannah seemed to be considering Ruby's words, giving them weight, but then she shook her head. "Maybe he wants you back. He's doing this to scare you back into his arms."

"I know him, Hannah. And he knows about the baby." The words came because they had to. "But we aren't in love. Neither of us want to get married. Him even more than me and you know how much I've always cherished my space alone at home." She couldn't tell Hannah that the father was being stalked and both Ruby and the father feared that if anyone knew he had a child on the way, that child could be in danger. But she had to get her sister's promise of silence. "Please," she said then. "Just give Fletcher a few days to work on these attacks. As soon as the person is caught, I'll tell Mom and Dad myself."

"And the father…he's okay with that?"

"He's not thrilled by the idea. After all, we're the Coltons, you know?"

Hannah's answering nod, the look on her face, held total commiseration at that point. And Ruby said, "But he knows it's the right thing to do. And I get the feeling he's going to insist on it once this violent behavior is solved."

"So he knows about the attacks?"

"Yes."

Hannah nodded again. She didn't look like she was ready to be done yet, though. "So why won't you at least tell me who he is?"

"Because we need some time to figure out how our parenting situation is going to work. Time without anyone else even knowing that we're going to be sharing a child." She met her sister's gaze head-on. Hannah knew all about the trials and tribulations of parenthood. "I'm going to retain full custody," she added. Something else Hannah would understand, being a single mother herself.

Hannah's face softened then, and she headed toward the door. But turned when she reached it. "By the way, Mom wanted me to remind you about Uncle Buck's birthday party next week. It's going to be at the ranch instead of in town because so many people accepted invitations. Mom asked me to cater it."

Ruby wasn't in a partying mood. Most particularly when one family member or another was bound to bring her a glass of her favorite wine and wonder why she wasn't sipping from it. But she nodded. Congratulated Hannah on the job offer.

And wondered, but didn't ask, if Sebastian Cross had been on the guest list.

And if so, had his name been on the acceptance list as well?

Sebastian had a visit from Fletcher Colton on Saturday. Watching the broad-shouldered man walking toward the training pen, seeing his dark hair, worn a little long, he was struck by the fact that Fletcher's niece or nephew was going to be Sebastian's biological child. Would the baby have blond hair like Sebastian and Ruby? Or darker hair like Fletcher and Wade? He and Ruby both had green eyes. Wade's were blue.

He had no idea what eye color the rest of the Coltons had. Including Fletcher.

Until the man got closer.

Green.

Sebastian was probably going to have a green-eyed kid.

Giving a "sit" command to the Labrador he'd been training, Sebastian held out a hand to his long-time friend's older brother.

Finding himself fighting a load of guilt, unable to shake the fact that he was the father of the man's younger sister's unplanned baby. If Fletcher knew...

When Wade found out...

Glen Steele, as the lead on the Crosswinds case, had called to let Sebastian know that Fletcher would be coming out. The Utah detective had been deputized by the Owl Creek Police Department in order to officially help find Ruby's attacker.

Being the father of the unborn child who could be in jeopardy with any further attacks, as well as the owner of the property involved and the friend of the woman who'd been put at risk, Sebastian kenneled the Lab and walked Fletcher around the property, pointing out every place an attack had happened. Fletcher pulled out crime-scene photos and Sebastian walked the other man through every one of them.

Gave him a full tour of the kennels. Introduced Ruby's brother to every one of his ten adult dogs. Including Fancy, the two-month-old shepherd mix Sebastian had determined had the scent skills to be trained for search-and-rescue. "I've got a few people who foster potential trainees for me," he told the man. "Ruby's friend Kiki Shelton and her grandfather, Jim, have agreed to take Fancy."

There, he'd put Ruby on the table.

Gotten the fact out there that Sebastian was indirectly responsible for Fletcher's presence in town.

As the two headed down to walk the shoreline, where, Steele was certain, the unknown assailant had been accessing Sebastian's land, Fletcher said, "This nastiness aside, you've saved my sister's life, man."

Sebastian pulled on his beard at that thought. If the man only knew...

When he knew...

"That woman had always had more of an affinity with animals than with people," Fletcher continued. "Probably had something to do with the way we grew up—has she told you about that?"

Indirectly. There'd been too many opinions, he knew that.

"You know that our mom's a twin, right?" the detective asked, his mind seemingly only half on the words he was saying as he perused every inch of land upon which they walked, while keeping an eye on the horizon, and occasionally turning to look back toward the house and other buildings, too.

"I didn't know that," Sebastian said. He'd been a summer pal of Fletcher's younger brother. They'd fished. Challenged each other to dive off docks into the lake. They'd shared freedom from parents—they hadn't sat around and talked about them.

Partially because Sebastian didn't do that with anyone. Or hadn't, until recently. With Ruby.

When a guy didn't want to share, he didn't put himself in a position to have sharing expected of him.

"Her name is Jessie. She was Uncle Buck's wife."

That was news. "The woman who ran off and left him with four kids to raise?" You didn't live in Owl Creek without knowing some of the history.

Buck and Robert Colton were brothers. Buck went off to the army, leaving Robert to take over the family's hardware store in town. Buck came back, sold his share of the store to Robert and used the profits to buy Colton Ranch. Then Robert saw Owl Creek's potential to grow into a tourist area and spent his profits buying land cheap and purchasing buildings in town under market value. When the market turned around, he'd amassed a small fortune of land and rentals.

And that hardware store now served as the lobby for Colton Properties, though Robert had left a lot of the shelving and the register in place for posterity's sake. He'd added two additional floors, still with the red-brick facade, but all decked out with modern offices and the best of technology. A newcomer couldn't miss the place. Other than the town hall, it was the tallest building in Owl Creek.

And Fletcher had been about to tell him something about Ruby's upbringing that had made her better with dogs than with people. He could argue that point, no matter what reasoning Fletcher gave. Ruby most definitely worked her magic on people as well as dogs. He had personal testimony to confirm that.

But he had no intention whatsoever of sharing. So he didn't ask any of the questions he suddenly had.

Fletcher had stopped to take a couple of photos with his cell phone. Of the house, and then, of the lake. From midyard.

"I think Mom always felt guilty, her sister leaving Uncle Buck that way, and with Dad traveling so much, she'd cart us six kids over to the ranch, to help Buck out with his kids and things around the house. We'd spend nights there, with Mom tending to all ten of us at once."

Sounded chaotic. Somewhat fascinating.

Why hadn't Wade ever said anything about that?

Or had he, and Sebastian hadn't thought it a big enough deal to remember?

He hadn't known Ruby well back then.

Hadn't been making a baby with her.

"Rubes, being the middle child in our family, and the same age as Uncle Buck's youngest, Lizzie, kind of got lost in the shuffle, I think. Or just figured the dogs were less trouble than putting up with the rest of us."

Sebastian figured he should feel guilty about listening to Ruby's older brother profiling her, but he was too interested to stop the man.

"We all saw veterinary science as the perfect choice for her," the detective jumped ahead before Sebastian was ready to leave the past behind. "Problem was, that's all she wanted. Worked seven days a week, on call twenty-four hours. She was starting to show signs of burnout until she began working at Crosswinds so much. Volunteering with your PTSD program gave her something she'd obviously been missing. She's more relaxed. Has hired a couple more doctors for her clinic, and, from what Mom and the girls tell me, she's taking complete days off, and sometimes whole weekends."

Like the weekend, two months before, when they'd dealt with Oscar, and then made a baby together?

Fletcher wasn't going to be thanking Sebastian, or thinking he'd saved anything, once he knew the truth. And to that end...

"I've got an idea to try and draw this stalker out," he said. He'd come up with the plan the night before. Lying on his cot, awake in the middle of the night, thinking about Ruby's near miss on the road the morning before.

He intended not only to draw out the fiend who was trying to ruin him, but also to keep the unknown assailant busy at Crosswinds, where Ruby absolutely would not be.

"I'm going to run a huge ad campaign for Crosswinds. I've already contacted a marketing firm my mother worked with in Boise. They'd offered to help before, but I'm already at capacity and don't need the publicity. Anyway, a film crew will be out from a local station in Boise to film what we do, interview me, that kind of thing. The crew will be made aware of the situation and will all be privy to the danger before accepting the job. They'll be provided bodyguards. We'll be doing other videos as well, paying social-media influencers to air them. I've got an ample supply of photos and some videos of our dogs out in the field. We'll be asking for permission to use those and include them in the campaign." They'd almost reached the shore. He just kept talking. "To begin, though, the firm is going to hit Owl Creek hard, with news that the marketing firm is honoring me and my parents for a lifetime of service to our communities. They wanted to do that when my parents died, but I needed my privacy."

He cringed at the idea, but to draw out the stalker, trap whoever it was and end the threat of violence… he'd do whatever it took.

"They'll get posters designed and printed, with the idea to put them up on trees on public property coming in and out of town, not involving any individuals or businesses. The plan is there. Ready to roll. I just want police buy-in before I give the final go-ahead."

They'd reached the shore. Stopping, Fletcher turned to Sebastian. "You're taking the offensive, egging him on, rather than waiting for him to strike again."

"And again," Sebastian said, nodding. "I've got three armed security officers here at night. I can bring in a day shift as well. And will work around the clock, if I have to, to keep running things here without staff, if it comes to that. I started out alone. I can do it again."

"You can afford all of this?"

Sebastian shrugged. "I'd spend my last dime if that's what it took to put an end to the reign of terror. This individual went after Ruby," he said, unable to keep the boiling anger out of his tone.

Fletcher studied him. Sebastian, holding the other man's gaze straight on, was up for it and then some.

"Let me talk to Steele," Fletcher said then. "While a bit more elaborate than I'd like, I think we can work with what you're planning. We'll need to assign extra officers to the case and I don't know what kind of staff he has on hand. And maybe we hold off for a few days. Steele's been looking at those hotel bills your father charged. He's got some leads on a woman who was also known to be there. And she later had a kid. A boy. Let us get a look at him."

Sebastian fell back against the tree behind him. Leaned there.

He'd been right? He had a half brother?

Who'd pushed Ruby off the road and could have killed her? And the child?

"Sorry, man," Fletcher said then. "Steele led me to believe you kind of figured your father had been having an affair."

Right. Fletcher would have no idea that he'd been thinking about Ruby at the hands of a deranged guy who resented Sebastian so much he had to take him down.

"I threw it out as a possibility," he said, straightening. "I never suspected it before now. I'm an only kid. The idea of a half sibling…"

"I've got five siblings, and the idea of a half sibling out there somewhere would throw me for one, too. Wrapping your mind around that one…hell, you gotta see your parents, your whole life different…" Fletcher was walking again.

Clearly trying to put a witness, and a friend of his brother's, at ease.

Sebastian would be at ease when the stalker was locked behind bars.

When he knew Ruby and the child were safe.

Until then, he was at war.

# *Chapter 13*

Ruby awoke Sunday morning to a text-message notification.

Thinking it was Sebastian, who'd been the last one to text her the night before, just to ask how she was doing, she rolled over and picked up her phone.

A smile on her face.

Not a horrible way to wake up.

The man got her. He not only accepted her right to make her own life choices, but he also understood her independence. Her need to be a single decision maker.

Not part of a twosome.

Lying on her back against the pillows, giving her stomach a chance to wake up before she started whirling it around, she held up the phone and tapped the text icon.

STAY AWAY.

Two words. All caps.

And her heart was pounding.

Sitting up, she pushed Fletcher's speed dial. Nodded when her brother told her to stay put. And away from windows.

With him on the phone, she walked to the bathroom attached to her bedroom. And when he hung up, she tapped Sebastian's icon.

He wasn't the police. Or part of the investigation.

But he was her partner, of sorts, on the new route her life was taking. If something happened to her, to the child she was carrying, he'd lose his own biological offspring.

"I just thought you should know, because Crosswinds is involved, that I got an eerie text a few minutes ago. Fletcher's on his way over."

Dawn was barely breaking on Sunday morning. He was probably still in bed.

"I'm on my way to Connors. Elise is bleeding. I've got a tourniquet on her, but I think she might have slit a vein—"

"Connors?" she interrupted, her text message an issue for later. "You bring her here, Sebastian. If it's a vein, she might not make it to Connors."

"I'm not involving you or the clinic…"

"Bring her to my house," she said. "I have my kit here. And anything else I need, someone can get for me." She was pulling on jeans and a sweatshirt as she spoke. And, as she heard a car outside and peeked out, added, "Fletcher's here. Bring her to me, Sebastian," she said, hanging up.

She wasn't going to argue with him. Elise might not have that much time.

Ruby already had a sheet in hand as she gave her

phone to her brother and went straight to the kitchen table, covering it.

"Sebastian's on his way with an emergency," she told him. "One of his dogs, whose handler is arriving this week to pick her up."

Frowning, Fletcher, whose hair was standing up at the back, in a bedtime cowlick, didn't say a word as he asked for her phone's password and then typed it in.

She ran for her bag, then laid out supplies.

Fletcher came closer. "I don't like this."

"I don't, either," she told him. "But it's the best I can do. He said a vein's been cut. Depending on which one, she could bleed to death before I can help her. She might need a transfusion…"

"The text, Ruby. I don't like the text."

Right. Fine. Neither did she. "You figure that out, I'll work on this," she told him, thinking of the girl she'd birthed two years before. Of all the hours of training Sebastian and Della—and her cousin Malcolm, too— had put Elise through. The golden retriever had shown more promise, from the beginning, than any of Sebastian's other dogs. She was going to a group of mountain rangers who lost lives every year when they couldn't find missing people in time.

"A dog is hurt and right afterward you get a text telling you to stay away?"

The thought had crossed her mind.

"We don't know that the two are connected," she told him. "If Elise got cut digging, I'm saying the chances are slim. But in any event, I *am* staying away. And ultimately, this guy is after Crosswinds for some reason, not me. Or Sebastian, either. If he was a murderer, why not just take out Sebastian and be done with it?" She was busy arranging, running a silent checklist through her mind. Preparing an IV. Antibiotic. Getting sutures ready. "This isn't just a dog I'm hoping to save here, although I'd do the same if it were. This animal is going to save human lives. It's her calling. And I'm not going to have people die because I got a text message."

Her text notification sounded again. She glanced at Fletcher, who was watching her screen.

"Sebastian's here," he said, and headed toward the door to the garage.

She heard the double garage door open. Listened while her brother told Sebastian to pull in. Counted seconds while she heard the truck's engine shut off and the garage door close.

And counted more as the men carried the injured dog into her.

"She's conscious," she breathed with relief. She showered the girl with praise, with reassurance, even while her heart thudded at the sight of the blood-soaked bandage around Elise's left ankle. "There's blood on her right foot, too," she said, taking a brief glance, seeing cuts, as she unwrapped the gauze around the dog's left front leg.

"Sebastian, stay at her head, comfort her. Fletcher, keep tight pressure right here." She moved her brother's fingers about an inch above the gauze.

And five minutes later, they were all breathing huge sighs of relief. Sebastian's quick thinking and the tourniquet had made the injury less catastrophic. "It's the cephalic vein," she told the two men, relieved to find that only the superficial vein had been nicked.

It took a while longer to dig small pieces of glass out of several cuts and incisions on Elise's lower front legs. She was still assessing damage, tending to immediate medical concerns, when Fletcher told Sebastian about the text Ruby had received that morning, finishing with, "I need to know what happened."

With a swift hard look to Ruby, and a new frown marring his brow, Sebastian said, "She's due to leave us this week. I was running her through all the courses one last time, in the dark, just to be sure I felt she was completely ready. Instead of hitting the spot where I'd buried her scent, she stopped on a hill and began digging frantically. Next thing I know she's spurting blood…"

Fletcher, who'd been dismissed from pressure application a few minutes before, pulled out his phone. Tapped. And then said, "Get a team out to Crosswinds." Talking to Sebastian, her brother received and relayed exact location coordinates to, she assumed, Glen Steele, and then hung up.

"Aren't you going to join them?" she asked Fletcher, adding a second, and final, stitch to another left-foot wound.

"You received a direct warning to stay away, Ruby. I don't think the guy cares about geography at the moment. He wanted you to stay away from the dog."

"Because every time he strikes, you save the day," Sebastian added through clenched teeth.

They didn't even know yet if the two were connected, which she pointed out, only to have two strong male voices come back on her at once.

Ruby felt ganged up on.

And…loved, too.

The text warning to Ruby had come from a burner phone. Off a local tower. No surprises there. But frustrating as hell.

Once again, Sebastian had to call an elite client and explain that his dog had been attacked, and would not be ready for delivery as soon as expected. Thankfully, he was dealing with law enforcement, and once they knew the details, they were not only willing to wait for Elise's cuts to heal, but were also offering suggestions to catch the fiend who'd deliberately harm dogs.

And a third piece of great news—Ruby found no muscular damage to the dog at all. If a small piece of glass hadn't pierced Elise's vein, her wounds would have been mostly superficial. Not that he gave his stalker any credit for that one.

The police had quickly located the spot where Elise had been digging and Fletcher had left to check it out, asking Sebastian to stay with Ruby until they knew more.

The hole Elise had dug was on an incline, coming up from the shore of the river. The land was fenced as part of a training course, and didn't appear to be obviously breached, but someone could have climbed the fence. The enclosure was made to keep young, eager dogs inside, not to keep humans out.

Steele had found pieces of steak with shards of glass embedded in them, buried just inches underground in three different locations along the incline. All out of range of cameras.

Clearly planted there.

And not for a good purpose.

Whoever was after him was smart. Watchful. And vigilant.

And, as Fletcher had pointed out on one of his calls to Sebastian, the subject seemed to have a lot of time on their hands. Or, as the visiting detective had suggested, the stalker worked second shift and Sebastian was the man's current after-work activity.

Ruby's brother had another interesting theory. That the person they were after had a place along the lake. Possibly even in view of Sebastian's property. The police were checking rentals. Not a small task, considering the tourist mecca Owl Creek had become.

Fletcher, in going over the case files the night before, had found another possible suspect as well. He'd been looking for anyone who'd had a history with both Sebastian *and* Ruby. There'd been a man a few years back who'd claimed to be a veteran in need of a PTSD dog—part of the volunteer portion of Sebastian's outfit. Veterans received trained dogs for free. The guy had lied about his military service. He'd never served his country and had no medical records to show he'd received any treatment, or even had a consultation for the stress disorder.

Ruby had been the one to raise doubts in the beginning. She hadn't liked the way the man related to the dog they'd been about to give him. There'd been no bond at all. More like someone who was going to turn around and sell the dog for a nice profit.

His name was David Pierce. Sebastian remembered him. According to police, the guy's last known address was the county jail, dated a few years before. He'd been in for a misdemeanor swindling charge of some sort. Meaning it had to have involved less than a thousand dollars. He'd disappeared upon his release.

Moved out of state.

Fletcher was attempting to find out where.

Sebastian was sitting at Ruby's kitchen table, his truck still in her garage, relating the gist of the most recent telephone conversation he'd had with her brother. Ruby was going over the dog's paws with a bright light, a magnifying glass and tweezers, looking for small shards of glass she might have missed.

It was her third time doing so—giving Elise breaks in between—and she was still finding little glints that turned out to be more shards.

"I remember him, too," Ruby said slowly, as though her mind was only half on her words. "The guy gave me the creeps. The way he didn't even seem to see dogs as living beings. He never looked any of them in the eye. As I recall, he didn't even talk to them."

Listening to her, Sebastian smiled. In some ways, the woman was his twin. Who else judged people by whether or not they spoke to dogs? Or looked them in the eye, as opposed to just looking at them?

"I like Fletcher," Sebastian said then, the other man's integrity pushing at him. Hard.

"Yeah." Ruby rubbed an alcohol-soaked pad on the paw she'd just been picking, and, praising Elise, helped the dog down. "I kind of like him, too," she said then, returning to her conversation with Sebastian.

Sebastian dropped to the floor with Elise, petting the girl, and said, "I'm thinking we should let him know about the baby."

He'd spent a good bit of time soul-searching after his meeting with Fletcher the day before. "When something doesn't feel right, it means you're in the wrong place, or with the wrong people, or doing the wrong thing," he said, paraphrasing her words to him during their Friday-night phone conversation. "It doesn't feel right to me that he doesn't know that when this guy goes after you, it's not just your life that's in jeopardy."

"Would it make any difference to his policing?"

It would not. The answer was a no-brainer. Fletcher would protect his sister's life with everything he had. Period.

"It could change how he thinks about me," Sebastian said, feeling a bit less proud of himself in that moment. "When he finds out…knowing that I knew…"

When had he ever made choices based on others' opinions of him?

But then, he'd never had his own biological kid's potential aunts and uncles swarming in the background, either.

"It doesn't make you any less trustworthy." Ruby's tone held the confidence that made a lot of people just nod their heads and do as she said.

It wasn't the tone that got him. It was the fact that she'd known what he'd been thinking. Or how he'd been feeling.

Which, strangely enough, brightened his mood some. "Just as a heads-up, which one of your three brothers is most likely to come looking for me with a baseball bat when they find out?" he asked, sending her a raised-brow look. With the beginnings of a grin.

There they were, with a stalker, threats, Elise hurt… and talking things over with her made the burden seem lighter.

"I'm guessing Wade," she told him, her tone holding no humor at all. "He won't hit you with it, though."

He'd already known that part. He and Wade had taken care of proving their physical superiority over each other as kids. Both had won some and lost some.

"He's not at his best right now," Ruby said, and Sebastian nodded.

"I tried to talk to him, but he's not ready," he told her.

"Plus, you guys have been close since you were kids. I'm guessing he's going to take our situation a little more personally than the rest."

"Because we aren't getting married."

"Yeah. I can see him taking offense that you don't think I'm good enough for you."

His hand on Elise's back paused. "You don't think that do you?"

"Do *you* think I think you aren't good enough for me?"

She didn't look at him. Didn't even slow her cleaning and disposing of the supplies she'd just used.

And he knocked off another reason to feel bad from his list. Ruby didn't want marriage any more than he did. He'd have thought the relief at that one would be palpable.

Finishing up with her supplies at the table, Ruby dropped down to the floor on the other side of the retriever. Elise wagged her tail, looking none the worse for wear.

Because, once again Ruby had saved Sebastian's day.

When he needed to be the one who saved hers.

# *Chapter 14*

With Fletcher home, Jenny Colton had insisted on having Sunday afternoon dinner with all her kids at the table. There was no way Ruby had been able to get out of going. Everyone was worried about her, and they needed to see that she was fine.

Her dad and oldest brother, Chase, who was vice president at Colton Properties, talked business. Fletcher and Wade took the boat out for a while. Her mom and two younger sisters talked cooking and food and coffee drinks. And Ruby played with Lucy.

She'd been worried that Hannah or Frannie would blow her secret somehow, even by trying to talk to her alone and being overheard, but neither one of them sought her out. Jenny had been too busy helping to plan the food for Buck's birthday celebration and both of her sisters were deeply involved with that. Apparently, Frannie was providing a full bar of coffee drinks to go along with dessert.

Sebastian had taken Elise and gone home shortly after noon. Della had been planning to train, but with the police there, she had fed the dogs and worked inside the kennel instead. And from what Fletcher told her at dinner, Sebastian had decided not to do any more training until he had someone out to check every inch of the other courses.

Fletcher insisted on having Colton Veterinary Clinic inspected as well. He brought in a K-9 officer, which Ruby saw as total overkill, but she had to admit she felt safer going into work Monday morning knowing that the place had been checked for any booby traps.

She wasn't so much afraid of being physically hurt. But living with the constant threat of criminal activity disrupting daily life and hurting dogs was taking its toll on her. She could only imagine what it was doing to Sebastian.

And she figured that the stalker had intended the emotional distress as much as anything physical he'd done.

Which meant, she thought, that the unknown assailant was after Sebastian, not her.

Sebastian had asked her to text when she got home Sunday night. She did, hoping that he'd call. He just texted back instead.

And she figured that was just as well.

He thanked her for letting him know and telling her that Elise had been out in the exercise yard several times and was doing just fine. He kept things on a less personal level.

More their usual style.

Other than the vein bleed, the retriever's wounds had all been fairly superficial. Because Sebastian had been out there to stop the dog from digging any further for the blood-covered meat she'd found.

Fletcher had let her know quietly after dinner that the blood on the meat had tested as human.

But as gruesome a warning as that sounded, he, Steele and Sebastian all figured it was the sign of a thorough stalker, someone who knew that human blood would be most likely to attract a search-and-rescue animal, not a warning of more human bloodshed to come.

They were testing the blood for a DNA match, though. Hoping that they'd have a lead on the assailant within a few days.

That blood could be the mistake they'd been waiting for.

And before she could fully begin to plan the next phase of her life, she needed the stalker caught. Overkill, maybe, but she was growing more and more adamant that she didn't want the person to know that she was carrying a baby. And most particularly did not want him even suspecting that it could be Sebastian's.

Still, having been with her whole family, in her parents' home, playing with Lucy... She couldn't help thinking how the family dinner would look next time Fletcher came home. If he waited for his next yearly vacation. There'd be a playpen, a car seat. She'd be breast-feeding. Changing diapers. And holding a baby. Her mom would be taking charge of the infant, holding baby cheeks up to her own and talking that sweet talk again...

Elation welled in her, mixing with panic. And other

things, too. Excitement. And an odd combination of sadness and regret that she didn't understand.

Which had led her to wanting to hear Sebastian's voice. To talk to him. Telling herself she yearned for him in particular because he was the only one who knew her full secret. Who had an idea of what her future looked like.

But Monday morning, as she left for work, seeing the empty place in her garage where his truck had been parked the morning before, she realized that it was a good thing she and Sebastian hadn't talked the night before. With emotions running abnormally high, they could lead themselves into a place neither one of them would want to be when the dust settled.

And the last thing she wanted to do was trap a man into being there for her.

But it wasn't just her who'd need him. Ruby might be the only visible occupant of her vehicle, but she wasn't the only living human there. She wasn't alone anymore.

Ever. Not even for a second.

And while her child would grow up, and apart from her, that new life forming inside her would always be a part of her.

The concept was mind-boggling.

Every aspect of her life was going to change.

Driving along the lake through her hometown, Ruby started to see the businesses differently, too, just as she had her parents' house the night before. The Tides, the high-end restaurant located on the lakefront, was rented out frequently for weddings and special occasions. Jenny had thrown a party for Ruby on the large open patio there when she'd graduated from veterinary school.

Would Ruby be arranging a high-school graduation party in that same space in eighteen years?

And Tap Out Brewery, with its local brews. She'd had some good times there, eating pub food with friends back before they'd all gone their own ways and her work had become her life. The place turned into more of a party venue after 8:00 p.m. Would she be driving by to make certain her teenager wasn't getting sucked into drinking underage?

As the muscles in her stomach tightened with tension, she passed Hutch's diner. And relaxed some. Hutch had always only made breakfast, but it was the best. She'd been going there since she was a kid. Hutch had been gone for four years, but his wife, Sharon, still ran the place, with the help of their son, Billy.

And maybe Ruby's child would one day join her at the clinic. Just like Chase had joined Robert at Colton Properties. And Wade and Malcolm both worked with Uncle Buck at Colton Ranch.

She'd love that. To have her own little one grow up to love animals, to want to care for them with her. And even after her.

There was a sense of permanence in the thought. Of continuity. For years she'd been pushed by the sense that if she didn't work hard all the time, her clinic wouldn't survive. The idea that it could possibly thrive even after she was no longer there was…nice.

Coming up to the newest addition on Main Street, she pulled over in front of the long, narrow three-story brick building and turned off the SUV. Frannie's bookstore and café, Book Mark It, wasn't open yet, but her sister had offered the night before to have tea ready for Ruby on her way to work if she wanted to stop.

Frannie hadn't said, but it would be decaffeinated. Because… Frannie knew.

And while Ruby could make her own morning beverage at work, and normally would have just to save the time, she went inside to see her little sister, instead.

Sebastian wasn't waiting on Ruby's brother, or anyone else, to start his lure-the-stalker-out campaign. He'd wait to involve anything in Owl Creek, but the filming, and interviewing was going to begin on Monday. And the first segment would air in Boise later that week. He'd called Andy, Bryony and Della to let them know they needn't come into work.

Not Monday, for sure. And, if they chose, they could take off until the Crosswinds attacker was caught. He couldn't require people to risk their lives.

Della refused to take any time off. And she brought her own two-year-old search-and-rescue black Lab, Charlie, with her when she arrived in time on Monday to help Sebastian with the feedings and kennel cleanings.

Neither of them ended up doing much of either as Bryony and Andy showed up, too, telling Sebastian they'd work extra hours to make up for James's absence.

His crew wasn't just there to make money. They cared about the Crosswinds mission, they told him, in an impromptu little meeting in the kennel that morning. They loved the dogs.

And maybe they cared about him, too, he thought, as, fueled with energy, he left them to their tasks and took Oscar home for a PTSD session.

He'd been working with the dog since Ruby had first suggested that Oscar could be cross-trained. He'd figured trying couldn't hurt.

If it worked, he could add cross-training to the list of Crosswinds services.

The film crew and cohost interviewer weren't due until afternoon, when it would be warmest outside.

Sitting at the table, Sebastian started bumping one heel up and down on the floor. Two seconds, and Oscar was there, nudging his knee.

"Good boy!" He gave the dog a treat. And repeated the process.

He'd noticed that the heel bump was something he did when he was starting to get tense. He'd always taken the movement as a rhythmic reminder to himself to relax. But if he could teach Oscar to cue him when it started, the dog's distraction and loving attention might calm him before the tension escalated.

He knew the ropes. Had been training PTSD dogs for a few years. It was different when he was working with his dog. For himself. The thought created a curious level of anxiety.

Except that…he wasn't just doing it for himself. What if he was around his kid sometime, fell asleep and had a flipping nightmare?

If Oscar was there, if he was trained to nudge Sebastian when signs of a nightmare began, there'd be an added level of safety for the kid.

Not that he planned to have the kid around and fall asleep. He wasn't a family guy. Just the thought of not having his space to himself created a level of anxiety.

But the thought of not helping Ruby? Of not being a part of his own child's life? At first, he'd gone there automatically. Had made the logical choice. But as he'd lain in bed at night, and went about his tasks during the day, as he faced the fact that Ruby could be hurt, and that his child would, too…

Oscar nudged him.

Hard.

And he relaxed. "Good boy!" he said, giving the dog a treat. Oscar had the calming skill down. Far better than Sebastian did, apparently.

He moved on to simulate a moaning sound that he knew commonly accompanied nightmares. Ruby had told him he was moaning. Showing Oscar a treat, and moaning, and giving the dog the treat.

Oscar, who'd already mastered search-and-rescue training, caught on quickly. A couple of more moans and the dog was nudging for treats.

Figuring he'd move on to serotonin-level change, getting up to retrieve hormones that would simulate the smell, Sebastian stopped when his phone beeped a text message.

He hadn't yet heard from Ruby. She'd said she'd text when she got to work. Just so he'd know she was there.

More eager than he should have been to hear from Crosswinds's veterinarian, he grabbed his phone off the table.

YOU CARE MORE ABOUT DOGS THAN YOU DO PEOPLE

The phone number was blocked.

Tapping the newest icon on his speed dial, Sebastian got Fletcher on the first ring.

He hadn't even started his campaign and the guy was escalating.

Hitting out at him and not Ruby. Because he thought

Ruby had minded his command and stayed away the morning before?

"Bring it on," Sebastian said aloud, standing. "Come at me and we'll get this done."

Facing the danger on his own, by himself, he wasn't afraid.

He was trained.

The day flew by. Other than breaks for proper nutrition to go along with her horse-pill-size vitamins, Ruby moved efficiently from appointment to appointment, enjoying her time with each client and patient, answering questions, advising, giving lots of hugs and getting plenty of nose kisses, too. Until late afternoon, the day was the kind she liked best—all well checks. And everyone checked out well. She never scheduled surgeries on Mondays unless there was an emergency.

She was just getting ready to sit at her desk and make notes in her charting system when she got a call from the reception desk telling her that a dog injured in a car accident was on the way in. A runaway beagle had been hit on Main Street.

Three hours later, tired, but filled with satisfaction, with the sense that she was living her best life, she headed home. The beagle had lost part of an ear, and one kidney. He might walk with a slight limp, but he should fully recover and live a normal life. Barney's elderly owners had both been in tears when she'd led them back to see the boy before going home for the night.

Maria would be spending the night at the clinic and would call Ruby if anything changed with Barney before morning.

Figuring her family should be proud of her—in prior

days Ruby would have spent the night on the couch in her office and sent her technician home—Ruby was looking forward to some of Hannah's homemade vegetable soup as she pulled into the nighttime traffic. Filled with tourists all year round, Owl Creek was always a happening place during the evening hours as people came in from days of boating, fishing, skiing, or climbing and were looking for evening entertainment.

The Tides was booming, as was the brewery. She figured the nightclub just outside of town would be, too. But not for Ruby. None of it sounded good to her. Her sister had made up several individual containers of her soup for freezing and had gifted Ruby, and the rest of the family, with them the night before. Ruby was having part of her share for dinner.

And maybe she'd hear from Sebastian. More than just a text message. He'd had a marketing crew in that afternoon, she knew. But she hadn't talked to him or heard from Fletcher or Detective Steele all day.

Didn't mean nothing had happened. Only that it hadn't directly involved her.

She didn't like not knowing.

So why didn't she ask? Who said she had to wait to hear? And if she wanted to talk to Sebastian, why didn't she?

Filled with self-righteous energy, she gave the voice command to call Sebastian. And grinned in the darkness of her car's interior when he picked up on the first ring.

"Have you eaten?" she asked without preamble.

"Nope. Just coming in from the kennels for the night." He'd had a long day. She wanted to hear about it. As a volunteer in his program. Her Dr. Colton persona wanted a rundown on her patients, too.

"You like vegetable soup?" she asked before she could get ahold of herself and change her mind. She was carrying his child. He wanted to be involved. They were friends. And she wanted to see him.

"I do."

"You want to come over?"

"Of course."

"I'm not there yet. I had an emergency come in at the end of my day. Spent three hours in surgery."

What in the hell was she doing? Sharing her day with him like they were a couple or something. She always went home alone after work. Long days and not so long. Grueling and easy. Her, alone. It's how she wanted it.

"I'm leaving now," Sebastian said.

Starting to doubt herself, she almost canceled the invitation she'd just issued, but he'd hung up. Too much was changing. Too fast.

She wasn't a woman who ever had a man over after work.

Or ever.

Her home was her haven.

It was soon going to have a new human being living in it full-time.

Sebastian was an offshoot of that little person.

And a big man with an appetite to match. Her servings of vegetable soup weren't going to be enough to satisfy the mountain man who'd been working all day and hadn't had dinner. She turned into the grocery store, then ran in and grabbed a loaf of freshly baked Italian bread from the bakery and a precut vegetable tray from the deli. Paid at self-checkout and was back at her car within minutes. Her little house, right on the lake, was only another couple of minutes away and he had ten to get to town.

She'd left her nightshirt on the kitchen counter, to remind herself to do a load of laundry when she got home. And hadn't put away the rest of the supplies she'd used for Elise the day before, either, which she needed to do to set the table for dinner.

For that matter, she hadn't emptied the dishwasher.

She had not thought the evening's events through.

She wasn't a woman who could just entertain a man on a moment's notice.

"He's not a man. He's Sebastian," she said aloud as she rounded the curve to her little lakefront home. Heard the absurdity of the statement, considering the fact that his manly part had very much changed her life, and...

Lights shone to the left of her. Blinding her in her rearview mirror.

Sebastian?

Already?

The vehicle wasn't behind her.

What the...?

It was there, up to her bumper, beside her, going to hit her...

Ruby swerved. Had no shoulder to turn on. And came to an abrupt stop in the ditch.

Heart pounding, she sat for a second. "I'm fine," she said aloud, checking to make certain her assertion was correct. The airbag hadn't deployed. She hadn't hit the steering wheel. She'd felt her seat belt, but hadn't been bruised.

Glancing in her mirrors, she unbuckled herself with shaking hands. All was dark around her. The vehicle had sped on past. She could see lights shining from homes down from hers. Their little access road didn't get a lot of traffic.

Taking a deep breath, she tried to calm herself. She needed to get home. But the nose of her SUV was stuck in dirt. And with the small but sharp incline she'd headed down, there was no way she could back up.

She'd have to walk. Or wait for Sebastian. Opening her door, she pulled out her phone to call him so he didn't miss her and drive on past. She couldn't stop shaking, missing his speed dial on the first attempt and...

She screamed as arms came around her from behind. Pulling up under her armpits. She saw black gloves. "No!" She got a word into the second scream.

"I've been told that land is mine," a male voice said softly into her ear. "I will have it. God says animals are here to serve man, not for man to serve them. It's blasphemy."

Scared, trembling, unable to breathe, she flung her head back as hard as she could, hitting her assailant in the face. He released her and pushed away, and she fell to the ground.

Lights came around the corner. She had a flash of the man's face. His bloody nose. Then he turned and ran off through the trees.

Gasping for air, trembling, Ruby crawled to her tire. Pulled herself up.

Saw Sebastian.

And started to cry.

# *Chapter 15*

Leaving Ruby's SUV nose-down in the ditch, Sebastian picked her up, cradled in his arms, grabbed her satchel and rushed them both to his truck.

"I'm fine," she said, but the way she laid her head against his chest, pushing into him, showed him the lie in her words.

He dropped her satchel to pull open the passenger door. Set her on the seat, pushed the button to ease it back, strapped her in and set her satchel on the floor of his truck as though he'd been through save-your-child's-mother basic training.

He just moved. On instinct.

Got himself in the driver's seat the same way. No thought. No feeling. Just do.

As soon as the truck was on, and headed back to Main Street, he voice-called Fletcher Colton, telling the detective in a few succinct words what he'd come upon, giving a description of the back of the fleeing man, which was all he'd seen, and let him know the direction in which the man had gone.

Fletcher had questions, spat out in the same manner.

He answered every one of them.

Including that he had Ruby and was taking her to be examined.

By the time he hung up, he was already heading toward the highway.

"I don't need to be examined." She was raising her seat as she said the words. "He didn't hurt me, Sebastian. He just scared the air out of me."

"I saw you on the ground." Emotion hit then. Hard. Full of anger. He'd find the man. And show him why he should never have touched Ruby Colton.

"I head-butted him," she said, sounding more like the woman he'd known since childhood. Controlled. Self-sufficient.

She'd been crying when he'd picked her up. It was a sight that was going to haunt him.

"I think I broke his nose." She sounded as though she might be bragging a little. "I know I made him bleed."

Sebastian's grip tightened on the wheel. "How do you know that?"

"I saw the blood coming out of his nose."

"You saw his face."

"Yeah, in your headlight as you came up the road. I think that's what made him run off." He heard the fear in her tone at the last remark. She shuddered.

And he gritted his teeth against the need powering through him to go hunt the guy down. Right then. Himself.

Because getting Ruby to the emergency room was more important.

"If you hadn't come—"

"You'd have been fine," he interrupted. He had to believe those words.

"I should talk to Fletcher," she said then, as though just coming into a full awareness of the situation. "Turn around. I'm fine, really. We need to get back so I can talk to the police. And I have to get my car out of the ditch. I have to be in early to check on Barney. And I have appointments starting at eight."

"You're pregnant, Ruby. Your SUV obviously hit the ditch with some force. And if you were close enough to head-butt the guy with enough force to land you on the ground, I have to assume he had some kind of hold on you, and then let you go in a way that caused you to fall."

She wouldn't have deliberately lain down for the guy. Sebastian would bet his life on that one.

She was fully dressed. Her clothes weren't torn. He'd just been on the phone with her ten minutes before he'd come upon her...

The man hadn't had a chance to...

He owed fate his life for sparing her...

Thoughts flew. Started and stopped.

"Fletcher and Steele will have people out casing the area. I had enough of a description for them to apprehend him if they find him soon. We need to get you checked out to make certain the baby is okay. That's more important than a police report," he told her.

They just needed the baby to be okay.

He repeated the words to himself. And then again.

Until he realized just how much he had invested in

the small being growing inside Ruby. Not just his biology, but the heart and soul of him.

He wasn't going to be a father. But he'd fathered a child.

And would give up his life for that tiny being, too.

She and the baby were both fine. Ruby had known they were, and yet, when the doctor came into her Connors emergency-room cubicle and told her so, she'd been flooded with relief, anyway.

There'd been no doubt, since she'd found out she was pregnant, that she was going to have the child. That moment alone with the doctor, waiting on the precipice of knowing what the ultrasound had revealed, she'd been shown just how much she wanted the baby. How deeply she already loved it.

The worried look on Sebastian's face when she approached him in the waiting room touched her heart, too.

He cared.

And that mattered.

"All good," she said, unable to stop the smile that spread on her face.

Or to stop the flip-flop her heart gave when he smiled back.

Reliving the near kidnapping, trembling, as she stepped out into the dark, she stopped her hand from sneaking around his elbow, forcing herself to keep her distance as she walked with him back to the truck.

They were friends.

Not lovers.

As she reminded herself on the forty-five-minute drive back to Owl Creek—Sebastian was all business, and there was no reason for her feelings to be hurt by that fact.

Her emotions were on overload.

She was not only hormonal due to pregnancy, but she'd also been through a near abduction. Sebastian was the guy who'd happened by to clean up the mess.

She'd be on top of the fear by morning. And would have the rest of her heart back in line by then as well. With all the upheaval she'd experienced growing up, she knew she could count on herself to be strong and step away from the drama.

As soon as they were in the truck, Sebastian started filling her in on news from Fletcher.

There'd been no sign of a man between five-ten and six feet in dark pants, a dark, long-sleeved hoodie and dark shoes anywhere in the woods or neighborhood surrounding Ruby's house. Officers canvassed houses and businesses on Main Street, too, but no one remembered seeing a man with that description.

They were requesting private security footage, both in the neighborhood and from businesses along Main Street, to go through.

"He had dark hair," Ruby said, when Sebastian paused for breath. "And he was white." She remembered his hands coming up from her sides, as his arms slid under her armpits, and shuddered again.

Glancing at her, his chin seemed to tighten, but in the darkness of the truck, she couldn't be sure.

"They found an SUV, Ruby," he said, his tone like a sergeant, reporting to the masses. She knew the tone. From Fletcher and Wade, too.

Wasn't overly fond of it.

But being one who sometimes had to be the bearer of bad news at work, she completely understood it.

"It fits the description you gave from Friday morning. It was abandoned in the woods across from your house."

"He ran me off the road," she said, as it occurred to her that Sebastian hadn't known that part. She'd been in panic mode when the father of her child had arrived. Was still trying to comprehend that she'd nearly been taken against her will.

Shivering, she wanted the memory, the horrifying sensations involved with it, to go away. Forever.

"Just like Friday morning…"

But that night she'd been in the ditch. "I wasn't able to turn out of it," she said slowly, reliving those moments, with darkness looming larger than the lights on the dash, the lights in the homes along the lake. "I sat in the ditch," she remembered. "Trying to figure out what had just happened. Deciding what to do. I was just getting out of the SUV, to flag you down, when…"

He'd grabbed her.

She was cold. Needed a warm blanket. Forced herself to think.

"My phone," she said. "I was calling you…"

He glanced her way again. Maybe it was her imagination, but he seemed pleased by those last words.

And in times of crisis, a little fantasy to get her through didn't hurt, did it?

"Fletcher's meeting us at your house." Sebastian repeated something he'd told Ruby on the way to the truck in the hospital parking lot.

She didn't respond. He wasn't sure how much she'd processed of anything he'd been telling her.

"He talked to me," she said softly, her entire body shaking, as though warding off a chill. He reached to the dash, turned up the heat in the truck. Kept his eye on his driving, and glanced at her, too. Back and forth. The road. Her. The road. Her.

She'd hadn't mentioned hearing a voice.

Was she imagining things?

It was only a couple of hours since she'd been attacked, and he knew what trauma-induced panic could do...

"It just came to me, the sound of his voice in my ear." She hugged her arms, her voice sounding almost childlike.

"What did he say?" Sebastian asked softly. With as much kindness as he had inside him.

"'I've been told that land is mine, I will have it. God says animals are here to serve man, not for man to serve them. It's blasphemy.'" The words rolled off her tongue with no intonation whatsoever. "It was him, Sebastian. Your stalker. The SUV, yeah, but those words. It was him." As she looked his way and continued talking, her tone rose, panic lacing every syllable.

And Sebastian pressed his foot on the pedal all the way to the floor.

He had to get her back to Fletcher.

And needed to hold on to her.

No way was he leaving her to drown in the panic all alone.

He knew how that felt.

And she was there because of him.

Ruby refused to go to her parents' house. Or to the police station. At ten o'clock at night, her big brother could come to her house.

She had to go home.

To be where she was the boss of the land.

She heard Sebastian relay the information to Fletcher while they were still ten minutes outside of Owl Creek.

"He doesn't think it's a good idea for you to go back to that neighborhood right now," Sebastian told her, hanging up.

"That's exactly why I *have* to go back," she retorted. "I won't let this fiend turn my home into a haunted house. Besides, if he was going to do something to me at home, he'd simply have waited until I got there," she added. "I was three houses down. If nothing else, he could have waited for me to pull into the garage and slipped inside…" Her voice trailed off as another wave of panic hit.

Sebastian shot a quick look at her. And then said, "I think you're probably right about that."

He almost sounded relieved.

"I guess it's better that tonight's…episode relates to my work at Crosswinds, rather than just that I'm un-lucky enough to be the target of a second madman." Dear God, let that have meant that he wouldn't have forced himself on her.

No. She wasn't going to borrow trouble.

She had enough real boogeymen chasing her mind at the moment.

As they passed the sign announcing the turn-off for Owl Creek in two miles, Sebastian blurted out, "We have to tell Fletcher about the baby. I've been trying to figure out a way to get your cooperation on this one, and I know it's not what you want or what would be easiest for you. I get that you don't need your family breathing down on you any more than they already are, or will soon be, but I'm not backing down on this one. Not anymore."

When he finished, finally giving her a chance to get a word in, she said, "I know." And then added, "But we don't have to tell anyone that you're the father."

He'd pulled to a stop at the bottom of the highway exit ramp. They had the road to themselves, and when he glanced over at her, he didn't seem to be all that concerned about turning into town. "Are you ashamed to tell them it's me?"

"No!" She'd screamed the word once before that night. Her throat still stung from the sounds she'd made. That second time, it wasn't filled with panic. But with exclamation. "No," she said again, more calmly. "I'm thinking of you, Sebastian."

"Then you don't know me all that well." He faced forward.

"What does that mean?" She could see the set of his chin in the darkness but little else. Avoiding the strong desire to unbuckle and touch that chin—it wasn't anything she'd know how to pull off casually—she continued into the silence, "Talk to me, please," she said, in her more professional tone.

"I'm a man of honor. I don't shirk my duties. And I won't have anyone in your family thinking that I do."

She wished she hadn't asked. Her heart fell as she heard the words.

It wasn't about her.

Or their baby.

It was about Once a Marine, Always a Marine. Wade's explanation anytime she told him he was getting on her nerves with his need to fight for and defend everyone in their family anytime he was home on leave.

With a nod, she accepted his explanation and waited for him to take her home.

# Chapter 16

*Are you ashamed to tell them it's me?* Where in the hell had that come from? If ever there was a man completely out of his element, it was Sebastian.

Fighting the enemy, he knew what to do every time. Whether that enemy was a terrorist in another land, or one in his own backyard, antagonizing his dogs. And his veterinarian.

But finding out that the night his friend had taken pity on him, he'd made her pregnant? In spite of the precautions they'd taken...

How did a confirmed bachelor go about figuring out how to deal with that? Most particularly in a small town that, along with his dogs, was the only family he had left?

She'd gone cold when he'd overreacted to her very sweet offer to keep his name out of her baby confession that evening. He'd have apologized if he hadn't thought it would make matters worse. If for no other reason than because they'd almost reached her house and had no time left to talk about it.

Her SUV was already back in the driveway, with her brother's right beside it. Fletcher climbed out as Sebastian pulled up out front. Half expecting Ruby to wish him good-night before she exited his vehicle, he was aware as she climbed down from the truck and then stood there, as though waiting for him to finish rounding the front of the vehicle.

No way he wasn't going to be present for the coming conversation. Just felt irrationally good that she'd seemed to take his presence for granted.

After giving his sister a thorough once-over glance, Fletcher took a seat at Ruby's kitchen table—still strewn with supplies from her attention to Elise the morning before—and announced that while Steele was running command on the officers out on the street, Fletcher would be recording the interview with Ruby.

Sebastian sat diagonally across from the detective and Ruby sat next to Sebastian. He didn't make anything of it.

The ten-minute conversation was straightforward. Ruby told her brother everything she'd told Sebastian in the truck. Adding more description to the man's face. With the light's glare she hadn't been able to tell an age, but she'd seen no age lines. He'd had facial hair, but no beard or mustache. Just stubble. Light-colored, not dark, like his hair. She agreed to sit with a sketch artist Fletcher was calling in from Boise in the morning.

Then Fletcher turned off the recording, putting his phone down on the table instead of back into his pocket.

Glancing between the two of him. The detective's frown, the uneasy look in his eyes, had Sebastian looking at Ruby. Gearing up to take the brunt of whatever was coming.

She seemed to be holding up fine. Hands folded on the table, tone strong. It was as though the attack had never happened.

"First, it's pretty clear to everyone that this guy tonight is the same one we've already been hunting," Fletcher started in. "The SUV they found tonight just yards from where Ruby was attacked fits the description she gave Friday morning and then again this evening." Fletcher looked at both of them. "The vehicle was stolen last Thursday from a big-box store in Connors…"

"Which means we've just lost our best chance at getting him," Sebastian guessed. "He's changing vehicles. Driving stolen ones."

"It looks that way. Which would explain why we haven't been able to find the same vehicle leaving town on all the nights there's been attacks at Crosswinds."

His enemy was a canny one.

"He's been told that the land is his," Fletcher said, glancing between him and Ruby, but settling on Sebastian. "We have to assume this means the land upon which Crosswinds is sitting. Which brings us back to the possibility that your father had a child outside of his marriage to your mother. From Ruby's description, he sounds younger as opposed to not—that would fit, too."

Sebastian nodded. He'd also gone straight to the idea of a love child after Ruby had told him what the guy had said.

"But this…" Fletcher referred to the notes he'd also

been taking on a yellow pad. "'God says that animals are there to serve men…and not for men to serve…'"

"Has to refer to the kennels," Sebastian mused. "Until James quit, there were five of us there, pretty much every day, taking care of the dogs."

"And Ruby most definitely fits the role of serving animals," Fletcher continued, glancing back at his sister.

Sebastian felt her stiffen beside him. She was no longer shaking. Whether it was because she had her fear under control, or just enough determination to remain strong in front of her brother, he couldn't be sure.

Suspected it was the latter.

The woman had certainly perfected the guise of being a rock on the outside. Growing up as she had, he couldn't blame her.

"He's after you, too, Ruby. And judging by his behavior, it would appear that he's no longer satisfied just going after the dogs and issuing warnings. Tonight's episode shows us that he's escalating. They found rope in the car. He wasn't going to just warn you and let you go."

She nodded, surprising Sebastian. And scaring him. Ruby rarely just acquiesced and that was the second time that night. First one being when he insisted on telling her brother about the baby.

But then, looking from Sebastian to her brother, she asked, "What possible reason would he have for kidnapping me? I volunteer at Crosswinds—I don't own it. I get that I've angered him. That my work has systematically undone pretty much every attempt he's made to put Crosswinds out of business, but what does he gain by taking me? There are three other veterinarians in my office alone…"

Sebastian glanced at Fletcher, who said, "How many do you think will be eager to service those dogs, knowing that they could end up like you? Or how do you think it will look in the news? 'Crosswinds veterinarian kidnapped…'"

She shook her head. "I can't believe someone would resort to such tactics…"

"He would if he was experiencing some kind of psychotic break." Sebastian issued the explanation softly, while inside, every fighting instinct he had was at the ready. "Assuming he's a result of this affair of my dad's they think they've discovered at this point…he's grown up on the outside looking in. Even if he didn't know that my dad was his father, he'd have grown up without knowing his real father. Somehow he finds out, either he's always known, or maybe his mother told him after Dad died. She could easily have known about the Owl Creek property. Maybe even told the kid he deserved to have it. For all I know some lawyer told him it was his. From what Ruby said, he seemed to have no doubt that what he'd been told was true. And yet, he gets here and finds out that I'm firmly ensconced. The only known heir, the only legal heir and running an elite training business on what he thinks is his land. Then you come along—" Sebastian looked at Ruby "—and thwart every attempt he makes to get me to tuck my tail and go."

"He hasn't done enough homework if he thinks you'd ever do that," Ruby said, her words more of a statement of fact than praise. His heart lifted a bit at the words, anyway.

"I see where you're going with this," Fletcher added then, his gaze toward Sebastian assessing. "You could be hitting it exactly right. Ruby's in his way. He's getting more and more desperate, maybe becoming more unhinged, and just sees her as someone he has to get out of the way. Which makes him even more dangerous. He's still thinking clearly enough to create all these issues without ever being seen or coming close to getting caught. He's wearing gloves, so leaving no prints. Other than the rope, there was nothing else in the car."

At her sudden intake of air, Sebastian sent her brother a look. Ruby was strong. She wasn't inhuman.

"I'm sorry," Fletcher said, then added, "But not completely. You can't stay here, Ruby. I don't care how much you argue. He clearly knows where you live."

Relieved that he wasn't the one bringing up the matter he'd been planning to discuss with her as soon as they were through with Fletcher, Sebastian said, "Your parents have state-of-the-art security. You'd be much safer there."

If her brother hadn't been sitting there, he'd have mentioned the baby. Even if she survived another attack, the baby might not get that lucky. If the man had hit her harder, if the seat belt jerked tighter across her belly, if the airbag had deployed...

He started to sweat again...as he had pretty much the entire time he'd sat in the hospital waiting room that evening. She had to see the sense in not staying home alone until the unknown man was caught. "You saw his face," he added. "He's going to know you can identify him."

"Which brings a whole new level of desperation to his thinking," Fletcher said.

"Did someone check the ground for blood splatter?" Ruby asked. "Or my hair? Maybe I got some of his DNA on me when I hit him with the back of my head."

Sebastian's tension increased. He needed her on her parents' property. Safely locked in. Not sitting here trying to solve the crime. But while Fletcher called Steele to check the dirt in the area of the attempted kidnapping for blood, Sebastian turned on his phone light and studied the back of Ruby's hair. It was tucked up in her usual messy bun.

"I hit him with the bun," she said then. He grabbed some paper towel off the rack in the kitchen and pulled out her scrunchie. He saw no sign of blood but gathered the plastic bag she told him was in the drawer, inserted the hair band and paper towel and handed it over to Fletcher when the other man completed his call.

"If your shampoo has peroxide in it, and many of them do, that will most likely falsify any result for blood testing," Fletcher said. But he added that they'd test the few hairs attached to the scrunchie, just in case.

And he asked Ruby for her clothes. Again, just in case.

While she went to change, Sebastian looked at Fletcher. "She didn't say she'd go."

The detective nodded. "If I have to, I'll stay here myself, but I'd rather meet up with Steele, compare notes, see what we can find on the few new leads we have. We know the guy was in Connors on Thursday. Maybe surveillance tapes from there can give us something."

"She can't stay here," Sebastian said. Almost bursting with the need to know that Ruby would be in a safe place.

"I can hear you," she said, joining the two and handing Fletcher a bag with her work clothes inside. She'd put on jeans and a sweatshirt. Sebastian hoped that meant she was planning to go out again that night. To her parents' house.

Ruby looked at him. A long, meaningful glance.

Gut knotting, he sat back down when she did.

"What's up?" Fletcher asked.

"I'm pregnant."

If Sebastian hadn't been so involved, so disturbed with worry and his inability to control Ruby's every move so that he could keep her safe, he might have felt a small bit of amusement from the way the detective's jaw seemed to drop down to the table.

"You don't have to look that astonished, Fletch. I have had sex now and then on occasion."

Her brother coughed. Glanced at Sebastian, as though looking to him for some kind of guy way to handle the moment. "Pregnant?" Fletcher said then.

Flipping back his chair with force the detective stood. "By who? For how long?" And then, turning a complete circle, he asked, "Tonight...is everything okay?"

"We're both fine," Ruby told him.

And that's when Sebastian jumped up. It was either that or grab the woman and hold her close and out of danger, her and his child, for the rest of his natural life.

Ruby didn't want a whole drawn-out thing. She'd had a long day. A horrible evening. And wanted her brother's piercing stare—and the knowledge that he was going home to their parents' house—gone.

She needed some peace. Time to recover. To relax, if she could. To think.

Standing, with her arms crossed, she said, "The father's a friend. A good one. The baby is the result of one night that was filled with tension, just like this one. We used protection. It didn't work. I was shocked when I first found out. I'm already in love with the child, Intend to raise it on my own, my choice, and Hannah and Lizzie know, but no one else does, and I really need you to keep this quiet." She finished the spiel she'd been working on, mostly subconsciously, for the past week, then added, "I've got enough on my plate at the moment."

"You have to tell Mom and Dad," Fletcher replied. "You're going to be staying with them."

The baby was one of the reasons she'd been fighting with herself to stay home. There was no way she could live with her mother, a nurse, and not have Jenny figure out something. The first time Ruby smelled coffee and threw up would do it.

"And how good a friend is this guy if he's letting you take this on all alone?" Fletcher's tone was sharp, but faded at the end. He glanced at Sebastian. "A night filled with tension just like this one." Fletcher repeated her words. And then added, "He's not leaving you to take this on all alone, is he?" The question was meant for Ruby, but her brother hadn't moved since he'd locked eyes with Sebastian.

"No, he is not," Sebastian answered for her. He wasn't moving, either.

The two men were like… She didn't know what— opposing forces that didn't ever back down or lose. And the last thing she needed at the moment.

When Fletcher said, "Okay," and took a step back, Ruby was the one standing with her mouth open. "And now that I know the full detail—" he very clearly meant just one "—I understand why we need to keep this quiet. We absolutely do not want this guy getting any idea that there's another heir in the making."

Ruby cringed and looked away, fearing Sebastian's reaction to the casually dropped phrase, until she felt his hand on her shoulder. "I do agree that your parents should know, though," he said, increasing the tension he'd just deescalated with his touch. "She can't stay there without them being aware..."

"Hello, I'm right here," she said, frowning at both of them. But deep inside, where she didn't want to look at the moment, she knew they were right.

But... "I'll make a deal with you," she said. "I stay here tonight. One of you stay with me. And tomorrow we go to Mom and Dad's. And we tell them about the baby. I just don't have it tonight to deal with them. Not on top of everything else. Please."

"I'll stay," both men said at once.

Ruby glanced at Sebastian, making her choice clear. And Fletcher let himself out.

# Chapter 17

Sebastian heard the door close as Ruby's brother departed. He didn't watch the man go. He couldn't take his gaze from Ruby. The past few minutes, the entire evening, had been so fraught with tension, and being alone with the slimly built, green-eyed woman, with her long golden blond hair, was doing things to him that weren't right.

Not given the circumstances.

Those being that he was her friend.

And nothing more.

In dress pants and doctor's coat, makeup fresh and hair shiny clean, or in jeans and a sweatshirt after a near kidnapping, she was a vixen, luring him into space he knew he could not occupy.

"How about some of that vegetable soup?" Ruby broke the spell, turning away, toward the kitchen. She mentioned a grocery bag that, last she knew, had been on the front passenger seat of her SUV, and he gladly went to retrieve it for her. To breathe the nippy fresh night air, which cooled his body, but not his mind. Outside, he was a soldier, checking every inch of Ruby's small property, knowing that he was on duty for the rest of the night.

So thinking, he called the night security team manning Crosswinds, had them coax Oscar through his doggy door and lock him in the big kennel room with that officer for the night. He didn't want the boy letting himself out in the middle of the night in the event of an intruder. Sebastian had been closing off Oscar's personal entryway into the house every night before bedtime.

By the time he returned inside, Ruby had the soup heated. He cut bread while she unwrapped the veggie tray and set the table.

Growing up, he'd been the one to set the table. Until he'd deemed the chore not manly enough and then been assigned to do the dishes every night after dinner.

Then he'd learned to cook and was the one who'd prepared dinner. More often than not, he'd eaten it alone. With his plate on his mother's expensive side table, he'd sit on the couch with Jerry right next to him, watch what he wanted on television, or play video games, taking bites as it suited him.

Good memories of easier times.

Much easier than being part of an intimate twosome preparing a meal in the smallest kitchen he'd ever done any food service in.

Ruby talked while she worked. Telling him about Barney, the dog who'd been hit by a car that evening, causing her to stay late at work. Which gave him pause.

Their attacker couldn't have hit the dog on purpose, could he? To keep Ruby late? So that he could attack, as always, at night?

The theory was far-fetched, he silently acknowledged. But he texted Fletcher, anyway, suggesting that they contact the dog's owners and get a rundown of the incident. If it *was* their guy, maybe there was surveillance-camera footage…

Figuring it would be too rude to eat standing at the kitchen counter, which was what he'd have felt more comfortable doing, Sebastian sat across from Ruby, as she indicated which place was his. He put his napkin in his lap as his parents had taught him. And wiped after every spoonful of soup inevitably left drops on his beard.

He'd been on more dates than he could count. Had spent full weekends in the company of whatever woman he'd been seeing. He had never, not even once, been self-conscious sharing a meal with any of them.

Or with Ruby, either, in the past.

He'd never been having a child with any of them.

"This is good," he said, motioning toward the soup.

Ruby nodded. Looked at him, and said, "It's weird, though, isn't it?"

"The soup?" He knew that wasn't what she'd meant. Was not eager for the conversation that was coming. Her brother knew she was pregnant and Sebastian was the father of her child.

Her parents were going to know in less than twenty-four hours.

"We've never even been on a date," she said then. "I've never had a man in my home for a meal, either," she added. Took another bite, almost as though glad for the distraction.

He knew he was. Helped himself to a celery stick and another piece of bread, too. And did what he'd been trained to do—march into battle, not run from it.

"Tell me how you want to play this," he said. "If you want everyone to think we've been secretly dating, or that we were dating and broke up—whatever you need to tell them, give it to me and I'll back you up. One hundred percent. You have family to answer to—I don't. So whatever you need our story to be, that's what it will be."

Ruby took a bite. Then glanced at him, her gaze soft. "I've been sitting here trying to figure out how to tell them that we aren't a couple, aren't in love, have never dated, and are having a baby," she said, her tone as gentle as her look. "And you're right—we don't owe anyone our intimate truths. We just give them what works for us, while staying within boundaries of the truth." Her sudden smile, like she'd solved the problems of the world, pulled an answering smile from Sebastian.

The woman had a way with him that no one else had ever had.

He prayed that it didn't turn out to be what killed him.

"We've been together a lot these past months, with my volunteering at Crosswinds. One thing led to another, and now we're having a baby." With Sebastian sitting across from her in her small dining room, late at night, smiling that way, the words just rolled off Ruby's tongue.

Funny how what had seemed impossible was easy, when shared with a friend. A caring, yet different perspective, that didn't try to force one particular way down her throat.

"Whether we're dating or not isn't anyone's business. We're friends. We know that, in whatever fashion you choose, you're going to be involved in the child's life. So we present ourselves as friendly with each other, sharing a child. Done. End of what they need to know."

She liked it. A lot. Felt a bit easier inside. Took a bite of bread. Enjoyed the homemade, feel-good taste.

"And when your father asks me when the wedding's going to be?"

Chewed bread stuck in her throat. She washed it down with the decaffeinated iced tea she'd served them both.

"We haven't set a date?" she asked, but was only half-serious. He was right. Their situation was bigger than she was making it out to be.

"We're adults, Sebastian," she told him then. "We simply tell him that at this time we aren't planning on getting married. I'll tell him when I tell them that I'm pregnant."

"He's still going to come to me," he said. "I'm not complaining here. Or trying to get you to do anything. I know your father well enough and have heard way more stories from Wade over the years to know that he's traditional. He cares about how he and his family look to others. Appearances matter to him more than, say, being close to your mother. And while he loves you all very much, he's not beyond a little ruthlessness if that's what it takes to make the world what he thinks it should be."

Setting her spoon in her not quite empty bowl, Ruby stared at him. Not sure whether she was angry with him for…what? His honesty? Because he'd been spot on.

But no one was perfect, and Robert Colton was her father. She should defend him.

So why wasn't she?

"He's going to try to force me, somehow, to convince you to marry me."

Force—no, her father wouldn't go that far. But he did wield a lot of power. And had the gift of persuasion down pat.

Robert was also traditional enough, old-fashioned enough, to think that a man could still sweeten a pot enough to get a woman to marry him.

As though being alone was not the better choice.

Enough. Enough. Enough. Enough was enough.

"How about if you come with me in the morning? We tell them together, and I make it very clear to my father that it is my choice not to marry and that there is nothing you can do, say or offer that would make me change my mind?"

She respected Robert. She didn't agree with him a lot of the time. And had no problem standing up to him. Most particularly when it came to the way he took her mother for granted.

He, in return, gave her space and supported her endeavors, even while he had her brothers keeping an eagle eye over her.

And did so himself as well.

Ready to pick up the pieces in case she failed.

At least, that was her take on their relationship. She couldn't speak for any of her siblings.

Sebastian held his bowl up to his mouth to scoop out the last bite. Set the bowl down. Wiped his mouth. And, hands on the table, very quietly said, "I don't need you to handle your father on my behalf, Ruby. Not now. Not ever. I will talk to him man-to-man. I'm asking how you want our story to be so that I have your back."

She blinked. Wasn't sure what to say. Except... "I didn't mean to offend you."

"I'm not offended." He gave an easy shrug. "But I'm also not having you bear the brunt of awkwardness due to our situation. I was fifty percent of the creation, and I will carry fifty percent of the burden." He stopped. Held her gaze, and then said, "There are obvious things that you have to do, like actually giving birth to the child, giving them a home, but I can handle all of the child's financial details, rather than a fifty-fifty split like the law generally requires. And anything else, as yet unknown, you're going to need from me along the way. Right now, I'll be standing right beside you as your parents find out about the baby, and later, when the town does."

Tears pooled in her eyes. She didn't mean them to. Hadn't known they were coming. Didn't know why they were there.

But she knew why Sebastian suddenly leaned over and ran a thumb softly along her cheekbone. It wasn't a gesture of love. Or even of affection.

He'd simply been wiping away the moisture on her face.

Apparently, he intended to reveal his future plans to himself in spurts without thinking ahead.

Sebastian hadn't considered the town, his employees, or anyone but Ruby's family finding out about the baby. Just hadn't gotten that far.

But there he was. Standing by her through all of it.

And feeling completely right about doing so.

"How do we do this?" Ruby asked, turning to him in the kitchen as she stood at the sink rinsing soup bowls.

As soon as he'd seen her tears, and attempted to wipe them, she'd jumped up and grabbed their dishes and spoons.

He'd gathered up the rest of the meal and had been silently seeing to storing it.

When she leaned back against the sink, he took a rest against the opposite counter, facing her. "I don't know," he said. "I guess we just do it."

How did they give answers to questions they didn't yet know?

Or explain what they hadn't yet figured out for themselves.

"One step at a time," he added, because that was what he knew. You assessed the enemy, or the problem, you figured out your end goal. And you took the first step toward reaching that goal. Sometimes the step was face-to-face meetings to reach a satisfactory conclusion for all involved. Sometimes mediation was necessary. And if all else failed, you fought.

Ruby's nod lessened some of the tightening in his gut. "For now, it's just my parents. And we tell them…" When her voice faded off, she was still looking at him, and Sebastian got all tight inside again.

"What?" he asked.

"How do you feel about the baby?"

Not the step he was expecting. "I'm not sure what you mean," he said, anyway. "I'd die for it, if that's what you're asking."

Her lips trembled on their way to a small smile. "That pretty much covers it," she said. And then added, "Are you angry?"

"No." Straight up.

"Sad?"

"No."

She nodded. He was relieved he'd passed her test.

"Happy?"

Of course not. The words were there. Didn't come out. "I'm not happy that it's creating such havoc for you," he told her honestly.

"And for you."

He shook his head. "The only havoc in my life where the child is concerned is this damned Cross-winds stalker and keeping the two of you safe until he's caught. And what telling your parents is going to do to you." Truth.

"Are you happy there's going to be another Cross, your flesh and blood, coming into the world?"

"Yes."

Oh. Well then. He was happy about the baby. He'd arrived in a new place. Because she'd known him well enough to know how to get him there.

She grinned at him.

And he grinned back.

That grin.

Not sure what to do with herself now that they'd eaten and the kitchen was clean, Ruby continued to lean against the counter, facing Sebastian. Wanting to get lost in his smile.

Just for a little bit.

She had a two-bedroom home, but only one of them held a bed.

Fletcher had said the couch was really comfortable.

But the night she'd spent at Sebastian's, he'd shared his bed with her. She wouldn't mind having him in hers. It wasn't like they hadn't done it before.

Or would have repercussions…

Feeling heat rise up inside her, she halted the thoughts. Prayed Sebastian hadn't gotten any hint of what she'd been thinking.

"I'm thinking we tell my parents the truth," she blurted. "That we're happy about the baby. That we are both independent people who never want to get married. And that we're going to be raising the child together."

As soon as she heard the word *raising* come out of her mouth, she froze. Stared at him.

He was nodding. His expression…calm. Easy. "I'm good with that."

He *was*?

He didn't just want to be a help to her, he wanted to be involved in raising his child?

"Why do you look so surprised?" he asked. "I told you I'd go with whatever story you needed to tell."

*Story.* Her heart sank.

# Chapter 18

Ruby, still standing against the sink, heard Sebastian say he was going out to do one more perimeter check.

Nodding, she went to get a sheet, pillow and blanket for the couch.

Having a furious conversation with herself as she did so. What in the hell was she doing? Building some kind of fantasy where Sebastian was a fully engaged, participating father to her baby? Was that what she was really hoping? That they were going to engage in shared parenting? That he'd be by her side, figuratively if not physically, for the tough moments?

Telling herself she was perfectly fine doing it alone... Had she been lying?

By the time she was in the living room, dropping the pillow on top of the bedding she'd just tucked in, she'd calmed some.

She hadn't been lying. She really could see herself mothering the child alone. Knew that she'd be fine. Happy. That she'd be a good mother.

"I was wondering," Sebastian said, coming back in through the kitchen. "Maybe we could..."

He stopped. Stared at the couch.

As if to put the bow on her handiwork, she dropped a sealed toothbrush and paste packet on the pillow. "I collect them from hotels," she said inanely. "When they're complimentary, I bring them home..."

Her words dropped off. And she asked, "Maybe we could...what?"

He looked at the couch. "You're ready to get some rest," he said. "I'm sorry, I should have realized...with all you've been through tonight, and being pregnant..." He shook his head. "I guess I'm going to need some practice at the support role."

"Maybe we could...what?" She repeated her question. And then, as though it made some kind of statement, she sat down in the middle of the bed she'd just made for him.

With a shrug, he sat down beside her. Leaving a few feet between them. "I was thinking we could talk about what the future might look at in terms of my role. But I wasn't thinking about your long day with the late emergency, the ordeal, you needing to get up in the morning and being pregnant."

"I'm fine," she said, feeling much better now that he was sitting there, talking to her. "Tired, but not ready to sleep just yet."

"I was thinking about talking to your parents. Maybe it would be easier if we started to talk about it all. You know. Just between us."

His voice, the look in his eyes, the shaggy dark blond hair… Those muscles…everywhere… Ruby liked every bit of it. A lot.

She particularly liked the *just between us.* Her life was overflowing with people, with family. But to be a part of something that belonged to no one but her and one other person—her and Sebastian…

The flood of warmth that the moment invoked in her was brand-new.

And like the seed he'd let loose inside her to make her pregnant, Ruby had a feeling that Sebastian had once again altered the course of her future.

She just had no idea where his road led.

And that scared her more than the attempted kidnapping had.

The expressions crossing Ruby's face were like a jigsaw puzzle. Sebastian watched them all, but wasn't sure how to put them together.

Or how to answer the question she posed in the midst of them.

"What kind of involvement do you want?" The medical-professional tone she'd adopted each time they'd reached this conversation in the past was absent.

He'd have done better with its presence. With veneers stripped away, all he had was "I have no idea."

"Would you want to know if the baby got sick?"

"Of course."

"To the point of a call in the middle of the night?"

"Absolutely." What did any of that have to do with their future, though? He wasn't getting it. "I already told you, I'm always here to support you, every step of the way."

"Say the child likes soccer. Would you want to be at games?"

He hadn't thought that far ahead. In terms of his own wants. But… "If we could work that out, sure." Who wouldn't enjoy that?

She shook her head. "What's there to work out? You're there or you aren't."

And it hit him. The problem.

"Who do we tell the kid I am?" As soon as he asked the question, he wanted to take it back. He didn't allow insecurities.

And most definitely did not take on anything that he couldn't handle full out.

Ruby's frown sent his turmoil into tornado mode. "I don't get it," she said.

"If this baby knows that I'm the father, then why am I not being a father?" He had the questions, but no answers.

Only…more sweat. More discomfort.

Mouth open, Ruby stared at him for long seconds. Too long. Way, way too long. "You intend to tell my family, and the town, that you're the father of my child, but you didn't think the child would know?"

"It's a baby," he said weakly. Hating his lack of attention to detail. His failure to have all the answers.

Or any at all.

The child was going to grow.

Would look up to those in their life for example.

He'd had a thoracic surgeon to model himself after. A man who'd spent a good deal of his adult life in operating rooms saving lives—and in his spare time, had taught others how to do so.

And Sebastian's kid?

He looked straight at her. "You really want your child to have me as a role model? The ex-Marine who had a panic attack when his dog was shot and in the midst of it, had sex with the angel who'd appeared to save him and got her pregnant?"

He didn't.

Ruby's day melted off from her as she sat there in the aftermath of Sebastian's painfully honest question. Heart open, she felt the compassion, the caring, emerge from her and pour outward, toward him. In an effort to flood him with it.

Used to allowing herself to give her whole heart to the animals she cared for, to all the dogs in her life, she wasn't quite sure what to do with herself.

How to act.

Who to be.

"Maybe you need to hire a different writer for your story," she said softly. Talking because the words were there and she had no other ideas present. "Maybe the example is one of a friendship between two loners, there for each other without question in time of need, and fate steps in and gives them both a human being to love as their own."

Intensity shone from his sharp blue eyes. Pulling more words out of her. "In that story it wasn't just the ex-Marine who got the woman pregnant. She needed something from him that night, too, which he so tenderly and unselfishly gave, and she was equally responsible for what happened."

For a man who wasn't moving at all, Sebastian managed to bathe the room in emotion. So much that she had to start swimming or drown.

"Now might not be the best time to say this, or maybe it's the exact right time, I don't know, but I need to rest, Sebastian…"

Of course. He stood, blinked, and it was as though he turned off the faucet and sucked all the fluid out of the room. "I'll just…"

"What?" she asked him, feeling a strange kind of power as she sat there looking up at the strong mountain of a man. "I'm sitting on your bed. There's not much you can do." Her words were almost a challenge as, empowered by the knowledge that her friend and co-parent had a whole lot of him hidden inside.

And had shown her a huge chunk.

Crossing his arms on that massive chest, he stared her down.

When she didn't do anything but stare back, he said, "Finish what you were going to say."

"What I got that night… I could use another dose. I'm finding that I don't want to go to bed without it."

He started, his head jerking back sharply, maybe in horror. But at her eye level, he had a different response. "Are you actually sitting there telling me you want to have sex with me tonight?" he asked.

She was saying far more than that.

She'd already given him too much. More than she'd ever given anyone.

Which scared her.

So for starters… "I'm not much in a position to have it with anyone else now, am I?" She had to be strong.

To keep her wits about her.

"No, I guess not, so, if that's what you want, then, of course…"

No way. Uh-uh.

"Is that what you want?"

"This isn't about me."

There. That bothered her.

"So it's not a good thing when you're in need, and I help, but it's okay if I'm in need and you help."

He sat back down. "We aren't talking about sex here, are we?"

She looked him in the eye. "Yes." And said, "On a practical level, I was mishandled by a man tonight. I'd like to have a pleasant male-female physical experience to replace the repulsion my skin is feeling. On another similarly practical level, I think you and I did sex remarkably well, and it makes sense for two friends who understand and respect each other, friends who don't ever want to marry, to be able to share physical pleasure with each other. And there's the third aspect, which I've already mentioned… The awkwardness of me having sex with another man when I'm pregnant with your child…"

She was losing control of the situation. She could feel it.

And see it in his expression, too. The shift in power.

Teetering on just letting go, Ruby pulled herself back. Something much larger than winning and losing, than staying strong and maintaining independence, hovered around them.

*We aren't talking about sex here, are we…?*

"And no," she said, giving him the deeper answer to his question. "The friendship you gave so tenderly, so unselfishly that night… I need it again, Sebastian. Tonight, at least. As you said, it's been a rough day…"

She hadn't finished speaking when Sebastian reached for her, sliding his arms under her knees and back, just as he had earlier that evening.

But this time when he carried her, it wasn't to drop her alone in a car seat.

Or to deposit her anywhere.

He strode to her room, sat and then lay down with her on her bed.

Never letting her go.

For the night only, she knew.

As his lips came down on hers, and she closed her eyes, opening her mouth to welcome him, her last conscious thought was a reminder to herself.

It was only for the night.


Sebastian was at his best Monday night. Holding Ruby in his arms, pleasing her, letting go and consciously allowing himself to take what she had to give him, energized him in a whole new way. She strengthened him, even as they wore each other out.

He entered her differently, too. Slowly. Reverently. Aware that in another space inside her, his child was growing into life.

He was a part of the two of them.

They were a part of him.

What it would all end up looking like, what it meant in a real-world sense, he had no idea. He didn't ask. For those hours in her bed, he just lived.

After she fell asleep, he allowed himself the light doze that came with living in a battle zone. He slept, but always aware that he was protecting precious cargo.

And yet, he rested better than he had in a long while.

Which was a good thing, he realized, when, just after six, Fletcher called to say that both Robert and Jenny wanted a meeting with Ruby at seven that morning, in the kitchen of the family home.

"You see how he played that?" Ruby asked, in her

work clothes, as she sat beside him in his truck. He'd showered, brushed his teeth, turned his underwear inside out. He had nothing but the jeans, button-down shirt and dirty socks from the day before.

"Telling your parents that you had to talk to them?" Sebastian asked, admiring the detective's grit where his sister was concerned. Ruby was not easy to love when it came to worrying about her.

Not that he loved her.

He was in the unique position of being a friend who'd made a baby with her who also happened to own a business being targeted, with her getting caught in the crossfire. He could see how it would be hard to also love her when she was so independent and mostly refused to let people tell her what to do.

As a friend, and co-loner—as she'd sort of called them in her little story from the night before—he admired her independence and spunk. Understood it, even.

Better to go down on your own terms than to live a life that wasn't right for you.

As long as you didn't get closed-minded and forget that you weren't always right. As long as you always sought the evidence and looked at it with an eye to finding truth.

He'd known Ruby Colton, peripherally, since she was a kid. "Did you know that you used to irritate the hell out of Wade, always asking questions about everything, wanting to know how he knew something, verifying facts?" he asked as they drew closer to Hollister Hills, the affluent neighborhood of mansions where her parents lived in the five-bedroom, three-bath lake home Jenny had designed.

He knew Jenny was behind the home choices because Ruby had mentioned the dark green that colored every building at Crosswinds the night they'd tended to Oscar. She preferred his color to the gray wood and dark gray trim of her parents' lovely home…and figured she was the only person on earth who didn't find the exquisite beauty in the grayness.

He pulled to a stop at a light. Looked over when she didn't answer his Wade question. Figured he'd stepped in his own crap again. But wasn't sure how to get out of it.

"Does it irritate you?" she finally asked. Not at all what he'd expected.

"It comforts me." The truth fell out with his relief. "You get the facts, rather than let yourself be swayed, and because you're open to the truth, you make good decisions."

Relief dissipated as he heard his own words. And saw the surprised look on her face.

Thankfully, the light turned green, and he didn't have to keep staring into that expression.

"I think that's the nicest thing anyone has ever said to me." Her words settled over him. Gave him added confidence as he prepared to square up with her father.

"And for the record," she continued, "of course, I knew. You think Wade would be irritated and not let it be known? Ad nauseam?" Sebastian heard the words and heard the note of deep compassion in her tone, too.

And was envious.

Not because he wanted her affection toward Wade for himself. Or in any way begrudged all her siblings her love. But because, in the end, no matter what happened between the two of them, she'd always have her family.

And he'd always be without one.

# Chapter 19

Ruby had made a deliberate choice in accepting Sebastian's offer of a ride to her folks' place. Her SUV was drivable. He'd be taking her back to it in time for her to get to work.

She'd ridden with him because it meant she could leave with him. If things went bad—and she gave a fifty-fifty on that—she didn't want to send Sebastian off alone without a chance to talk about things.

And thinking of which…

"Do we need to talk about last night?"

He'd already been in the shower when she'd woken up alone in her bed that morning.

"We didn't talk about it last time."

"Right." But had it been the right way to handle it?

"Do you need to talk about it?" His question surprised her. She'd thought they were done.

"No, unless you're regretting it." He'd been so distant. But then, he'd had the call from Fletcher before they'd even seen each other that morning.

He turned into her parents' neighborhood. "No regrets here."

"Good."

"It was good, wasn't it?" He didn't take his eyes off the road, but he seemed to be playing with a grin.

"Very." She didn't even try to rein in her smile.

Until he pulled into her parents' place. Then she shoved his teasing words into her private thoughts.

"You ready for this?" she asked, as she walked beside Sebastian up to the door.

His shrug, his easy stride, was so... Sebastian. He was who he was, no apologies. But no airs, either. She'd always liked that about him.

Figured his parents had done something right in that they'd raised a man filled with quiet self-confidence.

Real confidence. Not bravado.

Ruby had gained her own confidence through sheer determination and hard work. She'd had to prove to herself who she was. What she was made of.

And refused to revert back to being the girl who always had to please her parents as she walked into their home with a quick knock and headed straight to the kitchen. Sebastian had been in the home before, with Wade. For some reason, the idea was a comfort.

Taking his hand would have been a greater one.

She purposefully did not do so. She had to stand on her own two feet.

Her parents both rose as they stepped into the room, Jenny rushing forward, grabbing for Ruby's hands, looking her over with concern, checking her over, as she said how worried she'd been. While Robert, who joined them as well, kept up appearances in his welcome to Sebastian. Not expressing the surprise that he had to be experiencing.

Over her mother's shoulder, Ruby saw the coffee cups on the table—along with her father's Irish cream liqueur—and stopped short.

"This isn't exactly how I wanted to go about this, but can you please remove the coffee cups from the table?" she asked, not wanting to chance another step closer.

Frowning, Jenny studied her harder, like a nurse studied a patient, and then did as asked, taking her cup to the kitchen island before motioning Ruby and Sebastian to seats. Robert, retrieving his cup, stood with it at the island, then began sipping. "What's going on?" he asked in the commanding tone that had been giving Ruby security, and intimidating her, since childhood.

"I'm pregnant," she told them both. Just dropped it out there. "The smell of coffee makes me throw up." She could have worded it better.

Jenny stared at her, her mouth hanging open. "You're pregnant?" Shock was evident in her tone. Concern. And possibly a slight bit of pleasure, too. It was no secret that Jenny Colton, who'd basically raised ten children and only had one grandchild, wanted more.

Robert, cup frozen halfway to his mouth, bellowed, "You're what?"

"She's pregnant, sir." Sebastian's calm words made it sound like a piece of good news. "And I'm the father."

In that moment, going up against her parents with her, he was her child's father, but he was much more than that. He was her hero.

\* \* \*

There were some tense moments, but overall, "That went well," Sebastian said as he and Ruby headed down the walk toward his truck.

As predicted, Robert had asked about marriage, a wedding. Ruby had preempted Sebastian's ready reply with a version of what she'd said the night before about them being happy about the baby, independent people who never wanted to marry, and raising the child together.

"It went amazing," she said, grinning at him over her shoulder. She'd been leading the way all morning. He'd been fine to have her do so. Knew better than to help her climb up into the truck, but he did stand by the door and closed it behind her.

"That's the first time in my life I had someone sharing my situation as I faced off with my parents," she said, still grinning at him as he climbed into the driver's side.

"You had five siblings," he reminded her. "Surely there were times when you all banded together to further a cause." He'd always envisioned Wade and his brothers and sisters that way.

"Not really, no," she told him. "What just happened there, Mom and Dad meeting us together, that's not the norm. I'd have a session with Dad, or a session with Mom. They weren't close, you know. Didn't present a united front for us kids. The only time I can remember having the attention of both of them was when I announced that I was buying my house."

How being a member of a family with six kids and two parents could sound lonely, he didn't know. But right then, it did.

"My folks were gone a lot of the time, pursuing their separate professional interests, but when they were home at the same time, when there was some big decision or announcement to make in my life, they always presented it together. We'd talk things out, the three of us. All three opinions on the table, being heard." Something he'd taken for granted until just that moment.

"Not here," Ruby said, nodding toward the gorgeous lakefront home with walls of windows providing beautiful views of the water. "Maybe because there were so many of us…so much going on. But Mom and Dad… Sometimes I wonder how they ever made six babies. They're more like strangers in the same house, or business partners, than lovers."

Sebastian glanced over at her as he put the truck in Reverse. Had he just seen a glimpse of why Ruby preferred to live alone?

Not that the *why* mattered. She preferred it. He preferred it. And that made them a good team.

A team. He and Ruby Colton. A baby-having team.

Surprised at how much he liked the idea, he glanced at the other member of his unusual partnership. "I agree with them that I'd worry less if you weren't going in to work, but with the security you have there, and being right in the middle of town, and this guy only hitting at night so far, you're probably fine to go."

"There's a lot of security at Mom and Dad's and I see the sense in staying there at night, especially with Fletcher there, but it's right on the lake, Sebastian, and this guy…the way he got to the dogs—it really does sound like he approached from the lake. I figure I'm safer at work than alone out at their place all day."

He liked that they could talk to each other. Be honest. Maybe the future really was going to work as well as they'd just led her parents to believe it would.

He wanted it to.

And believed that she did, too.

"You sure don't let your father intimidate you any," he told her. "Telling him that he had no room to talk about you still working full-time while you're pregnant—did he really have a minor stroke four years ago?"

"Yes, he did. Doctors had been after him for years about the sallowness of his skin, the pouch. Years of working all hours, being on the road for a week at a time, hard living, eating red meat every day, the whiskey he consumes, those daily cigars... They took their toll."

"And he hasn't given any of it up?" Sebastian clarified what Ruby had hollered at her father when he'd tried to put his foot down with her. He'd seen the Irish cream whiskey on the counter.

"Nope."

"I'm surprised, with your mother being a nurse, she doesn't have something to say about that."

"I think she gave up trying years ago. As you noticed, he doesn't listen to her much."

"I like her," Sebastian said, feeling generous with his emotions. He'd been welcomed back to the Colton home, been invited for dinner every night that Ruby was going to be staying there, and had been told to come and go, treat the house as his own, for the duration as well. Robert had stopped short of saying he was welcome to spend the night, but in the end, the real-estate magnate had been gracious.

And, Sebastian thought, sincere.

The man might be hardheaded, but he knew when to capitulate. Both qualities necessary to build a small hardware store into an empire that owned half of Owl Creek and still be well thought of in the town he'd taken over.

"Mom's the best," Ruby said. "She's wealthy enough to travel the world and she's still here, looking after all of us, and Uncle Buck, and doing some private nursing, too. She just sometimes wants different things for me than I do."

"I'm guessing our kid will want differently from us as well." The statement just came off his tongue. He'd been in the role, being the dad, for her parents, sharing everything with her and…

He had to go. Get back to Crosswinds. To Oscar and the rest of his dogs. To his employees. He couldn't expect, or allow, Della and the others to carry his weight.

He couldn't leave Ruby alone at her house. He'd agreed, in front of her parents, to wait while she packed. He'd do it even if he hadn't agreed. He also thought he should follow her to the clinic to make sure she made it okay.

And then he had to go.

They were getting in too deep. Sleeping together. Spending the night together. Visiting her parents together. He'd even been invited to her uncle's birthday party.

He'd accepted the invitation. Had actually wanted to go. With her.

Like a real date.

He was letting the vague description of their future that they'd delivered to her parents lure him into a place he didn't belong.

Ruby didn't want to marry any more than he did. Watching her parents together, he kind of understood that—though, of course, all unions weren't like that. Still, she'd spent the first eighteen years of her life surrounded by a plethora of needs all vying for attention. Still had to brace herself against all the lovingly offered, but still intrusive, interference in her life.

She needed her independence. He'd just watched her go up against Robert Colton to defend it.

And Sebastian needed his, too. For different reasons, but the result was the same. She'd pegged it the night before. He was a loner.

Which made them perfect for each other.

As long as he kept his distance.

He'd been doing it for thirty-two years with complete success.

No reason to think he couldn't get it done for the rest of his life.

With his thoughts firmly back in line, Sebastian waited comfortably in his truck, parked outside Ruby's house while she packed.

He helped her carry her things to the back of her SUV.

Followed her to work.

And went home.

Where he belonged.

Alone.

Over the next couple of days, Ruby watched her back constantly. She didn't go anywhere alone, other than to drive to work, and wasn't at the clinic by herself, either. Until the kidnapper was caught, she was his prisoner.

She missed Sebastian like crazy. Which made no sense to her. He was in touch. Making sure she was okay. Asking if she needed anything.

It wasn't the same as the two of them alone together taking care of his dogs. Or eating soup. She wasn't safe at Crosswinds. And he wasn't coming into town.

He had a handler coming in from out west and, apparently, a load of work to go through, video to view and approve for the marketing campaign he was launching to try to lure out his stalker.

She heard more about his plans from her brother than she'd ever heard from Sebastian. With Ruby's attempted kidnapping, the Owl Creek police were planning to do all they could to help with Sebastian's plan, including having extra patrols in the area, both on land and on the lake.

The city had agreed on Tuesday to allow posters to be hung and distributed, too, advertising the celebration for Sebastian and his parents in Boise later in the month, with tickets available to attend the black-tie event. She'd heard from Fletcher that the honor was a real one. Sebastian had turned it down in the past.

Her brother talked as though she knew all about it. He'd just been reiterating details in terms of the investigation. Fletcher seemed to think she was going to the event.

Sebastian had never even mentioned it to her, let alone invited her to accompany him.

Because they weren't a couple. They were just friends who'd made a baby and were dealing with the situation as best they could.

Which was exactly how she wanted it.

Except that…she didn't.

She didn't blame him for withdrawing from her after spending time with her parents. She had a tendency to do the same after even a normal day at home.

And Sebastian's time with the Coltons had been anything but that. Their daughter was in danger because of someone stalking his business. And she was pregnant by him.

He'd handled the whole thing like a pro.

He didn't need her lying in bed panicking about him needing some space.

So on Tuesday night, she turned over and went to sleep. On Wednesday night, too. But she dreamed of him.

Of them together.

And woke up with growing discomfort regarding the future.

The time she and Sebastian had spent alone together over the past couple of weeks, the personal conversations, even when they got intense, eating together, touching…she craved more.

And yet…she loved her little house. Needed a place where she didn't have to fight to have her way. Her psyche relied on the peace she found there.

The baby was going to change a lot of that. Starting with no full night's sleep for a while. But she'd still have the final say in the house. Still be paying the bills. Making the choices. She'd still be in control.

Lying in her bed at her parents in the wee hours of Thursday morning, she remembered being out of control a couple of nights before, in her bed, with Sebastian.

Her thoughts flowed freely in the dark, and for a while there, she entertained the idea of a lifetime of out-of-control moments.

With desire pooling at dangerously high levels, she finally slid from beneath the sheets to wake herself up and find her reality, and was suddenly beset with the strangest feeling. Like someone was watching her.

Her gaze went immediately to the corners of her room. There were no cameras there. She knew that. But after days of living with the need for surveillance to keep herself safe, she sensed the presence of cameras everywhere.

Watching them.

Watching her.

Was that a twinkling out on the lake? The nighttime view from the lovely wall of windows across from her bed was generally dark. She blinked.

Had a spotlight just flashed across her wall?

She waited for it to come again. Some kind of talisman for a lost boat, she told herself. Or surveillance out on the lake.

Closing her eyes, she stood against the wall on the side of the window, hiding behind the curtains, and tried to picture what she'd seen in her blink. Had there really been a flash of light?

Not liking the darkness behind her eyes, she peered out at the lake again. Where was the small light she'd seen moments before? Had it been a boat?

Someone night fishing?

Or a lonely person locked in a private hell of their own smoking a cigarette on a dock?

She was tired. Exhausted. From lack of restful sleep, but more from all the uncertainty in a life that had been carefully planned to avoid all chance of surprise.

A streak of white spread across the water. The moon came out from behind clouds. She recognized it. Welcomed it, even, in its normalcy.

For all she knew, she'd seen the moon's glow in her mind's eye as she'd blinked, and not a flash on her wall at all.

So, thinking, she went back to bed, pulled the covers up to her chin and forced herself to breathe deeply, to replay an old TV show rerun in her mind over and over until it bored her to sleep.

The boogeyman was not going to win.

## Chapter 20

Sebastian woke up before dawn on Friday morning to the sound of his text message notification. *Ruby.* Phone in hand before he'd fully opened his eyes, his heart pounded as he pushed to open the app. This early, it couldn't be good.

It was a text, not a call, so not an immediate trauma. He was just reassuring himself as the message popped up on screen.

THE LAND IS MINE GOD SAYS PRIDE COMETH BEFORE THE FALL AND YOU ARE ABOUT TO FALL BIG FOR YOUR PRIDEFUL WAYS

He read, and read again. Calming even as adrenaline pumped through his veins. The two previous texts, one to Ruby and one to him, had come from burner phones.

Pinging from the Owl Creek tower. Whether the man was in town only in the dark hours, or full-time, no one knew, but it was likely he was close by.

After texting Fletcher, Sebastian was out of bed and into jeans, a flannel shirt and cowboy boots by the time he had a response. Ruby's brother was on his way out. Commercials had run on the local television station the previous day and were scheduled throughout the weekend, talking about Crosswinds, featuring photos of people who'd been saved by Sebastian's search-and-rescue dogs. One had a testimonial from a veteran who was able to take up life again thanks to a PTSD dog. Posters about the dinner honoring Sebastian and his parents were up all over town.

They'd pushed the guy's button another notch. His current text, all caps like the previous two, was less to the point. It was longer, more preachy, like someone who'd reached a stage of rambling thoughts.

If they were lucky, they'd have him in cuffs in the next hour.

And Ruby had to stay home.

He didn't even try to get an agreement through text. He dialed her cell phone.

And felt a twinge of fear when he heard her voice. If anything happened to her…

"He's on the move," Sebastian said, not even attempting to tone down his tension. "Fletcher's on his way out. The plan is working. And I'm going to beg if I have to, but please stay out of sight today, Ruby. Please."

The long pause on the line didn't bode well. Antsy to get outside, Sebastian stood in his kitchen, ready to remain in that spot for as long as it took.

"I've egged him on," he said. "I've purposely pushed

him over the edge. Please let us get this done without giving him a chance to get to you."

"Okay."

Knees suddenly weakened, Sebastian said, "Did you just say *okay*?"

"Yes. What you say makes sense. I'll ask Wade to come spend the day with me, at least until we get the all clear," she told him.

And Sebastian actually smiled. He was going to get his guy. And until he did, Ruby would be protected by the best of the best.

The woman knew him well. Knew how to deliver exactly what he needed. Just as he hoped he was able to do for her.

"Thank you."

"Anytime," she said, but the word wasn't issued lightly. There was a message there.

He just wasn't ready to hear it yet.


Ruby tried to go back to sleep. But the more she forced herself to lie still, the less sleepy she felt. Her stomach was in knots, and as they grew tighter, they started to swirl, too. Not wanting to wake her parents, she made a quick stop at the bathroom, and headed down to the kitchen for saltine crackers.

Her brother had left a light on during his hurried departure. She worried for him. And for Sebastian. Told herself over and over again that Steele and his men would be there, too. They were all well-trained.

Many against one.

But the one knew who and where they were, while they were against a phantom.

"Ruby? You okay, sweetie?"

Jenny, a few gray streaks in her dark blond hair, came into the room, her pajama pants and long-sleeved T-shirt top showing the body of the slim, fit woman.

"I'm fine, Mom. You don't need to be up at this hour."

"I heard Fletcher leave."

Because, of course, Jenny was on call in her home, for her children, 24/7.

Would Ruby ever be able to be half the mother her own mom was?

The thought almost tipped her stomach over the edge. She took a bite of the cracker she'd just pulled out of the wrap.

"You want to talk about it?"

"About what? Morning sickness?"

"If that's what's on your mind."

The shrewd look her mother gave her reminded Ruby that she was alone because she chose to be. Jenny was always available.

Having a seat on the kitchen stool, she asked, "How did you do it? All those kids. Social functions with Dad. Taking over for Jessie when she ran off, mothering her kids, too, and still having your own career?"

Jenny poured two glasses of milk, put one on the island in front of Ruby and kept the other in her hand as she perched on the stool next to her. With a shrug, looking at her milk, she said, "Love."

What? Ruby frowned. "Love," she repeated.

"I loved your father, wanted to spend my life with him, so I married him. Our love gave us six kids. When each one of you were born, I fell in love in a way I'd never imagined. You start to feel it when you get pregnant, but once that baby is out of you and you're holding this tiny little human...it's like a wand waves over you, sprinkling you with gold that doesn't ever get lost. No matter what happens, you just know that as long as your child is alive, you have the jackpot. Not in money. But in love. It's the love jackpot."

Her mother had never been a wordy woman. Transfixed, Ruby homed in on the glow in Jenny's eyes. "Way more than money has ever done, the love I was blessed with for each of you kids has carried me through every tired day, every sleepless night, every chore and every tear. And with poor Buck… I loved my sister. I was happy when they married. And I loved their kids. Love is what does it, Ruby. In the end, it's all that really matters."

And was it love that kept Jenny with Robert? Despite the chill in their mutual treatment of each other? Deep down, did her mother get strength from spending her life with the man she'd fallen in love with all those years ago?

Jenny didn't say. Ruby was afraid to ask. Not sure she wanted to hear the answer, either way.

"Do you love Sebastian?" Jenny's gaze wasn't judgmental. But it was direct. And filled with compassion.

Ruby shook her head. But couldn't get the word *no* to rise up through her throat. "I don't know," she told her mother. What was love?

She loved her entire family. Deeply. But didn't want to spend her life with any of them, in the same house, forever.

"He makes you feel things you've never felt before."

Was Jenny guessing? Or telling? Did her mother, in all her wisdom, see something Ruby was missing?

"Doesn't mean it's love."

"No." Jenny's head tilted to the side a bit, and then

straightened. "But if it is, fighting it is a losing cause, sweetie. Love comes through the heart, not the mind, and there's nothing your mind can do to stop it from coming."

Ruby wasn't sure she'd gained any clarity in thought, or even in understanding, but as she took a sip of the milk her mom had poured for her, her stomach settled some. And her heart felt stronger.

She might not get all of life's choices right.

But she'd make them.

And be able to live with them.

Sebastian saw the brief trail of sparks in the air and Fletcher had yet to make it to his place. After calling the security company on site until daybreak, he'd grabbed his gun, jumped in his four-wheeler and sped out to the kennel. Dialed 911 to report a fire, and then Fletcher, as he drove, then circled the big building housing his dogs and turned his vehicle toward the lake.

He could see the blaze already, an acre away. After jumping out of the off-roader, he grabbed a shovel out of the back and started to dig. Some of his land was going to burn. He'd likely lose some trees. But he was not losing any buildings.

Sweating in the early morning chill, he dug eighteen inches wide, and then down to mineral soil, his only illumination coming from the vehicle's headlights. One man, by himself, he might make enough of a difference to at least divert the flames. Della, Bryony and Adam should be on their way to get the dogs up to his house. And to be prepared to vacate the premises altogether if necessary. Fletcher had said he'd make that call.

And police were heading toward him by lake, as

well. They'd be looking at both sides of the shore for the detonator. He'd told Fletcher the flare had not come from his land.

He'd only dug about a yard before he started to see the flames coming toward him, far faster than a grass fire in the spring should have done.

Like it was following some kind of accelerant...

Heart pounding, shovel in hand, he ran toward the flame, stopping half an acre away to check the ground in line with it. And with the light from his phone, saw the primer cord lying in the unmowed mange.

He shoved his phone in his pocket with one hand, raising his shovel high with the other, and with both hands and arms fully engaged, slammed the tip of the blade into the line, again and again, so angry he felt as though he could have ripped the thing in half with his bare hands. He wouldn't be able to stop the fire. But if he could prevent the speedy projectile to his buildings...

He would prevent it.

The fire was coming toward him. More rapidly than he'd assessed. Bearing down. He slammed the shovel again and again, watched the flames continue to speed at him.

He slammed the shovel. Jumped on it. And felt a snap.

Digging with his bare hands, he took hold of one end of the line in both hands, the end leading toward the building, and, pulling so hard his muscles stung, he ran toward the lake. He didn't have time to get to the buildings, to the end of the line, but if he could get his section far enough away from the fire...

He heard sirens. Didn't turn to look. He just kept running.

For his dogs. For Crosswinds. For all of the people who'd yet to become lost and needed to be found. For the veterans who'd sacrificed all for country and come back broken. For Ruby.

For his little baby.

The human yet to be born that was as much a part of him as he'd been a part of his father.

Ruby heard from Fletcher while she and Jenny were still sitting in the kitchen. Her brother needed her to phone Della to get to Crosswinds and move the dogs. He'd said that Sebastian wanted his trainer to call in Bryony and Adam, too.

Ruby made those last two phone calls instead, letting Della concentrate on getting dressed and out to Sebastian's place.

And then she stood.

"Where are you going?"

"To Crosswinds," she said. "I have to help. The dogs will be panicked. They know me. And I can tranquilize anyone who might try to run. I can treat any if the fire…" Her words broke off as she reached the stairs.

"You can't go out there, Ruby. You're a target. Think of the baby."

The baby.

She stopped, one foot on the stairs.

Why hadn't she thought of the baby?

She'd been thinking about the dogs.

Thinking.

Not feeling.

And as she sat on the bottom step, calling one of the veterinarians on her staff and asking her to head out to Crosswinds, she had an inclination that she'd just been given a lesson in what her mother had been talking about.

Love came from the heart, not the mind.

She was smart. Learned. And she trusted her mind.

Her life was cerebral by choice.

But if she was going to make it as a mother, she had to let her heart take the reins.

No matter how scary that might be.

Someone was watching him. Sebastian slowed to a walk, still heading toward the river with the highly flammable line in his hand, but took in the area around him as though he was back in Afghanistan, in the desert during the night, expecting an attack at any moment, from any direction.

A leaf fluttered down out of a tree, and he stopped.

If the enemy was in the tree, he'd be dead in seconds. His gun would do him no good when he didn't know where to aim. He could shoot into the tree and hope.

The enemy could shoot right at him and win.

He was in the open. The other was not.

And it hit him. The line.

Resuming his trek to the lake, he veered on a diagonal. Threw the rope up over a branch and shot it all in one move.

The tree lit up in an instant blaze.

Giving Sebastian a view of wide eyes filled with horror, just before a skinny male body hurled down at him. The fiend had the advantage of gravity. Sebastian had the superior height, weight, muscular build and a trained warrior's mind filled with intent.

Taking the brunt of the man's weight with a severe blow to his chest, he dropped his gun, grabbed hold with both arms and rolled, while the fire blazed right above them.

He had to get to his gun before his assailant did. The enemy may have been skinny, but he was a wild man, kicking and throwing punches, hurling his body around, reaching toward Sebastian's gun.

The smaller hand got there first, grabbed hold, and just as he was raising his arm, Sebastian's hand slammed down on the man's wrist, lifting it again, and slamming it down, until the gun was free. With complete focus and clear thought, he grabbed his gun and pushed into the attempted kidnapper's chest, pulling back the hammer all in one move.

He heard voices in the distance. Had flashing lights in his peripheral vision. All just distant background.

"Who are you?"

"Your brother, come to save you from your sins…" The voice came out strong and solid. Deep, as though the man was channeling a sacred tone.

With a hand at the chest of the man's hooded sweatshirt, right next to the barrel of his handgun, Sebastian pulled up and slammed the man back down.

"Your name," he growled, feeling nothing but a need to take the man down. But he couldn't let go until he knew the truth.

"Leon."

"Who's your father?"

"God is my father and you are a sinner, worshipping animals instead of God. This land is…"

"Sebastian!" Fletcher's voice sounded from outside Sebastian's sphere, cutting off his prisoner's tirade. "Hold on, man," Fletcher said, running up to them. Aware of other feet starting to circle them, Sebastian felt a hand at his back. "I've got this, brother," Fletcher said, more softly.

Brother.

One on the ground beneath his gun.

And one who would never be his, not even in law.

With a knee on the man's chest, holding him down, he kept the gun firmly pointed, but handed it to Fletcher Colton. Nodding at Glen Steele and other officers as he stood, Sebastian turned his back on the man on the ground, the half brother he'd never known, and walked away.

He didn't look back.

His job was done.

Ruby was safe. The child she carried was safe.

His only living relative in the world was being taken into custody.

He had to get back to his dogs. To make sure everyone was okay.

They needed him.

And he needed them, too.

# Chapter 21

Sebastian wasn't picking up. Ruby had tried several times that day. He texted each time, to make certain she was okay, but didn't engage any further, even by text.

Fletcher had called shortly after dawn to let her know that since she didn't need Wade's protection, their brother was going to be at Crosswinds, helping to clear out fire debris with other townspeople.

An impromptu volunteer service for a member of their community family. Her brother had thought she'd already heard from Sebastian.

For some reason she didn't want to think about, she'd let her detective brother go on thinking she knew what was going on. And had called Sebastian.

And received a text asking if she was okay. Her *fine*, followed by a question to him, went unanswered.

Jenny had ended up being the one to tell her that her

kidnapper was behind bars. She'd heard from Chase, who'd heard from Robert after Glen Steele had called him at work to let him know that his daughter was safe.

She'd heard all about Sebastian's heroic actions, trapping the kidnapper in a tree, and then fighting him physically to subdue him until police arrived.

And she knew that the man who'd tried to ruin him was his half brother.

Sebastian Cross had family after all.

He had to be taking it hard. To find out he had a living relative, only to have the man be a criminal who'd attempted to kidnap the mother of his baby, and could have killed the baby, too.

A brother who'd tried to kill several of his dogs. More than once.

A man with evil inside him. One who wanted to take, not give. To steal, not earn.

Saddest part was, if the man had simply approached Sebastian, she'd bet her life savings that Sebastian would have gladly shared the land with his younger sibling.

Instead, on their first meeting, he'd held a cocked gun to the man's chest until law enforcement arrived.

Ruby moved back home. After only a short time away, the place seemed like a long-lost friend to her. She walked through it. Absorbing the peace she'd created through color choice and beautiful objects. She showered. And, instead of having to call off, she went to work.

At lunch, she drove herself to the police station next to the fire station at the west end of Main Street and was shown to a room to identify the man who'd attacked her.

He'd seemed smaller to her at the station, but Fletcher

said that wasn't unusual, given that he'd grabbed her from behind. He'd have seemed like a big specter at her back that night. The man, according to her brother, was incredibly strong. If she hadn't head-butted him, much worse things could have happened.

She'd reminded him that she'd been well trained through a myriad of self-defense classes. Her brother had helped her find the best ones.

She'd had a glimpse of the man's face on Monday night. In the dark, with headlights shining. The only thing she'd recognized, the only thing she'd really seen, other than the dark blue hoodie that he'd apparently been arrested in, had been the wild, glazed look in his eyes.

It was still there. Even sitting alone in a police interrogation room.

Fletcher offered to take her to lunch after the ID procedure was over. She'd been afraid she'd throw it up, so she went back to work and had an apple. And later some crackers and an orange. Thanking the fates that her sisters weren't there to see what she was consuming. Or rather, how much she wasn't.

By late afternoon, when she'd seen her last scheduled client and her most recent call to Sebastian went to voice mail, she signed herself out. Exchanging her white doctor's coat for a dark purple fleece coat, over light purple scrubs, she grabbed her satchel, climbed in her SUV and headed straight out to Crosswinds.

Being busy was one thing. Ghosting her was not okay. He got a point for keeping in touch to ensure she was well.

And dozens of them for the trauma, the emotional tension, the life-changing news of the past weeks. Things she mentally relived during the ten-minute drive out to his place.

The points in his favor were catapulted by him finding out that the love-child theory he and others had tossed around had become deadly reality.

Her frustration with him had pretty much dissipated by the time she pulled onto Cross Road. Along with any self-righteous anger that might have been mixed in there.

When she saw the land, by the lake, the charred remains of some trees and the blackened ground, she felt tears prick the backs of her eyes. She had no idea which tree might have been the one that Sebastian had lit afire himself. From what she'd been told, the police had run their prisoner away from the burning embers and a fire crew had taken their place, but that didn't mean they'd managed to put out the fire before the tree had burned to the ground.

Needing something to be normal, she pulled into her usual parking space, relieved that it could be hers again. That their attacker was safely, and quite firmly, from what she understood, in custody. The man was in chains and was assigned a twenty-four-hour watch. Not for his own good, but the peace of mind of all those who'd sought him. And for those who'd suffered at his hands.

There'd be no worry of escape.

Because she was there, she peeked into the medical building, but had already heard from her colleague, who'd returned to the clinic, that no dogs were injured in the morning's attack. The building was empty. From there she walked up to Sebastian's house. He'd been up since well before dawn. Had, from what she'd heard, trained that day. And had helped with fire cleanup, too.

Oscar greeted her at the door. As did Turbine, a dog leaving them that week to be adopted by a female veteran pilot whose plane had been shot down. She'd managed to land the plane safely, to get her and her crew out, but had been taken hostage overnight before her rescue.

"Where is he, boys?" she asked softly, stooping to pet them both as she looked around.

"I'm right here."

Rounding the corner into the kitchen, she almost wept as she saw Sebastian, in jeans and a checked, long-sleeved shirt and tennis shoes, standing at the stove, stirring a big wok, with his three other burners filled with huge saucepans.

He was okay. He'd come through the day and was either making himself a freezer's worth of meals, or was cooking for a very large gathering.

"Can I help?" she asked, walking over to look in his pots.

"I'm almost done," he told her. A nonanswer that she took as a *no*. He'd barely glanced her way. It could have been because he was clearly quite occupied, but she didn't think so.

"Is this it, then? We're done?"

"Now's not the time, Ruby." She got that, but her emotions wouldn't settle with the logic. The man had to be suffering. And even if he wasn't, he'd been distant since long before the day's activities. Ever since they'd been to her parents' house, to be exact.

"When is the time?" she asked, taking a seat at the kitchen table, quite sure that if she waited for an invitation she'd be standing until she grew tired and left.

"I can't make you be a part of my life, Sebastian. I wouldn't even want to. But I'm not going away until you tell me that our friendship is over, and you want no part of the baby's life."

She'd been through a hell of a lot, too. It would be a long time before she drove down her own road and didn't avoid looking at the ditch where her SUV ended up. Didn't shudder with the memory of those arms coming up behind her.

Sebastian just stirred. Browning what had to be several pounds of what smelled like—judging by the meat packages she could see in the trash—minced chicken.

"You having a party of some kind?" she asked then, getting frustrated with him again. And maybe a little panicked.

She could do the baby thing alone. She didn't doubt that for a second.

But the thought of not having Sebastian in her world, understanding the loner parts of her no one else got, was more than a little unsettling.

"I'm making dog food," he told her. "They've been through a hellish two months, continued to work hard, and so for the next few days, they're going to eat like the kings and queens, princesses and princes, that they are."

She teared up. Quickly blinked away the moisture. Asked about the recipe he was using.

And found out it was one of hers, posted on her website.

She should have known from glancing in his pans. The chicken. The rice. Mixed vegetables, also minced.

Perhaps she wasn't doing as well as she'd thought she was. Maybe not any better than he was. Just different. She was reaching out…to him. Only to him.

Needing him to be wrapped in compassion.

As she'd been that morning.

Her mind froze as she reached a new place. The major difference between her and Sebastian. He'd known it already. She put pieces together as thoughts and memories of conversations tumbled on top of each other. She'd never known a single day of her life without her family in her background.

Being surrounded by people who cared even when she didn't think she wanted them there. Having a mother who'd get up in the middle of the night, pour her a glass of milk and sit on a stool with her.

She was a loner by choice, always knowing she had her family.

Sebastian was a loner because…he was alone. Maybe even more so, having just held a gun to his newfound little brother's chest. Having just had confirmation that the man who'd fathered him, the man who'd taught him what family was, had had a separate son somewhere else.

Seeing the big can of dog nutrients on the counter—the brand she recommended, something she should have noticed walking in the door, something she *would* have noticed if she'd been as together as she'd thought she was—she picked it up, grabbed the scoop she needed and started dropping scoops into the rice Sebastian had just drained.

"You brought Turbine in with you," she said as he dumped the ingredients of his pots into two huge bowls, handed her a big metal spoon and took another for himself.

His silence was hard to take. But she did it. Stirred right alongside him.

If he didn't want to talk about why he'd opted to take home his best-trained PTSD dog for the night, that was his choice. Still didn't change the fact that he'd done so.

Or that she knew why.

Sometimes, that's what friends did. They knew and just stirred food in a bowl.

Being a friend, a daughter, a sister, a cousin, a parent—none of it was going to be easy all the time. Jenny was a living testimony to that.

And yet, if Ruby ever wanted to emulate another woman, ever wanted to hope she'd one day be as shining an example as any one woman she'd ever met, heard of, or read about, it would be her mother.

Jenny got up every single day to tend to those she loved. No matter what.

Those she loved…

Ruby looked at the tall, broad, bearded man standing next to her and could no longer deny what Jenny Colton had already seen in her daughter.

She loved him.

They'd used the four-wheeler to cart the containers of dog food down to the kennels, filling bowls and putting the rest in the refrigerator. And then, feeling as though he owed her a good turn, Sebastian offered Ruby a homemade chicken-salad sandwich.

He'd saved the cooked chicken and she cut up grapes while he diced onion and celery. He made the dressing from scratch. She spooned it over their mixture. Sitting at his kitchen table with glasses of milk, they consumed the entire bowl. She'd had hers on crackers. He'd had three sandwiches.

He hadn't eaten all day.

Hadn't been hungry.

He figured she was sitting there needing more from

him than chicken salad. And he was just waiting for her to leave.

She was safe.

He'd captured her kidnapper.

And cooked.

He'd done what he was trained to do.

What he could do.

They cleaned up the kitchen together. And she still didn't pick up her satchel to go. As he hung the dish towel on the oven-door handle, Sebastian was trying to figure out the best way to tell her he needed to call it a night.

And said, "He didn't look anything like me."

"I didn't think so, either."

Ruby leaned back against the sink, reminding him of the night at her house. The night of the attempted kidnapping.

The night they'd talked about the future.

The night they'd had sex.

The night that everything had flown out of control.

And... *I didn't think so, either?*

"You saw him?"

"Fletcher had me go to the station at lunchtime to identify him."

"Why didn't I know that?" He, of all people, should have been told. The woman carrying his child, facing her kidnapper? His half brother. "I should have been there."

"You didn't answer my call."

Since it was part of the case, Fletcher should have let him know. "You could have texted the information."

"You could have answered your phone."

Swallowing, he met her gaze, full on, for the first time

since he'd driven her away from her parents' house on Tuesday morning.

It felt like coming home. Shock waves went through his system.

The start of an episode? The panic after the attack was done? Turbine wasn't indicating, yet.

"Were you able to give the ID?" He belonged next to her, supporting her as she stared through the glass at the man who'd attacked her.

"He matches the description I gave that night. Today, all I could remember for certain was that glassy, wild look in his eyes. Your headlights were bright, and every time I think of those seconds, it's those eyes that get me."

And, selfish ass that Sebastian had been, he hadn't answered her repeated calls that day. Thinking that she was checking up on him.

And that he couldn't encourage her to expect more from him than he'd be able to deliver. After they'd left her parents, he'd been talking as if the two of them would be parents, together, to the child they'd created. He'd had to take a break from the situation to get himself in check. The idea of disappointing her, which those comments had set him up to do, was worse than any PTSD nightmare.

"I'm sorry I didn't answer my phone. I will always do my best in the future to answer any call that comes in from you."

She smiled then.

And he hoped he'd redeemed himself a little.

# Chapter 22

"Fletcher says he's not talking." Ruby stayed by the sink, just leaning there, a friend in conversation before heading out. Wanting Sebastian to know that he wasn't alone in his suffering. That even if they didn't talk about it all, she was aware.

And cared.

Something she'd learned from her mother just that morning. And through the rest of her life, too, she supposed. She'd just been too set in her own thinking to realize what else had been there.

"He told me he's my brother."

She'd heard that, too. Could only imagine the shock that must have reverberated through Sebastian in that second. But according to her brother, who'd been watching from afar as he ran to the scene, Sebastian hadn't so much as twitched the entire time he had the younger man on the ground.

"I'm sorry it turned out this way."

"Sorry that your child is related to an unhinged criminal?"

"Stop it, Sebastian."

"Stop what? Speaking the truth? You're the Coltons. Your reputations matter."

"Stop putting thoughts in my head. That man is not a reflection on you. He never even met you. There's no way you could have had any influence on him, or, for that matter, him on you. He was deserted by your father, not raised by him. And he had a different mother."

"Who's dead," Sebastian said. "Fletcher said they'd tracked down the woman my father was meeting with in that hotel. She died a couple of years after their last visit."

"And she had a son."

"Yes."

"Is your father listed on the birth record?"

"No. And the rest was sealed. He was adopted out after his mother died."

"I wonder if your father even knew about him?"

He shrugged. "Leon knew about me…"

Leon. Her kidnapper had a name. She swallowed. "He must have found your connection through one of the DNA companies…or maybe his mother left him something that his adoptive parents gave him when he turned eighteen. Maybe they knew all along…" She was there for him. Not to get herself worked up again.

Her part was done. The ordeal was over.

Sebastian's chin jutted, but otherwise he gave no reaction to her words. Because he didn't care how Leon had found him? Or because he was just that good at hiding the turmoil inside him?

He rubbed at the beard on his chin as he said, "Fletcher said the only question he's answered, period, is when they asked him who his father was. He just keeps saying God is his father now. And that God will save him because he's righteous." With a shake of his head, Sebastian ended with, "When he told me he was my brother, he said he'd come to save me from my sins. Which, apparently, have to do with worshipping animals..."

"He needs help," Ruby said then, glad that the threat was done. Fearing that Sebastian would be a long time in healing from the ordeal.

Turbine, who'd been lying on the floor, stood and moved to Sebastian's side, nudging his hand. Sebastian pet the dog as he said, "He needs a good lawyer. And I'm thinking about paying for it." His gaze challenged her.

Ruby just kept looking at Sebastian's hand on the dog's head. Petting, just lying there, petting again. And Turbine, leaning up against him.

The dog was working.

Sebastian's stress level had just raised.

She looked at him. "You think I'm going to have a problem with that," she guessed, glancing at the dog again, and then met Sebastian's gaze.

"Seems like a traitorous thing to do, from your point of view," he said then. "Paying for the defense of the man who's terrorized your life."

Yet he was going to do it, anyway. "So why are you?" Her tone was neutral. She wasn't sure how she felt.

"My reasons are twofold." As soon as he started talking, she knew he'd given the matter enough thought. He'd already made his decision. And was worried about her.

Just as she'd worried about her family's reactions when she'd known she was going to do something they wouldn't like.

Their opinion mattered because she cared about them.

Sebastian cared about her.

Ruby's heart softened, and filled.

"First," Sebastian continued, "I want to make sure that he has the best defense first time out so that when they put him away, he stays there." His words were clearly stated. His expression unflinching. "And second, I grew up with my father's love and all the financial benefits I'd ever need. He's been denied the love, but I can still see that money that morally should have been shared with him, benefits him."

Which just confirmed what she'd already figured. If Leon had just gone to Sebastian, his older half brother would have given him part of the land.

Just as Sebastian would always be there for her child. Sharing what he had. In any way he could.

She felt her expression lighten as her heart did.

He frowned. "Why are you smiling? I thought you'd be upset."

"I'm happy that you're the father of this child," she said, holding her still-flat belly.

And looked him straight in the eye so he'd know she meant every word.

*She was happy he was the father of her child?*

Sebastian didn't doubt Ruby. He just didn't get it.

Why couldn't she see that he wasn't great father material? He lived a far-from-traditional life.

When he was alone in that life, Sebastian was good.

He liked himself and the life he'd built. Around Ruby, all he could seem to think about were the areas where he was lacking.

Which made no sense to him. He'd never been a poor-me guy. Not when he'd watched his friend die. Not when his parents had been killed.

He'd suffered. But others had suffered far more.

"We aren't getting married. Aren't moving in together. The child is going to grow up in a single-parent home…"

"But this baby is going to be loved and protected and given opportunities to succeed," Ruby said. "I'm seeing it more clearly now," she continued. "In a way, Leon did us a favor, showing us what matters most. It's not the license or where our bedrooms are, or how many adults are in the house when a child goes to sleep at night. It's having someone there, having people to turn to, to be able to count on, to believe in you, support you, help you grow and you do all of that, Sebastian. All the time."

If he wasn't careful, she was going to have him believing he could celebrate his child's birth without guilt. Without feeling like a failure.

Without doubting his every move.

"We're human beings, not cookie cutters," she said then. "We're not all meant to be the same, feel the same, want the same. But we are all deserving and needing of love."

Throat tight, he had to restrain himself from reaching out to her, pulling her into his arms and spending the night showing her how very much he valued her.

"And you know what I need right now?" she asked.

"What?" He wasn't afraid to ask. She knew his limitations. Respected them. And, best of all, had her own set of rules by which she insisted on living her life.

She was as stubborn as he was.

"I need to put these past weeks behind me. To feel no fear. To have some hours in the darkness where only pleasure and happiness exist."

She wanted to go to bed with him.

If ever there had been a woman made for him, Ruby was it.

And… "I can't risk it, Ruby, not tonight. After what happened out there today, I'm like a time bomb here, ticking off until I have a panic attack, or go to sleep and transport myself to hell."

"You have Turbine and Oscar here. They'll be in the room with us. And if I have to jump out of bed, then I do."

"I can't risk hurting you." And it wasn't only the results of PTSD that scared him. He was a loner. He didn't answer his phone every time it rang. Or enjoy being surrounded by people all the time.

"There are some hurts that are worse than physical ones," she told him. "That cut deeper."

He was between a rock and a hard place. Needing to please her. Wanting her to please him. And trying to prevent a future of failure.

He didn't walk into losing battles.

"I need to know that you won't suffer because of me."

"Then invite me to spend the night with you."

She wasn't backing down. He couldn't, either.

"I've spent the past several nights in stark fear, Sebastian. Lying awake, reliving it all. And the only thing that takes away the ugliness is thoughts of you. Please, even if you don't touch me, just let me stay and get a good night's rest."

It was like she was reading his mind. Facing the night ahead alone—with visions of his half brother's wild eyes glaring up at him, with the internal fight to accept that he *had* a half brother, that his whole life with his father had somehow been a lie—he needed more than Oscar.

He needed human conversation to sort out the chaos inside him.

Ultimately, he needed to support her and their child. He'd made the promise.

And he was not going to fail.

"Just for tonight," he told her, and, opening his arms, grabbed her close as she fell against him.

His touch was urgent. Needy. Giving. Tender. And for a few hours, Ruby let herself believe that as she gave him her love, he gave his back.

She didn't weave fantasies about living together. Or marriage.

Her entire being was geared toward avoiding both.

But as she was lying beside Sebastian, fully satiated, wanting to know that she'd be in his bed again sometimes, she needed more than they'd agreed to share.

As exhausted as he had to have been, he wasn't sleeping, either.

"Fear's an insidious thing," she dropped softly between them. With the dogs at the end of the extra large king-size bed, she drew from their silent support. "It's the root of PTSD and panic attacks. And stops us from reaching higher, trying for more."

"You're talking about us."

Turning, the sheet up under her armpits, she looked at his head on the pillow next to her. His ear was facing her. She studied the half of his face she could see.

"I'm talking about all of it," she said. "There has to

be a balance. The dangers we run from, and the ones we take on because if we don't, we lose too much."

He didn't agree. But he didn't argue, either.

"And sometimes," she continued, "you manage them."

"I need to know what, in particular, you're hoping to manage."

She did, too. Wasn't quite there yet. But since he was listening, seemed to be open to consideration, she reached inside herself and found, "Like tomorrow night, for instance. Uncle Buck's birthday. It's going to be a pretty big affair. Lots of people we both know. And there's no longer any reason to keep my pregnancy a secret, or to not announce you as the father…"

She started out bigger than she'd meant to go, or even wanted.

He hadn't left the bed.

"I'm not suggesting any kind of formal announcement," she quickly added, for her own sake as much as his. "But maybe we attend together. Not holding hands, or arm in arm, just…together. And when I start to show and news of the baby gets around—which, with my family, it will—we just continue appearing together on occasion. We show the world who we are. Friends who enjoy each other's company and are going to be raising a baby to whom they are both parents."

The announcement—too much. The plan she's just laid out…not enough.

"We've both spent our adult lives carving out the existences we've wanted. We've established ourselves as the people we want to be. We're strong-minded enough to carry this off. There's no reason why we have to define ourselves or explain to anyone. We just continue to be who we are."

Except that she was deeply afraid that she was changing.

Fear again.

"You make it sound easy."

Yeah. But they both knew it wouldn't be.

Still… "What's the alternative? We live in a small town. We work together. Even if you decided not to have anything to do with me, you're never going to abandon your child, Sebastian."

The reality was right there. Both of them knew it. "We're in control of how this goes, is all I'm saying," she finished, as much for herself as for him.

"I'm never going to decide not to have anything to do with you." He turned his head then, looking at her. "You've become a part of me."

Her heart flooded and she blinked back tears. Reached out and touched his face, running a finger along the lines under his eyes. "You've become a part of me, too."

He kissed her. Long and full.

She kissed him back, pouring herself into the silent communication.

And for that night, it was enough.

# Chapter 23

Before Ruby left early Saturday morning, she'd asked Sebastian if he'd be at her uncle Buck's birthday party that night. Looking in her eyes, he gave her the only answer that he could get out, telling her he'd be there. And felt good about doing so when he saw the brief flash of relief, and then the pleasure in her eyes.

The Coltons were her family, so technically, they were her problem, not his. But this child was going to be a Colton. And he'd impregnated a Colton. He couldn't leave her standing by herself, period, let alone in a very public crowd.

His father had always told him that he gave his all to everything, which meant that he'd succeed at whatever he tried. Certainly, his time in the Marines had played out that way right up until his friend had died instead of him. And Crosswinds put truth to his dad's words.

And, he supposed, Ruby did, too. Leave it up to him to impregnate a woman whose father owned half the town. Could sic the entire town on him for what he'd done.

He fed the dogs. Got some training in. Cleaned up a bit more residue from the fire. Thanked his employees again for all their support over the past couple of months. Giving every one of them generous bonus checks for having done so.

And he tried not to think about the evening's event at Colton Ranch. His gut knew he didn't want to go. His mind knew it, too.

A new tension related to Ruby pushed at his back all day, calling him to the ranch. To be there to stand beside the mother of his child.

More, to support his very, very good friend.

Friend.

There would be baby talk now that everyone who knew also knew there was no longer any reason to keep the baby a secret. Sebastian realized he couldn't show up at Buck's place without telling his lifelong very good friend of a different nature.

Wade.

By two that afternoon, he'd been unable to fight off the emotions over which he kept such tight control. After calling Ruby to let her know what he was doing, to give her a chance to voice disapproval, he then drove over to Colton Ranch and told Wade that he was having a child with Wade's younger sister.

As talks between them went, it could have gone better. Compared to sparring they'd done in the past, it hadn't been so bad.

Once Wade knew his father and mother had been

told, and that all hell hadn't broken loose, he could hardly try to condemn Sebastian himself. And when he called Ruby, to hear from her that she was happy with the way things were turning out, Wade held out his hand to Sebastian and congratulated him on becoming a father.

That was when Sebastian should have felt a lightening inside him. Relief, certainly. And satisfaction with the reassurance that he and Ruby really were going to pull off the parenting thing without having to change their lifestyles all that much.

It was what they both wanted. And it was working.

The stalker had been caught.

Life was good again.

So why didn't his step feel any lighter?

The question hit him again early that evening as Hannah Colton came up to congratulate him. "I was scared to death for her when she wouldn't say who the father was, but when I found out it was you... I'm happy for both of you."

He smiled. Glanced at Ruby, who was in conversation with a couple from town he knew only peripherally, and then forgot the moment for a bit as he was pulled into conversation with Malcolm.

The evening wore on, and he and Ruby gravitated to each other more and more, as they stood together and received congratulations for news that had spread as quickly as he'd figured it would. But he was left more and more unsettled.

People were accepting. Excited. Seemingly truly happy for them. Showing no misgivings over their unusual arrangement—friends living apart and having a child. Even when he wasn't with Ruby, people came up to Sebastian and offered words of encouragement and advice. He couldn't have scripted it any better. But felt more deflated than not.

Those who knew about the crimes at Crosswinds, and Ruby's near kidnapping, were congratulating them both on a successful conclusion to a very bad situation.

It was obvious to Sebastian that people cared.

That he was one of them. A couple even mentioned his parents, saying they used to come into their shop every summer, saying how proud they'd been of Sebastian. And how much they'd have loved having a grandchild.

The words left him feeling gratified. And strangely empty, too.

Because the investigation was still ongoing until the perpetrator was formally charged, the police weren't yet releasing any information on the suspect. No one knew, yet, that Sebastian had a half brother.

Until nightfall, people mingled outside with an open bar and live music. Tables were set up in a barn with food in warming trays, buffet style. Balloons and banners gave the party a festive air. A mammoth cake sat in the middle of a table surrounded by small plates, napkins and forks.

Sebastian was glad he'd come. Most particularly when he was with Ruby. The woman had a way of lighting up the space around her. And not just because she was a Colton or owned the town's veterinary clinic. She was unique and strong and...

Jenny Colton brushed by him carrying a large birthday present toward the front of the room, where a microphone had been set up. Robert, across the room, was holding court with a group of five or six people circled around him.

"Here, Mrs. Colton, let me help you with that," Sebastian jumped in, then carried the package, and caught Ruby watching him. She smiled.

He smiled back.

And wanted more.

Jenny, Buck and Robert were the first to go through the food line. And had gone in that order. When Jenny sat at Buck's table to eat, and Robert headed over to a table on the other side of the barn with a group of people in line with him, Sebastian found himself thinking about his own parents. How, even during major social events, they'd always eaten together. And had a dance together, too.

Had his mother known about the affair?

Been hurt by it?

He and Ruby went through the food line together. He hadn't asked her to wait for him. Wasn't sure she had. But he liked them there. Doing that.

Even the fact that he'd noticed such a thing didn't make sense to him.

He was just leaning down to point out the vegetable soup to Ruby—more of what they'd shared at her house, he knew, because her sister Hannah had catered the event—when there was a commotion at the far side of the room.

Chairs pushing back. A collective gasp.

"Call 911!" Shouts came one after the other.

And beside him, Ruby dropped her plate.

"It's my father!" she cried, and ran off toward the crowd gathering around.

For the rest of her life Ruby would be grateful to Sebastian for his quiet presence during the couple of hours that followed her father's collapse. The big mountain man insisted on driving her to the hospital in Connors, where the ambulance was taking her father.

Once she'd seen that her brothers and sisters were traveling together in one vehicle, she'd gratefully climbed up with Sebastian. All that collective fear together in one vehicle would be too much for her.

Buck and Jenny, who'd both been at Robert's side almost as soon as he'd passed out, had ridden together in the ambulance.

Her cousins, with hugs, concern and pleas to be kept informed, had stayed back at the ranch to see off the guests and clean up, as best they could.

*He's alive.* Sebastian's words as they'd pulled out behind the ambulance came back to Ruby again and again while they waited to hear any news at all.

Buck and Jenny were inside the emergency room cubicle, where they'd first taken Robert. The rest of them sat in various chairs in the waiting room. Hannah called her sitter to let her know she might need her overnight. And she then sat holding hands with Lizzie, their heads bent together as they talked softly.

Wade was by himself, reading a magazine. Chase kept checking at the desk for news. And Fletcher was scrolling on his phone.

Ruby sat with Sebastian, not touching, but so glad he was there. After an hour passed with no real news, other than that Robert had not yet regained consciousness, but was breathing on his own, and tests were being run, Ruby reluctantly told Sebastian, "You don't have to stay. I can catch a ride home with either Mom and Buck, or the crew." She motioned toward her various siblings scattered about.

And yet, all together, too.

When Sebastian said he was fine right where he was, she didn't question him. Or offer again. She found herself more calm—frightened, but not panicked—with him sitting next to her.

Sebastian felt as relieved as if he'd been sitting vigil over his own family member when Jenny finally came out to tell her children that their father had suffered another stroke, but that he'd regained consciousness a couple of times and was holding steady.

The slim blond woman was clearly concerned—for her children as well as their father.

"Buck and I are both going to stay the night with him," she said then. "The doctor said each of you can come in for a minute, but that's it. They'll be moving him to a room and you can all come up tomorrow," she said, even glancing at Sebastian as she did so.

As though, because he'd fathered a Colton child, he was one of them.

He nodded at Ruby's mother, touched her shoulder as she passed and made a silent promise to her to watch over Ruby. Wanting to tell her that Robert would pull through just as he had four years before.

Like Sebastian, or Robert, had the ability to control fate.

He waited outside the emergency-room door as the siblings went in three at a time, to give their dad love, and was moved when Ruby, who came out first, looked to him as soon as she exited the door.

"I need to stop by Mom and Dad's," she said as they wished her siblings good-night and headed out into the night. "Mom wants me to pack a few things, including her pills, to bring up in the morning."

All business. Keeping a stiff upper lip. That was his Ruby.

He knew now, though, that underneath, she was as scared as the rest of them. He'd seen the chinks in her armor that no one else ever saw. With the exception, he suspected, of Jenny.

"I left my SUV there, anyway," she continued without a pause as they approached his truck. "I went over to help Mom load up decorations this afternoon, and rode to the party with her. Dad came straight from the office."

Sebastian wanted to just nod, keep his mouth shut. But said, "I can drive out to let Oscar out and put him in the kennel and meet you back at your place if you'd like." He didn't want her to be alone. Didn't think she wanted to be alone.

And since she didn't have a husband or boyfriend to call on, a friend was the next best thing.

He tried to wrap it all up nice and clean, but knew that he needed to be with her. To share the anguish with her, just as she'd sat with him through his own on a couple of occasions.

If ever a panic attack or nightmare could be better than another. Those two times with Ruby would qualify.

She hadn't given him a response and as he pulled out of the parking lot, he saw her wiping at her eyes. He stopped.

She glanced at him. Nodded.

And gave him the saddest smile he'd ever seen.


Ruby wanted more.

Seeing her father in that hospital bed, knowing he

could have easily died that night, could still die, had brought it all home to her.

Life didn't come with a single guarantee, other than that it would, at some point, end. Robert wasn't the perfect husband. He'd been an absentee father much of the time. But he loved them all. Had gone to battle for every one of them when they'd needed it growing up. Had always provided well, both in advice and monetary advantages.

"I just realized something tonight," she said aloud. "My dad, he's lived his whole life big. If not for his over-the-top dreams, maybe over-the-top energy, his need to always reach for more...we probably wouldn't even still all be together. He'd be running the hardware store with Uncle Buck. There'd be no ranch. No Colton Properties. Owl Creek would be the small town with no industry that it had always been. Maybe even be dwindling into nothing, if not for my father's vision of it as a tourist town. Us kids, if we'd been lucky enough to afford a college education, would have had to move elsewhere to get good-paying professional jobs. I sure would have had to. At least as far as Connors. If I'd even been lucky enough to get to go to veterinary school. Without the example I had, to dream big, to reach for what I wanted, I might not even have considered the possibility that I could be a vet..."

She was rambling. She knew it. Had to do it, anyway.

And wasn't the least bit worried about it, either. Sometime in the past weeks, or maybe slowly, over a period of years, Sebastian had become her safe place.

She wasn't looking at him. Stared at the road ahead of them, the headlights on pavement in a sea of darkness.

"I think that once I reached that dream, becoming

a vet, I quit reaching," she said then. "I do good work, that I love, that completes me, and I go home where I feel peaceful. But, you know, there'll be plenty of time for peace when I pass on to the next life, right?"

Sebastian glanced at her. "If you want to do more with your life, you absolutely should," he agreed.

"If you spend your life avoiding turmoil, if you don't take risks, then you miss out on the possibility that you could have it all, instead of settling for peace."

It was all becoming clear, there in the darkness.

"What more do you want?"

She wanted him. As a husband. A lover. A boyfriend. The father to her child. A housemate. Or, if all he could give her was friendship, she'd grab at that for all she was worth.

"I want love," she told him, remembering what Jenny had said the other day in the kitchen. "I want love," she repeated, almost to herself, with total conviction. "And if that means my siblings drive me up the wall, then, oh, well. What goes up, has to come down, right? I want this baby. I want to be the best mother I can possibly be. It's going to be messy and unpredictable, but I want it, Sebastian. More than that, I think I need it."

His hands were gripping the steering wheel so tightly she could see the whites of his knuckles in the dash lights.

"I want you, too," she told him then. Taking the biggest risk of all. "However we work it out, so it's good for both of us, I want you."

# Chapter 24

Sebastian had no words. His friend was in pain. Pouring her heart out. And he had no words. He'd known the time would come.

Her father had just collapsed and was in the hospital. Could yet die. She was pregnant with Sebastian's child. She'd been nearly abducted that week. Had IDd her kidnapper the day before.

And she wanted him.

*Say something, dammit.*

"I'll be here for you, for as long as you want me to be." More than he'd ever said to anyone.

And, he was sure, not nearly enough.

"I know."

She didn't sound like she was settling.

But like she knew better than to ask for anything more.

"It's not enough, is it?"

When she didn't answer right away, his gut sank. They shouldn't be having the conversation right then. They'd been through so much. Were both tired. She had to be worried sick about Robert.

Should probably be with the siblings who shared her agony as acutely.

But…he knew what it felt like to lose a parent. "No matter what happens, you'll get through it, Ruby," he told her then. "If you risk and fail, or risk and get an entirely different result than you planned… If you need your father's advice someday and he's not there to give it…you'll get through. You'll learn. And you'll grow. And you'll have a future in front of you, too." He'd found words. Maybe not the right ones, but they were better than a deafening, potentially hurtful, silence.

"If one thing doesn't work, you'll take another risk. You're as determined as I am to chart your own course, and I can promise you that what I'm saying is true. When my folks died, I was lost. I sat in our home in Boise, knowing that I was the only family left within those walls, and felt like I was through. I was having nightmares, and panic attacks, and couldn't see a future. I came to Owl Creek just to get away from those walls. The cabin was mine, no one would come looking for me there, or visit, like they were in Boise. And look at me now," he said, not in a bragging way, but in an attempt to give her hope where he'd just snatched it away. "I've got Crosswinds, a career that I love, a town that is peripheral family to me, a baby on the way…and I've got you."

He bit off the last bit quickly. They'd reached Owl Creek.

Would soon be at her parents' home.

"You've got me, too," he said then, restless, frustrated as hell. Filling with tension that he knew he couldn't assuage.

Pulling into the Colton community of Hollister Hills, he slowed the truck. "It's not enough, is it?" he asked again, when he knew the timing wasn't right.

Because he knew, too, that she'd needed to have the conversation. Which was why she'd brought it up.

Once again, she didn't answer.

So Sebastian did what he said he'd do. He pulled into her parents' drive. Dropping her off as she'd asked him to do. "Do you still want me to come over tonight?"

She nodded, jumped down, put her satchel on her shoulder and turned back to him. "You'll always be enough, Sebastian. You are who you are, and I want you in my life. I need your friendship. There just might be someone else, too. Sometime down the road."

With that, she shut the passenger door and walked, head high, with steady steps up to the Colton mansion front door.

He waited until she was inside, wishing he'd said differently. More.

But didn't know what he'd add.

Backing out of the driveway, he headed out to tend to Oscar.

She wanted him with her that night.

And so he would be.


She wasn't going to let herself cry. Her father was probably going to be just fine. He'd survived his last stroke without any adverse effects. The same could happen again.

He'd just been to the doctor, she reminded herself,

comforted herself. His tests had come back no worse than previously.

Yes, according to Jenny, Robert's doctor had continued with grave warnings in the event that Robert didn't change his habits, but the man was only fifty-nine.

And other than the effects of his hard living he was in good health.

And the rest of it?

She was out of danger, thank God!

As she climbed the stairs up to her mother's room, to collect the things on the list Jenny had texted to her, she made herself focus on the good in her life.

Thoughts of Sebastian's words, the deep honesty in them, as he'd told her about coming home from Afghanistan, having to leave the Marines early, to deal with his parents' tragic and unexpected deaths.

The Sebastian she'd always known never spoke of such things.

And the picture he'd painted—a man all alone, suffering from what was probably, at that time, acute PTSD, to have pulled himself up and out and built Crosswinds from the ground up, who spent his life giving to other veterans, and training dogs to save lives of those who've gone missing... She'd fallen in love with a good man.

She wasn't sorry about that. Nor was she sorry she was having his baby. To the contrary, she felt honored to be the mother of Sebastian Cross's child.

And she wanted more. She wanted love.

Maybe Sebastian loved her and just couldn't tell her. But she wanted marriage, too.

She was, after all, Robert Colton's daughter. She

wasn't going to settle for peace and quiet. She was going to risk failure to try to have it all.

To live big, as her dad did.

She'd reached Jenny's room. Found the overnight zipper bag right where her mother had told her it would be. Didn't recognize the black leather satchel, but saw it as something her mother would use. There was a change of underwear inside already, so she crossed that off her mother's list.

She wondered where Jenny had been overnight. As far as she knew, her mom hadn't left town in over a year.

Sitting on her mother's bed for a moment, she remembered a night when she'd awoken with a nightmare and crawled in bed with her mother. Jenny had wrapped her arms around little Ruby and she'd fallen back to sleep safe and secure.

She'd grown up in a home filled with chaos, but she'd been well loved. Had never doubted that.

It was that assurance, more than anything else, that she wanted to give her child. Whatever she had to do to accomplish the mammoth feat.

She took her time packing.

The pants and blouse were right where Jenny had said they'd be. The hospital was providing a toothbrush and paste for the night, but Jenny wanted her own in the morning, just in case she had to stay another night.

Her mom's hormone pills were in the cabinet.

And she added the few makeup items and the hairbrush Jenny had requested.

If Sebastian hadn't been coming over, she'd have driven the bag back that night. To sit with Jenny as her mother had been there for her so many times in her life. But Uncle Buck was with Jenny, and maybe it was best for the two of them to have some time alone with Robert. They'd all grown up together right there in Owl Creek.

Had gone to high school together.

Where, of course, Robert had been quarterback on the high-school football team.

Her dad was a competitor. A fighter. He was going to be fine.

With the bag on her shoulder, she wandered into Robert's room next door.

Separate rooms.

When had that happened?

After Lizzie was born?

Or had it been that way from the beginning?

Looking around, noticing the burned butt of a cigar in the ashtray on the nightstand by her father's bed, Ruby frowned, trying to remember how old she'd been when they'd lived in a house big enough for her parents to have separate rooms.

And then frowned again as she smelled something.

It was familiar.

And she didn't like it.

Heart pounding, she opened her father's nightstand drawer. Was she really searching her father's things for drugs? Of the illegal variety?

She'd been around marijuana in college. Had strongly disliked the sickly sweet smell.

It was illegal for any use in Idaho.

Or maybe it was just cut grass she was smelling. Leaving the drawers, she went to her father's open closet door, thinking maybe he'd been golfing earlier that day.

A Saturday in late April, made perfect sense to her...

"And now, my pretty, I've got you!" The familiar

male voice reverberated through her brain, through the clothes in her father's closet, as a gloved hand reached out from between them and grabbed her wrist.

Sebastian took his time getting back to Crosswinds. It was late. Traffic was nonexistent. The night was peaceful. And he wanted to give Ruby time to get home and have a minute in her own space.

It was an act of selflessness.

What he wanted to do was turn around and follow her home.

Just to be by her side.

Life had spiraled in so many directions. For both of them.

The two of them together was the constant. Through all of it.

The attacks were on Crosswinds, and her.

The baby was equal parts of both of them.

He had a half brother. Her father had a stroke.

For years, they'd been living peaceful, productive lives. Side by side, through her brother, and then through work, but separate. And suddenly, they implode together. It was like fate was out to force them together.

The last thought triggered a self-deprecating grunt. He was so tired he was getting punchy.

Oscar greeted him with happy whines and a wagging body when he walked in the door. He fed the boy, and found a sense of rightness within himself, too.

Dogs were another thing he and Ruby had in common. A deep understanding of the relationship between canines and humans. Of the bond that existed between them.

"You want to go for a ride?" he asked Oscar then.

He'd take the dog to Ruby's with him. Oscar would bridge the gap of need between them.

She'd told him once that she'd love to have a dog of her own, but just couldn't subject a precious canine to a life spent mostly alone. He'd suggested she take the dog to work with her every day. She'd seemed open to the idea. And then Oscar had been shot and he and Ruby had slept together and they'd quit talking like friends.

Grabbing food for the dog for the morning, and a clean pair of underwear and his toothbrush, Sebastian was just bagging his items to head out the door when his phone rang.

He'd only left Ruby a brief fifteen minutes before...

His entire being stopped flowing as he saw Steele's name come up. Close to midnight?

"What?" he answered.

"Working late here, and heard you were in Connors with the Coltons, so figured it wasn't too late to call," the detective began.

*Get on with it.* Sebastian kept his impatience to himself. Holding the phone to his ear with his shoulder, he shoved his things between paper handles, motioned for Oscar, and was heading out the door as Steele said, "A report just came through from Boise. Your father wasn't having an affair. The woman he was seeing was a patient. She didn't have health insurance and couldn't afford a hospital stay. He paid for her hotel and treated her there, on and off for a couple of years. When she got pregnant, he told her it would likely kill her to have the baby. She opted to have it, anyway. And when she died, the child was adopted out."

"Leon."

"That's what we thought because we thought he was

your brother, but we haven't been able to confirm that. It's what we were after when we had Boise checking on the woman. We still haven't been able to positively ID this guy. He's got no driver's license, his prints aren't in the system. We've sent out DNA samples but haven't heard back."

Sebastian's mind was ticking. His father hadn't had an affair. He had to tell Ruby. And… "If he's not my brother, why does he think the land is his?"

"We're still working on that. He's not talking. Just keeps saying God is his father. And spitting out renditions of bible verse that aren't accurate. Our theory right now is that he did some amateur checking and somehow thinks you're his brother."

The young man sounded delusional.

"Has his attorney been in to see him?"

"Today. Of course, I have no idea what was said."

Right. And knowing the kid was in good hands—hands Sebastian would continue to pay for now that he'd started—he could walk away.

And he did.

Ruby screamed, "No-o-o-o!" burst out of her as the man in the closet held a vise grip on her wrist. She kicked her elbow out like a chicken wing, striking him under his chin, and twisted her arm with a purposeful jerk as she did so.

In the split second that his grasp loosened, she was free. Slamming the closet door, she ran for the room's exit, pushing the lock in the knob as she shut that, too.

The lock wouldn't hold. The door was solid wood, and the jambs were standard, attached to trim wood. Her attacker was strong. She had two minutes, max.

Too late, she identified the stench.

The smell of the man who'd grabbed her from behind in the dark.

He'd been smoking dope before he attacked her.

Her kidnapper wasn't in jail.

He was right there in her parents' house. Like he'd been lying in wait. Watching all of them. Had he followed her to the hospital, and back?

He'd smelled like pot the night of the attempted abduction. How could she have forgotten that?

How he had gotten out of jail, and how long it would be before anyone knew, she had no idea. Just knew she had a baby to protect.

She had to stay alive.

She'd left her purse downstairs. Had to get to her phone. Her parents, like so many, no longer had a landline. Thoughts flew as she moved down the hall.

Seconds later, she passed the bedroom she'd recently used and was turning toward the stairs when she heard the loud crack of wood behind her.

Her attacker was already free, just around the corner.

She'd never make it down the stairs in time.

Instead, she slipped behind the door in the bathroom, prayed that he'd run past her toward the stairs.

Her heart thumped. Pressed against the wall behind the door, she could hear the beat in her head, feel the ends of every nerve. She could hardly breathe, but had to keep thinking.

To keep focused.

She was alone. Had to save herself.

She knew the house. The fiend after her did not.

How long would it be until Fletcher got home?

Her brother had a gun in his room. Fletcher was

wearing his personal gun in town, and had showed her the nine-millimeter, for her use if she needed it to stay alive, the first night she'd stayed with him and her parents.

She was going to need it to stay alive.

Doors banged against walls down the hall, followed by seconds of silence. The kidnapper searching rooms? He was coming closer. If he banged her door, she'd be dead.

Turning her cheek to the wall, she prayed for all she was worth. And saw the sink. The cupboard under it was empty. She'd stored her toiletries there.

Hearing another door slam, figuring she had seconds while the intruder was in the guest room, she used those seconds to crawl inside the small cupboard, scrunching up, with her head tilted to avoid the drain.

The door just outside her space slammed.

If he opened the cupboard, found her, she had one shot. A kick straight to the groin, or she was done.

She had to wait for him to open the door. To be that close, facing the cupboard, or she wouldn't have a shot at incapacitating him.

She could hear the man's heavy breathing.

Could feel his incensed desire to lay his hands on her.

And held her breath.

# *Chapter 25*

Sebastian wasn't even up Cross Road before he voice-dialed Ruby to tell her about Steele's call. Her kidnapper wasn't his brother.

Though, logically, he'd known the relationship wasn't his fault—wasn't a reflection on him, as Ruby had pointed out—the relief was palpable. Coursing through him with a newness of life. His child was not going to have an uncle in prison for heinous crimes against the child's mother.

Expecting her to pick up on the first ring, as she generally did lately, he waited impatiently through the second.

And then the third.

After the night she'd had, he was antsy to give her some good news.

By the fourth ring, Sebastian was fully focused.

The young man in jail sounded delusional. Was quoting bible verses wrong. He must have done his amateur sleuthing incorrectly to have come to the conclusion that Sebastian was his brother.

Even with desperation driving escalated behavior, the man in jail did not resemble a stalker shrewd enough to elude investigators, leaving no clues at all, for more than two months.

A kid spouting religious rhetoric. Like the kidnapper had spewed to Ruby the night of her attempted abduction, and to him via text, and with a clever plan to torch his place that fit the man's method of operation. Calling him brother. Maybe he was overreacting.

It would be way too much of a coincidence, some kid just happening to torch his place after he'd initiated a campaign to squeeze out the stalking kidnapper.

And it hit him.

With cold certainty.

A man who'd been pushed past his limit, who'd been forced out of his carefully calculated plans, might hire someone to be in one place, while he would lie in wait for what he'd obviously determined was the root of all of his problems. Ruby.

Why the guy wanted his land, why he thought Crosswinds belonged to him, he had no idea. And at the moment, didn't care.

Calling Steele back, Sebastian told the man to get to Ruby's house, while he broke all speed limits to get there himself.

She thought she heard her phone ringing.

Would it draw her attacker down the stairs?

What about the security system?

Where was Fletcher?

Her kidnapper had shoved the bathroom door against the wall. And then…nothing.

Had he left?

Was he standing there? Staring at the cupboard?

Had she left a trail?

Did he know she was in there?

Chest tight, she couldn't breathe. Hurt everywhere.

And…she heard the screech of rings against metal just feet away as he pushed aside the shower curtain.

He was going to find her.

Sebastian had just reached the outskirts of Owl Creek when his phone rang again. Steele.

"She's not at her house."

The words sparked a fear in him that he couldn't contain. Gunning his engine, he spit out the words: "Her parents." And, turning his wheel sharply to the left, screeching his tires, he told Oscar to hang on as he entered the private neighborhood of mansions.

Feeling sick, ready to kill or die, he saw Ruby's SUV still in the drive of her parents' home. And saw the light on upstairs.

"Please, God, let her be in Jenny's room, taking her time collecting things. Needing to be close to her mother."

Comforted himself with the thought of the security system.

He dialed her again as he pulled up the drive, stopping right behind her vehicle. Told Oscar to stay and was already heading up the walk as he heard the ring of the connected call. He could see her satchel through the window. On an ottoman not far from the front door.

And knew with dead certainty that something was wrong.

Very wrong.

With her father in the emergency room, Ruby would not let her phone go unanswered unless she had no other choice.

Not knowing if she'd fallen, was hurt, or if his worst suspicions were true and the man in jail was not their stalker, and the kidnapper had Ruby, he picked up a rock and broke the front window, using his shirted arm to swipe away enough glass to get inside.

Gun out, he surveyed the space, looking for... *Oh, God, not blood.*

"Ruby!" The call was a cry from the heart.

Then he saw curtains blowing through an open window in the back of the house.

And went into full battle mode.

She might already be gone.

He had to check the house first.

Maybe he wasn't too late.

Maybe there would be a clue to who had her, where he'd taken her.

He'd quickly canvassed the downstairs, was heading upstairs when he heard what sounded like wood slamming against a wall.

Gun pointed, ready to take out the fiend with one bullet to the head, he took the stairs three at a time, heard a grunt. Fear made adrenaline race through him as he rounded the corner.

"You..." A man's voice.

He swung around. Saw a jean-clad backside and shot. The wall at the end of the hall.

It was enough to make the man stand upright for

the split second it took Sebastian to shove the barrel of
his gun to the back of the intruder's head. "Move and
you're dead."

Ruby saw blood drip to the hallway floor. And didn't
move.

*Move and you're dead.*

She'd heard Sebastian's voice but could only see the
intruder.

And blood.

After looking in the bath, her kidnapper had left the
bathroom. Ruby had breathed a full breath. She'd heard
the door slam against the wall. And then nothing.

Until she'd heard Sebastian call her name.

Tears had flooded her eyes. She'd bit her lip to keep
from making a sound.

And had heard her kidnapper as he whispered, "I
know where you are. You're going to come out of there
nice and slow…"

He was going to use her as a human shield. She just
knew.

Would hold her up and make Sebastian let them walk
away.

The cupboard had opened.

She'd kicked, but the evil man had been ready for
her, keeping himself back far enough to ward off any
self-defensive blow. Her foot landed on his shin.

Painful, but not debilitating.

That's when she'd seen the gun. Held low, in one
hand, it was pointed straight at her. Still.

Did Sebastian know? He was behind the man. Could
he see the gun?

Did she warn him?

Hoping that Sebastian was a quicker shot than the man who'd been eluding police for more than two months?

The kidnapper had escaped chains and jail.

Her parents' security system…

She was going to die, right there in front of Sebastian…

"Turn around slowly." Sebastian's controlled, commanding tone brought more tears. If his voice was the last one she heard, she'd take it with her forever.

Staring unblinkingly at the intruder's feet, she waited for them to move.

They didn't.

She was still staring at a gun barrel.

She was going to die.

Sebastian would never know his baby.

Never give himself another chance to have a family of his own.

If he didn't know about the gun, he'd never forgive himself when Ruby got shot.

Her only chance was to take a chance.

The gun was two feet away.

She'd get one move. And it had to be quicker than a trigger pull.

She'd positioned herself to kick out and up. If she could knock the gun…

A quick movement, and the feet in front of her suddenly twisted away. "Drop the gun, you…" Sebastian's curse words sounded. She waited for the sound of another shot.

Heard… Was that Fletcher?

And Detective Steele?

"We've got this…"

"Ruby…"

Sebastian's voice. Warm. Worried.

She wanted to tell him she was fine.

But she lay there, curled up, her back to the wall, a drain in front of her face, her arms cradling her baby, and couldn't move.

She was shaking. But breathing. Reaching a steady hand in, Sebastian felt for a pulse. It was rapid, but strong.

Her gaze didn't seem to be focusing.

Fear struck through him again. "Ruby?"

When that beautiful, deep green-eyed gaze moved to him, he felt tears prick his eyes. He hadn't cried since Jerry had died.

While everything inside of him wanted to rip the vanity apart and lift her up against him, never to let her go, he remained on his haunches, holding her gaze. "Are you hurt?"

If the man had…

She was fully dressed in the same red jeans and black pullover sweater she'd had on all night.

"No."

She still didn't move.

And he understood. The chaos right outside the bathroom door. The sounds of police voices, sirens in the distance. He shut the door.

Flipped on the bathroom light.

And met her gaze again, immediately.

"You want to come out now?"

She shook her head. "Not until he's gone."

"Ruby!" Fletcher's voice sounded panicked, followed by a strong knock on the door.

Standing, Sebastian opened the door.

"Her vitals are fine. She's scared to death. Stay with

her," he said, taking the stairs down two at a time, and racing for his truck.

"Come on, boy," he said, slapping his thigh and racing back toward the house. The blue-hooded man was in cuffs, being led out of the house. Sebastian didn't look at him. Just slapped his thigh again and took the stairs back up, with Oscar keeping pace beside him.

"It's okay, sis, it's over." Sebastian heard Fletcher's voice.

And when there was no reply, he tapped the detective on the shoulder and motioned for him to make room. Seeing Oscar, Fletcher stood.

It took strength for Sebastian to stand back and let Oscar rescue the mother of his child. He watched as the dog put a paw on Ruby's leg, and then moved closer, laying his front paws in as much of her lap as he could get to.

But when he saw her hand move to Oscar's head, and then slowly start to pet the dog, he knew she was going to be okay.

And dropped to his knees with relief.

# Chapter 26

Ruby had no need for medical attention. An EMT on scene checked her out, but she'd have refused to head back to the ER in Connors even if it had been recommended.

Standing in her parents' front yard, looking at the crime-scene tape, the flashing lights, she could only think of one place she wanted to be.

"Take me home with you," she said to Sebastian, her hand on Oscar's head. "Please."

Her brother was going to be at the police station for a while. If she didn't detest the fiend who'd been terrorizing them for months, she'd have felt sorry for him. Fletcher was not going to leave the man alone until he had every answer he wanted out of him.

He'd do it legally. But her brother would not give up. He'd also said he was going to head up to the hospital in the morning to speak with their parents. Or at least Jenny, if Robert wasn't well enough to hear what had happened.

Steele agreed to put off that particular notification for the night.

By morning, they should have answers to give Jenny—like how the kidnapper got past the security system—along with the bad news that her beautiful home was a crime scene. Or even, who the kidnapper was. In the meantime, officers were going to secure the house for the night. Tape cardboard to windows and assign a watch so the place didn't get vandalized.

It wasn't until she and Sebastian were in the truck, on their way out to Crosswinds—Oscar sitting in the back seat with his head popping over the back of the seat—that Ruby remembered the blood.

"Did you crack him with the butt of the gun?" she asked. She'd heard his report to Steele and Fletcher, right after she'd given her own without Sebastian present.

They'd both been told to stay close in case they'd need to come in for further questioning in the morning.

"Nope. No way I was risking any chance that man has any cause to come after me again. I played it fully by the book."

She glanced at him. "I saw blood drip on the floor."

When Sebastian pulled up his red-checked flannel sleeve, showing her the gash on his forearm, she gasped. "Why didn't you have the EMT look at that?" she asked him. "It needs attention, Sebastian."

"And I have someone perfectly capable of taking care of it, if that's the case," he said, adding, "Right here in the truck with me." He glanced over at her. "I needed to get you out of there."

Yeah. Even just five minutes down the road, she was feeling better. Breathing easier. Her chest felt lighter.

"I think it's just surface," he said then, sounding calm. But she saw those white knuckles on the steering wheel.

In his own way, Sebastian was as agitated as she was. And she thought of something she'd just heard.

"Leon isn't your brother." He had to be feeling good about that.

He nodded. Gave her nothing more on the subject.

And then they were pulling into Crosswinds. She insisted on a stop at the medical building so she could check out his arm—cut from breaking the front window glass in her parents' home. She found herself picking out a couple of shards—remembering when she'd been similarly engaged treating Elise not so long before—and could hardly comprehend that it was really over.

She'd thought it was. Trusted it was.

But it hadn't been.

Sebastian didn't need stitches. She'd have insisted on a trip into Connors if he had. She patched him up with butterfly strips and looked up at him, to see if he was satisfied, only to catch him staring at her with the most intent look in his eyes.

An expression she didn't recognize.

And couldn't look away.

He didn't say anything. Just looked at her.

And then lowered his lips to hers. Showing her what he was feeling.

Because that was who he was and what he had to give.

And when she'd needed him, he was there.

He'd saved her life. Not once, but twice.

Maybe she wasn't meant to get married. Maybe a good friend, hopefully occasional lover and co-parent was all she was ever going to have.

Because she wasn't going to walk away from Sebastian.

Ever.

There was no one else on earth whose presence made her world okay. No one else who seemed to take the same comfort from her own nearness.

So what he had to give was going to have to be enough.

Lying in his bed with Ruby that night, Sebastian watched the expressions chase themselves across her face. Frowns. Looks of pain.

No smiles.

He'd dozed some. Had definitely rested, with her body lightly touching his. He'd refused to allow himself deep sleep. After all the trauma of the past few days— culminating that night when he'd seen the gun in the kidnapper's hands and had thought, for a split second, that he could very well lose Ruby and the baby—there'd been too much chance of a nightmare.

He'd been surprised at just how relaxed he'd been, from the moment they stripped down to their underwear and crawled in bed together.

There'd been no sex. She'd given him no hint at all that she wanted it. And he'd had no inclination for it, either.

They'd been through too much to put themselves through any more emotional upheaval. Even ecstasy.

But as dawn neared, he wished he'd made love to her. To have that be her last moments before sleeping, to chase away the demons that seemed to be haunting her in her sleep.

To have a pleasant memory be the first thing on her mind when she woke up.

And right then, in that moment, lying there watching her, focusing solely on her, he knew. And bent down to kiss her.

Her lips moved beneath his before her eyes opened.

And then she was lying there staring up at him, completely open. No filters.

It was a second that would be locked in his memory for life. The thing he would be striving to achieve for the rest of his days.

"Marry me," he said then. So easily.

She blinked. And when her eyes opened again, the smart, assessing, closed-off woman he knew was staring back at him.

"Don't, Sebastian."

Absolutely the furthest reaction he'd expected to get.

"Don't what?"

"All of it—just don't." She slid from the bed.

And he followed right behind her. "I thought you'd changed your mind, that you wanted to get married someday," he said as she pulled a flannel shirt out of his closet and slid her arms into it on the way to the kitchen.

He wasn't going to panic. He was going to be there. Period.

Turning, she stopped him in his tracks. "I want you," she said. "The real you. Not someone who gives me what I want when it doesn't fit. That's a recipe for failure."

Something she'd been afraid of her whole life, he realized. Thinking of all her questions, always. Needing to know. To be sure. To limit...

And he took a deep breath.

"Last night, when I saw his gun…"

She hissed in a breath, but he didn't stop. "I knew I could lose you. And that if I did, the light in my life would go out. You are my constant, Ruby. And… I saved your life. I was able to protect you, in spite of myself. You said not too long ago that there are dangers we run from and those we choose to manage. I'm asking you to take on the potential danger of living with a man with PTSD. I've started training Oscar. Our awareness of the situation, the potential triggers and a dog trained to stop me before I escalate out of control could be how we manage that. And when our child is young, I'm never left alone all night, or at least, I never go to sleep, without another adult present, just in case. I know your stubbornness, your strength, and know that if I'm ever out of control when you're there, the first thing you'll do is see to our child."

She was shaking her head. Not smiling.

He didn't get it.

"I love you, Sebastian," she told him, as if she'd said the words many times before. "And right now, I need you to take me home. To get a shower and head to Connors to see my mom and dad. And you need to feed dogs and train…"

"Della's going to cover Crosswinds for me," he told her. "I texted her last night when you were in seeing your father." And then, with his newly opened heart shattering a bit, he said, "I'm fine to take you home. I'd like it better if you'd let me get a quick shower, first. And then I can come to the hospital with you. Just in case."

He left that "in case" hanging there. Just in case there

were questions about Ruby's near kidnapping the night before. Or, just in case Robert wasn't doing as well as expected. She could take her pick. Both were there.

And when she nodded, saying, "I'll feed Oscar while you're showering," his heart started to piece itself back together again.

The man already owned her heart. There was no reason for him to give up his own path to walk hers. As badly as Ruby had wanted to throw caution to the wind, reach for what she most wanted and suggest that she and Sebastian go to the courthouse that day to complete marriage paperwork, she couldn't.

Maybe she'd never be a person like her father. One who could just take what he wanted, create what he needed by hard work, dedication and sheer force of will, and deal with the consequences later.

She was a woman who'd been too shut in, too cautious to dare to dream. But she was also one who needed to look for possible consequences and be prepared to deal with them in the event her reaching, her risk, brought them about.

And the consequences of marrying Sebastian, when he was so definitely not a marrying man, were too brutal to consider. She could lose him entirely.

She'd rather be his friend for life than his enemy.

Or, worse, his nothing at all.

An early morning proposal, out of the blue, after the night they'd had, preceded by the weeks they'd had... She'd have been nothing but selfish to accept.

But she kissed him when he came out of the shower. Deep. Long. Like a lifetime lover would do. Squeezed his arm before she got out of his truck at her folks' house and got into her own SUV. She waited for him to pull into her garage after her and walked with him into her house.

And smiled, an expression she felt to her soul, when he was waiting for her with breakfast made when she came out of her room. He pulled her into his arms then, kissing her as deeply as she'd kissed him earlier, and she started to rest a little easier inside.

They were going to find their way.

It might not be traditional. Or be exactly what she thought she wanted.

But in the end, what she wanted was him.

And if he wanted her as badly, they'd find a way to make it work.

Fletcher called just as they were getting ready to leave for the hospital. He was heading up after a shower, and asked that she wait to tell their parents what had happened until he got there.

A condition with which she was quite happy to comply.

She put him on speakerphone then, as he relayed what had transpired during the night. Sebastian drove, as they heard, together, that her kidnapper's name was Bob Thompson.

"I know that name," Sebastian said.

"His lawyer approached you six months ago with an offer to buy your five acres on the lake," Fletcher said. And Sebastian and Ruby frowned together.

"All of this is because Sebastian wouldn't sell his land?" she asked, incredulous. No matter how much research, how many questions asked, or how many foreseen risks she might have turned up on a land offer, she'd never, in a million years, have come up with such a potentially deadly consequence.

"Yes and no. Yes, if Sebastian had sold the land, the man wouldn't have gone after the two of you. But he'd have been living right here in Owl Creek and that would not have been good," Fletcher continued. And Ruby grew more and more incredulous, and horrified, too, as she listened. "He's an Ever After Church member, and claims that God told him that the property belonged to the church. That God wanted the land for a new church."

"I've never even heard of the Ever After Church," she said, glancing at Sebastian, who shook his head.

"Neither had we. Supposedly it was founded by some guy named Markus Acker. But this is where it really gets weird. This guy, Thompson, has a record. He ran an illegal gambling ring for years without getting caught. And when he was apprehended, he made a deal to turn in some of his clients who were mobsters to stay out of jail. Apparently, the second chance turned his life around, he found religion and has dedicated his life to the service of Ever After Church, claiming it saved him. To the point that he was willing to risk going back to jail to follow what he claims are God's edicts. He's been living in plain sight, staying at a cabin on the lake. Dressed in expensive clothes. Golfing. The blue hoodie was for his nighttime persona. Using a rowboat along the shore in the dark to access Crosswinds. He's a smart guy. Too smart for his own good. He was able to hack into the Wi-Fi on Mom and Dad's security system so if it went off, it dialed his number instead of the security company or police. He'd done that the day after the kidnapping, when you started staying there. He'd been following you ever since."

Ruby had no words.

Sebastian's were off-color. And pretty much expressed her own feelings. Shivering, she put her hand on the console between them, and he laced his big, warm fingers through hers.

"He's still claiming that we're all sinners and that God will make us pay," Fletcher said.

Consequences again. The thought hit Ruby. They were everywhere, those things that happened due to choices made. She was never going to be able to control them all.

And she sure as hell didn't want to try and end up losing sight of reality, as Bob Thompson surely had.

"What about Leon?" Sebastian's question brought her back to the moment at hand. And the man at her side. One who'd asked her to marry him when marriage hadn't even been a dot on his radar. And who'd been rejected by her.

"When he saw Thompson in handcuffs, being led by his open door…"

"Your suggestion, I'm sure," Ruby butt in.

"Yeah, well, when Leon saw Thompson, and knew that he'd been arrested, he was only too happy to tell us that Thompson had been a visiting minister at his church on and off, and had approached Leon, saying he'd had a vision, that God had chosen Leon to do a hard part of His work…"

"He duped the kid into setting my place on fire," Sebastian said. "But what about saying I was his brother?"

"This kid believes that all people on earth are brothers and sisters, per his bible readings. His last name's

Connolly. Turns out his dad's in prison. His mom abandoned him. He's been in and out of foster homes his whole life. Some of them abusive. And, in high school, landed in the home of a couple of zealots, who took him to a small, very strict church. He'd been looking for something to believe in, someone to believe, his whole life, and he thought he'd found his family. His home."

There it was again. Family.

Home. She placed her other hand over her stomach. Cradled her tiny but growing baby.

"And hey, sis, you'll be the first in the family to know—I've been offered lead detective here in Owl Creek. And I've accepted. I'm moving home!"

Ruby burst out with enthusiasm without even thinking about how it would be with one more sibling watching her. Giving her their opinion of her life choices. Butting in. Instead, she let herself be happy to have someone she loved back home.

And after they hung up, she asked Sebastian to pull into a mountain park not far from Connors.

He stopped in a small, deserted lot by a hiking trail. "What's up?" he asked, turning to run a finger through a few strands of hair that had fallen out of her always loose bun.

"Why did you ask me to marry you? Full-out honesty here, Sebastian…" she said, her tone filled with warning. Though she couldn't have told him to save her life what the consequences would be if he didn't comply.

Because the heart knew what it knew.

And was strong enough to deal with the consequences.

"Because I realized something last night on my way back to Owl Creek," he told her, looking her straight in the eye, his fingers remaining in her hair. "You and I—we're a constant. When life flew out of control for both of us, others were involved, in the picture, helping, but you and I were my constant. Us. Together. I'm good alone. I'm better with you. And I think you're better with me, too."

Her eyes flooded with tears. Her lips were trembling so much, her throat so tight, she couldn't speak.

"I love you, Ruby Colton. As much as I'm going to love that kid you're carrying. I don't want to go to bed at night without you, wondering about you. Or wake up in the morning thinking of you, when I could be lying there with you. This morning, it was all…just there. The battle I'd been fighting, to be independent and live alone… Maybe I was just afraid of losing love again. Maybe I was just plain uninformed. But I lost the battle, Ruby. I don't need to fight it anymore."

She swallowed. Tried to speak. And when she couldn't, she threw her body over the console, her top half landing against Sebastian, and her butt on the hard cover between their seats. It wasn't a well-thought-out plan. Or elegant.

It didn't work well.

And she didn't care.

Because it got her where she most needed to be. Her body in the arms of the man she loved. And her arms around the human who needed her just as badly.

He lowered his lips as she raised hers. And in that kiss, she found her future.

It wouldn't be perfect.

There'd be hardship and pain along the way.

Their child would grow up to disagree with them, go out into the world and take their own risks. And if they had more than one...then they'd all eventually go and there would be even more risks.

She had to take them.

When they both finally came up for air—only because they couldn't go any further to assuage their physical needs on the driver's seat of his truck—she whispered, "Ask me again."

"Marry me," he said, and this time she smiled.

He hadn't asked the first time.

He'd commanded.

If she'd heard that, she'd have understood.

Because she knew Sebastian Cross. He hadn't been commanding her. He'd just been that sure of his own personal course going forward. And that's all she'd needed to know.

"Marry me," she said back, in just as forceful a tone.

And this time, when they kissed, they did so around the smiles on their lips.

\* \* \* \* \*

Don't miss the stories in this mini series!

# THE COLTONS OF OWL CREEK

MILLS & BOON

# The Bodyguard's Deadly Mission
## Lisa Dodson

MILLS & BOON

**Lisa Dodson** is a nationally bestselling author and an Amazon #1 bestselling author of over nineteen novels in multiple genres. Lisa writes positive, realistic characters that she hopes readers can connect with while enjoying her novels. Lisa works as a business development manager at a technology consulting firm, is the mother of two adult children and a Maltipoo, Brinkley, and lives in Raleigh, North Carolina.

Visit the Author Profile page at
millsandboon.com.au for more titles.

Dear Reader,

Alexa King has been living in my head for quite some time now, demanding that her story be told. I'm elated to finally bring her journey to light in *The Bodyguard's Deadly Mission*. This story centers on overcoming personal tragedy, conquering obstacles in life and allowing yourself to trust again after your heart has been broken.

Alexa and Andrew are intense, passionate and laser-focused apart. But together, they are a powerful force of nature! I wanted their relationship to slowly grow and develop as the story unfolded because each of them had reasons for guarding their heart and trust takes time.

I love to travel, so I'm always going to work exciting new destinations into my stories. I had fun researching Chamonix, France, and the fun winter sport of skijoring! Thanks so much for reading! I hope my characters are memorable for you and that you end up rooting for them to find lasting happiness as much as I do!

*Lisa Dodson*

# DEDICATION

To my niece and brilliant forensic scientist, Jillian Lewis.
Thank you for the invaluable insight!

To the Alexa Kings and Brendas in the world.
Embrace your power!

# Chapter 1

Alexa King dropped the yellow rose she was carrying on the wicker casket. Unfortunately, mourners weren't allowed to stay and watch the casket be lowered into the ground, so the memorial service for her best friend, Tanya Singleton, was officially over.

Walking over to the row of white fold-up chairs near the grave site, Alexa knelt in front of Tanya's mother, Viola Singleton, and took her hand. Tall and athletic in build, Viola was deep in her grief, but it did little to minimize her timeless beauty. Her cream-colored dress with the blouson sleeves was cinched at the waist with a wide tan leather belt. Her curly brown shoulder-length hair was adorned with a single white lily. Viola looked like she was ready to enjoy a picnic in the grassy meadow as opposed to laying her only child to rest. Alexa knew that would be exactly how Tanya would have wanted it.

"You were such a joy to my daughter. She would have loved all you've done to honor her today."

Alexa struggled to get the words out over the lump in her throat. "She was my best friend, and I loved her dearly."

"I know, honey. Thank you for driving all the way here. I know Pittsburgh isn't exactly around the corner from Washington, DC, but this place fits Tanya." Her mother sniffled and dabbed her eyes with her handkerchief. "The environmentally friendly burial was fitting. Thank you for finding it."

Hugging Viola tightly, she said, "You're welcome. And you're right. She would've loved this place." Alexa kissed her cheek before moving off and letting others pay their respects.

The burial site was on the other side of a meadow. Some

people with health issues took advantage of the caretaker's golf cart while most attendees walked.

When she reached the other side of the field, Jake and Margot Stanton King took turns hugging their daughter. Alexa and her parents were all wearing black suits and dark sunglasses. Each had a lapel pin of a gold crown with diamonds. It was a family trademark passed down to each male heir and family for generations.

"How are you, darling?"

Alexa lowered her sunglasses. "My heart is broken, Mom."

Her mother touched her shoulder. "I know, honey. We're so sorry."

"Lex, why don't you come back home with us? Take a few days to rest up and recuperate?"

"I can't, Dad. I have to finish packing up Tanya's apartment."

Her mother frowned. "Alexa, isn't there someone else who can do it?"

"No, Mom. I volunteered. The Singletons have enough on their plate back home with Tanya's brother still in the hospital recovering from surgery."

"I'm sorry he had to miss the funeral."

"We all are, Mom, but there was no way he was well enough to travel."

"Any word from Byron?"

Alexa's hands bunched into fists at her side. "No, and if he knows what's good for him, he'll stay away."

Jake frowned. "It seems strange that he's just disappeared without a trace."

"Well, after the police cleared him of any wrongdoing and the district attorney rejected the case, he decided to make himself scarce."

Margot rested her hand on Alexa's shoulder. "Honey, we know how you feel, but there's no proof."

"I've got plenty of text messages about their arguments and his temper, Mom."

"You know that Tanya never called the police on him, nor did she file a report. He also doesn't have a documented history of violence against his girlfriend. So even if you could produce the text messages, they'd never hold up against cross-examination. The defense will say you could've sent those messages from Tanya's phone."

Alexa blanched. "That's not true."

"It doesn't need to be true, Alexa. All it needs to do is introduce doubt to a jury about their authenticity."

That gave Alexa pause. "He can't get away with this. I don't care what it takes. I'll find a way to ensure Tanya's death wasn't in vain."

"You will be careful," her father warned. "I don't want you getting in over your head, Alexa. Suppose it wasn't an accident? Who knows what Byron could do if he felt cornered. The last thing we need is you to voice your theories on this publicly."

"If there is anything more to find, you let the police handle it," her mother cautioned.

When Alexa didn't readily agree, her father said, "Alexa."

"Okay, I hear you. I won't do anything on my own. I promise."

Her parents relaxed.

"I want you to take some time off work, Alexa."

"Dad, I'm fine."

"You've been working nonstop since she died, Alexa. You need some time to rest and regroup."

"No, I don't. I've got it under control."

Her father looked skeptical but agreed. "Okay, but you take it if you need it."

"I will," she promised.

Alexa's father, a retired intelligence officer for the Defense Intelligence Agency, cofounded J.M. King & Associates with his wife. Her mother headed up the legal side at the risk management firm in Washington, DC. After college graduation, Alexa went to work there and rose in the ranks to senior cyber threat intelligence analyst. A third-generation corporate lawyer, Margot wanted her daughter to follow in her footsteps and those of her mother and grandmother, but Alexa chose her father's profession.

"I have to go." She kissed both parents. "I promised Tanya's landlord I'd be over in the morning with the movers. Most of her belongings will be donated to local missions and charities."

Jake squeezed her hand. "That's wonderful, sweetheart. Let us know if you need anything."

After their goodbyes, Alexa headed for the parking lot while her parents went to say goodbye to Tanya's family. She had almost reached her convertible Volkswagen Beetle when someone called her name. Recognizing the voice, she kept walking.

"Alexa, wait." The man beckoned. When she ignored him, he ran and jumped in front of her. "Please," Byron Monroe said, holding up his hands. "I just want to talk to you for a minute."

She stepped back. "We have nothing to say to each other. How dare you even be here," she hissed.

"I have every right to be here," he said indignantly. "Tanya was my girlfriend."

"Every right, huh? Is that why you're slinking around and weren't at the grave site?"

He shifted on his feet. His hands shoved into the pockets of his navy blue slacks. "I didn't want to upset the family."

She took in his haphazard suit and unshaven face. "Get out of my way, Byron."

When she went to step around him, Byron blocked her path.

"You must know I would never hurt Tanya—I loved her. We were going to get married. So why would I do her harm?"

"Spare me. That's the garbage you told yourself and my

friend, but I'm not buying it." Alexa's expression turned menacing as she jabbed her index finger at his chest.

"I don't know what you're talking about."

"Tanya's death may have been labeled an accident, but we both know differently, don't we?" Alexa pressed, ignoring her parents' warnings. "She finally decides to leave you, and suddenly, she has an accident, trips down a flight of concrete steps, puts herself in a coma and eventually dies from her injuries?" She scoffed. "I don't think so."

Byron wiped his hand across his jaw in agitation. "I won't lie, we were arguing, and she tried to leave. I attempted to grab her arm, but she snatched it away from me, lost her balance and fell backward. It was an accident, Alexa—I swear."

She eyed him with contempt. "I'm not buying that. Save the innocent act for someone who doesn't know your history of losing your temper and taking it out on my best friend. I can't prove it now, but the truth will come out, Byron Monroe. When it does, I'll see that you pay for your crime, and I promise you that I won't stop until you're under the jail."

All pretense at civility was gone. When Byron leaned over, he was so close to Alexa that she smelled his cologne and breath, a cross between stale smoke, cheap liquor and cherry cough drops. She almost gagged.

Knowing that his proximity was an intimidation tactic, Alexa stood her ground.

"Regardless of what you think, I loved Tanya. I didn't kill her, and if I were you, I wouldn't continue digging up imaginary dirt—it's not wise."

"Is that a threat?"

A hint of a smile curled on his lips. Then, standing to his full height, he said, "Merely a warning from a concerned friend."

"We've never been friends. I tolerated you in my life because of Tanya. Nothing more."

"Everything okay over here?" a man called out.

They both turned in his direction.

"Yes, thank you," Alexa said sweetly before turning to Byron.

"If you think I'm going to cower in fear and let this drop, you don't know me."

Alexa shoved past him and strode to her car. Using the remote to unlock the door, she slid inside and started the car. When she looked up after starting the vehicle, Byron was gone. Taking a moment, she composed herself.

"The nerve of him." Her heart was racing, and her hands shook with suppressed fury and grief. "I will not be intimidated by you, Byron," she vowed.

Her thoughts drifted back to her last conversation with Tanya. It was, of course, about an argument with Byron. She could tell her friend wasn't telling her the whole story. But just as Tanya began to open up, Alexa got called into an important meeting at work.

*I'm sorry, Tanya, I'm late for a meeting.*

*Okay, but you'll call me back?*

*Yes, I promise.*

Alexa had been swamped the rest of the day and into the evening. She'd missed several calls and text messages, two from Tanya. It was almost two o'clock in the morning when Alexa dragged herself through the front door of her condo. Kicking off her shoes, she padded across the room to the couch, where she collapsed in an exhausted heap. She realized almost fifteen minutes later that she'd never called Tanya back.

*It's too late to call now. I'll do it first thing in the morning. It's Saturday, and we'll have plenty of time to catch up,* she'd promised herself.

Alexa tried to call and text several times the next day but never reached Tanya. When she finally did get a call, it wasn't one she'd ever expected to receive. Instead, it was a police officer calling to inform her that her friend had had an accident and that she should get to the hospital. They had called Alexa because they couldn't reach Tanya's next of kin, and Alexa was listed as her emergency contact.

Hours later, Alexa's world wobbled on its axis at discovering that Tanya was in Intensive Care in a coma with severe head trauma. The prognosis wasn't good, and even worse, the only person with her at the time of the accident was her on-again, off-again boyfriend, Byron.

Flipping through Tanya's phone, police had discovered a text message that Tanya drafted but never got to send. Chills shot across Alexa's body when she could finally read it herself.

You're right. People don't change, and Byron certainly isn't going to. So I finally broke up with him. But, of course, he insists that he'll win me back. Tanya was in the middle of saying that it would never happen when the text stopped, incomplete.

A horn honk jolted Alexa back to the present. Startled, she saw a car go by with two people waving goodbye.

Resting her head on the steering wheel, Alexa closed her eyes. "I failed you," she whispered into the quiet. "I'm sorry, Tanya."

During the five-hour drive back to Washington, DC, Alexa pondered her conversation with Byron. It made her skin crawl.

*Just because I can't prove you're guilty doesn't mean you're innocent.*

She disliked Byron with a vengeance and only tolerated his presence because of Tanya. He had never been worthy of her friend's love, and she liked him even less after noticing his mean streak. But Tanya had loved him and defended him regardless. To her peril.

The thought was like a dagger plunged straight into her chest. Fresh tears flowed, causing her vision to blur. Alexa angrily wiped them away with the back of her hand.

The pain closed in around Alexa. It gnawed at her, overtaking her waking hours and invading her sleep. It was the second time in her life that she had lost a friend to a violent encounter—first Shelley Porter, now Tanya. The guilt was so intense it was almost incapacitating.

On the other hand, the fact that Shelley hadn't died was a blessing, but it was bittersweet because her family had covertly blamed Alexa for the encounter in the park. Like she had control over some vagrant man trying to rob them in broad daylight.

Then, as the days turned into weeks and Shelley still hadn't recovered mentally, her mother, Carol Porter, showed up on the Kings' doorstep and accused Alexa of causing the whole incident and not protecting her daughter. Alexa denied any wrongdoing, and her parents had defended her against their neighbor's accusations.

"Mrs. Porter was right. I should forget about having close friends. I'm like a magnet for disaster." She gripped the steering wheel so tight that her fingers went numb.

Initially, Alexa felt certain the rift with Shelley would mend, but it had only grown. Eventually, the Porters packed up and moved without warning. The severed friendship with Shelley broke Alexa's heart, but losing Tanya to another violent act had exposed the deep wound festering inside. She was the common denominator, and if it weren't for their association with her, Shelley would be free from mental torment, and Tanya would be alive.

Tentacles of ice felt like they had snaked out and surrounded Alexa's heart, making it impossible for Alexa to deny the truth any longer.

"This was my fault."

# Chapter 2

It was almost seven o'clock by the time she arrived at her condo on the Southwest Waterfront. After taking a shower, Alexa put on a pair of lounging pajamas and ordered take-out. While waiting, she sat on the couch and jotted down the action plan for the next day. She wasn't looking forward to being in charge of packing up Tanya's apartment, but she had promised Tanya's parents she would handle it.

Lighting a few candles, Alexa sat down for a quiet meal but moved the steak salad around in the mango wood salad bowl with the Moroccan blue-tiled inlay. It was a gift from her cousin, Zane King, and one of her favorites. Unfortunately, her appetite was as absent as a good night's sleep these days.

The cell phone ringing startled Alexa. Upon seeing the caller's name, she didn't bother with salutations when she picked up.

"I wish you were here with me."

"If it weren't traveling for work, you know I would be," her cousin replied. "I know today had to be rough for you."

"Yes, it was. I've realized that I don't need to have close friends."

"What? Lex, what are you talking about?"

"Bad things eventually happen to people that I love."

"First of all, that's merely a coincidence. Besides, I'm your best friend, and I'm still here."

"Yeah, but for how long, Zane?" she cried. "Plus, you're family. Maybe you all are immune."

"Lex, that's grief and fear talking. These are mere flukes, that's all. You aren't a magnet for danger. It's unfortunate, but sometimes bad things happen to good people. It's not your fault."

When she remained quiet, Zane said, "Quit ignoring me."

"I hear you, Z."

"You say you do, but do you believe it?"

"I had a run-in with Byron," she said, changing the subject.

"What? Why?"

"He didn't take too kindly to me ignoring him and refused to leave until he had convinced me of his innocence. I told him I didn't buy his act for a second and that I'd find a way to make him pay for Tanya's death."

"Easy, cousin. Don't underestimate that man. He could be dangerous."

"I know, but I'm not about to let him get away with anything, Zane. Tanya is gone because of his violent nature."

"We don't know that for sure."

Her eyebrows shot upward. "Zane—"

"Wait, hear me out before you jump all over me. Look, I agree with you, Alexa. Byron Monroe is bad news. I'm merely suggesting that you tread lightly. We can't prove that Tanya's death wasn't an accident, and you can't convict anyone of murder due to a feeling."

"Quit worrying. I promised Mom and Dad that I would be careful and will."

Zane audibly sighed. "Good. Hey, I've got to run. I've got an early meeting. Keep me posted on how things are going, okay?"

"I will," Alexa agreed before hanging up.

It had been three weeks since the funeral and clearing out of Tanya's apartment. The more days ticked by, the worse Alexa became. Sleep was a foreign concept. She practically lived at work and survived on bottled water and protein bars. But the one thing that provided Alexa with a modicum of peace was laps in the condo's swimming pool. It was the only time when her mind was at ease. It was her coping mechanism.

One night after work, Alexa was about to go swimming when her father called.

"Hey, Dad," she said as she maneuvered into her suit. "What's up?"

"We have to talk, honey."

Two things tipped her off this would not be a social call—her father's gruff voice and the fact that he placed her on speakerphone. Not having time for beating around the bush, Alexa jumped right in.

"Okay, what do you two need to discuss?"

"You, Lex," her mother replied. "We're worried about you."

"I don't know why."

"Then allow me to clarify," her father replied. "You haven't been home for a family dinner in forever, you're working a minimum of fifty hours a week, and from what I hear, you look like you haven't slept in ages. I won't even mention the mini meltdown you had at work."

Alexa was shocked, but that quickly drifted into anger. "What, are you keeping tabs on me? I don't need anyone trying to micromanage me, Dad."

"Alexa, that's not what your father is doing, and you know it. You're merely deflecting because everything he's said is true."

"It may be true, but I can handle myself."

"I should've insisted on this weeks ago." Her father sighed. "Alexa, you need to take a leave of absence and get yourself together."

"Dad, that's crazy. I don't need—"

"You know what we're dealing with at work. I need you operating at one hundred percent, Alexa."

"I haven't dropped one ball nor had a decline in my performance."

"Yet," he countered. "Something could happen at any time. That's not a risk I'm willing to take from any employee— especially not my daughter."

When they ended the call, Alexa was livid. Snatching up her bag, she slammed out of her condo and strode toward the elevator. Jamming her finger on the down button, Alexa paced in circles while waiting.

"I can't believe he benched me. Like I can't handle myself," she snapped, and took the steps down to the fitness center instead. She pushed the door open and almost slammed it off its hinges. Yanking off her clothes, Alexa tossed them on a lounge chair and dived into the cool water.

Swimming laps, Alexa lost count of how many revolutions she did. She continued until all the hurt, anger, guilt, pain and sadness had left her body, and her muscles ached with exertion.

Hovering weightless in the water, Alexa let her mind go blank and floated. Nothing mattered except the comforting silence and the next breath. Not just to sustain her life but to honor Tanya's.

When Alexa emerged from the water thirty minutes later, her skin was wrinkled like a prune, but she felt rejuvenated and lighter than she had in weeks.

"Dad was right. I'm in no shape to continue like nothing is wrong." Alexa hoisted herself out of the pool. "It's time to stop moving through life and reacting to things that happen. From now on, I have to get proactive," she said with conviction. "Everyone has a God-given talent. It's time I found mine."

Alexa stood at her parents' front door, her finger hovering over the doorbell.

"Once I do this, there's no going back," she said aloud.

Alexa had spent the last three weeks at the Serenity Wellness Center in San Jose, Costa Rica. It was a pristine white compound in the middle of a lush rainforest. It had exceeded her expectations. At the retreat, Alexa had spent the entire stay surrounded by professionals dedicated to creating a safe, welcoming environment that encouraged their guests to restore their minds, bodies and souls.

There, Alexa met Dr. Marena Dash-McKendrick, a bio-chemist from North Carolina. They gelled instantly and promised each other to keep in touch.

Another incredible outcome of her time at Serenity was that Alexa had discovered her purpose. It was the reason why she had come straight from the airport to her parents' without delay. Now that she had a direction, she was eager to begin her new life.

Alexa greeted her parents and eagerly discussed her trip. She answered questions and gave them gifts she had pur-chased on one of the group outings to town.

Now she sat perched on the edge of her favorite leather armchair in her father's office doing her best to summon the courage to jump into the abyss without a parachute.

Alexa laid out her plan in detail because Margot and Jake King were laser-focused when it came to setting the groundwork and laying out all the facts.

Once done with her well-thought-out argument, what concerned Alexa the most was that her parents just sat there staring at her in utter silence. Both were on the couch across from her with their hands folded in their laps.

After more painful seconds, Alexa felt compelled to de-molish the silence.

"Dad, I know how it sounds, but I'm not crazy."

Jake leaned forward, his elbows resting just above his knees. "I didn't say you were, sweetheart."

"Well, I was thinking it," Margot snapped before turn-ing to her daughter. "You want to be a bodyguard? Alexa, this is insane, not to mention dangerous."

"Not just a bodyguard. I did the research," she added. "I'll be a close protection officer."

Margot shook her head. "Oh, great, that's even riskier."

"I know, Mom, but it's what I want to do—what I have to do."

"Is it? Alexa, I know you feel guilty about losing Tanya, but you can't continue blaming yourself."

"It's not just about her, Mom. It's about protecting the Brendas in the world."

Margot glanced between her daughter and husband and then threw her hands up. "Am I supposed to know what that means?"

"Brenda was a woman at the retreat. She was in a horrible relationship that almost turned violent. It got to the point where she said she didn't even recognize herself anymore. There were so many similarities between her and Tanya." Alexa's voice trembled. "Family and friends begged her to leave him, but it wasn't until he threatened to kill her that Brenda found the courage to leave.

"It took a lot for her to tell her story. The counselor said that was why she founded Serenity. She felt that everyone needed the chance to open up. To release the pain holding them hostage and stealing their voice. To transform themselves no matter their circumstances. To heal. That's when I knew what my calling had to be."

"Alexa, there must be a better way to devote yourself to a cause that doesn't include peril. Why not volunteer at a shelter, or start a nonprofit? There are a million ways you can make a difference without risking your safety."

Jake turned to his wife. "Can you give us a minute, love?"

"Only if you plan on talking some sense into our daughter."

He squeezed her hand. "Please, Margot."

Nodding, she turned and strode out of the room, slamming the door behind her.

"I know Mom is upset, but I'm not changing my mind about this, Dad."

Her father stood and walked over to his desk. "I can see that, Lex. But what I need to know is if you have thought this through." He sat on the edge of the table and crossed his arms.

"I mean good and thoroughly through, Alexa. This isn't an easy path you're choosing. It's dangerous, and to become an expert, you'll have to know a great deal about many subjects. This profession is… We're talking life-and-death, but also risk assessment and mitigation, tactical, combat, movement safety—"

"Dad, we work in risk and threat assessment now. I know this job has much to learn, and I'll need specialized training."

"There's so much more to it than that, Lex. First, you'll be putting yourself in harm's way to protect someone else." Jake studied his daughter. "Do you understand the gravity of that choice? Hundreds of things could go wrong for each one that goes right in the field. Are those odds you can live with?"

# Chapter 3

Alexa stood resolute in front of her father's desk. "I'm not changing my mind, Dad. I want to be an executive protection specialist to protect women who can't protect themselves. It's what I want to do. It's what I *have* to do."

Jake pinched the bridge of his nose. His stern expression echoed the gravity of his only child's decision.

"If you're sure, Alexa, and you're one hundred percent committed—"

"I am."

He shook his head. "I guess I shouldn't be surprised. When you were at the university library, you almost made that Peeping Tom eat a book on constitutional law when he got fresh with your dorm mate."

"Well, he needed to study that book anyway," she pointed out.

Unable to help himself, Jake chuckled. "Okay, Alexa. If you're dead set on this path, all my resources will be at your disposal. I have an old friend who runs a training academy with his son and a few other buddies who can help. They each have decades of experience, so you'll have the best training available."

She visibly relaxed. "Thank you, Dad. And I'm sorry about leaving you short one senior analyst."

"Don't worry about it, honey. I'll make all the arrangements."

She rushed to hug her father. "Thank you."

He returned the embrace. "The only thanks I need is you to be safe, sweetheart." He glanced into her eyes. "Do you hear me?"

"Yes," she said tearfully.

He kissed her cheek. "Good. Now I have to talk to your mother. Which isn't going to be easy." He sighed heavily.

"No, this is my decision, Dad. I'll be the one to talk to Mom."

Alexa found her mother outside by the pool in her favorite chaise longue. As was her habit, she sat by her mother's feet at its end.

The lights were on in the pool and around the perimeter. They both sat transfixed as the nighttime shadows and the shimmering blue water vied for dominance.

"I know you're worried."

"That would be an understatement," her mother murmured, never looking up. "Alexa, this is dangerous. Anything could happen."

"I know, Mom. But I can't ignore this anymore. It's eating away at my soul. I wasn't there for Shelley or Tanya. Not when it mattered. I want to help other women feel protected and safe, at least when they're in my care."

Margot turned to face her daughter. Alexa saw that she had been crying. There was also undisguised anguish in her eyes. Her mother's pain tore at her heart.

"Why is this your cross to bear, Alexa? All this guilt is misplaced. What happened to Shelley was an unforeseen event caused by a desperate man's ill-considered actions. Tanya also had a choice to make, and she made it. To her detriment. You aren't to blame for either incident."

"Mom, I'm not trying to hurt either of you—"

"I get it. You have to follow your heart. Your tenacity is something I've always admired about you, Alexa. You've always been a fighter and willing to help anyone that needed it. And as worried as I am, I know you'll do well. You're my daughter, after all."

That garnered a smile from Alexa. "I learned everything I know from my mother."

"Not everything," Margot chuckled before reaching for

Alexa's hand. "Whenever you're obstinate and set in your ways, you remind me of your father."

She leaned in and hugged her mother tightly. "I love you, Mom."

"I love you, my darling daughter. I couldn't be prouder of the woman you've become. Promise me that you'll be careful and return in one piece."

"I'll do my best."

When she got home, the first thing Alexa did was call Zane and bring him up to speed on her decision.

"I couldn't be happier for you. When do you leave?"

"What?" Alexa lay back on her bed and crossed one leg over the other. "I thought you'd try to talk me out of it, too."

"For what? It wouldn't make a difference anyway. I'm nowhere near as persuasive in arguing as your parents, so why waste my time swimming upstream?"

Alexa couldn't fault her cousin's reasoning. Not when it was true.

She went upstairs and began brushing her teeth and prepping for bed.

"You realize you're putting a damper on my social calendar, don't you? How am I supposed to hang out with my best friend if she's in— Where are you going again?"

"Colorado." She paused while rinsing her mouth. "Dad said that his buddy James Riker Sr. and his son own a facility in Pagosa Springs."

"Uh-huh. For how long?"

"Twelve weeks."

"You can't be serious," Zane complained. "Three months, Lex? That's insane."

"It's going to take time. There's so much I have to learn. Functional movement, first aid, several martial arts disciplines, defensive and offensive evasive maneuvers—"

"While that all sounds very impressive, I'm still going to miss you."

"I'll miss you, too."

"I can't believe that Uncle Jake is arranging all of this. Who doesn't he know?"

"Seriously," Alexa agreed. "I must admit to being surprised myself. I knew Dad had a lot of connections and old military buddies, but I never knew how extensive the list was until now."

"I'm sure his contacts will be helpful later," Zane reasoned. "Count your lucky stars. You're getting the VIP treatment."

"Zane, I don't want anyone going easy on me because I'm Jake King's daughter. I plan on earning my place on my own merits."

"I hear what you're saying, but don't be crazy. It's a highly competitive world you're about to enter. You'll need all the help you can get."

"That's true."

"Lex, I'm proud of you. You're daring to envision a whole new life for yourself. You'll be making a difference in the world. Don't get me wrong, you were excellent in cybersecurity, but I'd always felt that was Uncle Jake's choice for your life and not your own."

"I loved my job, Zane. I'm not leaving because I'm unhappy with it. I'm going because I believe this will be more rewarding for me."

"I'm sure it will, Alexa. I can't wait to hear about how it's going."

"I promise to keep you in the loop on my progress."

"You'd better."

After hanging up, Alexa set her cell phone on the nightstand. Then, staring at the ceiling, she placed her arms behind her head. This was such a significant change in her life. She was excited, but she was terrified, too. Failure wasn't an option. She would go all in, and she would complete the program.

"Well, Tanya. Neither of us saw this coming."

\* \* \*

In the late afternoon, Alexa arrived at the Phalanx Training Academy in Pagosa Springs, Colorado. It was a seven-hour flight from Washington, DC, with a layover in Denver and an hour's ride from the Durango Regional Airport to the southwestern town. The academy had hired a driver to pick her up, for which she was grateful since it allowed her to stretch out after the long flight.

Upon sign-in, a young woman escorted her to James Riker's office.

When they entered, he was engrossed in paperwork.

"Ah, you must be Alexa King."

"Yes, I am."

James came around his desk and hugged her, which caught Alexa off guard.

"It's a pleasure to meet you finally. You can't imagine how your father goes on and on about you. I tell you, Jake would talk a dead man to death if you let him." He winked.

"I'm afraid Dad doesn't talk much about his military buddies other than they're his brothers for life."

"That we are. And don't you mind us old dogs. Once we get settled somewhere, we seldom visit each other, no matter how much we talk about it."

Alexa laughed. He reminded her a lot of her father. They were tall, muscular, good-looking men with infectious smiles, rich brown skin and salt-and-pepper hair that was cut close.

James took Alexa's luggage and ushered her outside to a nearby Jeep.

"Come on, let's get you settled, then I'll show you around. You'll meet my son, JJ, later. He's in the middle of teaching a class. Normally, we have a full house, but our summer session isn't as busy. He teaches several free classes if time permits. Come on, I'll give you a tour."

Alexa barely got in an "okay" before James was on to the next topic. She listened to him provide background on the academy while they drove. He reminded her of her father in many ways, just more talkative.

"We have about three hundred acres total, with a few lakes, the national forest nearby and spectacular views of the San Juan Mountains."

"It's beautiful here but kind of remote."

"That's by design," he replied. "At Phalanx, we teach many courses in ninety days. Executive protection officers put their life on the line for their principal." He turned to her. "That's the person that you're protecting. Depending on the contract, that may not be your actual client."

"I understand."

"Anyway, you must know the job's practical, functional and technical aspects. They must become instinctual, Alexa. Our reputation is without reproach because we hire the best instructors in the field, surpassing what other companies teach their students and offering continuing education to our graduates."

"I've read up on your company. You all have an impeccable track record, Mr. Riker."

"Please, call me James, or Jim."

"Okay. I wanted to say thank you for taking me on as a student on short notice."

"When your father called, I admit I was surprised by his request."

"Why? Because I'm a woman?"

"No, the number of women in executive protection is rising. It's because close protection isn't for everyone, Alexa. It takes a unique person to handle the job. It's dangerous work and solitary, with extended hours, not many holidays off or visits home."

Finally, he turned and pinned her with a stare. "You need to ask yourself if this is what you want to do in life and be clear on your answer."

"I understand."

"I don't know that you do, Alexa. I'm asking if you are

willing to turn your life upside down for this program. Are you willing to put your mind and body through pain, discomfort and being pushed to the limit of what you think you can handle? This program is more than just learning new skills and carrying a weapon. It's about mind over matter. Realizing that you can do things you never thought you'd be able to do, being responsible for another human being's safety and well-being. And most importantly, ask yourself if you're willing to take a bullet for your principal if it comes down to that? Are you willing to lay down your life to protect someone else, Alexa?"

# Chapter 4

After their talk, James drove Alexa to her lodgings. They pulled down a dirt road, the only one Alexa had seen for some time. It led to a circular drive and a small log cabin surrounded by trees. The red cedar home had a red tin roof with modest landscaping.

"This isn't too remote for you, is it?"

Alexa jumped down from the Jeep and looked around. The mountain vista was majestic, with not one wrong view from any direction.

James pointed toward the back of the cabin. "There's a lake just a few minutes' walk down that path. It's well-stocked, so there are a few poles and a tackle box in the shed if you're an angler. There's also an ATV. You know how to drive one of those, don't you?"

"Yes, I do."

"Great. We're having dinner at our place tonight if you're up to it?"

"Oh, yes, of course. Thank you."

"It'll be after JJ's last class. The ATV's out back. You can ride up to my office at about seven."

"Thanks, I'll see you then," Alexa replied, escorting him out.

Alexa gazed around the log cabin. It was an open floor plan with many windows to let in the natural light. The living room had a fireplace made from river rock. A well-worn maple-brown leather couch with two big pillows with an Aztec design was right across from it. A coffee table and two chairs with a side table completed the space. The decor was homey and welcoming. The wood dining room table had six chairs and was right under the window, giving guests a magnificent view of the mountains. Photographs of

Native Americans were displayed proudly on the beamed walls in color and black-and-white.

Expecting the kitchen to be understated, Alexa was pleasantly surprised to find it was high-end and well furnished. The countertops were black-green granite with white and gold veins across the surface. A stainless-steel KitchenAid gas stove with five burners took up one side of the kitchen with the built-in microwave and oven nearby. In addition, there was a coffee machine, an air fryer and a slow cooker.

She ran her hand over the beverage brewing system before peeking into the metal drawer underneath that housed apple cider, coffee and tea pods.

"I can't wait to use you," she said dreamily.

The stainless-steel farmhouse kitchen sink was under the window.

"Eye candy. Just what I need while I'm doing dishes."

Next, she headed to the bathroom and gasped when she saw a large corner Jacuzzi tub in the same river rock as the fireplace. Half the wall behind it was glass. There was a separate shower, double sinks and a toilet area.

The cabin had two bedrooms that were similar in size on opposite sides of the house. Both had en suite bathrooms, a sliding door leading to a wraparound porch, window seats and huge walk-in closets.

Going back to the other bedroom, Alexa unpacked and took a shower. The hot water beating her back like a drum solo felt heavenly on her tired muscles.

Alexa chose jean shorts and a short-sleeve T-shirt to wear for dinner.

She glanced at her watch. She still had two hours before dinner. "Good a time as any to look around."

She shoved the phone in her pocket and went to retrieve the quad keys. Alexa had always been good with geography, so she confidently followed the path and her instincts to return to the main building. When she passed a break room, she spotted a refrigerator case with drinks and healthy snacks. Thirsty, Alexa retrieved an iced tea and continued down the hallway.

Rounding a corner, Alexa was about to enter James's office but stopped short at hearing raised voices.

"Since when is Phalanx a vacation destination?"

"What are you talking about?"

"Dad, I saw Jake King's note about doing him a favor and getting his daughter enrolled."

"JJ, he was talking about—"

"So, Alexa King has nothing better to do than disrupt our lives by signing up for our program she'll drop out of after two days? Can't we give her a tour and a T-shirt and be done with it? These weekend warrior wannabes are a waste of time and space."

"Don't be rude, JJ," his father snapped. "Alexa isn't here to take up space. Jake was very clear on his daughter's intentions. He assured me that she would take our training seriously, and I believe him."

"Well, I don't. We haven't had a woman complete our training program since…in forever," James Andrew Riker Jr. finished abruptly. "She could get hurt or, worse, cause someone else to be injured while she's out proving to herself that she can cut it."

"Nonsense," James dismissed. "I've met her. You haven't. She's serious about being here and deserves a chance to prove herself. So she stays. End of story. And the favor you mentioned that Jake asked me for was to *not* treat Alexa any differently than anyone else. She must earn her spot here. If she doesn't he expects her to get cut just like any other student."

His son crossed his arms. "I say you're making a big mistake. I read her application. It's obvious that Daddy gives her whatever she wants. She works for his company, went to the best schools and was a military brat."

"So were you," James pointed out.

JJ's expression darkened. "She's nothing like me, and I'm not going easy on her just because. It may be a moot point anyway. Mark my words, she'll wash out within a week and go crawling back to her fancy condo in Washington, DC."

Alexa reared back as though she had been stung by a bee. Her chest rose and fell with the pent-up energy she held in check. It was all she could do not to barge into James's office and demand his obnoxious and rude son retract every haughty accusation he'd slung her way.

Angry didn't scratch the surface of how she felt. *How dare he!*

She had no clue what she'd done to deserve this man's venom, but Alexa was determined to shove her diploma under his sanctimonious nose when she graduated.

Hearing both voices coming closer, Alexa rushed down the corridor. Unsure where to go next, she was about to head outside when another sound caught her attention. Following the noise, Alexa opened the door and went into a studio. There were several older adults in a circle on the mat. They were sparring, so she hung back not to be intrusive.

An instructor was teaching them an evasive technique. The man was wearing a protective face mask along with protective gear. His voice was calm and encouraging as he explained the moves to the students and studied their movements as they practiced.

Spotting a row of bleachers in the corner, Alexa took a seat. The man seemed kind and patient as each person had a turn.

"There seem to be some trainers here that can be professional and courteous. Shocking," Alexa snarked.

When a buzzer rang, the man announced that the class was over. The group thanked him and dissipated as another man entered from a side door and strode onto the mat. Alexa observed him with curiosity.

After patting a few people on the back, the teacher walked over to where the newcomer was standing. He was also wearing a protective helmet over his face. Some participants filed out of the room, saying their hellos to Alexa as they passed.

A woman stopped in front of Alexa. "Are you joining our class?"

"She's not old enough," a man said patiently from behind. "This is a senior citizens' self-defense class," he explained. "She doesn't look like she has an AARP card yet."

"That's true," Alexa chuckled. "I'm here for another training program, I just heard the commotion and came in to check it out."

"What do you think it'll be today?" one of the seniors asked his buddy before sitting down on the bench next to Alexa. "Sticks or swords?"

His friend shrugged. "Beats me, but it's always good. My money's on Andrew."

"Oh, great. More of that invisible money you love to bet with."

A loud crash caught her attention. Glancing up, she saw the two fighting with long sticks.

A woman nudged Alexa. "Looks like it's bōjutsu."

"What?"

"It's Japanese for staff technique. It's a type of stick fighting."

The woman had to speak loudly because the instructors were going full throttle, and the noise was deafening. Fixated, Alexa watched in awe as one man used his pole to sweep the other's feet from under him. There were several passes before they threw down the sticks and started grappling. When the man on the bottom finally tapped out, his opponent helped him up. Taking off their masks, they slapped each other on the back before walking over to join the crowd.

Alexa noted that both men were tall, and very attractive. One looked like an older, heavier version of the actor Scott Eastwood. The new guy was Black, had a muscular physique, arresting brown eyes, a mole on his cheek just under his right eye, and a scar from his bottom lip to his chin. Alexa found herself wondering how he got it. She guessed that he was either military or a former serviceman by how he carried himself. Either way, he was swoon-worthy, and she would have had to be incapacitated not to have an immediate response to his physical attraction.

She tried not to stare, but at this point, Alexa felt it would've been easier to outrun a bear while drenched in honey.

Eventually, the man's gaze connected with hers from across the room. When it did, his demeanor shifted so fast it caught Alexa off guard.

Unprepared for his outward hostility, she choked on her tea, dissolved into a fit of coughing, and then spilled her drink down the front of her clothing. She yelped as the cold liquid met her skin.

Everyone in the room turned and stared. Including the man she was just gawking at.

Though struggling to breathe, Alexa stood there dumbfounded. From the hostile way he was staring at her, and the similarity in looks, this guy had to be James's son.

# Chapter 5

Mortified, she bounded out of the room and down the hallway to the break room. Grabbing some paper towels, Alexa wet them and vigorously dabbed at the front of her shirt.

*What a jerk*, she mused. *One minute he's smiling, and the next he's glaring like I spit in his coffee.*

"You must be Alexa King."

Alexa whirled around to find the rude man in question standing inside the doorway with his arms crossed. Despite just having had a rigorous workout, he was as relaxed as she was flustered. A towel was draped over his neck, with sweat still glistening on his face.

*Well, if he thinks he's going to intimidate me, he's in for a disappointment*, she said to herself. *He may be cute, but that doesn't give him a pass to be ill-mannered.*

Giving up on the shirt, Alexa threw the mound of wet paper in the trash and turned to face him like she was going into battle.

"And you must be James Riker Jr. Or should I call you JJ?"

"Andrew is fine. It's my middle name. Outside of family, no one calls me that."

He pushed off from the wall and came forward. He extended his hand. "It's a pleasure to meet you, Miss King."

Her arms stayed at her side. "I find that hard to believe given your behavior earlier," she replied with a calm she didn't feel.

That gave him pause. He lowered his hand. "Have we met?"

He may look like his father, but it was obvious he had not inherited James's easygoing nature.

"No, we haven't. Which is the reason why you dragging my name through the mud to your father was baffling."

For the first time, Andrew looked uncomfortable. "My apologies. I didn't mean for anyone to overhear."

"Interesting that you apologized for being overheard, and not what you said. Look, I don't know what your problem is, or why you've painted me with a broad brush. Frankly, I don't care. I'm not easily intimidated, Mr. Riker. Nor do I cower on command. I'm here to gain what's up there," she said, pointing to his head. "Not your approval."

"Fair enough. But I admit that I'm surprised to find you at Phalanx, Miss King. Based on your application, you don't seem the type that's interested in this kind of career."

"It would appear that you have a certain image in your mind of who I am, and what I would or wouldn't do. I can't imagine what's caused this fixation."

"Fixation?" Andrew laughed heartily. "I certainly wouldn't call it that. No, you just remind me of someone I know. She talked a good game, but in the end, she didn't have what it took for this line of work. My guess is neither will you."

"Ah. Biased and closed-minded." Her smile was as sweet as cotton candy. "Why should I be surprised based on your rudeness."

He returned the smile. Not in the least ruffled by her put-down. "Good to know. I see we're off to a great start."

"Thanks to you."

Before he could say more, Alexa turned on her heel and strode out of the room.

Andrew stood there a few moments, feeling like he'd just been dismissed. He had to admit that he was surprised that Alexa overheard his discussion with his dad. That was unexpected, and he chided himself for losing his temper at work. It was unprofessional and never should have happened. But he had seen her picture, and it had sparked a memory that wouldn't let go.

Alexa King was sure of herself. That much was obvious. And clearly, she wasn't overly sensitive because she had gotten angry instead of dissolving into tears. Andrew appreciated her spunk, but from the moment he read through her application and saw her picture, Alexa had rubbed him the wrong way. She reminded him of someone he would have preferred never to think about again. Despite that, meeting Alexa for the first time was startling. Andrew was surprised by her beauty and how she carried herself. Her photo had not done her justice.

Alexa was taller than most women he had met, with long, wavy hair that framed her face. There was a faint scar on her left cheek that made him wonder at the cause. Alexa had dimples and bright, welcoming eyes.

*Not exactly welcoming*, he corrected himself. Her gaze when he caught up with her in the break room was as brittle as frozen metal. Andrew could've kicked himself for stirring up this beehive. "Why did you have to look like *her*?" he groaned. Maybe Alexa would do them both a favor and quit by the week's end. *That would put us both out of our misery*, he reasoned. A man could hope.

Alexa gritted her teeth. She was so angry at Andrew Riker that she couldn't think straight. She had returned to the cabin and pondered not going to the welcome dinner, but Alexa had given her word. And once given, she never rescinded it.

Decision made, Alexa changed into a pair of brown linen trousers, a plain white oxford shirt that was open at the neck and a pair of black block-heeled sandals.

Dainty gold earrings with a matching necklace completed the semidressy look. Next, she swept her hair up into a high bun. If she was going into battle with Andrew Riker, she wanted to look good doing it.

Confident and relaxed, she headed out. Not wanting to arrive windblown, and with bugs stuck in various places, she took her time driving the all-terrain vehicle.

The Riker residence was a combination of wood and stone. Alexa marveled at its natural beauty and how large it was. She figured that it was at least six thousand square feet. A wraparound porch on the front, several rocking chairs and a two-seater swing allowed for plenty of conversation while admiring the mountainous views. By the time she parked the ATV and was heading up the steps to the porch, Andrew was already on the top step waiting.

"Welcome, Miss King. I hope you're hungry. Dad has never mastered just cooking for a small group, so there's a lot."

Confused by his congenial behavior, Alexa made an effort to reciprocate. "Thank you. And yes, I am."

"Mom died two years ago," Andrew explained. "I was hoping that Dad would take more time off, but he did the opposite. Instead, he threw himself into work and hasn't come up for air yet."

"I'm sorry to hear about your mother."

"Thanks." Andrew motioned toward the front door. "It's been rough, but we've done our best to be there for each other."

"I, um, have to ask. What's with the complete turnaround? Earlier you were—"

"Rude? Horrible? Loud and wrong?"

"Keep going, I'll stop you when I disagree."

He chuckled. "I deserve that."

An awkward silence crept into their conversation. Alexa struggled for something to say. "Do you have any siblings?"

"No, I'm an only child."

"Me, too," Alexa confessed. "You know when it's hardest to bear?"

"Holidays?"

"Yep. That's when I miss having brothers and sisters. Though I don't mind being spoiled," she joked.

Andrew stared at her for a moment. His expression darkened slightly, but it was enough for Alexa to notice.

"There you two are," James yelled from the kitchen. "I was beginning to think the guys and I would have to eat this super-scrumptious meal ourselves."

The lighthearted moment restored, Andrew looked heavenward. "He loves to brag about his cooking like some seasoned pitmaster. He just started grilling and smoking meats last year."

They went into the kitchen and greeted Andrew's father.

"I hope you two are hungry. Got enough to feed a bear."

Glancing at Alexa, Andrew mouthed the words *I told you* before saying, "Can't wait. It smells amazing in here."

The meal stretched out on the granite countertops was massive. There were six side dishes: smoked brisket, chicken and sausages, corn on the cob, potato salad, coleslaw and yeast rolls.

"Dad?" Andrew said in shock. "What in the world? You said a little something."

"Well, I got to grilling, and the grilling bug bit me, so I kept adding more stuff. Finally, I decided I'd better invite everybody." He grinned.

A woman came into the kitchen carrying an armful of folded napkins and a tablecloth. "You know how he gets once there's a burr under his saddle."

Alexa had to hide her smile as the older woman nudged past James to get several trivets from a drawer.

"Esther, this is Alexa. Alexa, this is my housekeeper and boss, Esther." James winked.

"Nice to meet you, Alexa, and don't mind him," she said, inclining her head toward James. Esther turned and handed the linens to Andrew. "Would you take care of the table while I finish up in the kitchen?"

"I'll help you," Alexa replied, and followed him into the dining room.

They worked as a team to set the table.

"Your housekeeper seems like she's time enough for the two of you."

"Esther is wonderful," Andrew agreed. "She has us toeing the line for sure. She's been with our family for decades and is like a second mother to me."

"Do you normally have students here for dinner?"

"We have a big dinner on the first night. We feel it's important that the students should get to know each other. You all will be working as a team for the next ninety days."

"Oh, I'm surprised you're not hoping I drop out long before that."

Slightly embarrassed at her guessing his thoughts, he said, "Being in the protection business isn't about being a lone wolf. It's about teamwork. Your team has to trust you, and it's the same for you. There are many moving parts, Alexa. Each must function independently but also as part of the whole. That's how you keep your principal, team and yourself safe."

"That makes sense."

When they were done, she followed Andrew back into the kitchen to help bring out the food.

James and Andrew were at ease entertaining and being cordial to their guests. Including Alexa there were twelve students, a lead trainer and several instructors who came to dinner. It was a loud, laughter-filled affair. The dinner was buffet style, so some were seated at the dining table, while others grabbed spots in the family room.

Being the only female student at dinner didn't intimidate or bother Alexa. Instead, she worked the room, introducing herself to each classmate, sizing them up as she went. Most were cordial and welcoming, but there were a few of the guys who weren't overly thrilled that she was there. One of them, Tate Bannon, was overtly hostile.

"You can't be serious," he said when she introduced herself. "You really think you're cut out for executive protection?" He practically laughed in her face.

"That's what I'm here to find out," she said, looking him straight in the eye. "This is a marathon, not a sprint, Bannon. And I plan to cross the finish line just like everyone else here."

"Wanna bet?" he remarked under his breath.

Alexa moved off before she said something to Tate that she would regret.

She wasn't about to make it easy for Andrew Riker to dismiss her. For whatever reason, both had assumed she wasn't cut out for the job. Which meant that she would do whatever it took to prove them wrong. *Loud and wrong*, she added for good measure.

Later that night, Andrew sat on the wooden swing on the back porch. He was absentmindedly swaying the rocker with the heel of his foot.

His thoughts drifted to Alexa. Despite their rocky start, Andrew tried to make up for his bad behavior earlier that day. He was engaging, sought her out on several occasions to ensure she was enjoying the party and offered to drive her home in his Jeep so she wouldn't have to drive the ATV at night, but she had declined, assuring him that she would be fine.

"Glad to see you've mended fences with Alexa."

He turned to see his father coming through the screen door. James leaned on one of the porch's support beams and observed his son.

"I wouldn't exactly call it that."

"One thing you'd better call it is finished," his father warned. "There's enough to worry about with the training and coursework. I need everyone focused and with a clear head, so no one gets hurt—that includes you, Andrew."

Whenever his father called him Andrew, he meant business.

"I know," he responded. "Business is business, Dad. I'm not about to jeopardize that for any reason."

"Good. Then keep whatever hang-up you've got about Alexa to yourself. I don't want it affecting your work, or her learning."

"It's not a hang-up," Andrew countered. "But come on, Dad. Don't tell me you don't see the resemblance."

"What I *see* is you stirring up trouble where there is none. And that's not something we can afford."

After a few moments, Esther joined them on the porch.

"It's a beautiful night," she breathed.

"Yes, it is," James replied, stepping away from the railing. "How about a stroll? Something tells me that my son here could use some alone time."

Andrew knew his father was right. He would do his job and train Alexa just like any other student. If she decided it was too much to handle and quit, that would be one less potential crisis later.

# Chapter 6

The next few weeks were grueling for Alexa. She loved every minute. After the preliminary introductory coursework, filling out a guard card application and other required documents, they watched videos on executive protection, legalities and government policies. From there it was straight into hands-on and practical applications. An entire world opened up before Alexa, and she embraced it wholeheartedly.

That afternoon's sessions were all about strength, agility and endurance. Their instructor drilled them on functional movements to help improve flexibility and speed.

Alexa's muscles were sore when they were finished, but she kept it to herself since no one complained about their workout.

One of her classmates waved. "See you tomorrow, Amazon."

Alexa waved back. Everyone in class had a nickname, and Alexa's was Amazon. She was hoping it would wear off after a few days, but no such luck. It had stuck, so she embraced it. Upon reaching the cabin, the first thing she did was run a hot bath. Scouring the linen closet, Alexa almost whooped for joy when she found another box of Epsom salts. While the water was running, she called her parents to catch up.

"I was beginning to think you'd forgotten our telephone number," Jake teased.

"I'm sorry, Dad. It's been hectic this week. And we had functional movements and hand-to-hand combat training all afternoon. I'm spent."

"Did you have Dixon?"

"Yes." She grimaced and instinctively massaged her arm.

"He's a machine. He's going to put you through your paces, Lex."

"I can see that," she grumbled. "I'm running an Epsom salt bath as we speak. It's the third one this week."

Her father laughed. "Get used to it, Booba. There'll be plenty more in your immediate future."

She grinned at hearing the nickname that only he used. "I know, Dad. Gotta take the bad with the good, right?"

"You got it, kiddo."

"Speaking of much-needed pain relief, I have to run. My tub is almost full. Say hi to Mom for me. I'm sorry I missed her."

Jake chuckled. "She will be, too, sweetheart. And take it easy. You're the only daughter we've got."

"Don't worry. I plan to return in one piece."

A week later, Andrew was in his office working on a lesson plan when his father came in and sat down.

"Hey, Dad. What's up?"

"Just wanted to check in and see how things are going with Alexa?"

Leaning back in his chair, Andrew crossed his arms. "She's doing great. Her firearms instructor said she's at the top of the class and is an excellent marksman." He caught himself. "Markswoman. She's inside the eight rings every time. She's got the aptitude for mastering the fundamentals, and Alexa is acing all her written exams and holding her own in the simulations."

James nodded. "But?"

Andrew frowned. "But something is holding Alexa back. The mechanics are there, but the passion isn't. Her focus is split, and that keeps her from giving it her all. From being in the zone, you know?"

"Does that have anything to do with Tate Bannon? From what I've seen, he enjoys giving her a hard time. A few of them do."

"I don't think so. Alexa seems like she can handle it. She can give as good as she gets."

"Still, keep an eye on that," his father warned. "Competition and ribbing go with the territory, but I want to make sure that's all it is. This is no place for bullies."

"Understood."

His father got up. "Whatever is going on with her, you'll have to find it, JJ, because we're getting to the drop-off point, and Alexa needs to make it over the hump, or she's done. And I'd hate to tell Jake King that his daughter washed out of the program at this stage in the game."

Andrew tapped his pen absentmindedly on his desk. "I know."

That afternoon, the students were taken a few miles away to a practice center. The group was split into two teams for tactical maneuvers. Their assignment was to find the hostage in an abandoned building and get them to safety while eliminating any threat. Everyone was required to wear tactical gear, but they would be using practice ammunition. Alexa's team was first up. Headsets allowed them to keep in contact as they fanned out. The building was dark and musty, and visibility was poor, so Alexa stuck to the walls as she made her way across the space toward the steps.

"Watch your backs," their instructor cautioned. "Anything could be a potential threat."

Alexa made her way up the stairs. Her heart was hammering inside her chest, and she felt the sweat gathering at the nape of her neck. The gear was heavy and the heat stifling. She took a few deep breaths to calm herself before proceeding to the second floor.

The sounds of gunfire and yelling erupted in the silence. Glancing over at her partner, he motioned for them to get moving. Following his lead, Alexa hurried up the stairs. At the top, she melted into the wall and followed it down the corridor. Her eyes were burning from the perspiration that ran off her forehead. She took a second to swipe it away before they were under fire.

Dropping down to make herself small, Alexa's partner

spun around to return fire before yelling, "Move," over his shoulder.

She was running down the hall now with him right on her heels. Alexa entered the first door she saw and barely had time to duck as something whizzed past her head.

Crouching down, Alexa saw two figures in the far corner.

"Help me, please," a woman cried out.

Alexa raised her weapon. "Let her go," she demanded.

A man had one arm around her neck while the other was holding a pistol straight at Alexa. "I don't think so. Drop your weapon, or she's dead."

Dozens of scenarios rushed through Alexa's brain as she struggled to keep her wits about her. Adrenaline coursed through her body, causing her to feel nauseous, but she ignored it.

"Do you have a clear shot?"

"Negative," her partner replied.

Before she could react, the kidnapper opened fire before dragging the hostage out a rear door. Alexa hit the floor before returning fire. She heard her partner yell, "I'm hit!"

Alexa turned around and saw that her teammate had a huge bright yellow spot on his chest.

She rushed after the kidnapper.

"Wait," her partner called after her. "Shouldn't we wait for backup?"

Alexa pulled him farther into the room and slammed the door. Grabbing a turned-over chair, she wedged it under the doorknob. "There's no time. We're not losing this exercise. You're fine," she said, checking her ammo. "Stay put. I'll go."

It was eerily quiet as Alexa ascended the stairs in front of her. The radio chatter in her ear confirmed that there was only a handful of students from both teams still left in the maneuver.

Crouched low, Alexa cautiously opened the door and proceeded into the room. Boxes and junk were everywhere. The rest of the area was cast in shadows, with only one window providing light. Recalling her training, she stuck close to the wall as she moved.

Someone jumped out from behind a box with a gun pointed at Alexa. She fired without hesitation. As she ran past, another assailant grabbed her from behind. Her rifle fell to the floor. Alexa barely dodged a blow to the gut. She took a swing, but it was deflected, and before she could recover, the man snaked an arm around her neck and tried to pull Alexa off her feet.

"Give up," the man growled in her ear. "You're not cut out for this. Just admit it."

"Not happening," she gasped, trying to break his hold.

"One day you'll be in over your head and cost someone their life, King. And you'll be powerless to stop it."

That got under Alexa's skin. She paused for a split second, but it was enough.

Her opponent flipped her, and she landed hard on her back, knocking the wind out of her. Alexa turned on her stomach. Slow to get up, she mumbled something.

"I can't hear you," he taunted. "Do you give up?"

Spinning around, there was a pistol in Alexa's hand. She fired at point-blank range. A yellow paint splatter surfaced across the man's middle section before he hit the ground with a groan.

"I said, not today."

Retrieving her rifle, she spotted the target running toward a narrow plank, pulling the hostage behind him. Alexa raced across the space, and when everyone was clear, she launched herself at the man and victim, knocking them both off-balance. With the assailant effectively separated from the woman, Alexa jumped to her feet ready to engage the man when the crack of a pistol shot rang out. She felt the bullet connect with her chest a second before the force of impact knocked her backward and sent her crashing into a stack of crates.

# Chapter 7

"Alexa? Alexa, can you hear me?"

She felt something tugging at her and a cacophony of sounds overhead. Alexa tried again to drag herself out of oblivion and back to consciousness, but it was useless.

"She's out again," the facility's doctor confirmed.

"How did this happen?" Andrew snapped.

Before anyone could answer, he continued his rant.

"Someone better tell me how in the world someone's gun had live ammo," he yelled as he paced. "We're supposed to have safety protocols in place to ensure that nothing like this ever happens. Alexa could've been killed."

Several of the instructors were hovering just inside the treatment room in the infirmary. Each looked incredibly worried, and nervous.

"We have our team looking into it," one of them replied, his face a mask of concern. "It was clearly an accident."

"An accident I can't explain," another man chimed in. "I double-checked all the equipment last night before locking up."

"Obviously, something was overlooked."

Everyone turned at the irate voice behind them.

The men scattered as Andrew's father rushed in and went straight to the hospital bed. He peered down at Alexa and then at the doctor treating her.

"How is she?"

"She'll feel like she got run over by a dump truck and likely have one heck of a bruise, but she'll live."

"I want a report on my desk in an hour—including a statement from the student who shot her."

Andrew didn't bother looking up to see if his employees acknowledged his command. The two teachers nodded to no one in particular before rushing out of the room.

Andrew sank into the chair next to Alexa's bed. He ran a hand over his face.

"This could have been so much worse, Dad."

"I know, JJ." He clapped Andrew on the back. "We'll get to the bottom of this."

"She could be out for a while," the doctor informed them. "I can call you when she comes to."

"You go ahead," Andrew told his father. "I'm going to stay."

James took Alexa's hand and squeezed it. "Okay. Let me know the moment you hear something."

"Roger that."

It was almost midnight before Alexa came to. Andrew was leaning back in the chair asleep with his arms crossed and legs stretched out in front of him. His eyes snapped open when he heard Alexa moan.

"What happened?" she asked. Her voice sounded like tires rolling over gravel.

"You had an accident," he confirmed. "Hang on a second."

He hopped up and went to get the doctor. They both returned less than a minute later. Andrew hovered while he examined Alexa and asked her a few questions.

"I'll give you something for the pain," he said as he injected her with medicine. "It will also help you sleep."

Alexa's worried gaze connected with Andrew. "I don't remember anything."

"Don't worry. Try to rest, Alexa. I'm sure it'll come back to you soon."

Her eyes drifted shut and seconds later she was asleep.

"You should call it a night, Andrew. She'll be out until morning."

He nodded and headed for the door. "I'll be back first thing."

Andrew glanced over his shoulder at Alexa. His expression was grim as he watched her chest rise and fall several times before he left.

Walking the short distance back to the house, he was grateful when he arrived to find it quiet and everyone gone to bed.

Silently, Andrew climbed the steps to the second floor. He was careful not to make noise as he headed to his bedroom. He was exhausted and had a pounding headache. The last thing he felt up to was a lengthy conversation with his father.

Aside from the clock on his nightstand, the room was pitch-black. The darkness was soothing to his head, so he moved around without light. Kicking off his shoes, Andrew stripped and dumped his clothes in the hamper just inside the bathroom before turning on the water for a shower. He placed a towel on the bronze hook on the wall outside of the shower and climbed in.

He welcomed the pounding hot water beating into his tired muscles.

While he soaped up, Andrew replayed the events of the day. He couldn't wrap his head around how a gun containing real ammo was used in one of their training exercises. In the history of their school something like this had never happened before.

If Alexa had not been wearing a bulletproof vest for precaution, she would have died.

That thought flooded him with anger, which was quickly replaced with remorse when he recalled his treatment of her when she had first arrived.

Andrew turned the water off and stepped out of the shower. As he dried off, his mind ran through various scenarios of how such a momentous mistake could have happened.

*What if it wasn't a mistake? What if Alexa's accident was intentional?*

Still moving around in the dark, Andrew retrieved a pair

of pajamas from his dresser and put them on. When he was done, he settled into bed.

After a few minutes of trying to go to sleep, Andrew rolled onto his back and placed his arms behind his head. He pondered several of his students who hadn't warmed to Alexa and had on occasion given her flak.

Tate Bannon was at the top of this list. It was no secret that he didn't want Alexa in the program and had even gotten into an argument with her after she bested him sparring during a martial arts class.

That thought made his jaw clench. If one of his students had purposely endangered another student's life, it would be grounds for expulsion. And Andrew wouldn't hesitate to nail whoever was responsible's butt to the proverbial wall. He wasn't about to risk Phalanx's reputation on a student's prejudices, no matter who it was.

Later that morning, Alexa was sitting up in bed when the doctor came in.

"And how are you feeling, Miss King?"

"Like an elephant sat on my chest all night."

With a smile, he examined his patient and then scribbled a few notes into her chart.

"I want you to take it easy for a day or two. And no physical exertion until you're feeling better."

"Thank you for taking good care of me."

"My pleasure, Miss King." His blue eyes twinkled as he wrote her discharge orders. "Try not to get yourself shot again, okay?"

"Believe me, it's the furthest thing from my mind, Doc."

"Glad to hear it," Andrew replied as he strolled into the room.

The doctor repeated her discharge instructions and then excused himself. Andrew observed Alexa, who was attempting to put on her shoes.

"Here, let me help."

He rushed over and helped tie up the laces.

"Thank you, for the change of clothes," she replied congenially.

"You're welcome. Though I admit I thought you were going to challenge me and say that you could put on your shoes yourself."

"I would have, but I'm too tired."

Alexa tried to sound lighthearted, but it came out sounding like she was exhausted.

"Let's get you up," Andrew replied, helping her to stand.

Alexa gritted her teeth against the soreness in her chest.

After helping her into his Jeep, Andrew hurried around the side and jumped in.

A man watched the sport utility vehicle drive down the dusty path toward Alexa's cabin. Retrieving the cigarette from his lips, he dropped it on the ground and stamped it beneath his boot.

"Close call, Miss King. Next time, you won't be so lucky."

Alexa had fallen asleep a few minutes after Andrew helped her to bed. When she woke up, the sun had almost set. She blinked a few times and cautiously raised herself up on the pillows strategically placed behind her head.

"Take it easy," Andrew said, popping up from his chair and rushing over.

"I'm fine," she replied after making a bit of an adjustment. She sighed with relief because it had not hurt as much as she had anticipated.

Esther came in an hour later.

"Changing of the guard," she announced before setting the tote bag she was carrying on the bench at the foot of Alexa's bed.

"I've got cards, movies and magazines in case you get bored."

"Esther, I'll be fine tonight. There's really no need to stay."

"Nonsense," the older woman dismissed. "The doctor

told you to rest, and that's what we're going to ensure that you do. Now, how about one of my homemade lemon bars?"

Andrew leaned over Esther and retrieved a sugary treat. He took a bite and sighed blissfully. "These are the best, Esther. You ladies have a good night. I'll check in first thing in the morning."

Ensuring the house was locked up tight before he left, Andrew drove back to his office to retrieve the requested report. He was sitting at his desk with his feet up, poring over the document, when his father came in and sat down. "Anything of import?"

"No. Velasquez confirms that all the weapons had dummy ammo when he transported them to the building."

"Then who secured them once they arrived?"

"Roberts did, but admitted there was a window of about fifteen minutes when he was instructing the class that his eyes weren't on the equipment."

James frowned. "So we've got nothing."

"Not yet. But I'm not about to let this go until we find our culprit. My gut tells me someone was deliberately targeting Alexa."

"How? No one knew who would get each weapon."

"That's not exactly true. The gear was all separated out by the time the students arrived. We started the maneuvers shortly after that."

"So it couldn't have been a student because they were all accounted for and receiving instructions," his father reasoned.

"We only had two teams there for maneuvers, but other training sessions were going on that day. Anyone could've had access during those fifteen minutes where the weapons were unattended."

"I don't like this one bit. We need to find this guy, Andrew, before anything else happens. Alexa shouldn't be fearing for her safety."

"I'll get to the bottom of this, Dad. Rest assured, this won't happen again."

# Chapter 8

"A perfect way to start the weekend," Andrew said as he set his helmet on the seat of his ATV and walked over.

"I thought so," Alexa replied.

"How'd baton training go?"

Her face lit up. "Loved it. They had me sparring against Big Mouth. I took great pleasure in sweeping his legs from under him—again."

Andrew laughed at the thought of Tate Bannon being bested again by Alexa. Getting behind her, he pushed the swing. He expected Alexa to protest, but when she didn't, he continued.

"I haven't been on a swing since middle school."

"Just like riding a bike," Andrew countered.

"I suppose you're right."

He pushed Alexa higher and higher until she laughed so hard she started hiccuping.

"Get me down," she yelled between gasps of air.

"Not until you say the magic word."

"Embussing."

"Nope."

"Cover fire?"

"Not even close."

"Chase car?"

It was Andrew's turn to laugh heartily. "You're terrible at this game."

"Andrew, please let me off."

Immediately, he took hold of the swing and began slowing her forward momentum until she came to a complete stop.

Alexa placed her feet on the ground, and Andrew extended his hand. She put her fingers in his firm grasp. When she stood up, she pitched forward into Andrew's chest. He wrapped an arm around her waist to keep her steady.

"Are you okay?"

"Yes, sorry about that," she said when she could steady herself. "Got a bit dizzy. So, what was the magic word? Please?"

"No," he said with a devilish grin. "It was Andrew."

"Andrew," she repeated slowly.

Gazing into his eyes, Alexa stood rooted to her spot, which meant there were mere inches between them. Andrew's arms were still wrapped around her waist. It hadn't dawned on him yet to remove them. Instead, the blush that inched up her neck and splotched its way across her face had him riveted.

He stared at her intently. His hands caressed her back before he moved one hand up to catch a wisp of her hair blowing across her face. Andrew twirled it between his thumb and index finger before placing it behind her ear and resting his hand on the side of her cheek.

"You scared me to death. Do you know I've barely thought about anything else but you since the accident?"

Alexa peered up at him. Whatever she expected Andrew to say, this wasn't it. Nor was the expression on his face that made her skin tingle.

"That wasn't my intention," she whispered once she could speak.

"Mine, either," Andrew said absentmindedly as his fingers outlined the curve of her face. "Yet here we are."

For a moment, Alexa gave in to the fascinating tingling she felt unfurling inside of her and leaned into his touch. When his gaze moved to her lips and his head lowered, Alexa closed her eyes in anticipation of a kiss she hadn't dreamt of wanting until this moment.

"Andrew."

A noise behind them broke the spell.

Alexa's eyes flew open. The shock of what had almost happened was enough to bring her back to her senses.

"Andrew, I'm sorry. I shouldn't have… This can't happen," she blurted out before backing out of his arms with such force she almost toppled over. "I had no right to lead you on like that. I'm—"

Andrew reached out to steady her before returning his arms to his sides. "Married?"

Alexa's face scrunched up in question. "No."

"Oh, you have a boyfriend."

"No," she repeated. "I'm not seeing anyone. I just can't get involved with anyone. I don't do relationships. It's dangerous to be near me."

His eyebrows shot up in surprise. "What?"

"I'm sorry, I didn't mean to be precipitous. What I should have said was—"

"I got it," Andrew cut her off. "Strictly professional. I shouldn't have tried to kiss you. The last thing I want to do is make things awkward between us."

For a moment, his expression was unreadable, but eventually, it returned to neutral and he offered up a reassuring smile.

Alexa wasn't making sense to him right now, but he understood that she had drawn a line between them, and he would respect it.

Though there was some chemistry there, Andrew had learned from past disasters that all endings weren't happy. It was a lesson that almost cost him everything and not one he would ever repeat. Not even for Alexa.

"Thank you," she said before putting some space between them. "That was fun."

"You're welcome." It took Andrew a moment to remember why he'd come over in the first place.

"Fishing," he finally blurted out. "How about going fishing with me? There's a stream not too far from the house."

"Sounds good. How about you get the equipment, and I'll be back in a few?"

"Sure," Andrew agreed.

Waving, Alexa disappeared into the house. She hurried to the bathroom and doused her face in cold water.

"What was that?" she said, staring at herself in the mirror. "You can't afford distractions, King—of any kind."

There was no doubt that Andrew Riker was good-looking with an enigmatic air about him, but that was no reason for Alexa to get off track. She didn't have time for playful banter or harmless flirting. She was there to learn her trade and that was it. *So how is fishing work-related?* Alexa asked herself.

"Good point," she said aloud. Brushing her hair, Alexa secured it into a bun at the top of her head. She retrieved a sun visor from the closet in her bedroom and then rushed outside to meet Andrew.

Alexa carried the fishing poles while Andrew took the tackle box and a bucket. He had tried to bring everything, but she refused.

"Do you have to do everything yourself? You know it's okay to get help sometimes, right?"

"I was raised to be self-sufficient," she replied. "My parents thought it was important to rely on your abilities to get things done. So I had my first job at six."

He looked surprised. "Doing what, a lemonade stand?"

"No, a cleaning business."

He arched an eyebrow. "Are you serious?"

"Yes. My friends would pay me to help them clean up their rooms."

Andrew shook his head. "Somehow, I can see that."

Reaching the stream, they set up and then searched for worms.

"These lakes are stocked with catfish, panfish, perch and bass, so we should stand a fighting chance of catching something for dinner."

"This is the perfect time to come," Andrew said after

they'd cast a few times with no luck. "Early morning or late evening is ideal."

As if to prove his point, Alexa got a hit.

"I've got a bite," she said eagerly. She waited until the third hit before reeling it in.

"That's a decent-sized yellow perch," Andrew remarked before dropping it into the water-filled bucket.

They chatted as they fished, and by the time the sun started setting, Alexa was bragging about her superior fishing skills as they packed up and returned to the cabin.

"Uh-huh. How about you save that boasting for when it's time to clean fish?"

"Please," she scoffed. "I slay at that, too."

Andrew burst out laughing. "The, uh, fish slayer?"

She joined in. "Now, doesn't that have a ring to it?"

Working together, it didn't take long to clean and prep all the fish for frying.

At dinner, Andrew took a bite and smiled. "This is delicious. You did a great job on the fish. Is there anything you can't do?" he teased.

"I'm not too good at relationships," Alexa replied, but clammed up. She was surprised that she had even said it aloud.

There was an awkward silence where the statement drifted in the air like an airplane circling the runway.

"Why not?" Andrew asked before he could think better of it.

Alexa was quiet so long that he looked up.

"It's a long story that I'd rather not go into tonight," she finally answered. "Suffice it to say, I've been known to have trust issues."

"You've been hurt before?"

"You could say that. I had a best friend that was in a toxic relationship. I saw firsthand how deadly the consequences can be. It's not something I'd ever want to experience."

Andrew's eyebrow rose at that. "Alexa, not every relationship is like the one you described. Look at your parents. They're still married. You've got a decent blueprint for relationships that do turn out well," he reasoned.

"True, but I've never known that kind of happiness. The boyfriends I've had were few and nothing memorable. It's better if I'm alone because at the end of the day, I'm just not willing to risk it."

He glanced over. "Risk what?"

"My heart."

"Well, in this line of work, you miss all those important get-togethers with your significant other. Like birthdays, anniversaries, holidays. It's hard on relationships."

"As I said, I'm not interested in a love life."

"Then you'd be the first woman I've ever encountered that wasn't."

Alexa cut her eyes at him. "I always say what I mean. I never lie. You think every woman is just waiting around to get swept off her feet by a man?" Before he could answer, she continued. "Well, not me. I'm good."

Andrew digested that information. Alexa may not lie, but something was lurking under the surface that she wasn't sharing, affecting her performance. *Don't worry, Alexa*, he said to himself. *Whatever it is, I'm going to find it*.

"Are you okay?"

He glanced up. "Yeah, why?"

"You have this intense look on your face."

"It's nothing, just an issue at work that I'm trying to solve."

"I'm sure you'll work it out. You seem to be resourceful."

Andrew grinned. "Careful, Lexi, that sounds pretty close to a compliment."

She paused. That was the first time he'd called her by a nickname.

Alexa made a face. "Oh, so we're friends now?"

He sat back and regarded Alexa. "I thought you weren't good at relationships?"

"I meant the romantic kind, and you know it."

Andrew stood and began clearing the dishes from the table. Alexa followed suit.

"Well, now that we have that cleared up," he teased as he placed the dishes in the dishwasher while Alexa put the rest of the food away.

Suddenly, he stopped and turned around.

"Yes, Alexa. I'd like it if we were friends." Andrew leaned closer. "That doesn't mean I will take it easy on you."

"The thought hadn't crossed my mind," she shot back before resuming her task. After a few minutes of working in companionable silence, she glanced at Andrew over her shoulder. "Besides, I'd be disappointed if you did."

# Chapter 9

Alexa was slammed back into the wall, and her opponent brought his arm to her neck.

"Get your back stabilized, Alexa. Break the hold before he chokes you out," her instructor cautioned. "And don't try to pry his arm away with your hand. You won't win just trying to go strength against strength."

Using the palm of her hand, Alexa struck the man she was fighting against in the face, but he didn't budge, so she did it again.

"If he doesn't drop his arm, what do you do? Come on, think. The average person is unconscious from lack of oxygen in six seconds."

She immediately used her fingers to simulate an eye gouge, took her other hand, shoved his arm away from her neck, wrapped it around his face, and pushed him up against the wall before following up with a knee kick to his middle.

In the following exercise, Alexa went for a strike, but it was blocked, and she was thrown to the mat so hard that it took her a moment to recover.

"You okay, Amazon?" her classmate laughed. "You gotta learn to take a punch."

"Knock it off, Bannon," her instructor warned before pulling Alexa aside.

"King, you're not concentrating. Try it again. This time, think about how you're going to take out a hostile that's bigger and taller than you. Sometimes an obvious response may not be the best—you need to improvise."

"Got it." Alexa returned to her place on the mat. This time she evaded Tate's frontal attack and responded with a combination of hits before taking him down to the mat and following up with a blow to the gut and the jaw.

She jumped to her feet. "You're right," she said, breathing heavily as her opponent slowly got up. "I gotta learn how to take a punch."

"Good job," a few of her fellow students remarked as she walked by.

"Okay, class. Hit the showers and report back in an hour. Your tactical mobility instructor will meet you out front."

Alexa left the training room and hurried to her ATV. The last thing she wanted was to have a classmate stop her for a chat. The instructors were sticklers for time, and anyone late usually got called on the carpet for tardiness.

At the cabin, Alexa went straight to the kitchen cabinet and retrieved a bottle of ibuprofen. It was hard to open the bottle because her hand was slightly shaking from exertion. It took some effort, but she got the bottle open, took two pills, then a swig of water from her bottle. Finally, she took a minute to sit on the couch and regroup.

When her cell phone rang, Alexa glanced at the table.

"You're lucky you're this close," she said tiredly before reaching for it.

"Hey, Lex," Zane said when she answered. "I haven't heard from you in a while and thought I'd check in to see how it's going?"

She leaned back and closed her eyes. "It's going. I'm just not sure in which direction yet."

"You sound horrible. Uncle Jake and Aunt Margot said they haven't heard from you in over a week, and before that, it was only ten minutes."

"I know. We've had a lot of work to do, Zane. There are only a few weeks until the course is over. So the pace has been pretty intense."

"Lex, are you sure this is still what you want?"

"Yes—one hundred percent. Training is insane, but I've never doubted that this is what I want to do with my life."

"Okay, just checking. I'd be a horrible cousin and best

friend if I didn't ask, right?" He chuckled. "So, is there anyone you want to take to the mat yet?"

"Not on your life. I'm here for business, not to fill my social calendar. But there's one superhot commando teaching us tactical and combat training and—"

"Wait, did you say superhot? Sounds like you're mixing a bit of fun and pleasure with all that business. I'm surprised at you, Lex. I didn't know you had it in you," Zane joked.

"What? No, it's not that at all. We're not— Nothing is going on. I meant cute in the loose sense of the word."

"Nice try, but I know you better than that, cousin. You meant it exactly as you said it."

"Since you *know* me, you know that nothing will come of it. I'm merely pointing out the obvious. Andrew is good-looking and knows his stuff."

"Alexa, you know it's possible to talk and chew gum simultaneously, right?"

"Not for me. I have a plan, Zane. After I graduate, I'll learn the ropes, build up my experience and eventually open an agency of my own. The dating game doesn't factor into my plan."

"I hear you chirping, Big Bird," he teased. "But life has a way of throwing curveballs we didn't expect. You should know that more than anyone."

She thought of Tanya and felt guilty for being so busy that she hadn't thought of her friend sooner. She was one of the main reasons she was there.

"Thanks for calling, Zane, but I have to go. I still have to shower and get ready for the next session."

"Okay, but call your parents sometimes, please. Of course they'd never say it, but they miss you, Lex. A lot."

"I miss them, too, and I will. Thanks for calling, Zane. It's good to hear your voice."

"Likewise, kiddo."

Alexa hit the shower when she hung up. She still had

thirty minutes left when she finished, so she took a quick twenty-minute nap. It wasn't much, but it helped her re-focus.

Defensive and tactical driving were two of Alexa's favorite classes. Unfortunately, the instructor announced that today's training was at a different facility, so a shuttle drove the group to a closed course.

"Your job will take you worldwide, so we don't want to assume that you'll only be driving in urban areas," their instructor reasoned. "For example, you may protect principals in Europe, where driving conditions may not be as congested as in the United States. Some maneuvers you'll learn, like a J-turn, barricade breach and pendulum turn, better known as a Scandinavian flick, will come in handy."

The drivers had radios in their helmets for close contact with their instructor.

"What we're going to practice in this turn is front and rear weight transfer and side slides. This maneuver is perfect if you find yourself on the wrong side of the road and need to bring your vehicle under control. You will be using both feet. The left for braking, and the right for the throttle to help shift the car's weight. With practice and calm, you'll be able to do this on multiple road surfaces and at speed."

After discussing the fundamentals, the instructor said, "King, you're up."

"Yes, sir."

Alexa got into the vehicle, secured her seat belt and took off. She executed the pendulum turn and skidded sideways around the curve without error. Alexa felt excitement as the car handled as she'd expected.

"Well done, Miss King. Try it again—faster."

This time, Alexa went through the course at a greater speed. Her face was a mask of concentration while she maneuvered the car through the turns. As she was coming out of a turn, Alexa went to hit the brake. The pedal went all the way to the floorboard.

Alexa tried it again, and it occurred a second time.

"My brakes are out," she said calmly into her headset.

"Don't panic," her instructor replied. "I need you to carefully engage the emergency brake."

"That doesn't work, either," Alexa confirmed after following his instructions.

Downshifting to a lower gear, she was coming up fast on the next turn. Alexa hugged the outside lane not just to shave off some speed, but to keep the car from sliding or rolling.

"You need to cut more speed," her instructor advised.

Easing the two right tires off the road and onto the shoulder slowed the car down even more. The car careened off the road and down an embankment, but it did not flip over. Eventually, the vehicle rolled to a complete stop. Her hand was shaking so bad that it took a few moments before she could put the car in gear and shut the engine off.

"Well done, King," her instructor said in her ear. "Hang tight. We're sending help to come get you. We'll tow the car back so that we can check her out to see what happened."

"Roger that." Alexa heaved a sigh of relief. Her hands shook as she removed her helmet. "It's going to be okay," she told herself several times while she tried to fight back tears.

Upon returning back to Phalanx, the class was invited to a picnic and given the weekend off from studies since Monday testing would commence. Alexa was still shook up by the incident and decided that she needed some time to compose herself. Back at her cabin, Alexa pondered whether she would go to the picnic.

It was a harrowing experience, but she did not want to appear antisocial or as though she was still spooked from the incident at the driving course.

Alexa was putting the finishing touches on her outfit

when she heard a knock at her front door. When she opened it, she was surprised to find Andrew on the other side.

For the first time since she arrived, Alexa was wearing a sundress. It stopped at her knees and showed off her shapely brown legs. She was wearing platform sandals, and her hair was still wet from the shower and slicked back in a high ponytail. The natural curls cascaded behind her, stopping just above her shoulders.

He stared at her for a few moments before saying, "Are you okay?"

Oblivious to the shift in the air, Alexa stepped aside and let Andrew enter.

"Would you like some iced tea? Or I've got lemonade?"

She would have walked by, but Andrew took her by the shoulders and turned her to face him. His expression was a mask of concern.

"Are. You. Okay?"

She took a moment to study Andrew's face. His eyes were wide, and his face was taut with worry. She could feel every point where his fingers connected with her arms.

Her stoic expression slipped. "No. Not really."

The words were coerced from inside Alexa as fluidly as a snake being propelled out of a basket by a snake charmer.

Before she could elaborate, Andrew swept her into a hug. After a moment's hesitation, Alexa relaxed into the embrace and held on tight.

"It's okay," he said softly. "You did everything right."

The tears fell faster than she could stop them. "I'm sorry. I'm here bawling like a baby."

"Shh," he soothed. "You're entitled."

Andrew swiped the tears from her cheeks with his thumbs. Before he could stop himself, he leaned down and kissed her.

# Chapter 10

Though his face was mere inches away, Alexa was shocked when Andrew's lips touched hers in a tentative kiss. Shock soon gave way to a rush of desire so unexpected and powerful that Alexa had to hold on to him for support.

The caress grew more intense by the second, making Alexa oblivious to anything but the warm feel of Andrew's lips moving possessively against her own.

*This can't be happening*, she chided. *This is too dangerous, and you need to stop.*

She heard the warning in her head and knew that no good could come of it, but at that moment in time, Alexa was oblivious to anything but the feel of Andrew's body. The scent he wore was the perfect blend of sexy, spicy and woodsy. Its distinct notes overloaded her olfactory receptors, making it hard to concentrate on anything but Andrew Riker and the sensations he evoked.

Somewhere in the distance, Alexa detected a ringing sound. For a moment, she thought it was her own ears, but eventually realized it was her cell phone.

It could have gone on ringing for an eternity for all she cared, but it was enough of a distraction to yank them both out of the haze of yearning they were caught up in.

Alexa came down as sharp as an elevator lurching to a stop. It was jarring.

"I'm…I'm sorry," she said, trying to find her bearings.

"No, I'm at fault. I promised I wouldn't cross a line and I did."

His breath sounded so ragged that it gave Alexa a start.

"We both got caught up in a moment," she murmured.

"You had a harrowing experience, Alexa, that would've upset anyone."

She smoothed her dress and tried not to focus on her shaky hands.

"Yes, but it's part of the job. I should learn how to handle the unexpected better than this."

A sheer look of discomfort passed across Andrew's face. He ran a hand over his jaw and cleared his throat. "It wasn't an accident."

She stared at him. "What?"

"The brakes on the car you were driving didn't just go out on their own. It was sabotage."

"But why? Who would've done something like this?"

With his faculties back under control, Andrew focused on the imminent danger from the attacks on Alexa as opposed to the way that brief interlude had made him feel.

"I don't know, but I promise you that we'll find out. Until then, it's probably prudent to suspend your training. I don't want any more accidents. Thus far, you haven't been seriously injured. I don't want to keep putting you in scenarios that will push the envelope."

She nodded and began thinking over run-ins that she had encountered with different classmates. There had only been three of them, but which one was responsible?

"Please stop doing that."

Startled, Alexa glanced up at Andrew. "Doing what?"

"When you're hyper-focused on something, you bite your lip. It's distracting."

Her mouth dropped open. She had not known that. By the intense way he was staring at her, it was a habit Andrew was trying his best to ignore.

"We should go."

"Sure, I'll just get my purse."

She hurried into the bedroom to retrieve her pocketbook from a chair. When she returned, the front door was open and Andrew was waiting on the porch. He held the door open as she stepped through it. Locking it behind her, Alexa dropped the key into her purse and followed him down the steps.

"Your dress is pretty."

"Thank you. I threw it in at the last minute. I wasn't sure if I'd even have an opportunity to wear it."

"You'll make quite an impression on the guys."

"Hardly. Most of them don't even notice me. Which is just fine," she added quickly. "I like being just one of the guys."

Andrew's step faltered. He waited to see if she was kidding, but Alexa looked like she believed what she'd just said. So, as crazy as it sounded, he decided not to point out that there was no way any man considered Alexa just one of the guys. Especially him.

Walking around to the driver's side, Andrew had to take a minute to compose himself. Alexa was wreaking unexpected havoc on his system. Was she oblivious to her effect on him and several other students at Phalanx? Everyone respected Alexa in class, but even Andrew noticed a few appreciative glances as she walked into a room. He caught a few men staring too long and gave them a look.

Not that he was trying to stake a claim or anything. They were just friends, and though he was attracted to Alexa, he would never take it further than that kiss. It shouldn't have happened in the first place. The last thing anyone needed while learning extensive training was distractions. Everyone's head had to be in the game. Mind-wandering could get someone injured or worse.

Besides, Alexa had made it clear that she wasn't open to a relationship. And as much as he had enjoyed that kiss, she was right. He wasn't up for getting his heart battered and ripped to shreds again, either.

*Just friends. Yeah, I hear you, Alexa.* Andrew smiled back. *A wise decision for both of us. Let's pray it lasts.*

"So, tell me some things about you that I don't know."

"Really?"

"How else is our friendship supposed to grow?" he countered.

After eating at the picnic, they decided to take a walk down to the lake. They had strolled in companionable silence before Andrew posed the question.

She glanced over at him. "Fair enough. I worked as a senior cyber threat analyst for my parents' company. I loved my job. I enjoy a wide range of movies, music and books. Except for horror movies—I never could get into them."

"Let me guess. You sleep with the light on after watching?"

"Uh, I so do," she laughed. "I enjoy being out in nature—always have. My favorite food is nachos, and sweets are my go-to food when I'm stressed."

She stopped walking. Andrew halted and turned around. "What's wrong?"

"I've had two worst days in my life. The first was when my best friend, Tanya, died a few months ago. The second day was at a park in Great Falls, Virginia. I was a teenager at the time. My friend Shelley and I got attacked while hiking on a trail."

Andrew's expression turned somber. "I'm so sorry, Alexa. I can't imagine how you must've felt in both situations."

She stared off into the distance. "It took a long time for me to come to terms with losing them. They were my best friends."

Andrew placed a hand on her shoulder. "You're still not over them, Alexa."

Their gazes locked. Sadness waded in the depths of her eyes, replacing the happiness that occupied them only moments before. She absentmindedly ran a finger along the scar on her cheek.

"No, I guess I'm not. But I try not to let the pain of losing my best friends engulf me. Instead, I try to focus on ensuring that Tanya's death and my lost friendship with Shelley weren't in vain."

He stepped closer. "Alexa—"

"Let's not," she cut him off. "I don't want to get melancholy and spoil this amazing day."

Her body language was a clear sign that those walls of protection were back up, so Andrew didn't push. Instead, he placed her hand on his forearm and guided her down the path.

"What you need right now is a distraction."

She beamed with excitement. "Then lead the way."

It had been ages since Alexa had enjoyed herself this much. Andrew had taken them to the other side of the lake with a paddleboat. As they moved around on the water, he told her a stockpile of funny stories that kept her laughing. It was hard to feel down around him, and she appreciated getting to know him better.

"You know, after Shelley and Tanya, I didn't think I'd meet anyone again. Now I've got two great friends in my life. You and Marena. It makes me…" She stopped suddenly.

"What were you going to say?"

"It makes me less hurt over the two I lost."

Reaching out, Andrew grabbed her hand and squeezed.

"Alexa, you aren't alone. I'm here if you need me—anytime."

Andrew knew it was true the moment he said it. He may not be able to connect with anyone again on a romantic level, but he could offer Alexa friendship. That was safe and predictable, and wouldn't break his heart. He was also recovering from a relationship that had left him in pieces. For Alexa, it was violence and grief that kept her at arm's length. For him, it was an overambitious ex-girlfriend who loved power, connections and prestige more than him.

"Thanks, I appreciate that." She closed her eyes and released a breath. "This day was exactly what I needed. You must read minds, too."

Andrew shrugged as he continued pedaling. "What can I say? It's a gift."

The two sat in silence for a long time and enjoyed their surroundings. Andrew studied Alexa when she was soaking up the sun. Then, as if sensing his scrutiny, she opened her eyes.

Watching her sunbathe brought back a similar outing. It started out as a wonderful day but had turned into a huge blowup faster than a summer rainstorm in Florida. Just thinking about his ex-girlfriend instead of the great time he was having with Alexa made him feel out of sorts.

She touched his arm. "Are you okay?"

He shook himself out of the memory. "Yeah, I'm fine. I guess it's time we headed back."

"Oh. Yes, of course." Alexa helped him paddle back to the other side of the lake.

On the way back to the cabin, Alexa tried not to ask about Andrew's sudden mood change while they drove home. He turned on music, but she remained quiet other than asking about an occasional song.

When he pulled around the circle in front of her cabin, Alexa unbuckled her seat belt and turned.

"Andrew, is everything okay?"

"Yes, of course. I'm sorry, Alexa. I was just thinking about some work I must complete tomorrow."

"Tomorrow's Sunday. I thought you were off the entire weekend?"

"That was the plan," he replied. "Until I remembered some tests I have to grade and post."

"Okay."

Before she could say anything else, Andrew jumped out and walked around to her side. He opened it and helped her out.

"Thank you."

"My pleasure." He followed her up the steps.

"I had a wonderful time today," she said after unlocking the door.

"I'm glad you enjoyed it."

She shifted from one foot to the other. Finally, she said, "Have a good night."

"You, too, Alexa."

Andrew watched her walk in and didn't move until she'd shut the door.

By the time she peeked out of the window, he was already in the Jeep and pulling off.

"What was that about?" she wondered aloud.

# Chapter 11

Jake King was in his study reading when his cell phone rang. Glancing at the screen, he set his book down and grabbed the phone.

"Alexa." He sighed with relief. "Are you okay, sweetheart?"

Alexa settled back onto the pillows. Hearing her father's voice caused a rush of emotion. She forced herself not to cry. "Just fine, Dad."

Standing, Jake moved to the couch. He sank into the buttery soft leather cushions, his legs stretched in front of him.

"Andrew said it'll be nose to the grindstone until graduation."

"Are you talking about JJ Riker?"

"Yes, everyone but James calls him Andrew."

"Got it," her father chuckled. "He seems like a very accomplished young man."

"He is, Dad. He's very knowledgeable on a lot of subjects. He's smart and very caring."

Grinning, Jake reclined farther into the plush cushions. His gaze traveled to his bookcase, where there were pictures of his daughter in various stages of her life. His favorite was one with the three of them after falling into a mound of leaves they had just raked. He missed his daughter's light, carefree nature. Listening to her talk in such an animated way provided a glimpse of the old Alexa. It warmed his heart.

"Sounds like you two have hit it off."

"We have. The Rikers have been wonderful hosts."

"Glad to hear it," her father said approvingly before leaning forward so his elbows rested on his thighs. "So, when were you planning to tell me about the accidents?"

There was a long pause. So long that Jake said, "Before you deny it, I should mention that James called me to tell me about both training incidents."

"He shouldn't have done that."

"Lex, it's obvious from the sounds of it that you weren't planning to tell us."

Alexa got up out of bed and started pacing. "That's because there's nothing to tell, yet. The Rikers are investigating what happened."

"Booba, I can—"

"No, Dad. You've done enough—and I mean that in a good way. There haven't been any incidents in the last week. Plus, I can handle myself."

Before her father could respond, Alexa heard a commotion and then her mother's voice in her ear. "We know you won't let anyone push you around, Alexa."

After ending the call with her parents, Alexa was too wound up to sleep. She decided to go for a walk outside. Changing into a pair of shorts, a T-shirt and sneakers, Alexa left out the back door. The landscaping and floodlights provided some illumination as she walked down the path toward the old wooden swing.

Alexa could hear crickets and the occasional woodland creature as she continued her stroll. The last thing she wanted was her father intervening to discover who was behind the attempts to scare her.

*Was that all it was?* she pondered. *Some person with a bone to pick? How is that even possible? I don't know anyone here.*

Sitting on the plank, Alexa pushed off so that she could gently sway to and fro. She thought back to the last time she was out there with Andrew.

Closing her eyes, she recalled their playful banter and the heightened awareness of him.

"He's a complication you just don't need," she whispered aloud.

Suddenly, Alexa stopped in her tracks. The hair on the back of her neck shot up and she had an uneasy feeling that she was being watched.

Turning to the left and then right, she attempted to hear anything that might give her a clue what was out there.

What if it was a bear? Or some other dangerous animal? Alexa was defenseless against that kind of attack. Her eye caught something at the base of the tree anchoring the swing. She stared at it for several seconds. There were several cigarette butts scattered on the ground.

That's when she heard the distinct sound of movement to her right.

"Who's there?" she yelled.

Silence.

It was too dark to make out a target, and with no weapon, she didn't stick around to investigate. Alexa jumped off the swing and took off running in one motion. Air filled her lungs and fear propelled her forward. Not once did Alexa slow down or look over her shoulder. Only when there was a door safely between her and the outside did she look back. There was nothing there.

Locking the door, she rushed to the front door and checked the bolt. Next, she checked each window latch. Everything was secure. Arming the alarm, Alexa should have felt safer, but she didn't. She was still plenty freaked out.

She glanced at the clock on the mantel. It was one thirty in the morning. She thought about calling Andrew. She knew he would come, but she didn't want to disturb him. For now, she was safe and in no danger.

Going into the kitchen, Alexa made herself a cup of tea, hoping it would calm her nerves. She was still in fight-or-flight mode and felt jittery.

She sat on the couch and tucked her legs under her. There was no way sleep was coming anytime soon.

\* \* \*

"What were you thinking? You should've called me, Alexa." Andrew knelt and examined the used cigarettes littering the ground. He used a plastic baggie to scoop them up. Turning it inside out, he secured the bag and placed it into his pocket.

"I don't care what time it was, you should've let me know what happened."

"I was fine," she countered stubbornly. "There was no reason to wake you in the middle of the night. I made it back to the house, everything was locked up tight and I turned the alarm on. Nobody was getting inside."

"Unless they wanted to," he pointed out before striding off toward the house.

Alexa fell into step beside him. "Okay, next time, I promise to contact you the moment something strange happens."

"There won't *be* a next time," he ground out. "Whoever the culprit was did a pretty good job of hiding his tracks. Until now. Your coming outside was unexpected. It startled him, so he took off to avoid being discovered but left these." He patted his pocket. "There will be mucosal cells on the tips of his cigarettes. I have a friend at the FBI that works in the lab. He'll get these analyzed. If your assailant is in the CODIS database, my buddy will find him."

"CODIS?"

"It's the FBI's Combined DNA System, which is a DNA database. It has multiple tiers, criminal, federal, local and international, that can be accessed to track anyone who has been entered into the system. If he's a student of ours, he doesn't have a criminal background, or he wouldn't have been accepted. So what we're looking for is anyone who has a reason to have their DNA samples in the database. Likely a state or federal employee."

"Will that take long?"

"Likely a few days. Depending on how many tiers have to be searched. In the meantime, you're coming back to the main house with me. It's not safe for you to be out here by yourself until we have the culprit."

"Andrew, is that necessary? I have the alarm, and I'll be careful."

"We're not taking any chances, Alexa. This could've gone differently last night. I'm not about to give him an opportunity to come at you a third time. Let's go pack your gear and get going."

Realizing he wouldn't be swayed, Alexa nodded and went to pack her belongings. When they arrived at the house, James and Esther were on the front porch.

"Everything taken care of?" James asked his son.

"Yes, the house is secure, and the alarm is on."

"I'm sorry to impose," Alexa began.

"Don't be silly," James replied. "We are here to ensure that our students are safe. We take that responsibility seriously, Alexa."

She nodded. "Thank you for your hospitality."

"Of course," Esther replied, taking Alexa by the arm. "Come on inside and let me show you to your room."

Andrew hung back with his father.

"How soon can we get the results?"

"I called in a few favors to get it rushed, but it depends. It could take a few days or a week or so. I'm driving into Pagosa Springs shortly, where my contact will be waiting. He'll get the samples to my friend at the FBI."

James held the door while Andrew took in Alexa's luggage.

"I want a lid kept on this. I won't risk Phalanx's reputation on some crazy with a personal grudge against one of our clients."

"I'll handle it," Andrew said tersely. He moved off to take the bags upstairs, but James stopped him.

"Hey, what's going on?"

"Nothing."

James stepped into his son's path, crossed his arms and waited. "Andrew."

Blowing out a harsh breath, he dropped the bags he was carrying.

"This shouldn't have happened. I let myself get sidetracked. If I'd followed protocol like I should have, I'd have continued the investigation after the first incident. Now we almost had a third occurrence. Alexa could've been accosted, or worse. This is unacceptable, and I'm not just talking about for our company's reputation. She could've been killed, Dad."

"I agree. How did you let yourself get sidetracked?"

Andrew frowned. "What?"

"You mentioned that you let yourself get sidetracked. How?"

He ran a hand over his stubbled jaw. "By Alexa. I've been spending time with her lately and—"

"And that's a bad thing?"

"Yes," Andrew countered. "If I'd been doing my job instead of getting to know her better, we may have caught this guy by now."

"Do you have a Magic 8 Ball or something?" James chuckled.

"I'm serious, Dad. I should've stuck with my original instinct and just stayed clear of Alexa King. She's all over the place, and I still get the feeling that she's holding something back. If she's not one hundred percent committed to this career it could cost someone their life. Plus, you'd think her reminding me of Olee would be enough of a warning. I should've listened to my gut and steered clear of her."

A gasp overhead drew both men's gazes upward. Alexa and Esther were standing in the interior balcony. Holding on to the rail, Alexa's face was flushed red with embarrassment. Realizing that she'd been discovered, she excused herself and rushed down the hall. Seconds later, the bedroom door slammed. Esther tsked and shook her head before following Alexa.

James scowled at his son. "And what does your gut say now?"

Andrew closed his eyes and shook his head. "That I've just made a monumental mistake."

# *Chapter 12*

For the next week, Alexa and her classmates didn't have time to come up for air. Instead, it was nonstop training and testing for the group. For her, the days began to blur together. She hadn't seen Andrew at all outside of his teaching capacity. He had attempted to knock on her door and apologize afterward, but she ignored him.

After a few days it had become weird. Alexa decided to confront him about what she had overheard, but he was gone by the time she got up, and not home by the time she went to bed. James and Esther had done their best to compensate for Andrew's absence and were model hosts. Alexa let it go. She was under a lot of stress getting ready for finals, and the last thing she wanted to do was increase the weirdness between her and Andrew.

In hindsight, Alexa would later recall that things being just weird would've been a cakewalk compared to the full-blown disaster that was about to occur.

After class, she went looking for Andrew.

"He left a while ago," James told her when she poked her head into his office. "Had a burr under his saddle about something. Try the sparring room. JJ usually goes there when he needs to blow off steam."

"Okay, thanks."

"My pleasure, kiddo."

Alexa found Andrew in the studio practicing on the Wing Chun dummy. The wooden athletic instrument cultivated fighting skills and chi in Chinese martial arts training.

Not wanting to interrupt him, she sat at the back of the room and watched.

It was some time before he stopped and said, "What's up, Alexa?"

Surprised, she said, "Sorry, I didn't mean to disturb you."

"I saw you when you came in."

Alexa thought Andrew must have used peripheral vision since he hadn't looked up once since she'd arrived.

She got up and walked over to the edge of the mat.

"Don't you think it's time we cleared the air?"

"What are you talking about?"

"About what I overheard and how absent you've been since then."

"I've been busy. This is the last week of the program, so it's been hectic."

"Yeah, you mentioned that before. I just wanted to let you know that it was never my intention to cause problems for you. I don't know who Olee is, but clearly whoever she is, being compared to her wasn't a compliment."

Andrew stepped away from the testing equipment and faced Alexa. He opened his mouth to say something but then stopped.

"What?"

"Nothing."

"Andrew, I know something's up. Even your dad said something's on your mind, and you're distracted. Please, just tell me what it is."

"Why do you want to be an executive protection officer?"

Her eyebrows shot upward. "What do you mean? I thought I'd already answered that. I want to help protect people. Especially women."

"I know what you said. I just question your motivation."

Alexa frowned. "What, you think I'm lying?"

"That's not what I'm saying," he countered. "You said you want to help women. So why not volunteer or work with already established organizations back home? In comparison, being someone's bodyguard and protecting someone's life with your own seems excessive."

"I want to help women in danger, whether from a person, a hostile situation due to work, or external forces."

"That's the *what*, Alexa, not the *why*."

She blew out a breath in frustration. "I don't know what you want from me, Andrew."

"The truth."

"You got it."

Without warning, Andrew grabbed her and spun her around so that his arm was around her neck. Caught off guard, Alexa struggled against him.

"You're the only one keeping me from getting to your principal and doing whatever I want. So what are you going to do to stop me?"

Immediately, Alexa used a jujitsu defense to break his rear choke hold. She tucked her head slightly, grabbed his arm, and pulled down heavily on it before wrapping her leg behind the calf of his leg. Then, she dropped her base and spun one hundred and eighty degrees before pushing against her blocked leg, causing Andrew to lose balance and hit the floor. In seconds he was up and coming after her again.

He tried to swing at her, but she blocked his arm and pushed it away from her face.

Alexa backed up to give herself some distance. She was baffled as to why he was forcing this fight, and she was getting angrier by the minute.

"Andrew, what are you doing?"

"Why, Alexa?" he asked as he moved to take her down again. "Tell me what's really at the heart of it?"

She evaded his takedown and countered with a blow to his midsection. Andrew doubled over. Sweat was dripping from his forehead now.

Alexa was getting angry at him. He could see it in her stance, in the way her chest heaved with exertion and by her expression. Behind the confusion at what prompted the altercation, she was mad. Good. It's the reaction that he was after. Irate people were more concerned with being irritated than hiding the truth.

"I don't know—"

"You're lying," he snapped before coming after her again and again.

"I told you that I don't lie," Alexa snapped back.

Andrew had gotten under her skin in a way that no one had before. Alexa's eyebrows scrunched together in concentration as she looked for weaknesses in his attack. Her nostrils flared from the anger rushing throughout her body. "Then tell me."

This time, it was he who was on the defensive as Alexa tried to back him into a corner. But her triumph was short-lived because Andrew countered the maneuver and knocked her off-balance. Alexa crashed to the floor. Her body protested in pain, but anger was a powerful strength booster. She was back on her feet in seconds ready to lunge at him again.

"What are you hiding, Alexa?"

The question caught her unawares, and was just the push he needed to cause her to erupt.

"I couldn't protect them," she yelled. Her face contorted with rage. "I couldn't stop us from being attacked at the park. Is that what you want to hear? Fine, I wasn't strong enough."

Frustrated, Alexa threw a punch at Andrew, but he used his hand to push her fist slightly past so that she missed the mark. She tried again, but he rotated his body to avoid the hit, countered and knocked her to the floor. She let out a howl of frustration. Next, he set up a mount.

"You said 'us.'"

"No, I didn't."

"Yes, you did. You said 'I couldn't stop *us* from being attacked.' This isn't just about your best friends, Alexa. Your decision to be a CPO is also about *your* need to feel safe and in control."

Setting up a guard using her forearm, Alexa placed her

other hand across her wrist to keep him from moving higher up her frame. "No, it's not," she gasped, struggling.

"It is. The man in the park took something from you, didn't he? Your innocence? Your feeling of safety and security? Losing Tanya took something from you, too. You've spent all this time trying to get it back. Trying to make yourself whole again, but deep down, you're the one needing protection—aren't you?"

"You don't know anything about it," she roared. Grabbing his hips, Alexa used the force of an upward thrust to launch Andrew off to the side before rolling out of his grasp and vaulting to her feet.

"Shelley's whole life has changed. She's a shell of the person she once was. And Tanya shouldn't have died. She'd be alive today if it weren't for her abusive boyfriend."

"How is that your fault?"

"I begged her to leave him, but she didn't listen until it was too late. So spare me your sympathy, because you have no idea how I feel—what I lost."

Andrew stood. "I do," he shot back. "I know what it's like to lose someone you loved and be helpless to stop it. I've felt the pain and guilt eating you from the inside out. It's all-consuming, and you'd do anything not to feel it— to be able to escape."

Andrew's voice broke. "Alexa, you have to let the baggage go." He placed his hands on both shoulders to keep her in place. She tried to pull away, but he held tight.

"Let me go."

"It's affecting your focus, and that's not good for you or your clients. You can't let anything distract you in the field. If you let your emotions lead, you'll make a mistake that can get you both killed." Andrew dipped his head so that they could make eye contact. "Do you *hear* me?"

"That won't happen because I'll never let my feelings jeopardize a mission."

"You can't say that," he countered. "One day, an enemy may discover who you care about and exploit that."

"Not if I've stopped caring."

Andrew stared at her a moment. "What does that mean?"

"Aside from my family, the people I love tend to sever contact or die, so now it's easier not to let anyone into my heart anymore."

"And you think you can just turn off your emotions?" Andrew said incredulously. "Alexa, that's not sustainable."

Exhausted from the sparring, she leaned over to try and catch her breath. Tears flowed down her face, making her gaze blurry. She blinked several times to clear her vision but eventually wiped her hand across her face as if the tears were an annoyance. "Loving people is a liability I can't afford," she said tiredly.

He loosened his hold but didn't let her go. Instead, he pulled her into his arms.

Alexa tried not to cry more, but it was pointless. She was too overwhelmed, so the tears just flowed.

"While I may not agree with your logic, I get it, Alexa."

"Who was it?" she finally murmured into his shirt a few minutes later. "The person you lost?"

His eyebrow arched in surprise. Olee came to mind, but he tamped that memory back down where it belonged. That betrayal was too raw to voice. "One of my buddies in the field," he whispered. "He was my best friend and was killed in the line of duty. I wasn't there when he died."

She raised her head to look at him. "I'm sorry, Drew."

He nodded. "It took me a very long time to get past it. Past the anger and the guilt over losing him."

"Of being spared?"

"Yes."

"I know how that feels."

He smiled. "Did you just call me Drew?"

"Yeah, I guess I did. Do you mind?"

"No. Can I call you Lexi?"

She scrunched her face up. "If you must."

Andrew laughed. "Does anyone else call you that?"

"No."

"Then I must."

She burst out laughing. He soon followed suit.

Suddenly, Andrew sobered.

"Alexa, I'm sorry about what I said last week. It wasn't about you. Well, not completely. I was feeling out of sorts because of what happened. It caused me to remember another time when I was in a situation where I didn't feel in control of what was happening around me. Let's just say I learned a painful lesson that I don't ever want to repeat."

"Thank you," she murmured.

Andrew's thumb brushed away the tears under one eye. "You're welcome."

"Are you ever going to tell me what happened with this mysterious woman from your past?"

Andrew looked like he'd just been sucker punched. "How did you—"

"You may not have provided details, but it's written all over your face."

"Maybe someday," he reluctantly admitted. "But not now."

"This," she said, waving her hand around the mat, "was you trying to find my Achilles' heel, wasn't it?"

He nodded. "The scab had to be removed so that the wound you're still carrying can heal."

Alexa inched closer. "Thank you."

Standing on her tiptoes, she pressed her lips against Andrew's mouth without warning. It took a moment before his arms wrapped around her waist to hold her tight.

A purr of contentment drifted out of her mouth before she grasped his shoulders like she was drowning and Andrew was the only life preserver for miles.

Eventually, Alexa pushed against his chest, and Andrew released her immediately. It was so sudden that the momentum propelled her backward. He reached out to stop her from falling.

"I'm sorry. I shouldn't have kissed you like that," she squeaked, moving away. "That's not exactly the kiss that friends give each other."

"Depends on the friends," he teased.

"Andrew, I don't want to complicate things. We're friends. We need to stay that way. Anything else would just get awkward."

His expression turned incredulous. "Kind of late to put that horse back in the barn, don't you think?"

# Chapter 13

"We have to," she replied. "I just poured my heart out to you about why I don't do relationships. I'm sorry."

She hurried across the mat.

"Alexa, wait," he called out.

She turned but remained where she was. "Thanks again for helping me, Andrew. And I want you to know that I heard you."

He observed her from across the distance.

"I meant every word, Lexi," he replied. "Including the unspoken ones laced in that kiss."

She rushed out of the room and didn't look back. It was hard for Alexa to think of anything on the ride home except the feel of Andrew's mouth covering hers in a kiss that ignited every dormant area of her body like an accelerant. Now Alexa felt like she was blazing out of control.

"What were you thinking?" she accused herself. "This is a disaster."

The move was reckless and crazy, yet at that moment, it was impossible not to do what she had been fantasizing about for a long time. The wonder of kissing Andrew had overridden all her carefully erected boundaries and common sense.

Parking the ATV, Alexa went inside and headed straight for the shower. As the hot water pounded against her back, she realized why she needed to forget Andrew Riker's mischievous smile and smoldering eyes.

"Because no good can come of it," she scolded, but then her thoughts of the kiss they shared caused Alexa to switch the hot water to cold.

Desperate for a voice of reason, Alexa called her cousin when she was finished.

"Hallelujah. It's about time," he said after hearing the account of what happened.

"Zane, this is no time to joke."

"You thought I was? Lex, what's the big deal? You like him, and clearly, the feeling is reciprocated, so why not see where it goes?"

"I'll tell you where it's going," she groaned. "Straight into a bona fide disaster."

Sitting on the bed, Alexa spun around until she was lying on her back with her legs stretched out on the headboard. "I'm not about to see that happen. I need Andrew in my life."

"You're telling me."

"As a friend," Alexa clarified. "He's important to me, Zane. I can't risk losing that."

"You realize you're overthinking this, right? By a lot."

"I'm being cautious."

"No, you're being crazy. You haven't talked like this about a man in eons."

"That's because work is my life."

"It's not your life, Alexa. It's your camouflage."

She turned right side up in the bed. "What is that supposed to mean?"

"You're hiding in plain sight, cousin, under the guise of socializing and spending time with people, but in truth, you're scared to have anyone get too close to you because you're afraid of what that kind of closeness could mean if things go pear-shaped."

"Zane, that's not true. I'm friends with Marena, and everything is going just fine."

"We both know that's because she lives in North Carolina, far away enough to keep her at arm's length. It's safe."

An uncomfortable silence descended on the telephone line.

"You may be mad at me for what I've said, but you know that all of it is true. I love you too much not to point out that you're self-sabotaging your life, Alexa. Our hearts aren't designed to be encased in plexiglass for fear of being broken. That's not how life works. Risking pain and heartache comes with the territory. It's time you came back to the land of the living because you can't spend your entire adult life waiting for the other shoe to drop."

After hanging up, Alexa recounted the conversations with Andrew and Zane. She didn't feel like she was self-sabotaging. In her mind, it was self-preservation. It was time for her to fess up about why she didn't let anyone new in too far past her defenses. It was simple. Her heart couldn't take another break regardless of Zane's statement about living without the plexiglass. After having two best friends ripped from her life, she wasn't strong enough to have it happen again.

So if that meant living the life of a hermit and only experiencing life on the periphery, one step below loving someone, then so be it. No one would end up hurt, damaged or dead. "I'm fine with those odds," she said before propping her arms behind her head and staring into the dark. Thoughts of what Tanya would say to that drifted into her mind.

*Lex, quit pretending to live and live.*

The expression on Tanya's face and the intonation in her voice played out in her head.

"Oh, Tanya," she cried softly into the soundless room. "I miss you. If ever I needed your advice about what to do, it's now, because I'm scared to death."

"You wanted to see me, sir?"

Andrew and his father glanced up as one of their students entered the office.

"Yes, Jeffries. Take a seat."

James grabbed the folder sitting on his desk. Not one to mince words, he got straight to the point.

"You're expelled, Mr. Jeffries."

The young man's eyebrows shot upward. "Excuse me?"

"This can't be a surprise," Andrew replied in a clipped tone. "You were behind the attacks on Miss King. Are you going to make us go over the evidence?"

He shifted in his chair. "What evidence? I haven't done anything that warrants you kicking me out."

James opened the folder and retrieved a document. He tossed it across the desk.

"We retrieved all the shell casings from the training exercises. Each student has color-coded ammo so that we can track their fire patterns and how well they did in the assignment. Your count was off by two rounds. Which, subsequently, was the number of live rounds fired at Alexa. In your statement, you said that you were nowhere near Alexa during any of the exercises that day, but surveillance cameras show you and Miss King engaged in hand-to-hand combat prior to your shooting her in the chest. She struck you in the face, after which your blood splattered onto her tactical gear. We had the sample analyzed, and you are a match."

His gaze shifted from Andrew to his father. "That was an accident," Jeffries stammered. "You can't be suggesting that I would purposefully try to harm her?"

"I'm not suggesting anything," James said curtly. "I'm flat-out saying you did it. We can't place you at the scene when her brakes failed, but it was you outside of her cabin smoking the cigarettes that you so carelessly left."

"So? I was merely watching her. That's not a crime," he shot back.

"Stalking is an escalated crime. And the DNA left on the cigarettes also points to you, Mr. Jeffries. Add the training incident, and it's enough to have you arrested and charged," Andrew informed him.

Edgar shot to his feet. "I wasn't trying to harm her," he repeated. "I was only trying to scare her. I wanted to prove that she'd crack under pressure. She doesn't deserve to be here, and everyone knows you all gave her preferential treatment. Just ask Tate and a few of the other guys. After a few mishaps the plan was she'd quit and prove my point."

Andrew glared at him. "Then you're as stupid as you are careless. Alexa is highly qualified and earned her spot—you just lost yours."

Two police officers entered the room to take him into custody. When he saw the cops, he tried to make a run for it, but didn't get far. Andrew anticipated his resistance and grabbed him.

"You can't do this," Edgar yelled, trying to break free. "My father has connections—"

"So do we," Andrew countered before shoving him in the direction of the two officers. "Get him out of here."

Edgar's face was contorted with rage as he fought against the police officers. The vein in his forehead bulged against his skin as he was dragged out of the room.

After the three men left, Andrew sank into an armchair. He pinched the bridge of his nose. "Glad that's over."

"Me, too," his father agreed. "Now Alexa is safe from that nitwit's schemes."

Three days later, the Phalanx students graduated. Everyone was dressed to impress in dark suits for the ceremony and could barely contain their excitement. Hearing her name, Alexa got her certificate and shook hands with James, Andrew and the instructors. It was their last night at the training academy, so the Rikers threw a party. Alexa stayed for about an hour but decided to call it quits. She said her goodbyes and was headed out when Andrew called her name.

"Leaving so soon?" he asked when he reached her side.

"Yes," she told him. "I'm headed back to the cabin to pack."

"Then allow me to give you a ride."

"No, thanks. It's a beautiful night out, so I'll walk."

Without another word, Andrew fell into step beside her.

It was dark out, so he retrieved a flashlight from his car. While they walked, Alexa gazed at the starry sky. "I'll miss it here."

"Me, too."

She looked surprised. "You're leaving?"

"I've taken a consulting job in Dubai. I'll be gone for a few months."

A frown wrinkled her forehead. "Oh. Well, I wish you all the best, Andrew."

"Thanks. You, too."

Alexa stopped suddenly and faced him. "I want you to know that I appreciate everything you and James have done for me. This has been the most amazing time of my life, Andrew. I'm a better, stronger person because of you."

"We just laid the foundation, Alexa. The motivation and raw talent were already there."

Shaking her head, she resumed walking. "Can't you take a compliment?"

"I'm just saying that you did a fantastic job."

"Drew."

"Okay, okay," he laughed. "Thank you."

By the time they reached the door, they were laughing and joking like old friends.

She unlocked the door and turned to Andrew. "Would you like to come in?"

He stepped forward until he was mere inches away. "I would, but I think I'd better go."

They stood rooted to their spots for a few moments staring at each other. They were so close that their breaths mingled. Finally, it was Alexa clearing her throat that severed the connection.

"Well, I'd better go in before we get attacked by mosquitoes." She hugged him. "Thanks for everything, Andrew."

He held her tight for a moment before letting her go. "My pleasure, Lexi."

Andrew searched her face a moment, committing it to

memory before he leaned down and kissed her. It was meant to be a light, quick action, but it quickly morphed into something hotter than he had expected.

Alexa's arms slipped around his neck, prompting Andrew to back her up against the side of the cabin and deepen the kiss.

Moments later, their embrace ended as abruptly as it began. He released Alexa.

"I'm sorry. I should not have done that."

"It's okay," she said quickly. "No harm done."

The sudden loss of shared body heat made Alexa shiver. She rubbed her arms to warm up. Everything in her screamed out to stop him. To not walk away without coming to an agreement, but Alexa ignored her own longing. Her stomach was tied up in a ball of knots over the decision. Feeling a sudden emptiness, she forced herself to back away. "Take care of yourself, Andrew."

He lingered for a moment, but then stepped back, too. His face showed his resignation. "You do the same."

She watched him head back down the path before turning and going inside. After she shut the door, Alexa leaned against it. Her heart was racing, and her lips tingled from their explosive kiss. She missed him already. "I have to walk away," she said aloud. "It's better this way because if anything happened to you, Andrew Riker, I might not survive it."

# Chapter 14

*Three years later...*

Alexa placed her SIG Sauer P365 handgun in its holster and slid the navy blue suit jacket over her white blouse. After fastening the buttons, she retrieved a dragonfly lapel pin from her jewelry box. Its wings were gold, and the body was garnet. She secured it to her lapel and then put on diamond stud earrings before sweeping her hair up in a chignon bun at the base of her neck.

Picking up a pair of glasses from her nightstand, she put them on and headed downstairs.

Before she had reached the bottom of the steps, her cell phone rang.

"Alexa King?...Yes, I'm heading out now."

She hung up the phone, grabbed her luggage and purse, and left.

There was a black Mercedes S-Class sedan waiting for her at the curb. When she reached the bottom step, a woman had exited the passenger seat and opened the back door.

"Thanks, Miranda."

"You're welcome, Miss King."

"Good morning, Valerie."

"Good morning, Miss King," her driver replied.

Her assistant handed her a gold folder.

"Is everything in order, Miranda?"

"Yes, ma'am. Your gear is in the trunk, the advance team has scouted out the route and car two is in place. Everything is green."

"Good. And how was your date?"

Miranda blushed. "It was great! Things are going along

well. His name is Apollo Hayes. He's tall, handsome and so attentive. I can't wait for you to meet him!"

Alexa's assistant was a stunning petite Hispanic woman. At five foot four, she stood below Alexa's shoulders. Miranda had long black hair and brilliant brown eyes and dimples. Her family was from Houston, Texas, and they were very proud of her moving to Washington, DC, and landing her dream job. Miranda was passionate about learning the ropes and working her way up the ladder at Dragonfly International. Her goal was to eventually become a close protection officer, and she relished the opportunity to learn and work under Alexa. To her, her boss was strong and smart, and cared about everyone around her. She looked up to her and was inspired by Alexa's strong work ethic.

"I'm glad you had a good time. Bring Apollo by the office sometime. I'd love to meet him," Alexa replied before she turned her attention to a file she needed to review.

Alexa's condo was a quick drive to the Salamander hotel on the Southwest Waterfront to pick up their principal.

When they arrived, Valerie pulled up to the front of the hotel. Alexa got out and walked into the opulent lobby. Spotting her CP officer, Dyan Grayson, standing to the side while her principal checked out, Alexa walked over to her operative.

Dyan was one of Alexa's good friends. They met when Alexa was just starting out. Both had worked at the same firm while on assignment and had hit it off. Dyan was five foot eleven, and had a strong, muscular physique. She had smooth, dark brown skin and vivid gray eyes. Most people who saw her became mesmerized. They often mistook her for a model. Which Dyan would graciously deny and keep moving. Occasionally, she would wear contact lenses in the field to allow her to blend into the background when needed.

As serious about exercising and weight training as she was about protecting her clients, Dyan was always training.

When Alexa decided to start her own agency, she instantly gave her notice as well, telling Alexa that it wasn't even a question of if she were coming to work for her.

"How is everything, Dyan?"

"Uneventful night, Miss King. The principal had an early dinner, worked until about eleven thirty and then called it a night."

Alexa nodded. "I'll see you on the plane."

"Yes, Miss King," she replied before her team walked past Alexa and left.

Dyan was a regimented person and never called Alexa by her first name when they were in mixed company. Alexa knew she wasn't going to budge on that, so she did not try to dissuade her.

A woman in a red pantsuit turned around. When she saw Alexa, she smiled.

"Thank goodness you're here, darling. Dyan is nice, but she never lets me have any fun."

"Good morning, Mrs. Crawley. I'll be sure and speak with her as soon as we're wheels-up."

As they walked to the car, Alexa had to smile. Veronica Crawley was an heiress to a large private equity firm in Zurich, Switzerland. She was one of Alexa's top clients.

She guided her principal out of the door and into the Mercedes.

"I hope you've packed evening wear, Alexa. I've been invited to several parties while in Chamonix."

"Of course, Mrs. Crawley."

"Good. It will be good to get back to Beauté Majestueuse."

"Yes, ma'am, it will."

The chalet Beauté Majestueuse was one of her client's residences. It was in the luxurious resort area of Chamonix-Mont-Blanc at the junction of France, Switzerland and Italy. A gift from her late father, the seven-thousand-square-foot villa with six bedrooms and seven bathrooms boasted picturesque views of the Alps.

Alexa watched the scenery whiz by on the way to Washington National Airport, also known as Ronald Reagan Washington National Airport. She glanced at her watch. Unfortunately, Alexa would not get a chance to let her parents know she would be on an assignment out of the country. Typically, they preferred a phone call instead of texting if she traveled, but Alexa was pressed for time, so she typed out a message on her cell phone.

A few seconds later, her father responded with a frown emoticon. Since she and Shelley got accosted years ago, her parents' protectiveness was expected. When she pointed out that she was in her thirties now, her mother replied that she failed to see the relevance of that argument because she would always be her daughter.

Alexa wondered if her grandmother acted like her mother but refrained from asking. She didn't have time for one of her mother's lengthy rants.

When they arrived at the airport, Alexa thanked her driver before her team of close protection officers headed to Mrs. Crawley's private jet. Their client received numerous death threats and required around-the-clock detail when she traveled. As a result, several bodyguards and close protection agents worked directly for Crawley's company. Still, Veronica preferred that her immediate detail be all women, so Alexa and her team were on point with the others as secondary protection.

Once they were wheels-up, Alexa and her associates reviewed their operations plan. It listed everyone's assigned roles. For example, the drivers, surveillance officers and personal escort section all played a role in protecting Veronica. Alexa was the primary protection officer, also called PPO, and once she was satisfied that everyone was up to speed on all the plans, safe houses, maps and multiple routes reviewed, she allowed her team to take a break and relax for the remainder of the flight.

"What's troubling you?"

Glancing up, she saw Dyan take a seat across from her chair.

"Nothing. Why?"

Dyan secured her seat belt and then relaxed into the plush leather.

"You look a little edgier than usual."

Alexa shrugged. "I don't know why. I'm fine."

"You know Clive likes you."

"Say what?" Tilting her head to the left, Alexa briefly observed him. He was one of her client's main bodyguards. He was a mountain in a single-breasted suit.

"No, I didn't know that," she said dismissively. She did, but she wasn't about to tell Dyan that. Ever the romantic, her colleague would try to read more into it than there was.

As far as Alexa was concerned, Clive was efficient, professional, he knew his stuff, and he could keep a cool head in a crisis. She wasn't interested in him for anything more than that, so personal details about him were irrelevant.

The look Dyan gave her said she didn't believe her. Alexa shrugged, almost as if Dyan had voiced her opinion aloud.

"I'm going to get some sleep," she announced, stretching her legs and getting comfortable.

"You just don't want me plying you with questions about Clive," Dyan mumbled.

"You're right. I don't. Besides, there's nothing to say on the subject. I don't date. End of discussion."

"Alexa, there's no reason you shouldn't entertain the idea of having a relationship with someone. It might be good for you. You know it's good to have a work-life balance—not to mention a horizontal workout now and then."

Opening her eyes, Alexa pinned Dyan with an annoyed glance. "Why this sudden interest in my love life?"

Her friend took a sip of her hot chocolate. "You mean besides the fact that you don't have one?"

"I don't have one because I don't *need* one," Alexa

countered. "So quit worrying about me, please. I'm fine—couldn't be better."

"What couldn't be better?"

Both glanced up to see their topic of discussion hovering over their seats. He leaned in as if waiting to hear the punch line of a joke.

"Not what. Who." Dyan smiled sweetly and waited for Alexa to answer.

Letting out an exasperated puff of air that could have leveled a tree, Alexa scowled at Dyan before turning her attention to Clive.

"I was just telling Dyan here that I don't have the time, or the inclination, to date."

"Oh," Clive replied, relaying his disappointment at her news.

Alexa didn't want to, but she couldn't help gazing at Dyan. Her smug look said *I told you so*.

"Yeah, I get that," Clive said, finally rallying to offer a reply. "This line of work is all-consuming."

"Exactly what I've been saying." Alexa nodded in agreement. "We have enough to tackle without worrying about missing date nights or forgetting your significant other's birthday or anniversary. There is no way I'd want to deal with that kind of pressure."

"Unless the man was extraordinary," Dyan remarked.

"He'd have to be."

At that, Clive bowed out under the guise of getting some food.

When he left, Dyan observed Alexa so long that she shifted in her seat.

"What?"

"You've never been in love."

Alexa scoffed. "First of all, that's private."

"And true."

"Okay, I've never been in love in the romantic sense." Alexa stared out of the window. "I've never met a man that

I wanted to get close enough to in order to develop those kinds of feelings. Well, at least not someone I would turn my life upside down for, put him first above everything else and sacrifice my life for."

"Well, at least?" Dyan said, homing in on the statement with zeal. "So, there was someone."

It wasn't a question.

Alexa remained tight-lipped, but Dyan crossed her arms and waited.

"Okay, fine," she replied, admitting defeat. "Yes. There was someone that I was attracted to, but the timing was wrong. I was just starting my career and had a plan to follow—it didn't include a serious relationship."

"Or any relationship from the looks of it," Dyan snickered.

"Exactly."

"Alexa, it's been three years. Dragonfly International is thriving. You're one of the top woman-owned businesses in our field and on the Top 10 Executive Protection Companies list this year. Business is beyond great, and you've garnered respect in what was once a strictly male-dominated field. So I think you can stop and smell a rose or two. Or should I say a man's cologne?"

Reluctantly, Alexa had to laugh at that one. "Dyan, I know you mean well, but I love my life the way it is. So for now, Dragonfly is my top priority and the only thing on my mind."

"It's not your mind that I'm trying to help out."

Shaking her head, Alexa decided to get some sleep. But before she drifted off, Andrew materialized before her eyes. He was smiling at her with his usual self-assured air. Next, she pictured how soft his mouth would feel at the base of her neck.

That thought jolted Alexa upright. Her gaze darted around as if she expected Andrew to be sitting across from her with a smug look on his face.

"No, no," she whispered before wiping her face, simultaneously feeling hot and cold. Why did Dyan have to talk him up? Alexa had been doing well for years without thinking about what could have been. He was a friend and a colleague. Nothing more.

It didn't matter how tall, well-built and incredible he was or what he did to her blood pressure. Andrew Riker was a heartthrob of a distraction Alexa simply couldn't afford.

# Chapter 15

Andrew sailed through the air. Seconds later, his back connected with the training mat. The dull thud from his body coming in contact with the thick padding ricocheted around the room.

"Dude, you're not concentrating. Do you want to spar, or don't you?"

Andrew's eyes shut, and his face wrinkled as he tried to work through the pain in his midsection. He could've kicked himself for not being ready to absorb and redirect the energy of that punch.

Slowly getting to his feet, Andrew tightened the belt on his gi. "Sorry, man." He returned to his position. "Let's go again."

This time, Andrew anticipated his friend's moves and did well to counteract them and deliver blows until he got caught with a roundhouse kick.

"Okay, that's it for today."

A bit slower getting up this time, Andrew bent over and took a moment to even out his breathing. "I'm fine."

"Come on, man. Where's your head at today?" Sanjay Kholi groused. "You could've easily dodged both those shots."

"I know." Andrew went to grab a towel. He dried his face and neck and then drained half his water bottle. "Seems I'm a little preoccupied today."

"How many times have you told me that split focus gets you killed or worse—"

"Puts your asset in danger," Andrew finished for him. "You're right. I have no defense for not concentrating."

"I'm not looking for a defense, my friend. More like an explanation."

Sanjay followed Andrew down the hall to the men's locker room. They both stripped and headed for the showers.

"It's Alexa," Andrew finally announced over the loud whooshing of water barreling out of the showerhead.

"What about her?"

"I can't get her off my mind. Especially lately."

"What's that got to do with it?"

It was hard for Andrew to explain something that he didn't understand. On occasion, they ran into each other, and Alexa had always been cordial and happy to see him, but something was off. It was as if they both were waiting for something. He couldn't call it mixed signals, because she had always been clear on not wanting to be anything but friends. Still, there were moments when she'd call to ask his advice about something and they would… Andrew paused to find the right word.

"Linger," he finally said.

"Who's lingering where?" Sanjay roared.

Andrew shut the water off. "It's nothing."

"You aren't making any sense, my friend."

He snatched the towel from the peg outside the shower and dried off before securing it around his middle.

"Tell me about it," Andrew muttered. "I need to forget about it."

Sanjay looked confused. "About lingering?"

"About Alexa," Andrew clarified.

"Oh. If she causes this much dismay, my friend, that would probably be wise."

Sanjay was right. He knew it. It was time to let Alexa go. No more wishing things were different. They weren't, and it was time he stopped wishing things would change and accepted the reality of how things were.

"You're right. Time to quit pining."

Decision made, Andrew felt lighter than he had in

months. He whistled a cheerful tune while he dressed. Then, after bidding his friend goodbye, he went home.

"JJ, I need you," his father called out from his study not even a minute after Andrew came through the front door.

When Andrew poked his head in the doorway, his father motioned to the chair across from his desk.

"Sure, what's up?"

"There's a security consulting assignment for an old client. But, unfortunately, I've got a scheduling conflict that's come up, or I'd go myself."

"No problem."

James glanced up from reviewing the contract when his son didn't continue. He eyed his son curiously. Then, with a slight nod, he sat back in his chair.

"Okay, what's going on?"

Andrew's expression turned quizzical. "I'm not sure what you mean."

"This is the first time you've agreed to cover an assignment for me without asking for a whole heap of details."

"Does it matter? You asked me to help."

"And I appreciate it," his father acknowledged with a wide smile. "But this isn't like you, son. I'm just wondering why the change-up?"

Andrew crossed his leg, resting his ankle on his knee. "Just feeling the need for a change of scenery lately. Something to take my mind off a few things. Besides, we're on a break, so now's a great time to go."

"A few things, or one specific thing?" James inquired. "Or should I say someone?"

"What do you mean?"

"Come on, JJ, I'm your father. And even if I weren't, I'm still a very observant man. You like Alexa, and you've been on a slow burn since you met her. So I say it's time to stop dragging your feet before someone else stakes a claim."

"Dad, first off, I'm not discussing my love life with you—"

"Good, because it's hard to talk about what you don't have."

Andrew shook his head. "Second, stake a claim? I'm not prospecting for gold. Besides, we're just friends. I can't make her interested in more than that. She's been clear since the beginning on how she felt. So there's nothing more to do."

"Balderdash," James replied, then stopped short. "Are people still saying that?"

Andrew snorted. "No one under eighty."

"I've seen you two together. And the fact that she is still in your life tells me that you've gotten past her looking like—"

"Don't say her name," Andrew warned. "It's better if you don't talk natural disasters up."

"I hadn't planned on saying it," James countered. "I was merely going to say that whatever hesitations you seem to have had early on seem to have resolved themselves, no?"

"No. There's still the very big hurdle of Alexa herself. Like I said, she's made herself crystal clear."

"Alexa likes you, son. Regardless of what she says."

"I'm sure she knows her mind, Dad," Andrew countered. "Not that it matters. I will be on assignment, and I'm sure that wherever Alexa is, she's working. So, let's forget it."

"Consider the matter dropped." Then, handing his son the client folder, James waited until Andrew left before relaxing into a smile.

"Molasses may not be the best way to catch this particular dragonfly. Time to shake things up for you and Alexa, my boy, and see what happens."

*Five days later...*

Andrew adjusted the black bow tie until he was satisfied. He glanced in the mirror before sliding on the midnight blue tuxedo jacket. The black satin lapels provided a subtle contrast between the two. He retrieved his pistol from the nightstand and slid it into his gun holster before buttoning up the jacket.

There was a quick knock at his bedroom door.

"Coming." Andrew strode across the room to open it.

"Good evening, Mr. Riker."

"How are you, Etienne?"

"Very well, sir. Mr. Simms is ready."

He followed the butler downstairs to the group assembled in the foyer.

"There's my security expert," Mr. Simms's voice boomed. "I told a few of my colleagues that you're here to revolutionize my security detail."

"Thank you, sir. I'll do my best."

"Now you're just being modest," Mr. Simms replied. "Phalanx is one of the best in the business, and you know it. That's why you're here." He pulled Andrew to the side.

"I'm sure you heard about that unfortunate mishap a few weeks ago. One of my men got sloppy, and some disgruntled former employee almost caused a scene. Unfortunately, incidents like that tend to have a snowball effect. I can't shake my stakeholders' faith in my abilities to lead or tarnish my company's reputation."

"No, of course not. I intend to observe your team and provide any necessary alterations to processes. You understand that may result in additional training or even staff changes?"

"Whatever you need to do. You have complete operational control, Andrew. I've known your dad for years, so I know I'm in great hands. James didn't even rake me over the coals for not hiring Phalanx in the first place." Mr. Simms chuckled. "I wouldn't have blamed him in the least."

"Don't worry, sir. We'll get things back on track."

He clapped Andrew between the shoulder blades. "I don't doubt it."

Several Range Rovers were on hand to transport the

businessman's entourage to the nearby chalet for a formal charity event. Andrew was there strictly for observation of his client's team.

When they arrived, there was a reception already in progress. Andrew's gaze roamed the luxurious great room, taking in the immaculately dressed guests and uniformed waiters serving drinks and canapés. Before they had come, Andrew sat in on the operations meeting for Mr. Simms's protection officers. The chalet Bruyère was at the foot of the Alps. The residence belonged to one of his client's business partners, and while the view was spectacular, the team was more concerned about entry and exit points, the guests attending and safe houses along the route.

Keeping a low profile, Andrew waved off the flute of champagne a waiter had offered him. He didn't drink while on duty, so he asked for a glass of club soda instead. More to have something in his hand while walking around. When on assignment, Andrew worked hard to blend in. Granted, he was in the Alps and noticed the only people of color at the event were on Mr. Simms's security detail, so there wasn't but so much being a wallflower he could do. That thought made him chuckle.

He was about to take another sip of his drink but stopped. A weird feeling settled into the pit of his stomach. His body's early detection system that something wasn't right.

When Andrew got these hunches, he never ignored them. Instead, he paid close attention to everything happening around him.

That's when he saw it. There was nothing unusual to the untrained eye about the two elegantly dressed people standing there talking, but Andrew could tell the man was upset by his body language. The woman's back was to him, but he saw her leaning into the man to speak with him. Then, when the man tried to step around her, she placed her hand on his biceps and guided him down the corridor.

Before he'd even registered, Andrew was moving to follow them. He set his drink down on the table along the way. He spotted them moving away from the guests and down a flight of stairs. Glancing around, he confirmed that everyone was engaged and enjoying the party.

Silently, he crept down the stairs. At the bottom, Andrew walked into a wood-paneled theater room with two large couches, several plush beanbags and a large projection-screen television. Continuing down the corridor, he poked his head into a sauna and the adjacent steam room.

*Where could they have gone?* he questioned himself. That's when he heard two muted voices. Silently, Andrew strode toward a room at the end of the hall. He could hear the raised voices and see that the once-agitated man was flat-out belligerent.

"No, I will not calm down. I have every right to talk to her. This is a free country, you know. You can't prohibit me from speaking to whomever I please. Now step aside."

The woman remained planted in front of him. Nothing about her body language seemed excited. Instead, she appeared calm and spoke to the man slowly, soothingly.

"I'm sorry, sir, but Mrs. Crawley is here to enjoy the charity event. If you would like to give me your name, I would be happy to relay any message you have for her tomorrow."

"And I said I'm not doing that. I am going to give her a piece of my mind. I was a good employee. I didn't deserve to get fired over some stupid misunderstanding, which she'd know if you'd let me speak to her. But you know what, why am I wasting my time with you? I don't know who you are, but this conversation is over. Now move."

He reached out to shove the woman out of his way. Andrew watched in growing amusement as she used the man's momentum when he tried to grab her to flip him to the floor by the arm. Before he could utter a word, she hauled him to his feet and grabbed him by the scruff of his collar. When she turned around, and they saw each other, both froze.

Alexa and Andrew were speechless and stood rooted to their spots. Her aggressor tried to use the opportunity to make a run for it, but she was still holding his collar, plus Andrew was blocking their path.

"Andrew?" Alexa said when she'd recovered herself. "What are you doing here?"

He grinned. "You know me. I have a habit of turning up where I'm least expected."

# Chapter 16

Alexa crossed her arms. "I'm serious."

"I'm here on business," Andrew explained. "So, how are you, Lexi?"

"I'm doing great—and you?"

Alexa's detainee was incredulous. "Who cares how he is? Let go of my neck."

"Shut up," they both said in unison.

Andrew's gaze returned to Alexa. "Of all the places we could've run into each other."

She nodded. "Who'd have guessed Chamonix, France?"

"Not me." He turned to the man struggling to get free. "I see you're on duty?"

"Yep. I have a client here for a few weeks. And you?" she inquired.

"I'm doing some security consulting."

"Well, that's exciting."

"No, it's not," her captive groused.

"If I have to tell you again to stop talking, you'll be walking home with a limp," she promised.

The man snorted. "And I'll sue that sequined dress off your body."

"How do you stand it?" Andrew asked seriously. "I've only known him two minutes, and I'd love to deck him already."

The man went to say something, but Alexa cut him off.

"You've tried to threaten and intimidate my client, and you took a swing at me, so by all means, call your lawyer," she countered.

He grumbled but remained quiet.

Escorting him through the patio door, Alexa guided him

along the wooden deck to the front of the house. Then, spotting one of her employees, she headed his way.

"Is the principal on the go?"

"Yes, Miss King. Dyan took Mrs. Crawley in the lead car. We left car number two here for you."

She nodded. "Escort this gentleman to his vehicle and see that he leaves the premises."

"Yes, Miss King."

When her employee left, physically pulling the protesting man behind, she turned to find Andrew standing with his arms across his chest.

Shaking her head, Alexa went up to him. "Enjoying the show?"

"Oh, yeah," he laughed. "You were impressive, Miss King."

"Thank you, Mr. Riker. Fishing for compliments considering Phalanx taught me everything I know?"

Andrew fell into step beside her. "Not at all. I'm pleased you're doing well and Dragonfly International is thriving. You've made a solid name for yourself in our community, Alexa. That's all my dad and I ever wanted for you."

"Thanks, Andrew. That's high praise coming from you. And it's good to see you."

Their shoes tapped out a staccato beat on the wood decking as they returned to the entrance at the back of the house.

"It's good to see you, too, Alexa."

When they went in, Andrew noticed the slightly blue tinge to her lips and her shivering. Rushing to the couch, he grabbed one of the thick sherpa throw blankets and draped it over Alexa's shoulders.

"Thank you," she said through chattering teeth.

"You're freezing. Why didn't you say something? I could've escorted the whiner outside to your team."

"That's my job, and I'm fine," she retorted.

Andrew studied the floor-length V-neck sequined gown

that she was wearing. The flutter sleeves and slit above her right leg exposed some of her skin to the elements.

"Alexa, your lips almost match the gray of your dress. If you don't warm up soon, I will be forced to escort you to the sauna. Better yet, that might still be a good idea."

"Don't you dare," she cautioned before a shimmer of a smile peeked through a stern frown.

He helped her sit down on the couch closest to the fireplace before he flipped the switch to turn it on. At the same time, Alexa rubbed her shoulders vigorously, trying to warm up. Finally, the gas ignited with an audible whoosh, and flames shot to life.

Andrew sat as close as he could to help with the transference of body heat. He placed an arm around her shoulder and drew her close. Her body wasn't shivering as much as before.

"You'd better not catch pneumonia."

"That's not in the schedule."

His chest shook with delight while he rubbed his hand up and down her blanketed arm. Andrew was startled when Alexa moved closer, resting her head on his shoulder.

The room was eerily quiet save for the occasional muffled voices and footsteps coming from the first floor.

"Always by the book, huh, King?"

"It's easier that way. Everything is predictable—no surprises."

"Yeah," he agreed. "But where's the fun in that?"

It was two days later when Alexa received a text from Andrew. Both got a break in their schedules, so they decided to meet. Dyan was on point as the CPO for the day and took Mrs. Crawley to the spa.

"So, where's he taking you on your date?" Dyan had said when she heard about Alexa's plans.

"It's not a date. We're simply two friends getting reacquainted on our day off."

Dyan pulled out her phone.

"What are you doing?"

"'A date is time spent with another person that is enjoyable and allows you both to grow closer.'"

Alexa's mouth dropped open. "Did you just google that?"

"Yes, I did. And as you can see, by definition, you two are on a date."

Alexa's eyes shot heavenward as she excused herself to go and get ready.

The forecast was for a clear day with a high temperature of forty-seven degrees. Alexa didn't know where they were going. Andrew suggested that she dress comfortably and in layers, so she wore black stretch leggings, hiking boots, a fleece jacket and a long-sleeve Henley shirt. Pleased with her appearance, Alexa grabbed her coat, hat and gloves and headed to the family room to wait.

When the butler announced that Andrew had arrived, Alexa followed him outside.

Several of Alexa's team were walking the perimeter of the house. Each looked surprised when she and Andrew walked by but refrained from comment. The snow was piled high on either side of the shoveled driveway. Andrew's car was toward the entrance of Beauté Majestueuse, so they walked down the road. While they strolled, Alexa took in the snow-covered trees and glorious mountain view. Retrieving her cell phone from her jacket pocket, Alexa took pictures of the snowy scene and a few of Andrew. "How are you this afternoon?" he greeted her, opening the silver Range Rover door and helping her climb up.

"I'm wonderful."

She waited while Andrew walked around to the other side. Then, when he slid behind the wheel, Alexa said, "Okay, so where are we going?"

"Come on. I can't tell you yet. Then it wouldn't be a surprise."

Andrew started the car and entered an address into the

GPS. He used his hand to block the screen from her view, which caused Alexa to arch an eyebrow.

"Yeah, about that. I'm not big on surprises, Andrew. It helps when I'm prepared and—"

"Uh-uh," he interrupted as he pulled off. "You're not working today, so come back off high alert. Besides, you'll like this surprise," he said confidently.

Alexa couldn't argue with his logic. She nodded her agreement and allowed Andrew to continue with their journey while she enjoyed the scenery.

They chatted as he drove. "How are your parents?"

"Doing well. Not happy I'm over four thousand miles away," she explained. "But they're supportive of my career. They always have been."

"That's valuable to have."

"Don't I know it," Alexa agreed. "Our family isn't that large, so it's always special when we get together."

Andrew parked and cut the engine when they pulled outside their destination.

"Where are we? Come on, now is a great time to fill me in."

"Fair enough. We're going skijoring."

Her expression was blank. "What?"

"It's a winter sport that means ski driving, and you're pulled along on skis behind a horse." He stopped. "You can ski, can't you?" Andrew frowned. "I suppose I should've asked before now."

"Yes, I can ski," Alexa responded with a laugh. "This sounds like fun. I'd love to try it."

Thirty minutes later, Alexa was holding on tight as a horse gently galloped through the snowy trails. Her cheeks were hurting, not from the cold but from all the laughing and smiling.

Eventually, their guide led the horses back to the stables.

When they turned a corner, Alexa lost her grip and her balance. She went careening off the path and into a snowbank.

"Alexa," Andrew yelled as he let go of the harness. He came to a complete stop before he undid his skis and went after Alexa.

"Hey, are you okay?" he said with concern.

"Fine," she giggled. "Except for the fact that I'm stuck."

"Here, let me help you."

"No, I've got it," she said quickly.

He watched her attempt to stand twice before going over and grabbing her hand to hoist her up. Off-balance, Alexa was stable for a few moments before the skis began to slide.

"Wait, I've got you," he said, trying to keep her steady.

Before either could stop it, Alexa fell backward, taking Andrew with her.

He lay sprawled on top of her in a tangle of limbs. Once Alexa recovered, she started laughing so hard she began hiccuping.

Unable to stop himself, Andrew joined in.

They finally sobered. He gazed down at her. Suddenly, he lifted his gloved hand and moved a wisp of Alexa's hair out of her face.

She stilled.

"Why do you do that?"

A look of confusion crossed her face. "What?"

"Never accept my help? Or, as far as I know, anyone's help?"

"I like doing things myself. It's better that way."

He touched her cheek. "Better or safer?"

All of a sudden, the air between them grew dense with tension. Andrew's face was mere inches away. Alexa could feel his breath mingling with her own, and his eyes were intense, as if he were trying to peer into her soul. She worried that he could hear the hammering of her heart. Alarm bells went off in Alexa's head. Every inch of her warned that this was dangerous. That *he* was dangerous. Her gaze drifted to his lips. His upper lip was a cupid's bow and matched his full lower lip perfectly. There was a bit of razor stubble along his jawline, and the scar from his lip to his chin still mesmerized Alexa. They were so close that all she needed to do was tilt her head up, and their lips would be locked in a kiss.

The moan that drifted between her traitorous lips left her mortified.

She tried to push him off, but his body weight held her firmly in place.

"Andrew, I think we'd better get up," she said, still struggling to free herself.

"Answer me, Lexi."

She blinked several times. She was so affected by his proximity that she had forgotten the question.

"What?" she said, trying to stall.

"Why do you keep me at arm's length?"

"You don't appear to be at the moment, do you?"

"Alexa, what are you afraid of?"

Before she could respond, their guide called out from about one hundred yards away.

It was the proverbial splash of cold water needed to break the connection. Andrew glanced at her a final time before he got up. This time when he held out his hand to help Alexa, she accepted it.

"There you are," the worried man said when he reached them. "Is everything okay?"

Andrew glanced at Alexa with a heated look so intense that it took her breath away. She could only nod her head in response.

# Chapter 17

When they returned to the stables, Andrew unsnapped his snow boots from his skis. He turned to help Alexa, but she was already undoing her boots.

One of her buckles was stuck, so Alexa tugged on it sharply.

"Here, let me."

She started to refuse but stopped. Instead, she gave him a demure smile. "Thank you for bringing me. It was a great surprise, Andrew."

The mutual attraction still hummed between them like a powerline, but for now neither acknowledged it.

He grinned. "Glad you liked it," he replied as they returned their gear. "But the day isn't over. How about some lunch?"

"Are you kidding? I'm starving. Lead the way."

Andrew chose Neopolis, an Italian restaurant in the Centre Commercial Alpina in Chamonix city center with an impressive view of Mont Blanc and the banks of the Arve river.

The restaurant was cozy, with wood tables and brown leather chairs. White walls were decorated with paintings, and wood ledges held carafes, baskets and other artifacts from bygone eras.

Alexa ordered the capricciosa pizza while Andrew ordered the spaghetti Bolognese. The restaurant was busy, making intimate conversation difficult, but they enjoyed being there and eating delicious Italian food.

A walk along the river followed lunch, which allowed them a chance for quiet conversation.

"I've enjoyed my day, Drew. Thanks again for suggesting it."

"My pleasure, Lexi," he said, grinning.

Alexa observed the shops as they walked by. Eventually, she said, "To answer your question, it's safer."

Andrew didn't stop walking. After a moment, he said, "You are always safe with me, Alexa. Don't you know that by now?"

Alexa's cell phone chirped. She checked her text message and frowned.

"What's wrong?"

"That's Dyan. We have an issue with the driver in car two. He ate something that didn't agree with him and was forced to make a pit stop."

Andrew nodded and ushered Alexa back to the Range Rover.

"Where's your backup team?" he asked along the way.

Alexa's stride was almost as long as his as they rushed back to their parking space. Andrew's mind was racing with possible scenarios.

"They're en route."

When they got to the SUV, Andrew started the engine and turned to Alexa.

"Where's the lead car?"

Alexa tapped out a message to Dyan and waited.

"On la Mer de Glace," she finally said.

Andrew looked at the navigation system. "That's only four minutes from here. We can intercept them."

Dyan gave Alexa their coordinates, and she added them to Andrew's GPS.

It didn't take long to spot the lead car, but Alexa pointed out a black BMW 7 Series that had pulled up parallel to Dyan's car. They gave it a few moments, but when the other vehicle matched their speed, Alexa turned to Andrew.

"I see them," he said before she could say a word and sped up to intercept the chase car.

Alexa called Dyan's cell phone. "We're right behind you. Have the driver execute maneuver E."

"Will do," Dyan replied before hanging up.

"The driver will speed up so that you can take his place and deal with the other car," Alexa explained.

"Got it," Andrew replied.

Both were all business as they worked together to deal with the immediate threat to Alexa's operation.

He sped up and got behind Dyan's car so that when the driver hit the gas and took off, they quickly slipped in to deal with the BMW. Alexa used the time to write down the license plate number.

The other car sped up to pass, but Andrew's Range Rover connected with the left panel of the vehicle and pushed it to the right. The BMW veered sharply and ran off the road. Andrew shot past to catch up with the principal's car.

"Alexa, are you okay?"

"Yep, I'm fine. Great driving," she replied with a smile.

Andrew caught up to Dyan's car and dropped behind her while Alexa called to check on their second car's driver and let the backup car know that she and Andrew were following the lead.

She ended the call and turned to Andrew. "He has food poisoning."

"Coincidence?"

"Unlikely. He ate the same meal as the other CP officers, and they're all fine. I'll check it out when we get back and my principal's secure."

The two cars pulled into the driveway at Beauté Majestueuse, and Dyan assisted Mrs. Crawley into the house. Alexa and Andrew got out of the car, and he checked the damage on the rental car.

"It's not too bad."

"I'm glad. Thanks for helping me out today."

He grinned. "My pleasure. Never a dull moment, hey, King?"

"That's true," she replied. "Which is one of the things I love about my job."

Andrew nodded. His smile was brilliant. "Thanks for a lively day."

"That it was," she agreed. "I enjoyed the food, skijoring, the walk along the waterfront and the car chase."

Andrew laughed. "Of course."

There was an awkward pause before she said, "I'll see you later?"

He nodded. "I'm headed to Geneva tomorrow, but it'll only be a two-day trip."

Alexa frowned before she caught herself. "Oh. Then safe travels, Drew."

"Thanks. I know you'll hold the fort down, Lexi."

She chuckled. "Always do."

Turning, she strode into the house to find her team waiting in the living room. She returned to all business.

"How's the principal?"

"She's fine," Dyan replied. "Most of the time, she was on her phone conducting business and wasn't paying attention to her surroundings."

Alexa pinched the bridge of her nose. "I'd like an incident report in thirty minutes on what went wrong, how this could've been avoided and what steps we'll take to ensure that things go smoother next time. If Andrew and I hadn't been close, this could've had a different outcome."

Her team agreed and dispersed, giving her time to return to her suite to shower and change clothes. When she returned thirty-five minutes later, everyone was at the dining table waiting.

"Okay," Alexa said, claiming the spot at the head of the table. "Let's begin."

A few nights later, Mrs. Crawley hosted an intimate dinner party for some friends. There were various glass jars and vases filled with water, cranberries, green twigs and floating candles placed as centerpieces on the table and around the room. The warm glow of the candles replaced the bright overhead lighting that illuminated the dining room and complemented the solid custom acacia wood dining table and chairs. There was a runner on the table that included winter touches of evergreens, pine cones and holly. The red and green were a beautiful contrast to the cream-colored china plates with gold chargers and crystal glasses.

Alexa was the CP officer on duty and remained at a distance from her principal for the entire evening. Since they were in a controlled environment and had cleared the guest list, Alexa gave a few of her team the night off. The remaining employees were strategically placed around the chalet to avoid drawing attention. To anyone observing, she was merely one of Mrs. Crawley's employees.

Alexa had her laptop out and appeared to be working, but she observed everyone attending the party to ensure there were no surprises and that the night ran smoothly.

Her cell phone vibrated. Alexa glanced at her principal before she checked it.

How's everything?

She smiled, and her heart fluttered. *Andrew.*

Great. Principal is having a dinner party. Pretty sedate. How's Geneva?

I just finished a training session. Have some paperwork to do, and I owe Dad a call.

I do, too. My parents get antsy if I don't check in often on assignments. You'd think I was still a teenager.

You, too? LOL. How about dinner when I return? I promise it'll be a less hectic day. No car chases or overzealous fans.

Don't make promises you can't keep.

That garnered her a smiley emoji from Andrew.

Fair enough. There might be some chaos and mayhem involved.

That's more like it.

Can I ask you a question?

Sure, Alexa replied.

Did you smile when you saw it was me texting?

Alexa's cheeks flushed with excitement. She pondered if she should be truthful or not. Finally, she typed her answer.

Yes, I was happy to see it was you.

So, you miss me?

Alexa pondered his question. Try as she might, she couldn't deny that she had been thinking about Andrew a lot since he had left. Their ski outing played nightly in her dreams. Each time, they ended up kissing. It was hot and explosive, and always left Alexa wanting more when it was over. Each time she woke up feeling strung tighter than a violin string. It was disconcerting to her. She was placing her toe in water that was sure to burn.

Are you there?

She glanced down at the screen before turning around. Alexa noticed that everyone was enjoying the party and not minding her.

Yes, I miss you. I enjoyed spending time with you, Andrew. It has been a pleasant surprise.

How pleasant? he texted back.
Alexa almost grit her teeth in frustration.

Andrew, why are you fishing for compliments?

I'm not. Merely seeing how truthful you'll be in answering my questions.

I told you that I never lie.

We'll see if that's true when I return and I'm standing right in front of you.

Alexa felt her body growing warmer just recalling the last time Andrew was so close.

Andrew, I have to go. It looks like the guests are leaving.

Duty calls? Fair enough. We will continue this conversation later. Good night, Lexi. Sweet dreams.

There was no doubt that her dreams would be even more intense thanks to him.

Alexa shifted in her chair, suddenly feeling the need for some fresh mountain air. It was time to admit the truth. She was falling and there was no way to stop it.

Good night, Drew.

# *Chapter 18*

Alexa had off the next day, so she went into Chamonix and treated herself to a spa day at one of the luxury resorts. She had received a bamboo deep-tissue massage, followed by a detoxifying body wrap, a eucalyptus steam room session and a few minutes in the hot tub. While she was getting a deluxe pedicure, she called her friend Marena to catch up.

"Alexa, it's been forever since we've spoken. Bring me up to speed. What's been going on with you?"

She watched as the woman sitting on a stool at her feet massaged a cold, blue-green invigorating scrub into her legs. The rhythmic motion lulled Alexa into a further state of relaxation. Alexa leaned back into the soft white leather massage chair and pressed a button to start a combination of rolling and kneading her muscles. A blissful sigh escaped her lips.

"Well, I've been in Chamonix, France, for a few weeks. I leave for home in a few days. Let's just say this assignment has been full of unexpected surprises."

"Really," Dr. Marena Dash-McKendrick remarked. "And what do you mean by surprises?"

"Not all what," Alexa replied, feeling so relaxed that she yawned several times. "Some are a who."

"You don't say? Would one of those whos be Andrew Riker?"

"Yes." Alexa tried not to gush, but it was hard to do with the smile encompassing her whole face. "He tops the list, yes. I mean, figure the odds of us running into each other in France?"

"Seems predestined if you ask me."

Alexa choked on the seltzer water she had been offered. "Predestined? That's laying it on a bit thick, isn't it?"

Marena snickered.

"Oh, stop. It's not all dreamy. We just reconnected, and we're simply getting to know each other better."

"And has this time playing twenty questions changed your opinion of him?"

Alexa paused before she answered that. "No. Quit reading more into this than it is. We're still just friends."

"You're a terrible liar."

"Now you sound like my cousin, Zane."

"He's not wrong. Besides, I can hear what you're still trying to deny in your voice. You *like* him."

"Okay, yes, I do like Andrew. But there's so much going on with work, I can't afford to split my focus," Alexa dismissed. "Before I forget, we have a new client, Ruben Tyndale, who will come in shortly. A very VIP client, I might add."

"Congrats, Lex. I'm glad business is doing so well. Oh, Lucas is here for a visit. He wanted me to make sure I told the 'Amazon' hello."

Alexa laughed. "And how is your brother doing? I knew I shouldn't have told him my nickname when we were on that mission in London."

"Oh, you're never going to hear the end of it. Lucas said it suits you too much. And he's well. He and Coulter have decided to build me a larger workspace in the backyard for all my inventions."

"Speaking of which, anything new that Dragonfly can acquire?"

"Of course," Marena said gleefully. "I'm working on a ring that shoots out a burst of a sleeping agent."

"I know of a few people I'd love to put to sleep," Alexa joked. "If you need someone to test the prototype—"

"Don't worry, I'll send it as soon as it's done. And don't get too excited. It doesn't last that long," Marena added. "Now, back to my original question before you decided to redirect."

The woman doing her feet was rubbing hot stones on

her legs. Alexa sighed blissfully. "I wasn't redirecting," she finally managed to say. "And business has been booming. Dragonfly has had steady repeat business and word-of-mouth recommendations. And now that we're about to sign this new client, we're finally out of the red."

"I'm happy for you," Marena exclaimed. "You deserve it."

"Ruben mentioned the person we would be taking on is an ultra-high net asset. We'll go over the details in our operational meeting when I return home. First, we'll determine why the principal needs protection and how long. Is it because of a digital stalker, angry ex-lover, corporate espionage, or if it's for business travel—"

"You know I'm not applying for a job, right?" Marena laughed.

"Oh, am I boring you?" she countered while accepting a proffered glass of sparkling water with lime.

"To death."

"What? The world of close protection is so exciting," Alexa gushed while adjusting her massage chair. "It's amazing that you never do the same job twice. Every client and operation is different. You know, like when you're making serums in your lab, designing tech gadgets or antidotes to save your husband from certain death by poison."

"Touché," Marena replied. "So what's Zane's take on your latest client?"

Alexa chuckled and pointed to the nail polish swatch that she wanted. "You know Zane. He's betting whatever Ruben Tyndale wants to discuss involves some supermodel with a stalker."

"He would pick the scenario with a supermodel.

"Speaking of people we love to look at, tell me more about Andrew. Has he come to Washington to visit?"

"Uh, segue much?" Alexa teased. "And no, he hasn't come to DC. He's been tied up with work lately, too. He's in Geneva right now but will be returning to Chamonix. I'll get a chance to see him before I go."

"I bet he'd come if you asked him."

"Marena."

"Okay, okay. I'll let it go—for now. But only because I've got to run. Congrats again on landing the new client. Let me know how it goes."

"Thanks, and will do," Alexa promised.

Alexa hung up and had to laugh at her friend. Marena hadn't changed since they met at the retreat years ago. *The one that changed my life. Who would have thought I would decide on this career after going to a transformational retreat that Tanya had suggested?* Her mind drifted to Andrew again. Yes, life did have a way of trying to throw curveballs.

Andrew ended up detained and made it back on Alexa's last night in France. They dined at Le Matafan in the heart of Chamonix. It was a relaxed atmosphere with primarily wood decor with bright red as an accent color used in the tableware, lighting and seating.

Alexa marveled at the hundreds of pieces of wood logs flush on accent walls around the restaurant. It was unique and, paired with the fireplace, added to the romantic flair.

While they dined on pumpkin gnocchis with butternut cream, and octopus cooked in bouillabaisse, they talked about their upcoming assignments.

"It sounds like a wonderful opportunity to showcase Dragonfly. I wish you all the best. Let me know if you need anything."

"I will," she promised. "What about you? Thailand sounds exciting."

"I've been there a few times, so nothing out of the ordinary. Just babysitting a few businessmen for a summit."

"And what's next after that?"

"That would depend on you."

Alexa was about to take a bite of her gnocchi and stopped. "Me?"

"Despite your dire warnings as to why we wouldn't work together, Alexa, I get the feeling that you're not so sure that still rings true."

"Andrew—"

"Before you deny what I know as facts, hear me out. I propose a trial."

Her mouth dropped open. "A what?"

"When our assignments are over, let's schedule some time together. Uninterrupted time to get to know each other better. Without work getting in the way."

"Andrew, I—"

He took her hand, turned it over and kissed the pulse point of her wrist. Instead of releasing it, he held her hand captive, caressing her fingers with the pad of his thumb.

"Don't think. Feel, Alexa."

At the moment, Alexa could barely breathe. She stared at Andrew stroking her hand as if she had just grown the appendage out of thin air.

"That's a good sign."

Alexa felt warm and tingly all over. "What is?"

Andrew leaned in closer. "The fact that I'm not on my knees in a headlock right now." His gaze held a hint of playfulness. "I'd say you're at least amenable to my proposition."

Truthfully, Alexa's answer was yes the moment he suggested it. She'd find a way to deal with those subconscious worries later. For now, there was no way she was refusing anything this man offered.

Alexa leaned in to give him her full attention. His cologne wafted into her nostrils. The woody, masculine scent was heady and lulling her like a seductive siren song.

"Andrew?"

"Yes?"

"I don't like you."

His expression was so intense his gaze could have melted cheese without a fondue set.

"I'm glad. Because I don't like you, either."

# Chapter 19

A week later, Alexa was in her office reviewing the operational manager's detailed report on Ruben Tyndale and his company, Tyndale Global Holdings. Their latest annual report was quite impressive. Tyndale had business ties in entertainment, fashion, media and banking.

She was making discussion notes when her administrative assistant buzzed her office to let her know Mr. Tyndale had arrived.

"Thanks, Miranda." Standing, Alexa smoothed her dark gray pantsuit and ran her tongue over her teeth. Seconds later, the door opened, and he was ushered into her plush office.

"Good afternoon, Miss King," Ruben said as he strode across the room.

"Hello, Mr. Tyndale." They shook hands before Alexa motioned for him to be seated.

"Let me start by saying how thrilled I am to meet you finally. Your track record is stellar, Miss King, and I need the best."

"Thank you, Mr. Tyndale. We appreciate your business."

"Please, call me Ruben."

"If you'll call me Alexa," she returned. "Now, how can Dragonfly be of assistance?"

He shifted in his chair. "It's not for me—at least not directly. I have a high-profile business partner and client who needs your company's specialized protection. She's a young lady whose career has taken off. She owns very successful jewelry, makeup line and fashion accessory businesses and recently made the Forbes billionaires list. She will be traveling to several shows in the US and Europe, so I want her safe—especially from her boyfriend."

Alexa sat back in her chair. "Mr. Tyndale, while this isn't outside my company's skill set, I'm curious why you didn't mention to our operational manager that you aren't the principal?"

"Miss King, it's a rather delicate situation, and I didn't—"

Before Ruben could explain, a tall woman burst through the door. She walked in like it was her office. Her winter-white wool pantsuit was adorned with a diamond-and-gold belt. Her bracelets, earrings and necklaces were gold as well. The black suede red-bottomed ankle boots were devoid of adornment, as was the black suede handbag providing an understated anchor to the opulence of her ensemble.

"I'm sorry for the intrusion, Miss King," her assistant, Miranda, said, rushing in behind the woman. "I told her that you were in a meeting, but—"

"It's okay, Miranda," Alexa said, rising out of her chair.

The woman stopped in front of her desk. "Whatever Ruben has arranged, you can forget it. I have no intention of going along with this insanity." She scowled at him. "There is nothing that I'd ever want from this woman."

Before Alexa could reply, the woman removed her black sunglasses and glared back.

The color drained from Alexa's face, and it took several moments for her to recover from seeing her ex–best friend Shelley's baby sister. "Sophia?"

"So, you remember me," she said with a mocking smile. "Good. Then you know that there's nothing I'd ever want from you after what you did to my family."

Sophia spun around and pierced her business partner with a murderous glare. "Ruben, I don't know what you thought coming here, but I don't need *her* help. Nor will I ever need anything from Alexa King. I'm leaving."

"No, you're not," he countered. "You will stay here, and we will work this out."

"How could you?" Sophia accused. "She left my sister to die at the hands of some madman while she saved herself."

"You know that's not true," Alexa shot back. "I went to get Shelley some help. She's here today because of me."

Sophia leaned over Alexa's desk. "You mean she's psychologically damaged because of *you*."

Ruben bolted up and took hold of Sophia's arm. "Okay, let's calm down, ladies. Sophia, this isn't getting us anywhere. I'm sure we can find a way to—"

"Don't you even act like I'm the one being unreasonable when you've blindsided me like this." Sophia yanked her arm away.

"I'm sorry, Mr. Tyndale, but under the circumstances, I don't think this is going to work," Alexa said firmly. "I'll be happy to recommend another—"

"Excuse me, Miss King, can I have a word?" Dyan called from the doorway. "We have a situation regarding a client that I need to speak with you about."

Alexa hesitated.

"It's imperative."

"Certainly, Dyan." Ignoring Sophia, she turned to Ruben. "Please excuse me for a moment."

"There she goes running away again. Typical."

Alexa forced herself to refrain from commenting as she strode to the door. Instead, she turned her attention to Dyan when she got on the other side.

"Okay, what's going on?"

"That's what I'd like to know. So, because of a principal's temper tantrum, you're about to blow a ridiculously lucrative contract for us?"

That brought Alexa up short. "Potential principal. And you interrupted a client meeting for this?"

"He's already paid a retainer fee, and a screaming match was more like it," Dyan retorted. "Alexa, this isn't like you. You can get along with anybody. I've seen you do it."

"This is different," she shot back. "This is Shelley's younger sister. I'll add who is just as vicious now as she was almost fifteen years ago." Alexa stopped talking and sat down at Miranda's desk. She searched through a few drawers before pulling out a bag of chocolate chip cookies from the numerous snacks her assistant kept in her desk. Ripping open the foil bag, Alexa popped a few into her mouth. Closing her eyes, she chewed in blissful silence. Then, almost as an afterthought, her eyes flew open to find Dyan staring at her in stunned silence.

"Stress eating?"

"It's warranted," Alexa countered. "Dyan, you have to understand, there's no reasoning with Sophia about anything. She thinks I'm fully responsible for Shelley's deterioration." She ate a few more snacks before saying, "Maybe she's not wrong."

Dyan leaned against Miranda's desk. "You know that's not true. You told me you were teenagers at the time. I know you did the best you could because you're a fighter, Alexa, and you don't give up. Yet you're ready to throw the towel in now and walk away from a contract with Tyndale Global? Boss, think about it. Anything they touch skyrockets to the top, and regardless of how annoying she is, Sophia Porter has the Midas touch right now. If everything goes well, Tyndale's referrals and possible follow-up work could be phenomenal. It's just the exposure we need."

Leaning back in Miranda's chair, Alexa stared at the ceiling. Her ragged sigh ricocheted around the quiet space like a Ping-Pong ball. "Dyan, this dredges up so much from my past," she said softly.

"You can handle it, Alexa. No one I know is stronger than you when you set your mind to something."

Her friend stood there and waited. Finally, Alexa stood.

"You're right. If Ruben still wants to hire Dragonfly, we will do it. One thing I won't do is let Shelley's sister cost my company a contract. I'll do whatever is necessary to make this work."

Dyan touched her boss's shoulder. "That's the Alexa King I know."

Alexa smiled and threw the empty bag in the trash. She rose and smoothed her suit before turning on her heel to head back to her office. She stopped and glanced over her shoulder. "Dyan?"

"Yes?"

"Can you get a replacement bag of cookies for me? And go find Miranda? She's probably hiding in the break room. Tell her that I'm not mad about Sophia barging into my office. It wasn't her fault. Sophia Porter is like unstable air moving over warm water in September on her best day. At some point, you realize that a hurricane is imminent."

Stifling a chuckle, Dyan agreed and went off to find their younger associate.

When Alexa strode through her office double doors, it was to find Sophia sitting in a chair next to Ruben. The barely controlled anger was emanating from her body like a force field. Alexa ignored the invisible daggers being thrown her way and turned her attention to her client.

"I apologize for the interruption. Unfortunately, it couldn't be helped."

"No problem at all, Miss King. At best, I know this is a tenuous situation, and I apologize for not providing you with advance notice."

"Mr. Tyndale, crisis management is where we excel." Alexa smiled and returned to her desk. "Now, I believe we were discussing why Miss Porter requires protection?"

"That's funny. I thought we were at the point where Ruben and I leave, and you return to your miserable little existence?"

Ruben paled. "Sophia!"

Alexa dug deep to generate a serene demeanor. "But that doesn't solve your security problem, does it?"

"Fine," she capitulated. "But if you ask me, Ruben is being paranoid. I'm in no real danger. Nico likes to be a drama king at times. He and I argued, but it isn't like we don't always kiss and make up."

"Over what?"

"Excuse me?"

"What did the two of you argue about?" Alexa clarified.

"That's none of your business."

Alexa grabbed a pen and Ruben's contract, signed it and then set it aside.

"Now it is. I've been hired to protect you from this day forward. Every move you make is my team's business, Sophia."

She placed her feet up on the coffee table. "Fine. We fought about some stupid investment. Nico wanted me to be a silent partner in some club he's trying to buy with a few friends. I think his friends are useless, and I wasn't about to go along with pouring my money down a bottomless drain, so I told him I wasn't interested. Especially not with the wastrels in tow.

"I've declined business ventures with him before, but this was different. He blew up and threatened that I'd regret my decision. A few days later, one of his friends cornered me at an event and thanked me for changing my mind and bankrolling Nico's portion." She glanced up at the two of them. "I didn't."

Alexa made some notes on her tablet. "What happened next?"

"Nico left for Portugal, and I flew back to the States for a fashion show. I haven't seen him since."

"Do you have arguments often?"

Sophia shrugged.

"Has Nico ever become physical with you?"

"Not if he values breathing."

"Good to hear," Alexa replied, making more notes. "Did you tell him about your conversation with his business partner?"

"No, not yet."

"We'll need to drill down further into your daily schedule, the places you go and the people you meet. The process will take a few hours, so you'll meet with a member of my logistics team."

"Fine. Are we done?"

"For the day, yes."

"I'll be in the limo, Ruben," Sophia replied. She turned to glare at Alexa.

"I'll work with you because I have to, but that doesn't mean I'll ever forgive you for your part in Shelley's issues."

Without another word, Sophia stormed out.

The room was draped in awkward silence.

"I'm sorry about her behavior, Alexa," Ruben said quickly. "Of course she'll never say it, but this latest falling-out with Nico is more significant than Sophia lets on. He's made more than a few missteps concerning business ventures, making me fearful of her getting involved in his harebrained schemes."

"Do they have any joint accounts?"

"Yes, but I don't think it's a significant amount that she keeps in the accounts she shares with Nicholas, but I can't be sure."

"I understand. Dragonfly is on the clock now, Mr. Tyndale—Ruben. We have a team of forensic accountants, so we'll check everything. Rest assured, we'll have a full picture soon."

Her client visibly relaxed. "Thank you, Alexa."

She stood up and walked around her desk to shake his hand. "My assistant, Miranda, will contact you when we have created our operational plan for Miss Porter's protection."

Her client nodded. "I appreciate you continuing with the contract. I know she can be caustic, but I care about Sophia like a daughter. Her father and I are old friends, and with Ralph and Carol wanting to stick close to Shelley, I promised I'd look out for Sophia. Her brand has expanded exponentially, and some might look to exploit her however they can."

"Ruben, I assure you that regardless of our personal history, while in our care, Sophia Porter will have every resource at our disposal to ensure her safety."

Satisfied, he bid Alexa goodbye and left. When her doors shut behind him, she sank to the sofa, flicked off her heels and placed her stocking feet on the coffee table. The surprise encounter left her utterly exhausted. Unable to help herself, Sophia's accusations came to mind. The years had done nothing to temper the sister's animosity. Clearly, she was still to blame for Shelley's plight as far as the Porters were concerned.

There was a lot at stake with this contract, and the earlier bravado about being able to work with Sophia fizzled out like a bottle of sparkling water that sat out too long.

Then, thoughts of her long-lost friend came to mind as if summoned. From Sophia's rant, Alexa surmised that Shelley was still having problems.

That thought didn't sit well with her, and she burst into tears before she could stop herself.

# Chapter 20

Nicholas Michaux settled on the black leather sofa in the dimly lit club. The electronic dance music summoned many beautiful people to the dance floor like a beacon. He toyed with the drink in his hand, swirling the amber liquid around in the glass tumbler, but it remained untouched. Usually, he'd be out there dancing and feeding off the crowd's energy, too. Lisbon was famous for its nightlife, and he enjoyed partying with the best of them, but tonight he had more significant problems. Life-and-death problems.

Nicholas shifted uncomfortably. The venue was suddenly too everything. Too hot, claustrophobic and loud. Slamming the glass on the table, he bolted up from his seat. The need for air drove him past the packed space to the second floor. Once he made it down a dark hall, Nicholas turned a corner and headed up another flight of stairs to the club's rooftop. Thankfully, it was empty.

He walked over to the edge and stood there, hungrily inhaling the cool night air while trying to gather his thoughts.

Nothing was going according to plan. Nicholas had suffered countless setbacks, starting with his father's refusal to bankroll his latest project and Sophia pulling out of partnering with him for a nightclub venture with his friends. Both denials were unexpected. He'd made dicey moves to get his portion of the money, and if any of those markers came due before he convinced Sophia or his father to reconsider, he was a dead man.

The picturesque skyline was lost on him as he stared at the brilliantly lit night with unseeing eyes.

"Enjoying the evening?"

Nicholas froze. His jaw clenched in annoyance at the intrusion. "I was."

"She wants to see you."

"She who?"

Turning, he found two well-built men in black suits directly behind him.

"The Siren."

He shook his head. This was not how he envisioned his evening shaking out. "Sorry, fellas, but I don't know who that is."

"She knows you, so let's go."

"I'm not about to go off with two goons I don't know to speak to some woman I've never met."

"When my boss wants to see you, you go."

"Maybe I didn't make myself clear. I don't respond to a summons from some stranger like a trained seal."

The man nodded. "Maybe I didn't make *myself* clear. You, Mr. Michaux, don't have a choice in the matter." He patted his right jacket pocket. "Not if you want to live."

Livid, he motioned for them to proceed. One man took the lead while the other fell into step behind Nicholas.

"I don't need an escort," he snapped. "I'm capable of getting there on my own."

"Our orders were to bring you to Torre de Pérolas, which we're going to do. So quit stalling and get moving."

Nicholas was ushered outside and into a diamond-white Mercedes G 550 SUV.

Torre de Pérolas, the "Pearl Tower," was located in Torres Vedras, a municipality almost an hour's drive from Lisbon. Thankfully, the silence was as luxurious as the vehicle. He was not in the mood to make small talk when his life could be on the line. He hadn't been entirely truthful. He had never met her, but everyone in his circle knew of the Siren.

An arms dealer, a procurer of stolen art and a thief, Siren had several illegal and legitimate enterprises. Not one to be crossed, it was well-known that she had a penchant for setting examples. Nicholas wasn't sure how he had stumbled onto her path, but being known by this dangerous woman was not good.

"We're here," the passenger called from over his shoulder.

Even in the distance, Torre de Pérolas was impressive. The uplighting around the white mansion only added to its stately appearance. Nicholas heard rumors that Siren conducted all her business at the Pearl Tower.

The main house was over ten thousand square feet and sat squarely in the middle of a massive acreage. It was a working farm with stables, a vineyard, several outbuildings, a pool, multiple gardens, a winery and an impressive turret with a wraparound balcony on the back side of the house. It was also well fortified with guards, and word on the street was that the tower was equipped with prison cells.

The car pulled into a circular driveway, stopping at the front door. His escorts got out, with one holding the door open for Nicholas, who didn't bother to thank the man as he exited.

The three men went through the massive wooden door and walked down several corridors. Nicholas checked out the interior on the way. The walls were white except for a great room with a stone fireplace.

Ushered down a floating staircase to a lower level, Nicholas found himself at the entrance to a modern dojo.

"Take off your shoes and follow me," one of the men said.

It was a stark contrast to the warm and homey feel from upstairs. However, the decor was still luxurious, with red-painted accents, rich wood walls and floors with Japanese tatami mats around the room. In addition, there were wall shelves that held swords and other sparring weapons and black lacquer room divider screens. The space exuded controlled power.

At the end were several chairs on a raised dais. The one in the middle was more impressive than the others.

A woman was in the top spot, looking very relaxed and at ease. She was an older white woman with flaming red hair swept into a tight bun. She wore black leather pants, matching knee-high boots, and a long silk balloon-sleeve floral duster in turquoise, gold and black paisley. She sipped a cup of what he assumed was tea with the exaggerated slowness of someone who has the luxury of time.

"Good evening, Mr. Michaux. Welcome to Torre de Pérolas," the woman said.

"I would say thank you, but I don't know why I'm here."

"Have a seat." She signaled for one of her employees to bring a chair.

After sinking into the comfortable black lacquer chair, Nicholas turned to his host.

"Come now, Nico. You can't be oblivious to why you're here?"

He frowned at her use of his nickname. "I don't have a clue. And you have me at a disadvantage, Miss…?"

She chuckled. "Come now, don't pretend you don't know who I am." The Siren sat back and crossed her legs. "Does Gates Budreau ring a bell?"

His jaw ticked. *Yep. You've got a clue now*, he told himself.

"I can tell by your expression that you do indeed know my colleague. Lovely. That saves us some time. Now that your memory has been restored, where is my eighteenth-century Bellasini emerald, ruby and sapphire bracelet?"

Nicholas shrugged. "I'm sorry, but I don't have it. Gates showed it to me one time, but that's it."

"Mr. Michaux, everything you've heard I'm capable of is grossly underestimated. I assure you that I'm much more dangerous than you realize. Now, I want my sixty-three-thousand-dollar bracelet you stole from Gates before I carve you up like a Christmas turkey."

Shifting in his chair, he held her gaze. "I promise you

that I don't have your bracelet. I never stole anything from Gates."

"Your *promises*," she sneered, "are of no consequence to me. He said you have it, and I want my jewelry."

Her bodyguards yanked Nicholas from his seat and forced him to kneel while Siren strode over to the wall and retrieved a katana sword from its holder. She swung it through the air in graceful yet powerful movements.

"Whoa, wait a minute," Nicholas said quickly. He attempted to fight against his captors. "I'm not lying. I didn't steal anything from Budreau. Ask him yourself."

Siren walked toward him. "I'm afraid he won't be talking—or eating solid foods for quite some time. No one steals from me and doesn't face the consequences, Mr. Michaux. It's a lesson you're about to learn. The hard way." She smiled.

Widening her stance, she was about to swing the blade at Nicholas when he screamed, "Stop! I know where to get it."

She paused. "Ah, motivation does work. Tell me where, and I suggest you hurry, because my patience is wearing thin, Nicholas. The next time I swing, my blade won't be halted."

"A friend of my girlfriend, Sophia, has it," he said in a rush. "Gates sold it to them, and I was just the middleman that delivered it. Just give me some time, and I swear I'll get it back to you."

"If you're double-crossing me—"

The burly man released him suddenly, causing Nicholas to pitch forward. His hands flew out to keep from face-planting on the wooden floor. Then he wiped the sweat from his brow with a shaky hand before rising cautiously. "I would never do that," he said hoarsely.

Siren handed the weapon to her bodyguard and then embraced Nicholas. "See that you don't," she whispered before nibbling on his earlobe. "Or I promise you my face will be the last thing you see."

* * *

Andrew was awakened by the vibrating sound of his cell phone. When he was on duty, he never turned it off. He glanced at the time and groaned aloud. It was two in the morning. He had just gotten to sleep two hours before thanks to a six-foot, deliciously sexy protection officer who periodically occupied his waking and now unconscious hours.

Grasping the device, Andrew lay back against the pillows. When he saw the phone number, sleep left him faster than water circling a drain.

It was Alexa. The object of his desire and the disruptor of his sleep.

Got a minute?

Yeah, sure.

Sitting up in bed, Andrew wiped his hand across his face and took a sip of the bottled water on the nightstand before pressing a speed-dial number.

"Hi," Alexa replied after picking up on the first ring. "I'm sorry to disturb you, but I could use a friend."

"No, it's fine. Alexa, what's wrong?" Andrew bolted upright. "Are you crying?"

"Something happened today," she sniffed. "It was unexpected."

"Where are you?"

"At home."

"What's wrong?" Andrew immediately started calculating how fast he could get there.

Alexa relayed her encounter with Sophia. Andrew remained silent while she spoke. Most of the time he spent trying to calm down. Her waking him up in the middle of the night and crying put him on edge. Before he had heard the cause of her distress, Andrew was prepared to land on her doorstep ready to do battle if necessary.

It wasn't a matter of if Alexa King was under his skin; he'd made it clear in Chamonix that she was.

"Well, that's a surprise," he replied when she'd finished.

"Tell me about it," Alexa muttered before blowing her nose. "Andrew, I don't think this is a problem I know how to handle."

He smiled at that. "I disagree. Alexa, you deal with split-second decisions, danger and life-and-death situations daily. This assignment would be no different."

"But it *is* different."

"Alexa, you're trained to compartmentalize your emotions and face them later. I know this is childhood trauma that you're dealing with, but you've learned to categorize your feelings. There are exercises we can go over to reinforce it. Don't worry. You can handle this."

She blew out a breath into the phone. "I don't think I can."

"Why not?"

"Because this is personal. Sophia gets to me, Andrew. I don't know why I ever agreed to do this," she cried. "Nothing good can come of it. She's like a walking day of reckoning that I can't escape."

Andrew swung his legs over the side of the bed.

"Listen to me. I've watched you over the years. I know how you think, how you move, and what you can accomplish when you get your mind, body and soul behind it. Lexi, I know you're scared, but you can do this. I have faith in you."

The line went silent for a few moments before Alexa said, "Why? Why do you have such faith in me when I can't even muster up enough for myself?"

"Because I care about you," Andrew replied simply. "And I'm your friend, remember?"

Alexa's silence tore at Andrew in a way that was unfamiliar to him. It made him feel utterly helpless, and that was something he wasn't used to. He also wished he were there with her in his arms instead of thousands of miles away.

"Alexa, if you need me, say the word and I'm there."

"I know. Drew?" she choked out.

"Yes, Lexi?"

"Thank you." Her voice trembled. "For being here when I needed you."

"You're welcome." For now, Andrew would let Alexa set the pace between them. However long it took, he wouldn't rush her. Now that he had acknowledged wanting their relationship to move forward, he was all in.

"I don't know what I'd do without you in my corner."

He chuckled. "Then I guess it's a good thing you'll never have to find out."

# Chapter 21

Alexa climbed up the steps of Ruben Tyndale's private jet. It was a Gulfstream G550 business aircraft that was as elegant as it was functional. The interior had six well-padded cream-colored leather captain's chairs in the front, and a tan suede sofa with cream-and-brown silk accent pillows. The plush rug was off-white in a geometric design. At the far end of the room was a large table with two of the same chairs on each side. The walls were white with the darker cream inlay around the windows and a rich mahogany on the walls separating the seating areas. There was also a bedroom and bathroom.

Handing her bag to the flight attendant, she kept her briefcase with her and headed down the aisle. She greeted several team members before walking to the back of the plane. Then, taking a seat, she secured the seat belt.

"What are you doing?"

Sophia barely glanced up. "What do you mean? I have a flight to Los Angeles, and I'm on it."

"No, *we* have a flight. As in you and your security detail," Alexa replied as calmly as she could.

"Look, they were taking too long. I got tired of waiting around, so I left."

"We've been over this before. You don't get to leave whenever you feel like it. That's not how protection works, Sophia."

"Like I care," the younger woman groused. "I can't help it if your guys can't keep up."

"Can't keep up? You climbed out a bathroom window at the fashion show. But, trust me, if you want us more up close and personal, we will accommodate you."

"Hey, I didn't ask to be here."

"Neither did I," Alexa snapped before she could catch herself. "But for better or worse," she continued, "you are under my company's protection as long as there's a threat. So I need you to cooperate and stay with your detail. Is that clear, Sophia?"

Sophia yawned and lightly nodded. Alexa caught the barely-there agreement, so she let it go. She missed Sophia's smirk.

Alexa reached into her purse and retrieved a pendant. "Here." She handed it to Sophia.

"What's this?"

"It's a dragonfly pendant."

"I can see that, but why are you giving it to me?"

"Because I need you to wear it. It's for security. If there's ever an emergency and you need me, press the wings together for five seconds and release. That activates the emergency beacon, and I'll be able to find you anywhere."

Sophia examined the diamond dragonfly with the emerald wings. "This is so lame," she complained, securing it to her jacket. Her fingers ran over the wings. "Not bad for an imitation."

Alexa shook her head before turning her attention to some briefings she needed to review.

Sophia had several business engagements in Los Angeles and was a guest judge at a contest for aspiring jewelry designers. After landing, Alexa's local team waited to escort them to the Beverly Wilshire hotel. The competition was held in the Burgundy meeting room. Afterward, several fans asked for a picture with Sophia or her autograph. To Alexa's surprise, they stayed until she was done with every fan's request.

"It's time to go," Alexa gently reminded her. "The club opening is soon, and we still need to change."

Sophia was attending a friend of Ruben Tyndale's grand opening for his new nightclub, so they stayed at a guest house in Pacific Palisades that belonged to Alexa's colleague Alejandro "Dro" Reyes. He owned a crisis management company in Chicago. The two often collaborated on assignments with Dr. Marena Dash-McKendrick. Alexa was thrilled to see them working with her. In the field, Dragonfly operatives relied heavily on Marena's tech inventions, while Alejandro's network of global assets provided them with an edge.

Alejandro's house was in a quiet neighborhood, far from the street, and had a fenced backyard that aided in privacy.

Alexa's room was next to Sophia's, making it easy to watch the headstrong young woman. Or so Alexa thought. When it was time to go, Sophia could not be found.

Alexa's team scrambled to locate her and was about to go on a massive search when Alexa's communication manager alerted her that she had spotted a post of Sophia on her social media page from outside by the pool and grotto.

Taking a deep breath, she counted to five. "Go retrieve Miss Porter," she quietly informed one of her officers.

The dance club was packed by the time they arrived. Sophia was ushered to a VIP area at the back of the club that Alexa was happy to see was away from the heavily populated main dance floor. It was a younger crowd, so Alexa chose younger-looking operatives who were easily able to blend in. The club was U-shaped, with bars set up around the perimeter of the room and the dance floor in the middle. Strobe lights danced off every surface, along with the DJ's light show that was synced with the music he played. The repetitious thumping of the club music made it difficult to carry on a conversation without having to yell.

"Stay sharp," she cautioned her team before escorting Sophia to her table.

Sophia didn't take long to announce that she wanted to dance. Alexa allowed it but had several people placed strategically around the dance floor, watching their principal's every move. The man Sophia was dancing with kept putting his hands on her rear end, which she kept moving.

Finally, he got tired of that and attempted to wrap his hands around Sophia's shoulders to pull her close. Alexa saw Sophia struggle against him and rushed to her side. In one fluid motion, she maneuvered herself between her protectee and the dancer.

He reared back in surprise. "Hey, what is this?" he demanded. "I'm dancing with what's her name, not you."

"I'm afraid your time's up," Alexa replied with a smile. "I suggest you find someone else to occupy your time."

"I don't think so."

He went to step around Alexa, but she shifted until she was in front of him again. He was shorter than she was, so he had to glance up when he spoke.

"What are you doing?" he complained. "Look, lady, you're pretty, but I'd have gone outside if I wanted to climb a tree."

Alexa smiled. "Why, thank you. Pick a new dance partner."

He stood his ground. "I don't think so. I like the one I have. This chick is hot."

He tried to force Alexa out of the way, but she grabbed him as if she would hug him. But instead, she grasped his wrists, twisted them around so they were facing upward and applied pressure.

"Ow, that hurts," he roared over the music thumping around them.

Alexa smiled sweetly. "It's supposed to. Now get lost."

She passed him off to another agent and went to Sophia's side. "We're leaving," was all she said.

"But why? The night's still young, and I'm having a good time. Well, I was until that man couldn't take a hint."

"Sophia, that's not likely to improve the longer people drink."

"Well, you handled him, didn't you? So what's wrong

with me staying? You seem to have everything under control."

"Yes, and I'd like it to stay that way."

After escorting Sophia back to the car, Alexa held the door while she got in, then slid onto the seat next to her charge. During the ride, the only thing that could be heard was Sophia's music playing on her cell phone. Eventually, she turned that off and faced Alexa.

"Are you planning to sit and not talk the entire ride home? Is that supposed to punish me? If so, you're falling a little short."

Alexa didn't bother to reply. Instead, she focused on the passing scenery.

Sophia kicked off her shoes and pulled her legs up under her. "I just wanted to enjoy myself without the entourage in tow."

Praying for calm, Alexa said, "You can do that after the threats have ceased. Ruben hired us for a reason—remember?"

Sophia snorted and began to flip through the pictures on her cell phone. "How can I forget? My style has been permanently cramped ever since."

Incredulous, Alexa turned to face her. "And isn't your life worth a little inconvenience?"

That gave her pause. Sophia instantly looked contrite. "You're right," she said grudgingly. "I apologize."

Satisfied, Alexa added, "Make sure you relay that to those officers that you ditched. They're the ones who got reprimanded for your disappearing act."

"Alexa, we have a challenge car." Her driver glanced at his rearview mirror again. "Two cars back on the right. At five o'clock."

Turning around, she spotted the dark sedan. "I see it, Anthony. Where is car number two?"

Dyan got on the radio. "Stuck one light back," she reported after a moment. "ETA five minutes."

She turned back around. "We need some air, Anthony."

"Yes, ma'am."

The twin turbo engine roared to life as the driver sped up to put some distance between them and the other vehicle.

"Who is it?" Sophia kept glancing back over her shoulder.

"We don't know yet," Alexa replied. "Don't worry. We'll lose them."

The BMW 750i cornered well as Anthony maneuvered in and out of traffic.

"Time?" Alexa asked.

"They're coming up now," Dyan confirmed.

Their second car, a Cadillac Escalade ESV, dropped in behind them and stayed at a safe but close distance.

Heading west on Interstate 10, Anthony used the opportunity to whip past a few slower-moving cars. Then he hit the gas, and the powerful sedan roared to life and took off down the highway. Traffic wasn't heavy, so they made it home in twelve minutes.

They drove up the long driveway and parked out front. Team members were waiting to assist. One opened the back door for Alexa. She got out first, then escorted Sophia inside and straight to her room.

"What was that all about?" Sophia inquired.

"Don't worry, we'll find out," Alexa assured her. "Get some rest. I'll see you in the morning."

Returning downstairs, Alexa entered the kitchen and got some hot tea. Dyan was already there.

"The passengers in the sedan following us were some overzealous fans. They were trying to get close enough to get some photos of Sophia."

"They were being reckless and dangerous," Alexa argued. She chose a tea pod, dropped it into the brewing machine and pressed the button. "They could've caused an accident—or worse."

Alexa rubbed her shoulders while she waited for her cup to fill.

"There's something else," Dyan replied, scanning over her notes. "It may not be anything, but one of them had a tattoo on his hand that I've seen before."

Opening the pantry, Alexa glanced around for a snack. "Tattoos are pretty common."

"Not this one. Let me do some research, and I'll let you know."

Finding a pack of Pepperidge Farm Chessmen cookies, Alexa picked up her mug and took a seat at the table across from Dyan.

"Have we found her boyfriend yet?"

"No, but we did a preliminary report and background check on Nicholas Michaux. We're still waiting to hear back from the forensic accountants."

"Thanks, Dyan. Keep me posted."

Alexa's cell phone rang. "Sorry, I've got to take this," she said before answering.

"No problem." Dyan got up and waved goodbye on her way out.

"Hi, Dad."

"Hey, Lex. How's everything? You haven't called in a while, so I wanted to check in to ensure everything is okay?"

"We wanted to check in," Margot corrected over speakerphone.

Picking up her snack, Alexa moved into the living room and sat down. "It's good to hear both your voices. I've missed you."

"We're only a phone call away, honey," her mother replied. "So what's got you so tied up that you can't call home?"

Taking a sip of tea, Alexa closed her eyes and leaned back against the plush cushion. "Not what, who. I've been hired to protect Sophia Porter."

There was a considerable pause before her parents spoke.

"Are you serious? After all that's happened, you've taken Sophia on as a client? Lex, what were you thinking?" her mother hissed. "That family has caused you nothing but pain."

"Mom, I didn't know she was the client when I took the contract."

"Well, now you do, and you can recuse yourself."

She sat forward. "Dad—"

"Alexa, I'm with your mother on this one. Why put yourself through this?"

"Because it's my job," she countered, pinching the bridge of her nose. "Regardless of my feelings, I was hired to protect Sophia. Which I'll do to the best of my ability."

"You're asking for trouble," Margot interjected. "Sophia Porter is selfish and cruel, and tried to make your life a living hell after the attack. And if I know Carol's daughter, she's probably still trying to make you suffer."

# Chapter 22

Andrew drove up to the Capital Grille, an upscale steak-house on Pennsylvania Avenue in Northwest Washington, DC. Across the street from the Federal Trade Commission and the National Gallery of Art, the well-known restaurant was also in view of the United States Capitol and a regular haunt of the District of Columbia's political and business scene. After getting out, Andrew adjusted his suit jacket, handed the keys to the valet parking attendant and went inside. Rich African mahogany paneling and art deco chandeliers were an apropos backdrop to the dark leather chairs and stark white linen. The superlative service was to be expected from a restaurant that was famous for its dry-aged steaks, fresh seafood and worldwide acclaimed wines. While he scanned the interior, he tried to contain his excitement. He would be meeting Alexa for dinner.

The hostess escorted Andrew to a booth at the back of the main dining room. Alexa stood and enveloped him in a hug. His arms encircled her waist as he returned the embrace.

"Welcome to DC, Drew."

"Thanks, Lexi," he replied warmly before sliding into the booth. "I was pleasantly surprised to receive your invitation."

"Why surprised?"

"Well, as busy as you've been with your new client, I thought you'd be tied up until further notice."

She placed the napkin back in her lap and took a sip of her water with lemon.

"Dyan's with Sophia for the next few days at another event."

"She seems to be keeping you busy."

"That's an understatement," Alexa replied. "When we're not arguing over her intense dislike of me, we are working overtime to keep her out of trouble. She enjoys trying to find new ways to ditch her protection detail. I swear sometimes it's like guarding a toddler."

He grinned. "Sophia Porter sounds like the perfect assignment to test your mettle."

"That's an understatement," Alexa shot back.

After the hostess had provided their menus and departed, he turned back to Alexa. "I must admit that I was surprised to get your invitation."

"Well, you did say you wanted us to get together soon."

"True," Andrew agreed. "But a weekend at your parents' house? Won't that send the wrong message?"

"Of course not. They've been briefed," she explained. "And they're fully aware that we're the best of friends without any romantic entanglements."

A humorous expression jetted across his face. He refrained from pointing out that they were way past the "just friends" stage, but he merely said, "Sounds good."

The waiter arrived to take drink and appetizer orders.

Alexa chose the lobster bisque and a glass of chardonnay.

"I'll have an iced tea and the calamari," he said, handing back the menu.

"So, how's work?" she asked when they were alone.

"Busy as usual, but I can't complain. With Dad scaling back on his hours, I've been interviewing for a director of operations at Phalanx."

"Married life must be treating him well if he's reducing his workload."

"I think everyone is shocked at him and Esther deciding to elope. The way he tells it, they didn't have time for a long-drawn-out wedding."

"Hey, there's nothing wrong with wanting the rest of your life to start sooner rather than later after declaring your feelings to the one you love. On the contrary, I think it's romantic."

"At least there were no whispers of a shotgun wedding," Andrew joked.

Alexa almost choked on her water. "Yeah, I think that ship has sailed."

"Seriously, though, I couldn't be happier for them. I'm glad that Dad put himself out there. It's been so long since Mom died. I didn't think he'd find that type of connection again, but Esther is a wonderful woman, and I'm pleased to call her my stepmother."

"She is exceptional. When I was there for training, I remember how warm and welcoming she was to me—to everyone."

"At Phalanx, Esther is everyone's mother. That's one of the things that makes being there special," Andrew pointed out. "She helps keep the trainees from being homesick."

When the waiter delivered their food, they lapsed into companionable silence while they ate.

"Oh, thank you for introducing me to Marena," Andrew said between bites. "Her devices have come in handy on several occasions."

"You're welcome, and I'm glad. She's so talented and has made my job much easier."

"Don't I know it," he agreed. "I've already used one of the cuff links that can be used as an infrared device."

"I've got a compact that does the same thing," she said excitedly. "And I've had to use it twice already."

"I think Marena will never be at a loss for business."

"Don't I know it," Alexa laughed. "But I've already told her she must continue using Dragonfly as her proving ground."

"Oh, she needs to add Phalanx to that list!"

Andrew was interrupted by a cell phone call. It was work, so he excused himself to take it. Alexa watched him walk away. She took a moment to appreciate how good he looked in the dark gray suit and a black shirt unbuttoned at the neck. The cut of his jacket accentuated his broad shoulders. Watching him made Alexa flustered to where she took a healthy sip of ice water.

It was getting difficult for her to deny that thoughts of Andrew had been plaguing her lately. So much so that she'd invited him to DC to her parents' Winter Serve Weekend on a whim. She hadn't thought he'd say yes, and when he did, it filled Alexa with excitement that he was coming and trepidation that her parents might bombard him with questions all weekend.

It was a family tradition they had been doing since her grandfather's time. Friday, guests would arrive and get settled. Saturday, her family would spend an afternoon passing out winter coats and supplies at the homeless shelters, followed by a black-tie fundraiser event at a country club in Upper Marlboro, Maryland. Sunday was church service followed by an afternoon of board games. Alexa's family was competitive, which she'd warned Andrew about in advance. He merely smiled and assured her that he would be fine. *Famous last words*, she thought to herself.

They headed to her parents' house after dinner. Alexa had been dropped at the restaurant by a rideshare service so that she could go back with Andrew. She was excited to use the drive home to spend some alone time with him before her parents swooped in to bombard him with questions and likely embarrassing stories of her childhood. She loved them dearly, but they could go overboard at a moment's notice.

When he got into the car, he grunted. It caught Alexa's attention.

"Are you okay?"

"Yes, for the most part."

She turned in her seat. "What does that mean?" she said warily.

"I hurt my back a few days ago. Sometimes it flares up when I move wrong."

"Oh." Concern for him caused Alexa to reach out and touch the back of his head before resting her hand on the nape of his neck. "Did you get injured during training?"

"No."

"On assignment?"

"Sort of."

She let out a frustrated sigh. "Drew."

"Okay." He chuckled while keeping his eyes on the road. "I was trying to break up a fight, and a large, angry woman decided to use me to break her fall."

Alexa tried to hold in her laugh, but it was pointless. Instead, she dissolved into a fit of giggles.

"I'm glad my hernia amuses you," he said dryly.

She wiped the tears from her eyes with the back of her sleeve.

"I'm sorry, I just… I can see the visual in my mind and can't get rid of it."

Despite his stern expression, Andrew eventually shared in the laughter.

When they arrived, Alexa directed him where to park. After opening her door, he retrieved his bag from the trunk.

"If you'd rather sit out on some festivities, I completely understand."

"No way," he said as he walked with Alexa to the door. "I've carried a wounded, unconscious woman on my back for miles. I think I can handle a little muscle strain."

"Very funny," she shot back. "And it wasn't miles."

"How would you know?" he countered. His eyebrows arched with merriment. "Weren't you passed out?"

Alexa found out after the shooting incident that it was Andrew who'd rushed her to the on-site infirmary after Edgar Jeffries had shot her during the training exercise.

With an indignant huff, Alexa glided past him and went to open the front door, but her father beat her to it.

"Perfect timing," Jake King announced as he stepped aside to allow them to enter. "Everyone just arrived."

Margot joined them in the vestibule. She hugged her daughter.

"Hello, sweetheart."

"Mom, Dad, I'd like to introduce you to Andrew Riker."

"The last time we met, I believe you were seven," Jake replied, shaking his free hand.

Andrew set his bag down. "It's been a while, sir."

"Welcome to our home," Margot enthused before giving him a big hug. "I hope you don't mind, but we're huggers," she explained.

"I don't mind at all." Andrew returned the embrace. "Thank you for having me."

"Of course," she replied before eyeing her daughter. "Any friend of Alexa's is a friend of ours." She turned to her husband. "Jake, this is a precedent, wouldn't you say?"

"Mom," Alexa hissed.

"What?" her mother responded sweetly. "I know you didn't expect us to fall for that 'we're just friends' thing, did you?"

Alexa closed her eyes and tried to remain calm. "It's not a thing. It's the truth."

"Andrew," her father said quickly. "Come on in and make yourself at home. Don't worry about your luggage. We'll take that upstairs later. My brother Curtis, his wife, Ernestine, and my nephew, Zane, arrived not too long ago and are all dying to meet you."

The moment the two men headed down the hall to the family room, Alexa spun around to face her mother.

"Did you have to blindside him two seconds after we stepped through the door?"

"That's not what I did."

"Mom, it's exactly what you did."

"Honey, your boyfriend will be fine. You know it's trial by fire around here. Can I help it if you didn't warn him?"

"He's not my… I already told you both that Andrew and I are just friends."

"I'll reserve my judgment for later," her mother replied before hooking her arm through Alexa's and heading to the family room. "Do you *really* want him to have a separate bedroom, or was that just for show?"

Before Alexa could open her mouth to protest, her mother chuckled. "Did you know that your right eye still twitches when you're about to have a conniption? Oh, Lex, this will be such a fun weekend!"

# Chapter 23

"Gates, I don't know where you are, but you need to call me ASAP!" Nicholas snapped before pressing the end-call button on his cell phone.

*This is insane*, he told himself. *How could Gates set me up like this?* This wasn't just a simple misunderstanding. If he didn't find Siren's bracelet, he was a dead man.

"No luck?" The Siren's henchman snickered. "Personally, I hope you don't find it. I'd love to rearrange your face, pretty boy."

"Will you shut up?" Nicholas groused. "This isn't helping."

The man bolted out of his chair.

"Spare me the flexing," Nicholas said tiredly. "We both know you're not going to hurt me."

"Yet," the man snarled. "Sooner or later, Siren will get tired of this goose chase you're playing and give me the approval to end you."

"Until then," Nicholas stressed in a bravado he didn't feel, "I'm untouchable."

His aggressor patted his jacket pocket. "For now."

Thinking of another number, he turned his back and called another contact.

"Bruce." He sighed with relief when the phone was answered. "I need a favor—"

"Oh no you don't. You haven't paid me for the last favor you owe me. If you were here right now, I'd have you killed."

"Get in line," Nicholas said dryly. He got up and moved to the opposite side of the room to get a modicum of privacy.

"Look, I know I owe you money. I'm good for it. You know that. But right now, I need to know where Gates is at."

"Uh-uh. I don't know anything anymore. Especially not for free."

Nicholas turned and faced the wall. "Come on," he pleaded. "This is life-and-death."

"Not from where I'm standing."

"Bruce, I'm serious. Gates stole something. From the wrong person," he added. "I need to get it back—or else."

"Or else what?"

"The Siren will come looking for anyone that Gates knows or has come in contact with, whether they have her bracelet or not."

"Wait, Gates lifted jewelry from the Siren?"

"Yes."

Nicholas was tapped on the shoulder. He turned around.

"Time's up. Siren wants to see you."

"I gotta go. Think about what I said," he whispered into the phone. "You aren't safe, either."

"I'll see what I can do," his friend replied noncommittally.

"Yeah, you do that—and fast."

"Give me twenty-four hours," Bruce replied, and hung up.

Nicholas didn't know if he had twenty-four minutes, much less hours.

This time he was taken to a garden. He found the Siren pruning a rosebush.

*Oh, great. She's a green thumb in addition to being an assassin.*

"How's progress, Mr. Michaux?"

He shifted on his feet. "I'm not going to lie. It's slow. I need more time if you want me to locate this bourgeois bracelet of yours."

Siren smiled and removed one of her gloves. "I thought I was clear in my intent," she said with a baffled expression.

Without warning, she walked over to Nicholas and punched him in the solar plexus, followed by an uppercut to the jaw. With a grunt and then a round of violent coughing, he dropped to his knees.

"I have killed men smarter and cuter than you. Your logistical problems are not my problems, Mr. Michaux."

"I get that." The metallic taste of blood in his mouth wasn't the only thing that made him queasy. He was still having difficulty breathing.

Turning to her employee, she said, "Take him to my office. If he doesn't provide Miss Porter's account number the moment after you've arrived, cut off a finger every minute that I don't have what I want."

"No, wait," Nicholas yelled as he was grabbed by the arm and escorted out. He fought every step of the way. "Don't do this!"

The Siren grinned. "Ah, nothing like motivation," she called after him before returning to gardening.

Alexa, her family and Andrew were in the kitchen when she received a telephone call.

"Excuse me, I have to take this," Alexa replied when her phone rang.

"How's everything going?" Dyan asked when Alexa answered.

"Not bad. We're having a great time."

"I'm sorry to disturb you at your parents' house."

"No worries, Dyan. What's up?"

"We heard back from the forensic accountants. I emailed you the report of findings."

"Hang on a sec," she said, rushing up to her bedroom. Sitting at her desk, she opened her laptop and checked her email. After reviewing the document, Alexa leaned back in her chair.

"Well, this likely won't go well."

"I don't doubt it," Dyan agreed. "Do you want me to tell her?"

"No, I'll do it."

"Given your history, Alexa, do you think that's wise?"

"Probably not," she said truthfully, "but it's my responsibility. Can you ask Miranda to call me? I need to speak with her on a few things."

"Sure. Have you spoken to her lately?"

"No, why?"

"Yesterday, I ran into her coming out of the ladies' room and she looked like she'd been crying."

Alexa furrowed her brow. "She hasn't said anything."

"To me, either. I asked her what was wrong, and she tried to brush it off. I think it has something to do with her new boyfriend."

"Apollo?"

"Yep. Miranda is as pleasant and cheerful as lemonade in the summertime. But lately, she seems distracted."

Alexa could've kicked herself for not noticing. It didn't sit well that one of her employees was in distress, and she wasn't aware of it.

"Would you ask her to call me?"

"Will do."

She hung up with her associate and reread the report. Alexa let out a weary sigh before tossing it aside. She did not relish Sophia's reaction to hearing about Nicholas's hidden agenda. "And Mom talks about me having a conniption."

Her thoughts turned back to Miranda. Alexa couldn't recall one day when she wasn't her best. Grabbing her phone, she texted Dyan and asked her to do a preliminary background check on Apollo Hayes. Something was up with him, but Alexa couldn't say what. His not meeting Miranda's friends and her not meeting his didn't sit well. For Miranda's sake, she'd look him over to make sure he was everything he claimed to be.

"Hey, you okay? Your mother asked me to come up and check on you. She said we're leaving in fifteen minutes."

Alexa glanced over her shoulder to see Andrew standing just outside the doorway.

"Yes." She set her phone down. "Just an issue at work that I need to take care of."

When he remained, Alexa said, "You can come in, Andrew."

He eased into the room, peering around as he walked.

Alexa's bedroom looked like she hadn't been in it since leaving for college. Two nightstands flanked a full-size canopy bed against one wall. There were multicolored lights draped around the top, a white comforter set with yellow and green flowers, and a few throw pillows. Three books were stacked on one nightstand with a lamp and an alarm clock.

Across the room was an alcove with a plush white couch and flat-screen television mounted to the wall. A large built-in with a vast collection of books anchored the space.

French doors led out onto a balcony with white wicker furniture and floral-colored cushions. The walls were white, but there were colorful landscapes and pictures of animals hanging around the room. The space was neat, orderly and composed, just like Alexa.

"Finished scoping out my old room?"

A glimmer of amusement sparkled in his eyes. "Not yet."

Andrew walked over and sat on the love seat. "How long has it been since you've slept in here?"

"Usually just holidays."

"That's cool."

Shutting her laptop, Alexa joined him on the couch. "Yep, one of the duties of an only child. Make yourself available for all family functions."

He laughed. "True." He curled a lock of her hair around his fingers.

"It's nice seeing another piece of the Alexa puzzle."

Her eyebrows shot up. "I'm a puzzle?"

"Yes, indeed," he replied. "And I'm enjoying learning how the pieces fit together."

"I'm hardly as exciting as you make me out to be."

He inched closer, regarding Alexa as if he was studying something intriguing. "You are to me."

Alexa found it hard to breathe under the sheer weight of his gaze. Her heartbeat pounded in her ears. She wondered if he could hear it.

Andrew held out his hand. Alexa didn't hesitate to lock her fingers with his. He kissed the back of her hand. "I have to admit, I'm feeling kinda honored right now."

"Why?"

"Because I'm the only man that's been in your inner sanctum."

"How do you know that?" Alexa tossed back. "I've had a man or two in here before."

"Your family doesn't count. Besides, your mother told me."

Alexa closed her eyes and tried to contain her embarrassment. She and her mother were going to have a talk about boundaries.

When she felt the touch of his fingers along her cheek, her eyes flew open.

She wasn't prepared for her reaction to the desire in Andrew's gaze or the way his hand drifted down to her neck.

His fingers touched the pulse point. "Your heartbeat is elevated."

"You don't say?"

Alexa's voice drifted out like an intimate caress. Their eyes locked briefly before he lowered his head and replaced his fingers with his lips.

Her hands closed around his neck and held his head stationary. Leaning into his touch, Alexa didn't protest when Andrew deepened the kiss.

Andrew's weight pinned her back against the cushions.

Her body hummed with excitement as her hands roamed his back, shoulders and the nape of his neck.

"Lexi," Andrew murmured against her lips, trailing kisses down her throat. "You don't know how incredible you feel."

"About as good as you do right now."

Everywhere Alexa caressed, Andrew's skin felt hot to the touch. At that moment, she wanted him with a passion so consuming that it took her several moments to realize he was saying her name.

"What?" she finally managed to say.

He kissed her a final time and said, "Your mother is calling you."

Alexa didn't think. She just reacted.

"Yes?" she yelled so loud that Andrew scrunched up his face in reaction.

"I'm now deaf in one ear."

"Let's go, you two," her mother bellowed.

Alexa moaned. "We have to go."

He smiled at the genuine frown on her face before kissing the tip of her nose.

"Yes, I know."

"I don't want to," she said frankly.

Andrew buried his face in her neck. "And you think I do?"

Alexa took another moment to enjoy the closeness with Andrew before nudging him.

"We'd better go before she comes looking."

He reluctantly got up and helped Alexa to her feet. After she had adjusted her clothing, Andrew reached up and traced the path she had made to guide the few errant strands away from her face. He continued along her neck and down her shoulder.

Not once had their gazes disengaged. They continued to stare at each other in mutual fascination.

Alexa felt her body swaying closer to Andrew.

*When did that happen?* she wondered. When had she relaxed her "no relationship" policy so completely?

"We should go before your mom sends up a search party," he warned softly.

"Uh, yeah," she replied, clearing her throat. "I wouldn't put it past her."

Alexa moved past Andrew and headed for the door. She didn't need to turn around to check if he was following. The hair tingling at the back of her neck told her all she needed to know.

When they reached the foyer, everyone was putting on their outerwear.

"Perfect timing," her father said gleefully. "We're ready to go."

"Great, I'll go get our coats," she said quickly and bolted to the hall closet. But truthfully, she needed a few moments to gather the wits scattered around her head.

She placed her hand on her heart and felt the rapid staccato beat hammering against her chest. She blew out an exasperated breath.

*Get a hold of yourself, Alexa*, she chided.

For the first time since Andrew arrived, Alexa started doubting her bright idea to open a box she couldn't close. Now that she had tasted a sample of the fruit, she wanted the entire bowl.

Retrieving their coats, Alexa turned around to find Zane standing right behind her with an amused expression on his face.

"You say one word, and I'll put you in a choke hold," she snapped before shoving past him.

"What?" he countered sweetly before dissolving into a fit of laughter.

# *Chapter 24*

The event ended late, so they hurried home to prepare for the black-tie event across town. When Alexa came downstairs after getting dressed, only Andrew was waiting. She glanced around.

"Where'd everyone go?"

"Since your mother was the event chair, they went on ahead so they wouldn't be too late."

"Oh. Not like I took that long," she muttered, reaching the bottom step.

She finally noticed that Andrew was wearing a black tuxedo with a red bow tie and red silk pocket square. Alexa had to force herself not to gape. He looked more handsome than when she'd seen him in Chamonix, and that was saying something!

Alexa watched him look her over from head to toe before saying, "Lexi, you look breathtaking."

Her face lit up at his praise. It had taken her forever to get dressed, and up until that moment, she had second-guessed every choice. Now she was glad that she had chosen a black satin floor-length gown. It had an hourglass design that was outlined by rhinestones. The arms and low-cut back of the dress were sheer.

"Thank you," Alexa responded as he helped her into a long velvet coat. "You look wonderful, too."

Not releasing her lapels, Andrew backed Alexa up until she was against the wall. Startled, her expression showed her surprise.

"What are you doing?"

"Admiring the view," Andrew quipped before touching her cheek. "You are so beautiful, Alexa King."

She did not get a chance to reply before Andrew kissed her with a heat that could have lit a wet match.

"Drew, we have to go," she whispered against his lips. "Any longer and they'll think we're not coming."

"If the alternative is staying here with you in my arms, I see nothing but upside."

Eventually, he released her coat, but did not let her go. Instead, he rested his forehead against hers.

"Thank you," he whispered against her lips.

"For what?"

"For allowing me to know you better. For a glimpse into your personal life—to *see* you."

Alexa was ready to dissolve into a puddle on her parents' marble floor.

Her line of sight moved from holding his gaze down to his lips. Instead, it lingered on the rapidly beating pulse at his neck.

"Lexi, that's dangerous," he warned.

Her glance traveled back up to his eyes. "I deal with danger every day, remember?"

"Not this kind."

Before she could retort, Andrew held her wrist out of the way before crushing her body against his chest. His mouth claimed hers for a searing kiss. The power of it took Alexa's breath away.

"That wasn't dangerous at all," she murmured against his mouth.

In a flash, Andrew picked Alexa up. Her legs locked around his waist as he backed them up against the closet door. Her gown bunched in yards of silky fabric between them. Before she could react, he kissed a trail from her lips to her neck. He lingered at the spot where her pulse beat out a rapid staccato against her skin.

"Are we just friends, Alexa?"

"Hmm?" she said in a dazed whisper.

Andrew leaned closer. His lips floated just above her

skin and hovered over her ear. His warm breath caressed her as he spoke.

"Tell me that you feel nothing but friendship for me. Say you don't want me as much as I want you, Alexa, and I will never mention it again."

She gravitated toward his touch. A small moan escaped her lips.

"Andrew."

Andrew Riker would run away with her heart if she let him. And right now, Alexa wasn't sure she would stop him, and that scared her to death.

When they arrived, the party had already begun. They picked up name tags at the entrance, where there was a long-stemmed red rose for each lady. A hostess directed them to their family's table, where she found her aunt and uncle sitting.

"Where's everyone?" Alexa asked as Andrew helped her out of her coat.

"Zane and his date are on the dance floor. Your parents are making the rounds," Ernestine replied. "My, don't both of you look gorgeous."

"So do you," Alexa replied with a kiss on her cheek.

Andrew placed a hand on her back and leaned in. "What do you say, Alexa? Will you dance with me?"

"I'd love to." She beamed at Andrew, allowing him to lead her to the floor.

"This is 'Corcovado,'" she informed him as he swept her into his arms. "It's one of my favorites."

"Mine, too."

Andrew guided her into a bossa nova dance. Alexa laughed as they glided together in unison. "You're full of surprises, Mr. Riker."

"So are you, Miss King."

After the dance, Alexa went to the ladies' room to freshen up. As she was coming out, a woman called after her.

"Alexa King, is that you?"

Turning, Alexa's mouth dropped open. "Andi?"

"Yes," the woman cried and, throwing up her arms, rushed across the room to gather Alexa in a loose bear hug.

"My goodness, it's wonderful to see you!"

When she finally released her, Alexa stared at Oleander Barlowe, her former roommate, with genuine shock.

"How have you been? Honestly, you haven't changed a bit since college," the woman gushed.

"I hope that's not the case," Alexa retorted. "So, what are you doing here?"

"A client of mine invited me. You know me, always working, and stuffy events like these are the perfect place to land new clients."

*Same old ambitious Oleander. She would never let a roomful of rich people go to waste*, Alexa noted.

Latching arms with Alexa, Oleander said, "So, what have you been up to?"

She grabbed a glass of champagne off a waiter's serving tray as they walked.

"Still working for your dad's company, married with a slew of kids, a minivan and a quaint Cape Cod in the suburbs?"

"Not exactly." Alexa brought her up to speed on life since college.

"No kidding? How fortuitous that we ran into each other."

Setting her empty glass on a high table, Oleander retrieved a business card from her velvet clutch and handed it to Alexa. "Let's keep in touch, I can definitely send some clients your way—if you return the favor, of course." She winked.

"Oh, uh, sure."

"Thanks, love. You always were dependable."

Alexa glanced around for Andrew so she could introduce them. When their eyes connected across the room, her hap-

piness was crushed by his look of surprise and then pain.
A second later, Andrew stormed out of the room.

*What just happened?* she asked herself.

Disentangling herself from Oleander's arm, Alexa excused herself and rushed out of the room to find Andrew.

Slamming out of the ballroom, Andrew strode down the corridor and out the back door. It was frigid outside, but it didn't register. His emotions were a jumbled mess of broken promises, betrayal and regret.

There, right in front of him, was Alexa talking to the woman who had smashed his heart to pieces before devouring it like chocolates on Valentine's Day. His worst nightmare had just come true. Now he knew why there was a reason Alexa had reminded him of Olee. They were the best of friends!

Bile rose into his throat, and his palms grew sweaty. He hadn't listened to his gut instinct trying to warn him about Alexa King, and now he was paying for it.

Taking a minute to get his anger under control, Andrew eventually went back inside. When he did, he was brought up short by a woman blocking his path.

"Hello, Andrew."

"Olee."

The one word was laced with a perfect balance of surprise at her audacity and hatred. If Oleander was affected at his tone, she did not show it.

She smiled. "I'm surprised you still remember that nickname you gave me."

"I haven't forgotten anything over the years," he said in a barely controlled voice. "What are you doing here?"

"Isn't it obvious? Hobnobbing with the wealthy benefactors, same as you."

"That's not why I'm here."

Her voice grated on his nerves, making him long to get

away. Not willing to bear her presence longer than necessary, Andrew got straight to the point.

"How do you know Alexa King?"

"Alexa?" she shot back with a raised eyebrow. "I could ask you the same question."

Seeing that he was waiting for an answer, Oleander shrugged. "We met in college. We were best friends and roommates. We were inseparable. Can you imagine running into each other again? It's like the years just melted away."

Seeing Andrew frown, Oleander continued. "So, what's your story?"

"We're colleagues," he said, not elaborating.

"Ah. Alexa and I are meeting for lunch in a few days. I have a joint venture I wanted to discuss. It should be very lucrative." She gleamed.

Andrew let out a contemptuous laugh. "You haven't changed a bit, Oleander. Ambition still overrides everything else—except your love of money."

"Neither have you," she shot back. "Still holding grudges. You plan on taking what happened to your grave, I see."

A couple walking by spared the two a curious glance. Andrew took her elbow and guided her down the hall back toward the party.

"I can tell you now that Alexa isn't interested in any proposition you might concoct."

She yanked her arm free of his grasp and stopped walking. "I'd wager that I know Alexa a lot better than you do," Oleander threw back.

His jaw ticked. "Alexa is nothing like you."

Oleander went to slide her hand under his tux jacket. "If you say so," she said smugly. "We couldn't have been besties all those years and not have a few things in common."

Capturing her wrist before she could touch him, Andrew leaned in.

"You know, I don't know what's worse. The fact that

you don't even acknowledge your part in our breakup, or the fact that you're still only interested in using people."

Her once-amiable expression darkened. "People in glass houses should steer clear of stones, lover."

Not bothering to respond, Andrew looked at her disgustedly before leaving. When he rounded a corner, he almost collided with Alexa. His hands instantly reached out to steady her.

"Andrew. I've been looking everywhere for you." She sighed with relief. "What's going on? I looked up, and you'd disappeared."

"Did you invite Oleander Barlowe here?"

Alexa was taken aback by his tone. "No. We went to college together. I haven't seen her in years."

"What did she want?"

Alexa frowned. "She asked to meet with me in a few days to catch up and discuss a business venture.

"Andrew, what is going on with you? You're acting strange."

"Don't do it. Olee can't be trusted and has only ever cared about herself."

"That's not true. We used to be best friends in college."

"So does that mean the two of you are cut from the same cloth?"

Alexa took a step back. His accusation hurt. "Why would you ask that?"

"Because I know her," he snapped. "She'll end up betraying your trust. I'm warning you, don't entertain any business proposition she has for you. You'll jeopardize your reputation fooling around with Oleander Barlowe."

Alexa felt her anger rising. "Andrew, I appreciate your concern, but I don't appreciate you implying I can't handle myself where Andi's concerned."

He threw his hands up in frustration. "Are you that naive? She's a professional grifter, Alexa. She won't hesitate to eat you up and spit out the bones."

"And how would *you* know?"

"Because she did it to me!"

The words shot out of Andrew's mouth like a cannonball. Alexa's eyebrows shot upward. "Andrew, I—"

He held a hand up to stop her. "I don't need your sympathy. You know what, suit yourself, Alexa. You're going to do what you want anyway. It's obvious you don't need me trying to look out for you, right?"

"You're not being fair, Andrew."

"Just admit it. You don't need anything or anyone. You don't *need.*"

The color drained from her face. "That's not true."

"Yeah? You could've fooled me."

# Chapter 25

Andrew stared out the hotel room window. A towel was slung low around his middle. His warm body in proximity to the cold window caused it to fog up, but he was oblivious. There was nothing about his evening that had gone according to plan.

Rubbing a hand over his jaw, Andrew retreated from the window. He padded to the bed and fell back onto the fluffy mattress.

He realized that he had overreacted to Alexa's conversation with Oleander, but at the time was powerless to stop it. He would apologize for his behavior, but the fact that Alexa didn't set him straight only reiterated his point that it was Alexa's pride and fear of commitment keeping them apart. Could he be content waiting for her to accept they were perfect for each other? Should he throw in the towel and walk away? That thought didn't sit well. Andrew had never given up on anything in his life. Especially not something he wanted with a passion that kept him up at night and made him restless.

He cared for Alexa unlike anything he had experienced before. Even his relationship with Oleander paled by comparison, and he had thought himself completely in love with her. Alexa was different. His feelings for her had been way past the level of friendly since before she graduated from Phalanx. He was all in the moment Alexa stared at him with a perfect blend of lust and fascination.

"Come on, Riker. You gotta double your efforts to win her over." And he would, but it was hard to overcome Alexa's trust issues and the past. She was complex, stubborn and trapped in a cycle of fear like a spider's prey dangling from its web. But regardless of how long it took, he'd help her break free. The first thing he would do is give her space. As much as it would kill him to distance himself from her, it was necessary. Alexa needed to come to terms with not just their relationship, but the past. Their future happiness depended on it.

Alexa spent the next week at work putting out fire after fire. Several members of her staff were on leave. Either sick or scheduled, it meant they were short-staffed, so Alexa had to fill the gap. She didn't mind. In truth she was glad for the distraction.

It had been two weeks since she had spoken to Andrew. After their argument at the Christmas fundraiser, she returned home to find him gone. He had left a note thanking her parents for their hospitality and wishing everyone happy holidays. Hurt, Alexa had tried to call, but he didn't answer. Unable to deal with the questions from her parents, Alexa pretended that nothing was wrong and Andrew was called away on an unexpected assignment.

She had regretted her words to him, but his behavior had gotten under her skin. Now, he had retreated behind a wall of cool indifference that made her grit her teeth in frustration.

*What did you expect? You basically told him you didn't trust him and didn't want a relationship*, her inner voice scolded. Plus, pride kept her from setting the record straight on working with Oleander Barlowe. She didn't trust Andi, but she had neglected to tell Andrew that, which in retrospect had only made matters worse. *You got exactly what you wanted, so leave it alone.*

With her relationship with Andrew in tatters, Alexa threw herself into the job. Everyone at work had noticed the change in her mood, and that she had not mentioned Andrew, but no one pressed her on it. Not even Dyan and Miranda.

Her latest assignment was protecting a widowed businessman, Nigel Weatherby, and his young son while they were going to London for a tech conference in Kensington. His company rented out a luxurious seven-bedroom house in Chelsea, an affluent area in central London. It was close to the River Thames, Harrods and Michelin-star dining. In addition to Alexa's team, his nanny accompanied him, as did his assistant. Her principal enjoyed jogging, so they would go out at night after his son went to bed and the house was quiet.

The rental was close to Chelsea Embankment, a road and a walkway along the river's north bank.

While jogging and running weren't two of Alexa's favorites, she did them if it was a client's preference.

They jogged almost two miles in silence before Nigel slowed the pace to cool down. It was cold out, so their walk was brisk.

"So, why does a woman like you get into executive protection?"

She fell into step beside him. "A woman like me?"

"Tall, beautiful and pleasant to be around. From your looks, though, you don't look like you've been in many fights."

"I assure you that I have. It takes more work to avoid physical altercations than to get into them."

"Then you must have a knack for it, because you look like you've been behind a desk all day," Nigel observed. "So, is there a mister bodyguard at home?"

Alexa laughed. The heat from her breath caused a cloud of condensation. Was he flirting? If so, she would firmly shut him down. It was her company policy that employees never got romantically involved with clients. And even if it weren't, Nigel wasn't the one.

Alexa snapped out of her daydream. "No, there's not," she said quickly. "Just a lot of houseplants that keep dying off."

"I know the feeling," he responded. "Luckily for me,

I have a live-in housekeeper who keeps on top of all the greenery."

They continued to chat while they walked. Alexa enjoyed his company, and though relaxed, she was alert. After walking a short distance, she spotted two men approaching, so she stepped in front of her client while continually chatting.

"Pardon me? Do you have a light?" one of the men asked.

"No, sorry, I don't," her client replied.

The stranger glanced over at Alexa. "What about you?"

"What about me?"

"Do you have a light?"

"No," she said sweetly. "I don't."

"How about that watch?" he countered, motioning to her client's wrist.

"If you think I'm—"

Alexa rested her hand on her client's forearm and squeezed lightly. He stopped talking, but his anger was still evident in his stance.

She raised both hands. "We don't want any trouble," Alexa said, keeping her eyes on his hands the entire time.

"Too late," the man in front of her replied with a grin before he lunged.

His hand came up, and Alexa saw the knife. Immediately, she grabbed his wrist and pinned his hand against her leg while rotating with him to get him away from her client. Then she struck him under the chin and didn't wait to see him collapse before turning on the other assailant going after her client.

Grabbing the back of his jacket, Alexa yanked him backward and down to the ground, where she delivered an elbow strike to the stomach. Unfortunately, his coat was thick, so she had to hit him twice.

"Let's go," she commanded, pulling her client along as she broke into a run.

Alexa glanced back twice to ensure they weren't being followed.

"We're clear," she announced at the end of the block.

Two men were running from the house to intercept them.

"Miss King," one of them huffed. "We saw you running. Are you both all right?"

"We're fine, thanks," she said, ushering her principal up the walkway and through the front door.

"Thanks to you." Nigel leaned over to catch his breath. "Your quick thinking kept that situation from being much worse."

"That's what we're here for," she countered.

He reached out for the wall. "I feel a little light-headed."

"That's the adrenaline rush. It'll go back to normal soon."

He nodded. "I'm going to go take a shower and then check on my son. Thanks again, Alexa."

"You're welcome. Good night."

Alexa was surprised to find her bed turned down and a fire roaring in the fireplace when she came into the room.

Decorated in taupe and cream with rose-gold accents, the room was relaxing.

After a shower, Alexa donned a pair of fleece pajamas, climbed into bed and snuggled under the thick comforter. Lying in the luxurious bed wrapped up like a burrito, Alexa's thoughts kept drifting to Andrew. He was the one she always called when she had something on her mind, or after a particularly stressful day or a run-in with a bad guy. Speaking to him made her feel better.

When she heard the indicator for a request for a video chat, Alexa's heart thumped wildly in her chest. *Andrew.*

Alexa grabbed it excitedly. Her elation was dashed when she accepted the call and found Dyan's face on the screen instead. "Oh, hey, Dyan," she said with as much excitement as she could muster in the wake of her intense disappointment.

"Wow," Dyan replied. "I've had more excitement coming from bad guys I've had to beat up than you."

"Oh, I'm sorry. It's not you. I just—"

"Thought I was Andrew?"

"What? No," Alexa countered quickly. "I just had a rough evening. Had a run-in while out with my principal on a late-night jog. Nothing I couldn't handle."

"If that's true, then what caused the rough night?" Dyan countered.

Alexa ignored the knowing grin on her friend's face. Confessing that she missed Andrew with a vengeance and hadn't thought of anything else since he went radio silent wasn't a truth that she was ready to share.

# *Chapter 26*

When Alexa scheduled a meeting with Sophia a few days later, she was exhausted. Jet lag and work were starting to take their toll. To make matters worse, she hadn't connected with her family since returning from London. She had called Andrew and was surprised when she got him. At a loss for what to say, she wished him a happy new year. Andrew had thanked her and wished her the same. He was cordial but distant. After hanging up, Alexa's mood tanked for the rest of the day. Later that afternoon, she had a meeting with Sophia.

As usual, Sophia glided into Alexa's office like she owned it.

When she sat down and finally looked at Alexa, she gasped. "Good grief, you look horrible."

"Thank you," Alexa retorted tiredly. "Sophia, we need to talk."

"Presumably that's why I'm here?"

Ignoring the sarcasm, she retrieved a folder from her desk.

"Are you aware of a joint account with Nicholas in Portugal?"

"What?" Sophia sat forward. "I never opened an account with Nico."

Alexa spun the report around and pushed it across her desk.

Sophia read over the pages before tossing them back. Her face was a mottled red. "This is ridiculous. Clearly, it's a mistake."

"So, you're saying that's not your signature?"

"Uh, what part of forgery isn't coming across? No, that's not my signature. Close, but not exact."

"That's not the only suspicious activity Mr. Michaux has been up to while you've been apart. Didn't he tell you that he was in France?"

Sophia shifted in her chair. "Yes. Why?"

"Well, his cell phone records indicate that he's in Portugal. Just outside of Lisbon."

"So he's not where he said he'd be. He could be hanging out with some friends. We did argue. Likely he's just blowing off some steam."

"Is this one of his friends?" Alexa asked, handing Sophia a photograph.

She scanned the picture of a red-haired woman with Nicholas. Her aloof facade started to slip. "None that I know."

"Her name is Eileen English. Her nickname is the Siren, and she's a dangerous woman. She spent several years in jail for fencing stolen items, extortion and kidnapping. She's been brought up on multiple charges in the last few years, but there was never enough evidence for an arrest. We don't know her connection to Nicholas just yet, but—"

"Why are you investigating my boyfriend? Aren't I the one you're supposed to keep tabs on?"

"Yes," Alexa confirmed. "And those around you who could be potential threats."

"We fought. I'd hardly call him a threat," Sophia scoffed. "You're taking this to the extreme, don't you think?"

"This is what we do, Sophia. We look for suspicious activity that could cause problems for those we protect."

"Well, this has been more intrusive than helpful," Sophia complained. "We've been at this for weeks, and nothing has happened. Clearly, whatever threat I was under is no longer an issue, so it looks like I don't need your services anymore."

"Sophia, we don't know if you're out of danger yet. Therefore, ending your protection is unwise."

"I disagree. I'm done with your team snooping into my

private life. Whatever outstanding balance you have, send me the bill." Sophia jumped up.

"Wait a minute," Alexa replied, rising. "Sophia, I know you're upset about Nicholas, but that's no reason to be reckless and—"

"Oh, *I'm* reckless?" Sophia sputtered. "That's rich coming from you. I knew this was a mistake from the beginning. You haven't changed one bit."

Digging into her purse, Sophia retrieved a checkbook. She filled one out, signed it and slammed it on Alexa's desk.

"Here. I'm sure this more than covers any owed amount."

Alexa didn't bother to take it. "You can't fire me, Sophia. The contract is with Ruben."

"Trust me. He'll side with me when he realizes there's no way we can continue working together. Have a nice life, Alexa King."

Sophia stormed out of the room, almost slamming the door off its hinges.

Alexa bolted out of her chair. "No amount of money is worth this aggravation!"

"Do I even want to know what that was about?" Dyan called from the doorway. Miranda hovered right behind.

"Same Sophia, different day," Alexa muttered. "Just when you think she couldn't act brattier and more entitled, bam! She exceeds your expectations."

"Should I contact Mr. Tyndale for you, Miss King?"

"No, thanks, Miranda. I'll handle this."

Her assistant nodded, then retreated to her desk.

Dyan sat down.

"Alexa, do you—"

"Don't you dare say you think I'm overreacting," Alexa fumed. "*We* are putting our lives on the line for a woman who doesn't appreciate it. And you know what else?"

"You're going to tell me," Dyan said calmly.

"She doesn't waste an opportunity to undermine our efforts." Alexa paced like a caged panther looking for a way out.

"I'll admit that part of the reason I took Sophia on as a client was because I felt guilty about Shelley and wanted to help their family in any way I could, but this is cruel and unusual punishment, Dyan. I'm done putting my employees' lives on the line for someone who doesn't appreciate or deserve the sacrifices we're all making."

"Alexa, I understand. And of course, this is your call. Whatever you want, you know we'll make it happen."

"Thanks, Dyan," Alexa said, plopping onto the couch. "I appreciate the support—and you letting me rant," she added with a smile. "I hope you know how invaluable you are to me."

"Sure I do, Alexa." Dyan came over and hugged her boss and friend. "I'm here if you need me. Oh, by the way. Have you noticed anything off with Miranda?"

"No, like what?"

Dyan shrugged. "I don't know yet. She's just not acting herself. I have to repeat things several times, and she's been jumpy."

"No, I haven't, but I've been meaning to circle back around regarding Apollo Hayes."

"Don't you think you'd better deal with Sophia first?" Dyan reasoned.

"You're not wrong," Alexa agreed before calling Sophia's business partner, Ruben Tyndale, to explain their latest run-in.

"I'm sorry, Alexa. Truly I am," he said ruefully. "I had hoped that Sophia's animosity would have diminished."

"As did I. I gave Sophia some news about Nicholas that she wasn't expecting, and it set her off. I've had time to think about it, and I can understand her lashing out. Even growing up, she was never good with surprises."

Alexa relayed their findings to Ruben.

"What? I can't believe he'd do that to Sophia," Ruben snarled. "I knew he had bad points, but forging documents and possibly embezzling money from her? That's insane— and criminal."

"Sophia is sure there's an explanation for it. So the first order of business is to learn more about why he's hanging out with a dangerous criminal, and how it ties into this new bank account—that is, if we're not fired."

"Earlier, it sounded like you were happy to see her go."

"I was," Alexa admitted. "But that wouldn't solve any of Sophia's problems, would it?"

"No, it wouldn't. And for the record, I was never going to let you go, Alexa. She may not know what's best for her right now, but I do. You and your folks stick by her side. At least until we get all of this mess sorted out."

"How long do you plan to hold me hostage?"

The Siren sat across from Nicholas and waited while one of her servants set a dinner plate in front of her. "Flower Duet" from the French composer Léo Delibes's opera *Lakmé* piped through in-ceiling speakers.

She leaned over and smelled the savory aroma of her chef's latest culinary delight. Her face radiated pleasure as she bit into the medium-rare meat perched on her fork. Siren slowly chewed the food and swallowed before washing it down with a sip of red wine.

"That's a rather harsh word, Nicholas. I'd like to think of you as my guest."

"A guest that isn't allowed to leave of their own volition," he tossed back. "And one that you were more than happy to maim if I didn't provide you with a bank account number. That hardly jibes with my definition of the word."

Nicholas sliced the large rib eye steak and took a hefty bite. It was perfect, but he would never tell his captor that.

Siren motioned to the glass decanter between them. "Wine?"

"No, thank you."

He had no plans to drink anything around the Siren because he'd need his wits about him to come up with a plan to get that bracelet back.

Nicholas wondered about Sophia. Their relationship would be over if she somehow learned about the bank account and him helping the Siren clean her money. He was playing a dangerous game, but his deranged captor had to believe he was on board and getting her bracelet back. She had threatened to chop off his fingers if he didn't.

Desperate for cash to fund his business, he'd done Gates Budreau a favor. Gates had a copy made of the eighteenth-century Bellasini bracelet to sell to some unsuspecting rich man as a gift for his wife. He was mortified to discover the man's wife was Sophia's friend. What if she found out he was involved in the bait and switch? Their relationship would be over.

Nicholas had no idea what his friend had done with the original. He felt like killing Gates himself for involving him in his scheme and putting his life at risk, but how could he blame him? If he'd been the one being tortured instead, he would've said just about anything to save himself.

*Gates must've been betting that I'd be able to get back the counterfeit bracelet*, Nicholas reasoned. *Why else would he say I had it?*

It was a dangerous move trying to trick Siren. After all, she was bound to realize a fake from the real deal. No. It was too dangerous. He needed the original. If not, he had better be on the other side of the world when the Siren found out she had been duped.

Originally, Nicholas had flat-out refused to help, but changed his tune when one of Siren's goons hung him over the tower railing by his ankles.

*At least Sophia is safe*, he told himself. Nicholas knew that Siren's threats were far from idle, and the last thing he wanted was to endanger Sophia's life.

*This is all your fault*, he scolded himself.

Nicholas had been desperate to get his business off the

ground and had no plans to crawl back to his father for more money or involve Sophia. *Now look at me*, he thought bitterly. *That streak of pride may cost me my life. First, I have to find Gates to see who has the original bracelet, and get it back.*

Nicholas didn't know how, but he would convince her to let him go under the guise of getting her precious bracelet. He'd see Gates and force him to give up the whereabouts of the original. If his friend resisted, he'd make him see reason. The first thing he would do if he made it out of the Siren's lair alive would be to contact his father. It was time to put pride aside. He would tell his father that his life was in danger, minus all the details, and pray that his father would assign him a security detail to keep him safe until he located Gates. He was not going to die for anyone.

# Chapter 27

"We're here, sir."

Nicholas completed the payment on the ride-sharing app and thanked his driver.

He still couldn't believe that the Siren had let him go. Not that he was under any illusions. He was only free so that he could convince Gates to give him the bracelet and return it to her. It was also likely that he was being followed, and that his life would be in jeopardy once she got what she wanted.

He got out of the car and walked up to the black wrought-iron gate. Next, Nicholas entered the six-digit pass code and stepped aside while the gate opened. Then, before it fully extended, he ran up the stamped concrete driveway and rang the doorbell several times. Finally, after another minute, he walked around to the side of the house. Spotting the large stone planter, Nicholas picked up one of the decorative rocks and twisted it. Then, after shaking the house key into his hand, he returned the faux stone hide-a-key to its place. After unlocking the door, he let himself inside the Spanish-style house.

"Gates?"

Nicholas set the key on the credenza just inside the door. The first floor was completely dark, save for a few lights plugged into outlets. Entering the kitchen, he turned on the light and spotted several dishes on the granite counter and a skillet on the stove. He floated his hand over the pan.

"It's still warm," he said aloud. "I know you're here, Gates," he called as he turned on lights around the house.

The interior was painted white with dark brown wood beams on the ceiling. The home was luxuriously decorated, but Nicholas wasn't paying attention to the open floor plan and decor. Instead, he was zeroed in on the sound of a gun being cocked behind him.

"Don't move."

Nicholas held his hands up and said, "I'm unarmed, Gates. Lower your weapon."

"Nico, what are you doing here?"

"I'm here to talk. That's it. Now, can I turn around without being shot?"

"Okay, but no sudden moves."

He turned around to find a gun pointed at his torso. His friend immediately lowered it but didn't set it down. Nicholas's gaze roamed over his friend. He looked like he had been in a car accident. His right arm was in a sling, his face was bluish yellow in some places from bruising, and he had a black eye and swollen lip.

"Jeez, Gates," Nicholas said in dismay. "You look terrible. Siren's thugs did all this?"

His friend bristled. His expression turned fearful. "What do you know about it?"

"Relax, I'm not here to hurt you. I just want information."

"How do I know that? You break into my home—"

"No, I didn't. I used the spare key. Remember you showed me where it was and gave me the gate code?"

He still looked suspicious. "How did you know I was here?"

"It seemed like a logical place for you to go. You told me once that you come here when you want to disappear for a while."

Gates nodded and relaxed. He sat the gun on an end table before limping outside onto the balcony.

Nicholas followed. The setting sun gave them a breathtaking view of the La Jolla coastline. In addition, his home offered an uninterrupted view of the Pacific Ocean.

Gates gingerly lowered himself to the cushioned sofa. He retrieved a remote from the table and turned on the firepit across from the seating area.

Nicholas sat across from him and leaned back against the plush padding.

"How are you feeling?"

"How do you think?" Gates said bitterly.

"What were you thinking?" Nicholas eyed his friend. "Why would you steal from Siren?"

"Do you honestly think I would've bought that bracelet if I'd known who it belonged to?" Gates snapped. "My contact told me it was in his family for years and was purchased at an estate sale. I had no reason to doubt him. Next thing I know, I'm being picked up at my shop by two of her goons and roughed up because I said I didn't have it anymore."

"Trust me, I know. I've been there."

"She almost killed me, Nico!"

"I'm sorry, Gates. Those same thugs kidnapped me and took me to her villa in Lisbon. The only reason I'm not fish food is that I told her I'd get it back. So I'm going to need that bracelet."

"I wasn't lying, Nico. I don't have it. By the time she darkened my doorstep, I'd already sold it. Who knows where it is now."

"Well, we'd better find out. If I don't, we're both dead."

Gates almost turned apoplectic. "Are you crazy? You brought her men here with you?"

"No," Nicholas assured him. "No one knows I'm here. Her men were tailing me, but I lost them."

Gates was almost hyperventilating. "So you say." He leaned back against the cushions and tried his best to calm down. Wiping his sweaty brow with the back of his hand, he sat forward.

"I'm sorry to bring you into this mess, man. This is not how I expected things to turn out."

"Yeah, well, now we're both screwed." Nicholas stood up and paced around the terrace. "She wasn't just bluster, Gates. Siren will kill everyone standing in the way of her getting that Bellasini bracelet back." He ran his hand shakily over his jaw. "When I did you a favor to get some quick cash, I had no idea it would risk my life—or put Sophia in danger."

Gates's face turned red with embarrassment. "I thought it was a sure thing. We'd make a profit and go. I had no idea things would go south." Gates broke down in tears. "I'm sorry, man."

He sat down next to his friend and gingerly patted him on the hand.

"Look, if we're going to both get out of this alive, we have to work together," Nicholas reasoned. "And the first step is finding the fence that you sold the bracelet to. Our lives depend on it."

Alexa strolled into the office with a decorated box of doughnuts in her hand. She dropped them in the break room and headed to her office.

"Miranda, I've brought your favorite doughnuts in. They're in the break room," Alexa said as she walked past her assistant's desk. Miranda was not there.

Glancing around, Alexa checked her watch. It was after nine. Thinking that she was just away from her desk, Alexa went into her office.

Thirty minutes later, she was working on a briefing when Dyan came in.

"Good morning, Alexa. Where's Miranda? She and I had a meeting fifteen minutes ago. Did you pull her for another assignment?"

"Hey, Dyan. No, I didn't. I came in earlier and she wasn't at her desk. I just assumed she was working on something."

Alexa and Dyan walked out of Alexa's office and over to Miranda's desk. Everything was as pristine as she usually kept it. Right down to the rose-gold monthly planner on her desk with a white pen with a fuzzy tip.

Alexa picked up the desk phone receiver and dialed her

assistant's cell phone. When she didn't answer, Alexa tried again.

"Nothing," she said, hanging up. She turned to Dyan. "Do we have an emergency number for Miranda?"

"Hang on." Dyan called Human Resources and got Miranda's emergency contact.

Alexa dialed Miranda's mother.

"Have you spoken to Miranda today?" Alexa inquired after introducing herself.

"No, I haven't. I was starting to get worried myself," her mother replied. "This isn't like Miranda. Normally, I speak to her twice a day. I haven't spoken to her the entire weekend. I'm very worried, Miss King," her mother said tearfully. "This isn't like her."

"Don't worry, Mrs. Travers. We'll check on Miranda immediately. It's possible she is home sick. I'll contact you the moment I find out."

The second she hung up, she turned to Dyan.

"Let's go."

Miranda lived in Northwest Washington, DC, right off Sixteenth Street, a historic and prestigious road that runs from the White House to the Maryland border and is home to over fifty churches, synagogues, shrines, temples and embassies.

Located on a quiet street, her house was a single-family redbrick home with a black door and shutters and a small, well-manicured yard and a one-car garage. They didn't see anything unusual, so they walked up the steps and rang the doorbell. Dyan pressed the buzzer several times.

"I don't like this."

"Neither do I," Alexa replied.

Retrieving a lockpick and torque wrench from a tool set in her purse, Alexa quickly unlocked the door while Dyan watched out for curious neighbors.

"You ready?" she asked when the door opened.

Dyan nodded and followed Alexa inside.

The house was barren except for a few broken chairs and a lamp on the floor. Paintings hung on the wall askew, and a plant was knocked over.

"Miranda?" Alexa yelled, retrieving her pistol from her purse. She dropped the bag and her coat on the floor so she wouldn't be hindered.

Also armed, Dyan called out as she cautiously moved around the first floor.

Once they had done a sweep, they took the steps to the second floor. There were three bedrooms, so they split up.

"I don't understand," Dyan replied when they met back up in the hallway. "Miranda never said anything about moving."

"My gut tells me that's not what this is."

Alexa retrieved her cell phone and dialed her office.

"I need a trace on Miranda Travers's cell phone—right now."

Dyan rushed down the steps behind Alexa.

"Text me the location when you have it."

Five minutes later, they were heading through Rock Creek Park toward the C&O Canal.

"Thirteen minutes," Dyan said as she maneuvered through traffic. Luckily, it wasn't rush hour so there weren't the usual delays.

The Chesapeake and Ohio Canal operated from 1831 to 1924 along the Potomac River between Washington, DC, and Cumberland, Maryland, to transport coal using mules on a towpath to pull the boats along the canal. It was now a popular running and cycling path, and picnic area for residents and office employees. There were also boat tours during the summer months.

Alexa was on the phone with a member of her operations team as they directed her to Miranda's location.

Parking the car, the two raced down the walkways on one side of the canal. Scanning the area, it was Dyan who spotted her first and pointed.

"There she is."

The two took off running. Their heels tapped out a rhythmic beat on the concrete as they dashed past several restaurants and down the brick-paved walkway that ran across the canal.

"Miranda!" Alexa yelled.

When she didn't turn around, she called out again.

Slowly, she turned to face them. When she did, Alexa stopped and gasped aloud.

Her assistant looked haggard, like she had not slept in days. Her clothes were disheveled, her eyes bloodshot, and her face puffy like she had been crying for just as long.

"Stop," Miranda croaked out. Her voice sounded like gravel being scraped across cement.

"Miranda, what's wrong?" Dyan called out. "Tell us what's happened. Whatever it is, we can fix it."

"You can't fix this," she cried out. "I'm ruined. My life is over."

Alexa held her hands up and moved forward as slowly as she could without being detected.

"Miranda, please talk to me. I want to help you. We both do," she said, nodding toward Dyan. "But we have to know what's wrong."

"I'm wrong. I messed up, and there's no way out."

She inched closer to the railing.

"No, no, no," Alexa called out. "Nothing you could ever do can't be undone, Miranda. I promise you. Just tell me what's happened."

"He's taken everything from me," she sobbed. "My money, everything in my house—things that can't be replaced. And I allowed him to. I fell for all his lies. I let him in and he destroyed me."

She grasped the railing and peered over the edge. Dyan began speaking to Miranda, which gave Alexa precious time to close the distance between them without being detected.

"You know what we do for a living. We can undo anything he's done, Miranda."

"No, you can't," she lamented, not bothering to look up. "My credit is shot, I'm behind on everything. I may even lose my house over this. I was so blind. I thought Apollo loved me, but I was just like all the others, he said. Gullible. Convenient. Easy."

Miranda said the word with contempt.

"I just want it to be over," she whispered.

Hearing his name caused Alexa to pause. Apollo Hayes. The man she had been suspicious about because of his evasiveness at meeting them. She closed her eyes. She was supposed to have looked into his background and got sidetracked by other things. She had dropped the ball. She had failed Miranda. She fought back tears as she moved closer.

"Listen to me, this is not the way, Miranda. Your parents are frantic with worry. I promised I'd call them the moment we found you to let them know you're okay."

"No! They can't know about this! No one knows about this. I can't tell them I've been duped by Apollo and I've had my life stolen from me. I can't hurt them like that. I won't."

In a split second, Miranda hoisted her leg up over the railing and was trying to pull herself up. Alexa sprang into action. She reached her assistant just in time to grab hold of her coat to keep her from falling into the freezing water below.

"No!" Miranda screamed. "Let me go."

Alexa was half over the railing trying her best to hold on to Miranda. Before she could call out, Dyan had reached her side and was helping to pull their distraught friend back to safety. All three landed in a heap on the ground.

"We've got you," Alexa said, breathless from the exertion, but trying her best not to fall apart. "You're going to be okay, Miranda. I promise you'll be okay," she said as her assistant's body shook with despair. Miranda's sobs zeroed in on Alexa's heart and broke it in two.

# Chapter 28

Alexa sat on her living room couch engulfed in a loden-green comforter that she'd taken off her bed. She stared at the fireplace, watching the flames greedily devour the wood log she had stacked there. Her doorbell chimed, interrupting the silence like an unwelcome guest. She didn't even bother to look up. When it echoed around the room a second time, she yelled out, "Just leave it at the door." Annoyed that she had to repeat something that she had specified in the instructions when placing her food order.

The firm knocking was the last straw. She groused as she got up and shuffled toward the front door. Unlocking it, she wrenched it open with enough fire in her eyes to go to battle, her blanket draped around her like a medieval cloak.

"I said leave it!" she stormed, but the rest of her tirade died on her lips as she realized it wasn't the delivery person with her dinner order.

Her eyes bulged with shock, an action she instantly regretted because they were puffy and painful.

"Andrew."

"Hello, Alexa. May I come in?" he asked after a few moments of silence between them.

She nodded and shuffled aside. "Watch your step." Plates and glasses lay over every table in her living room. The floor was littered with empty carryout boxes, along with the plastic or paper bags they had been delivered in.

As if the state of the house wasn't alarming enough, Alexa looked like she hadn't slept or showered in a week. She smoothed her hands over her wrinkled clothes.

He motioned toward the couch. "Do you mind if I sit down?"

Shaking her head, she staggered back to the couch and

sat, pulling her blanket around her like a shield. Andrew followed behind, and after removing some magazines and papers from the seat across from her, he sat gingerly on the edge.

She regarded him cautiously. "What are you doing here?"

"I was worried. I haven't spoken to you in weeks. And it's been even longer since I've seen you."

"And now you're worried?" she scoffed. "If memory serves, *you* ghosted me."

"I know. I'm sorry about that. I thought it would be easier for you. Less complicated."

"I thought we were friends. Clearly, I was mistaken."

"Alexa, of course we are. That's why I gave you space. Time to sort things out."

"Well, don't do me any favors," she snapped. "I don't need them. Frankly, I don't know why you're concerned."

"Alexa, no one has seen you for over a week and you haven't been to work. So, yes, that caused me to worry."

"I took some time off."

He glanced around the room. "Yes, I can see that."

"And you can also see that I'm just fine. Who called you? Let me guess. Either Dyan or my parents."

"Both."

"That wasn't necessary." Alexa pulled the blanket closer.

"Alexa—"

She stood. "Thanks for stopping by. You can report back to everybody that I am doing great."

"I'd be happy to, if that were true."

She glared at Andrew with annoyance. "What is it you'd like me to say?"

"How about how you really feel?"

For a second, her face relayed her pain. It was enough to make Andrew feel like he had been gut-punched.

"Please leave," she whispered.

"I'll leave once you level with me, because I know you're not fine."

Something inside Alexa snapped. "Fine, you want to hear the truth? Here it is. I am ripped apart inside! I am devastated!" She started pacing in front of the mantel.

"I can't sleep, and I can barely keep food down. All I can think about is Miranda. Her face. The fact that she was moments away from trying to end her life! She wanted to die, Andrew. And I could've stopped all this. I could have kept her safe and prevented her pain and suffering at the hands of some grifter who saw her as another mark. He took everything from her. And I handed it to him. How does that make me feel? Horrific," she cried, sinking to the floor.

Andrew came over and joined her on the floor in front of the fireplace. He tried to take her hands in his, but she pulled away.

"Listen to me. What happened to Miranda is not your fault."

"Yes, it is. My gut told me that something was off about him. So I was going to have my team investigate him. And I didn't. I was so caught up with Sophia's histrionics that I forgot. I let the ball drop, Andrew, and it almost cost Miranda her life. Everything that's happened was my fault."

"That's not true, Alexa."

"It is! I didn't protect them!" she yelled. "Not Shelley, Tanya or Miranda. I failed them all. They would've been better off without me in their lives."

"You don't mean that."

"Yes, I do. I couldn't even protect my friends. People that I love, Andrew. How in the world am I supposed to protect perfect strangers?"

"By doing the best job you can. By showing up and being present, Alexa. You can't hide from who you are or what you've been called to do. This is a temporary setback. You will find your center again."

She shook her head. "You should go. You're safer not being around me. As a matter of fact, I should just quit the business. I'm no good to anyone."

Andrew touched her cheek. Encouraged when she didn't pull away this time.

"That's just your pain and grief talking. The Alexa King I know has a heart of steel."

"The Alexa King you know is dead. She died from a thousand cuts."

"No, she's in there," he said, pointing to her chest. "You are a guardian to those you love and the ones you protect. And you always will be. No one is better without you. Do you hear me? Not me or anyone else."

"That's not true. You said some hurtful things at the Christmas party and then left me without a thought. You said I didn't need anything or anyone, remember? So spare me the fake concern and just leave."

"I was wrong," he said flatly. "I was hurt, angry, and should never have pulled away. I'm sorry, Alexa. I thought giving you some time was what you needed."

"What I *needed* was you."

When the tears came, Andrew didn't budge. He sat there with Alexa and held her as she cried. After she fell into an exhausted slumber, he picked her up and took her upstairs and put her to bed. Back downstairs, he took a few minutes to contact her parents and Dyan to give them an update.

"Keep us informed," Jake replied in a worried voice. "If she needs anything, you let us know."

"I will, sir."

Dyan had told Andrew that she would continue taking care of things at Dragonfly.

"I've never seen her this lost before. Any progress she had made since Tanya has just been blown out of the water."

"She needs time and space to heal. She'll get there, Dyan."

When he hung up, Andrew sat on the edge of the coffee table and put his head in his hands. There were so many emotions rushing through him that he couldn't get a handle on just one.

Over the years, Andrew had witnessed many facets of Alexa's emotions. Fear, happiness, desire, anger, love and self-confidence. Never had he seen her bereft of hope. It was devastating. Guilt ate at him for his part in her feeling abandoned.

Angrily, Andrew swiped away the few tears forming in his eyes. He was ready to punch something. If he didn't find a task, he would lose it.

For the next hour, Andrew threw himself into cleaning up Alexa's apartment. When she finally awoke, it was to find him seated in a chair across from her bed. A suitcase at his feet.

"How long have I been out?"

"Two hours."

Sitting up, Alexa leaned back against the headboard. She gingerly tapped at the swollen flesh around her eyes. "I feel like I've been punched a few times."

He went to the bathroom, and returned with a wet washcloth. Sitting next to her, Andrew laid it across her eyes.

"Better?"

She nodded.

After a few minutes, she took it off. She gazed around her now-pristine room.

"You've been busy. And what's with the luggage?"

"You're coming home with me. And before you protest, I'm not taking no for an answer. This isn't a time where you should be by yourself and swimming around in your own head. That's a dangerous place to be, trust me."

"I can't just up and leave everything. Sophia—"

"Dyan has been handling Sophia and everything at Dragonfly for the last week. She'll call you if anything requires your immediate attention."

He touched her cheek before letting his hand drift to her shoulder. He gave it a firm squeeze.

"You need to regroup, Alexa. Let me help you do that."

* * *

She studied every inch of his face. From the brow furrowed with concern to the firm cut of his jaw. Her heart constricted in her chest. She had missed Andrew. Everything about him. He was her best friend and had grown to mean much more. They needed to work some things out. But for now, Alexa sat in the moment with him and soaked up his strength. She allowed it to wash over her and soothe her crushed soul.

In that split second, Alexa realized that she was tired. She was too tired to think, to feel or to come up with reasons why she should turn Andrew down on his offer. Instead of protesting, she merely nodded in agreement.

Alexa spent the next week at Phalanx recuperating. James, Esther and Andrew were perfect hosts and went out of their way to ensure that she had everything she needed to rest, relax and heal. She spent most of her days walking along trails or sitting on the porch while Andrew trained the latest group of students.

"You know that I'd be happy to help."

"You are our guest," he clarified. "One that is in need of some downtime."

"And I've had it. You all have been wonderful to me."

He stopped walking and faced her. "Alexa, you must know by now how much you mean to me—and Dad and Esther."

She reached out a gloved hand and touched his face. "The feeling is mutual. I was in such a bad place after what happened with Miranda. I didn't think there was a way I'd find my way back, but then you arrived—you were my anchor."

Andrew pulled Alexa into his arms. "Correction. I *am* your anchor."

He kissed the bridge of her nose. When he stopped there, Alexa realized that he hesitated in deference to her, so she made the next move and kissed him. She felt him hold back for a split second before he was all in.

It was unlike the previous embraces she had shared with Andrew. This one held a lot more than tentative exploration. It quickly shifted into a heat that threatened to singe Alexa from the inside out.

"Well, that was…" Andrew stopped to search for the right word when they finally came up for air.

"Yeah, it was," she agreed. "This changes some things."

"We're going to be okay," he promised. "We'll figure everything out."

"I know," Alexa said with confidence. "But right now, I feel like I need to cool off."

"You've got a point," he chuckled before sweeping her into his arms.

"Andrew, what are you doing? Put me down!" Alexa shrieked. Her voice echoed off the white-topped trees as he carried her over to a mound of snow.

Wary, Alexa tightened the hold on his neck as she eyed him and the snow suspiciously. "James Andrew Riker II, don't you dare," she warned, inching higher in his arms.

"Oh, I dare," he laughed before depositing her into the flaky heap with a flourish.

She screamed and crawled her way out and got to her feet. She slapped the caked snow off her jeans and winter coat. Alexa's expression promised retribution.

"You're going to pay for that."

"I can think of several ways I'd like to do that," he declared with a wicked grin.

Laughter and taunting were the only sounds heard in the snowy meadow as they engaged in a snowball fight.Andrew gave up after one of her well-thrown missiles hit the tree branches above and dropped a mound of snow on his head.

"Yes!" she exclaimed in victory as she watched him stagger to his feet. "Do you yield, sir?"

"Okay, okay." He howled in laughter while shaking himself vigorously. "I give up. I think I got snow down my shirt."

"Don't expect me to feel sorry for you," she shot back. "Yay, Team King!" Alexa ran around the yard exclaiming victory but tripped on a piece of wood buried under the snow. She yelped in pain as she went down. Andrew was at her side in seconds.

"Lexi, are you okay?"

"Yeah, I'm fine," she assured him. "I just twisted my ankle."

Andrew tried to help her, but she got up alone. Hobbling a bit, Alexa walked around testing her foot.

"You know you don't have to do everything on your own. It's okay to accept help when it's offered."

"You're right," she agreed. "It's been difficult for me, you know? But I'm here, aren't I? So that's proof that I'm trying, right?"

"True," he conceded.

He helped her back to the cabin and had her sit on the kitchen counter while he examined her ankle.

"Looks like it's just a twist. Some ice and elevation should do the trick."

"Thanks for looking at it for me."

"My pleasure."

Andrew pulled a clean dish towel from one of the cabinet drawers and then grabbed a freezer baggie and filled it with ice.

"So, how are your parents?" Andrew finally asked while he wrapped her ankle with the floral towel.

"They're great. Relieved that I'm feeling better and wondering when I'm bringing you back with me to visit."

"Just name it," he replied. "You know I love visiting Washington, DC."

"Be warned. I'm sure Dad will bring up the fact that you caused him to owe Mom twenty bucks."

"Why?"

"After you came to stay, my family had a pool going on if we'd end up together. Dad was doubtful, but Mom never wavered."

His shoulders shook with mirth before he grew serious. "And are we?"

Alexa grasped his hand. "Andrew, I didn't know if I was even capable of having a relationship given my past. But, through it all, you've been patient and allowed me the space to figure things out. I want you to know that I'm grateful for that, Drew. I'm not afraid anymore. I want us to be together. Time isn't promised to any of us, and I don't want to let another day pass without declaring that I care about you, Andrew. Deeply."

He took her face in his hands. "And I care about you—deeply."

Andrew slid her closer to him for a kiss. "Was there an expiration date on that wager?" he murmured against her lips.

Alexa scrunched her face in concentration. "No, I don't think so."

"Good. Then I hope Jake knows that his baby girl caused him to lose."

Alexa poked him in the ribs. "Very funny."

They were still laughing when Alexa got a call.

"It's Dyan," she said after Andrew handed her the phone from her jacket pocket.

"Hi, Dyan. What's up?"

"Hi, Alexa, I'm sorry to disturb you while you're on leave, but we've got a situation."

"Okay. Let's hear it."

"Sophia was abducted."

"What? How was that possible? There should've been two teams guarding her at all times."

"There were, but we were outnumbered. The intel we received was faulty. By the time we arrived at the venue, several teams were waiting. We took on heavy fire. Two of our men didn't make it, Alexa."

Alexa closed her eyes for a moment then slammed her fist on the counter.

"Where was Sophia's last known location?"

"Paris. Not far from her apartment. She was supposed to meet Nicholas Michaux there after her show."

"Why?"

"I don't know, but our advance team said he never showed up."

"I want him found, Dyan. Send the jet to pick me up. After that, I'm going to Paris. I expect the team to have laid out a tactical plan to get her back by the time I arrive."

"There's one more thing, Alexa."

"This isn't bad enough?"

"We know who kidnapped Sophia. One detained man had the same tattoo as the men in Los Angeles. After some painful coercion, he admitted that everyone that works for the Siren has this tattoo."

"Are you certain?"

"Yes. He refused to tell us where Sophia's been taken. He said he'd be killed if he gave up her location. So we contacted the authorities, and he's been taken into custody. Maybe they'll get him to talk."

"Thanks, Dyan. I'll see you soon."

"We'll get her back, Alexa," her friend said firmly.

"I know we will."

After ending the call, Alexa shoved her phone back into her pocket and hopped off the counter. She landed on one foot before gingerly testing the other out.

She could tell by Andrew's expression that she didn't need to elaborate.

"I have to go pack."

"You can't go after Siren, Alexa. She's extremely dangerous."

"She has my asset, Andrew. Which makes *me* extremely dangerous."

He stopped her. "I'm serious."

"So am I." Alexa stared at him in surprise. "I've never seen you look spooked, Andrew. Have you crossed paths with her before?"

"No. I know her only by reputation. She's bad news, Alexa. Bad, deadly news."

"Precisely why I plan on getting Sophia back before she gets hurt."

"Then I'm going with you."

She resumed walking. "No, you're not. This was my operation, Andrew, and it went south. Sophia is Dragonfly's responsibility. My team didn't keep her safe, which means I'm the one who's going to get her back."

# Chapter 29

They were still having a heated discussion when Esther and James arrived.

The elderly couple exchanged glances as they set groceries on the counter.

"What's going on?" James asked when he could get a word in.

"Your son doesn't think I'm competent enough to handle a threat," Alexa snapped as she hobbled over and sat at the kitchen table.

Andrew's expression turned incredulous. "Whoa, I said no such thing. Don't put words in my mouth."

"And don't treat me like I'm a child who needs to be rescued!" she shot back.

He threw his hands up in frustration. "Alexa, where is this coming from? I've never once treated you like you couldn't handle yourself."

"Until now."

Andrew's jaw clenched, and an almost painful silence descended. The couple stood glaring at each other so long that James cleared his throat and would've said something, but Andrew turned to his father and Esther and said, "Excuse us."

Without another word, he swept Alexa up in his arms and carried her upstairs to his room.

"I can walk," she groused.

"You need to rest that ankle."

A few moments later, the door shut firmly behind them.

Esther glanced over at her husband. "Well, I've never seen that before."

"Me, either," James replied with a barely disguised smile.

"It looks like JJ has finally met his match—and so has Alexa King!"

\* \* \*

Alexa sat at the foot of Andrew's bed, her arms crossed and looking ready for battle. But it was the first time she had seen his bedroom, so despite her mood, she was curious.

His room was spacious, clean and extremely masculine.

"I can tell by your silence that you're still angry."

Alexa turned back to Andrew. "Yeah, I am."

"That makes two of us," he shot back. "Do you know how much I value who you are and what you've accomplished? I've never seen anyone as smart, capable and adaptive as you are. For you to even suggest that I didn't think you could handle yourself is crazy. I'm only worried about you because things are different now, Alexa."

"How?"

"Because it's not you and me anymore. It's *us*." The word shot out of his mouth like it was ejected from a cannon. "We're together now. In a relationship, and I had hoped both committed to seeing where this thing goes."

Some of Alexa's anger ebbed away. Despite her ankle, she hobbled over to him and touched his shoulder.

"Of course we are."

"Then don't go after Siren alone. Being together is hard enough without one of us going off and getting ourselves killed."

"I won't be by myself, Andrew. I'll have operatives with me and—"

"Do you think that gives me one moment of peace or eases the dread that settled into my gut when you said you were going after that lunatic?"

"Andrew, I don't—"

"I can't lose you, Alexa!"

He said the words like they were ripped out of him by force. Andrew ran his hand over his jaw as he struggled with his emotions.

Alexa was stunned. She remained ramrod straight as if her feet were welded to the floor.

Before she could get her bearings, Andrew grabbed Alexa by the shoulders and kissed her as if she'd just asked him for mouth-to-mouth resuscitation. Something uncoiled deep inside Alexa as if Andrew were breathing life into her body. She clung to him like she never wanted their embrace to end.

"Stay with me," he whispered against her lips.

"Drew, I want to, but I have to leave tomorrow. I don't want to make that any harder. For either of us."

"I just want you by my side. That's all, Lexi."

She knew he was telling the truth. Alexa trusted Andrew 100 percent. With her life, if it ever came to that.

Standing on her tiptoes, Alexa kissed him with a newly acquired possessiveness.

Some of the edginess left him. He squeezed her hand and stepped past her to light a fire in the fireplace. Alexa sat on the bench at the end of his bed and watched him. When Andrew was satisfied that it had taken hold, he extended his hand to Alexa. She didn't hesitate. He sat on the chaise longue by the fireplace and pulled Alexa into his lap. They both stretched out and, releasing a collective sigh, watched the fire.

After a few minutes, Alexa said, "Andrew, we both chose our professions for a reason. I temporarily lost sight of why I do what I do, but you helped guide me back from the edge, and for that I'm forever grateful. We want to protect people and keep them safe. We put our lives on the line every day to achieve that goal. So you must know I will do everything possible to protect my assets—and my team."

He stared at the fire as if hypnotized. "I know."

"But," she added, looking up at him, "I promise that I will also do everything in my power to come home—to you."

He touched her cheek and grazed her bottom lip with his thumb before he kissed her.

"And I promise you that I will always do the same."

Eventually, Alexa fell asleep. Carrying her back to his bed, Andrew took off the shoe on her other foot and eased the covers over her. Kicking off his shoes, he got in the bed next to her, but instead he sat up against the headboard and let out a tortured sigh. Nothing about this scenario sat right with him. Sophia being kidnapped and two of Alexa's operatives getting killed were bad enough. But Alexa was walking into the Siren's lair, and that shook him to his core. Andrew leaned over and moved a lock of hair out of her face. There was nothing that he wouldn't do to keep her safe. He had known it for some time, but now that statement truly hit home.

After breakfast the following day, Andrew drove Alexa to the airport to meet her plane. One of the men on her team retrieved her luggage while Andrew walked her across the tarmac to the plane's airstairs.

He hugged her goodbye. "Call me the moment you land," he whispered.

"I will."

"If you need anything—"

"I will let you know," she promised.

He nodded, kissed her a final time and moved away.

Dyan was on board, as was the rest of Alexa's team. Once at her seat and buckled in, she glanced out the window to find Andrew still standing there. Waving, Alexa held eye contact until the pilot announced they were ready to take off. Only when she could no longer see Andrew did Alexa settle back against the seat.

After the plane left, Andrew retrieved his cell phone and dialed a number as he walked back to the Jeep.

"Daniel, it's Andrew Riker. I need to call in a favor, buddy."

\* \* \*

It was a fourteen-hour flight from Colorado to the Humberto Delgado Airport in Lisbon. After landing, Alexa's group was met and taken to a rented house near Torres Vedras. Alexa's dragonfly pendant she'd given Sophia indicated that she was not being held at the Siren's compound, but in a farmhouse nearby.

To ensure the best possible outcome, Alexa contacted her colleague Alejandro Reyes again. Alejandro had painstakingly cultivated a network of allies from around the world. With his help, Alexa had access to resources to ensure they had the best possible extraction plan with minimal collateral damage.

After their briefing, Alexa's team would move out around two o'clock in the morning to get Sophia back.

Though she was tired, Alexa still called Andrew before bed and brought him up to speed.

"Sounds like you have everything fully mapped out."

Yawning, she settled under the covers and tried her best to remain awake.

"Hey, did I lose you?"

"No," Alexa replied, trying not to yawn again. "I'm here."

"Not for long," Andrew teased. "I'm glad you called, but you need some sleep."

"I know," Alexa murmured.

"Be careful, Alexa."

"We will be. Alejandro's men will be on point tomorrow and lead us in. Of course, we'll have the usual complement of body armor and Marena's tech, so don't worry. We'll be ready."

"Sweet dreams, Lexi," he said softly.

Alexa said good-night and hung up. She thought of Andrew and couldn't help the smile that crossed her face.

She thought of her deceased best friend. "You'd have liked him, Tanya," she said before falling asleep.

\* \* \*

Andrew hung up the phone, but he was wide-awake. He had a meeting scheduled for the next day himself, and if all went well, the Siren would no longer be a threat to Alexa or any members of her team. It was a calculated risk he was taking. One that had the potential to go very wrong, but if it meant Alexa would be safe, it was worth it.

# *Chapter 30*

Dyan rechecked the signal. "It's still strong," she confirmed. "She's in the west wing of the house. It looks like a back bedroom based on the map."

"Okay. Let's move out," Alexa announced.

She grabbed her gear and followed the group outside into the cold night air. It was forty-five degrees in Torres Vedras that morning. Clear skies aided in visibility as they loaded into a van. Dropped a good mile from the location to avoid detection, they went the rest of the way on foot.

Every precaution was taken as they approached the house from the woods. They used thermal imaging to determine that the point of entry would be a back window. From there, they would need to ascend to where Sophia was held, retrieve her and exit the building without alerting anyone of their presence.

Dyan and her team would secure the perimeter and hold off anyone advancing to the house.

Getting inside without incident, Alexa followed Alejandro's men upstairs.

The bedroom had minimal furniture, only a twin bed, a chair and a small table on the other side of the room. The full moon illuminated the area with small pockets of light, helping them navigate. Sophia was asleep, so Alexa knelt down and lightly shook her arm.

"Sophia?"

Her eyes flew open in an instant. Fear and confusion were there in equal measure until her gaze rested on Alexa. She blinked a few times and sat up.

"Alexa?"

"Yes, it's me," she said soothingly. "Come on. We don't have much time."

Sophia nodded before she launched herself into Alexa's arms. Her arms clamped around her neck. "You found me!" she murmured tearfully. "I didn't think you would come."

"Shh. It's okay, but we have to go," Alexa whispered. "Now."

Nodding, Sophia got up and put on her shoes. Her jeans and red shirt were crumpled, but clean. When they were ready, the men motioned for them to follow.

Alexa put Sophia between her and the first man. The other two were behind Alexa, bringing up the rear. They had just reached the top of the stairs when someone opened a door behind them.

Startled, the man yelled, *"Pare!"* Stop! in Portuguese.

"Move," the man behind Alexa commanded. They all rushed down the steps and were met by several of the Siren's men.

Their escorts laid down cover fire and immobilized the assailants while Alexa pulled Sophia behind her to the window.

"Wait, where are we going?" she said frantically.

"Down," Alexa explained.

"On what?" Sophia shrieked.

"We're rappelling down. You'll be okay, Sophia. I'll take the lead, and you follow me."

"No, I won't," she countered quickly. "I can't do this, Alexa. I'm scared of heights."

When a bullet whizzed past Alexa's head, she didn't hesitate to shove Sophia to the floor.

"Sophia, follow me," she commanded. They crawled behind a high-backed chair, and Alexa returned fire.

"Alexa? Are you on the way out?"

"Negative, Dyan. We're pinned down," she whispered, turning toward the earpiece. "The window's no longer an option. Sophia is scared of heights. We'll be target practice trying to get her out the window. The front door is our only option."

"Then you'd better hurry. We'll have company in two minutes."

"Punch a hole," she replied. "I need a clear path."

"Roger that," the team leader replied. "Sixty seconds."

Alejandro's men were back and crouched by Alexa's side. One checked his watch. They had heard the exchange and got into position.

"Fifteen seconds."

"Get ready to run when I say go," Alexa told Sophia. "And don't stop, no matter what."

"Okay," Sophia replied quietly.

Suddenly, the front door exploded, and many pieces of charred wood flew like projectiles into the foyer and around the first floor. Stunned, Alexa's ears were ringing. Still on the ground, everything appeared in slow motion to her. Men who were close to the blast lay either motionless or screaming and writhing in pain.

Rolling over, she checked on Sophia. There were a few cuts on her face, and she was disoriented by the blast.

"Are you ready?" one of the men crouched beside her asked. "It's time to go."

Alexa nodded before turning to her right.

"We have to move." She grabbed Sophia up by the arm.

The five of them sprinted for the gaping hole that seconds earlier was a well-guarded barrier.

Alexa ran ahead with Sophia in the middle, where it was the safest. They had to jump over a few bodies, inside and outdoors, but they met no opposition.

Dyan and her team were waiting near the tree line. Alexa glanced over her shoulder to see the blaze had spread to the second floor.

"Let's go," their team lead called out.

Everyone took off for the waiting van and piled inside. Watching the scenery whiz by, Alexa instructed everyone to check for injuries. Sophia had not said anything during the ride, for which she was grateful. Sometimes she was a bit irritable and nauseous coming down from an adrenaline rush, so she appreciated the quiet.

When they arrived at the safe house, Alexa felt better but tired. Dyan took Sophia upstairs while she debriefed her team. Afterward, Alexa went to her room and showered.

She was too tired to talk, so she grabbed her phone and texted her friend first.

Hey, on a mission. I just wanted to say your dragonfly pendant worked like a charm. The signal remained strong, and we had no incidents. Sophia is safe.

Glad to hear it, Dr. Marena Dash-McKendrick replied. Where are you?

Lisbon.

It's early there, isn't it?

Yep. Haven't gone to sleep yet. I just wanted to say thanks for the tech. I'll call when I get back to DC. Say hello to Coulter for me.

Will do. Talk to you soon, Alexa. Stay safe.

Always am.

Next, Alexa texted Andrew.

Hey, Drew. Op went well. Exhausted.

Good to hear from you. How's Sophia?

Better than I expected. I'll talk to her later after I've slept a few hours. Right now, I'm running on fumes.

I hear you. I'm glad you're all safe. Get some rest, sweet-heart. Call me later today.

Will do. How are your dad and Esther?

Well. I'm in the field, so I'll tell them you asked about them when I get back.

Oh? I didn't know you were on assignment.

I know. This just came up. I'll tell you about it later.

Okay. I miss you.

Miss you, too, Lexi.

Alexa set her phone on the nightstand and got under the covers. She was thankful for the dark curtains that would be blocking the sun once it rose.

Closing her eyes, she thought about Andrew. Alexa felt more at peace than she had in a long time. He was the balm that her heart had needed to heal and come to terms with the pain of the past. Shelley and Tanya were losses Alexa never thought she would recover from, and the incident with Miranda, while still fresh, was easing now that Miranda was doing better. Her team was working on locating Apollo Hayes so that he could be brought to justice for his crimes. Whatever it took, she would make Miranda whole again.

Now Alexa wasn't in it alone. This time, she had an ally. She had Andrew.

Despite her initial apprehensions about opening up to someone new, Andrew was constant and dependable, and cared about her in a way that allowed her to drop her guard and be herself.

Suddenly, a sense of dread came out of nowhere, causing her uneasiness. As did the next thought that popped into her head. *Dropping your guard is usually when something goes wrong.*

"Let me get this straight. You two stroll in here with some sob story and expect me to violate my client's trust and anonymity to ask for a bracelet back that Gates sold me weeks ago?"

"More like borrow," Nicholas added.

"How long do you expect me to be in business doing stupid stuff like that?"

"Look at me, man," Gates demanded. "This isn't a game. Our lives are at stake. You bought a stolen Bellasini—"

"Something I do all the time," his associate added.

"But not belonging to the Siren," Nicholas shot back.

The man was thoughtful. "Yeah, that was unexpected."

Gates shifted on his crutches. "Gee, you think?"

"If I help you, what's in it for me?"

"How about your life? You're delusional if you think she'll let us live if we don't give her what she wants. And how long do you think Gates and I will hold out before dropping your name?" Nicholas added.

"And trust me, she has spies and connections everywhere. Who knows, we could be under surveillance right now."

Gates's contact gasped. A look of terror on his face as his gaze zeroed in on the front door of his shop.

"Hey, how'd I know it belonged to her?" he stammered. "In our line of work, it doesn't pay to ask too many questions."

"Then you'll help us track it down?"

Nicholas's cell phone rang. He excused himself and went to answer it.

"Do you have my property yet?"

He paled and shot Gates a worried look. "Not yet. We've run into a few problems and—"

"Your problems don't concern me, Nico. However, you should know that some of my men are babysitting your girlfriend."

"What? Wait, that's not what we discussed," Nicholas roared into the phone. "Where is she?"

"Call it added collateral to ensure you give me what I want—Sophia in exchange for my bracelet."

"How do I know you haven't killed her already? I want to talk to her."

"You're in no position to demand anything. But if you and Gates keep stringing me along, I'll be forced to start mailing your beloved back to you. One lovely piece at a time."

She hung up before he could respond.

Nicholas shoved his phone in his pocket and stomped across the room. Then, grabbing two fists of that man's shirt, he hauled him up so they were eye-to-eye.

"Whoa, what are you doing?" the man sputtered. "Let go of me!"

"Nico, put him down." Gates hobbled over to his friend but didn't get close enough to risk a fall. "What's going on?"

"That psychopath has my girlfriend!" Nicholas thundered before glaring down at the store owner. "Your time is up. You find that bracelet, or I swear, I'll kill you myself."

"Okay," the man cried out. "I promise I'll get it back, but it will take some time. I'll need at least forty-eight hours."

Nicholas shoved him away. "You have twenty-four."

# Chapter 31

"Where is she?" the Siren stormed as she threw a tray with her afternoon tea across the room. It hit the wall and shattered. The tea dripped haphazardly down the wood paneling. "When I checked in earlier, you told me everything was under control."

The man sitting across from her shifted on his feet. "It was, but then we had a situation."

"*Your* men are the incompetent fools that couldn't hold on to one tiresome hostage. So I think *you* should be responsible for this excessive lapse in judgment."

"I lost several good men in that break-in, boss," he said defensively.

Siren reclined in her chair, her feet propped up on a small footstool as a servant handed her a new cup of tea. "Well, they can't be that good—they're dead."

The man blanched. "I'm sorry. I won't let you down again, I promise."

"I should hope not. I won't be as forgiving the next time."

Bowing, he rushed out of the room with the remainder of his men in tow. Sipping her tea, Siren turned to one of the employees standing off to her right.

"I don't think he showed the proper amount of remorse. Go explain it to him."

"Yes, Siren. Right away," the man agreed before signaling for a few men to follow.

"Mr. Riker? Mr. Livingston will see you now."

Andrew stood and followed the woman down a dim hallway. She knocked once and opened the office door. Andrew followed her inside.

A large, well-dressed man was sitting at his desk. The

room was elegantly furnished with dark wood paneling. Though it was a long and narrow room, no expense was spared. The oval desk was placed at the end of the space. The window behind it was dressed in floor-to-ceiling black silk drapes.

Above the desk was a large circular wrought-iron chandelier with rows of hanging teardrop oval crystals. Built-in bookcases flanked the desk with recessed can lighting in the paneled ceilings.

To Andrew, it was a luxurious yet claustrophobic space that seemed better suited to be a library than an office of one of the wealthiest landowners in the world.

Randolph Livingston's family was one of the top procurers of stolen art that grossed about six billion worldwide, but Randolph's father began investing in legal businesses decades prior. Eventually, his branch of the Livingstons turned to real estate and managed to triple the size of their fortune. So when his father retired and Randolph took over the company, he made significant gains in keeping their operation legitimate.

"Mr. Riker, it's a pleasure to meet you." He extended his hand. "Though I must say a surprise."

"Thank you, sir. Likewise."

"Please, have a seat."

Andrew unbuttoned his suit jacket and sat opposite the desk in the patterned brown leather chair.

"I won't take up too much of your time."

"When one of my business partners asked for the meeting, I must say, I was intrigued as to why. He said that you worked for him on several occasions."

"Yes, I provided security for him on a few overseas trips to precarious destinations."

"Well, you must be exceptional, because Arthur had nothing but praise when I inquired about you. So, what can I do for you, Mr. Riker?"

Andrew opened the briefcase at his side and retrieved a folder. He slid it across Randolph's desk.

"I found something that I thought would interest you."

Mr. Livingston sighed before he picked it up. "If this is another investment request—" he began.

"No, but it is something valuable to you."

He reclined in his chair to hoist his feet up on the desk. The chair creaked in protest. When Randolph opened the thick folder and started flipping through the pages, he gasped in shock.

The color drained from his face and, after a few moments, was replaced with splotches of red that disappeared below the collar of his crisp white shirt.

"Is this accurate?"

"Yes, sir."

The older man rose from his chair as fast as his large frame could. He eyed Andrew shrewdly. "Why are *you* bringing this to me?"

"Because I now have a vested interest."

"Do you know how long I've had my men on this? And you stroll in here with information I've been trying for years to get?"

Andrew shrugged. "I have a lot of assets at my disposal."

"And I don't?" Randolph stood up and walked over to the window. He stared out at the cold, rainy day. Then, with a loud sigh, he turned around.

Andrew noted that he looked years older.

"I don't care what it takes or how many resources you need. I want you to deliver the Siren to me—alive."

Alexa was exhausted but upbeat as she sprinted down the sidewalk and into her condominium's front door. She retrieved the key from an inside pocket on her exercise pants, unlocked the door and stepped inside.

A few minutes later, Alexa was enjoying the first sip of her favorite smoothie when her doorbell rang.

Disappointed, Alexa set her drink on the counter and strode to the door. Staring through her peephole, she looked surprised.

"Okay," she whispered, and opened it.

"Sophia. This is a surprise."

"Hi, Alexa," she said, standing awkwardly in the hallway. "I hope I'm not disturbing you. Oh, are you about to go out? If so, I can—"

"No, you're fine," Alexa assured her. "I just got home from a run. Come in." She stepped aside and let her enter. Alexa hadn't even been aware that Sophia knew where she lived much less would ever come by to visit.

Taking her coat, she hung it on the freestanding coatrack by the front door. Something told Alexa that she wouldn't be staying long enough to hang it in the closet.

"Would you like something to drink? Hot chocolate, coffee or tea? Unless you want something cold?"

"No, thank you. I'm fine," Sophia replied congenially.

Motioning to the couch, Alexa said, "Have a seat. I'll be right back."

Going into the kitchen to retrieve her smoothie, she took a moment to compose herself. Sophia was not her usual brash, hurried self, which had Alexa feeling wary. When she returned, she sat on the couch next to Sophia.

"This is a surprise," Alexa remarked while sipping her drink. "What brings you to Washington, DC?"

"You."

"Come again?"

Sophia looked like she was in physical pain. She shifted a few seconds and wrung her hands nervously before she finally got to the point.

"My actions placed my team in danger, and I was kidnapped because I didn't listen to anyone when you all were just trying to keep me safe, and I'm sorry," she got out in a rush.

Alexa's mouth dropped open in shock. Whatever she

had been expecting to hear from the younger woman, it wasn't this.

When Alexa didn't immediately reply, Sophia bolted off the couch and began to pace. Tears streaming down her face.

"I've been angry at you for so long, Alexa, that it's been hard to bury the pain and forgive." She took a deep breath. "I was the annoying little sister who was always trying to hang with my big sister and her friends. And then, after the attack, everything changed. I felt like I had a huge part of my childhood ripped from me and I was forced to grow up overnight. We all had to care for Shelley and be there for her. And then weeks turned into months, which turned into years. And I just felt lost—and angry." Sophia glanced at Alexa. "I took that anger out on you, and it wasn't fair. I finally see that."

Alexa was floored by Sophia's acknowledgment. She had not realized that she was holding the smoothie container so tight that her fingers were going numb. She set it down.

For years Alexa had dreamt of a reconciliation with the Porter family. Eventually, she had lost hope of it ever happening. But Sophia was here bearing her soul and explaining how the incident had changed her life, too. Some of the hurt Alexa had carried with her began to lift.

"Sophia, I honestly don't know what to say. I—"

Her client rushed to her side and grabbed her hands. "Please say you'll forgive me for lashing out at you about Shelley, for getting kidnapped, and that you won't terminate Ruben's contract."

"Of course I forgive you, Sophia. I'm not ending Ruben's contract, and I don't want you blaming yourself for being abducted. That wasn't your fault."

"None of this makes sense," Sophia replied with frustration and sat down again. "There were no demands when they grabbed me. I overheard one of the men holding me talking on his cell phone. He said they were supposed to babysit me while the Siren waited for Nicholas to get her bracelet."

"Did he mention details?"

"No. Just that it was priceless to her, and that she'd do anything to get it back."

"She was using you for collateral," Alexa surmised.

Sophia jumped up. "See, this is why you have to help him, Alexa."

Alexa stared at Sophia in shock.

"What?"

"It's obvious he's in over his head. Nico tends not to focus on the big-picture items. He gets lost in the weeds on things sometimes. Whatever he's doing for the Siren, it's obvious that it's dangerous and needs an extraction."

"An extraction?" Now it was Alexa's turn to start pacing around her living room.

"First off, I'm not in the spy business, Sophia. The only people we *extract* are the clients we've been hired to protect. And if we're doing our job properly, this isn't even something we'd need to worry about."

"Alexa, I want to hire you to protect Nicholas."

"Sophia—"

"I'm serious. Granted, he annoys me more times than not, he's fickle and doesn't have a head for business, but I love him, Alexa. I don't want him to end up dead, courtesy of some lunatic woman robbing and killing people to get what she wants. Please, Alexa."

Alexa didn't know what to make of this new development with Sophia, but she was just grateful that they could finally stop being at odds with each other. That they would be able to finally heal the wounds of the past.

She sat sideways to face Sophia.

"I can't, but I have someone in mind for the job."

"You do? Who?"

"Andrew Riker. He trained me a few years ago. He's the

best regarding strategy, tactical, protection and weapons—besides his dad."

Sophia launched herself at Alexa.

"Thank you," she cried.

"It's okay." Alexa patted her back while trying to sit them both upright. "I'll set everything up with Andrew. Nicholas will be in good hands, I promise."

Nodding, Sophia went to stand up, but Alexa stopped her.

"Wait, before you go." Alexa took a deep breath and forged ahead before she got cold feet. "I wanted to ask you how Shelley is doing. I've hesitated to ask because I didn't want to cause you any pain. And I've also been too chicken to inquire," Alexa confessed.

"It's okay, Alexa. I think it's time to talk about it anyway. Shelley has good and bad days." Sophia sighed. "But she is taking care of herself. She is a gardener and landscape designer. Shelley says that she feels most herself when working with the soil and in nature."

"She always loved it," Alexa added. "I'm glad she's doing something that brings her joy."

"It's been hard for her, Alexa. Mom hovering all the time hasn't helped." Sophia's expression turned sad. "What happened put such a drain on our family. I thought my parents would divorce from the strain. But they didn't. It seems like we all turned a corner. Each in our way."

"You don't know how happy I am to hear that Shelley is—doing well. I know it's not perfect, but she's dealing with what happened on her terms. In her way. Shelley is a survivor."

Sophia glanced at Alexa and smiled. "And so are you."

# Chapter 32

"Are you sure this is gonna work?"

"Relax, Gates. We have a plan. We stick to it, and we'll be good."

"I don't know if breaking in is the best way to go about this. Why not level with the guy and make him a counter-offer?"

"Do you have sixty-three thousand dollars to give this dude in exchange for the Siren's bracelet? Because I don't."

"I'm sure he doesn't know its true value." Gates rubbed his bearded jaw. "Maybe we could lowball him?"

"Neither one of us has the cash to be waving under his nose nor the time to barter. Have you forgotten about Sophia? The clock is ticking, Gates. I put her in danger, now I have to make this right, and the fastest way to do that is to steal the Bellasini. Now, are you going to help me or not?"

Gates shifted on his feet so long that Nicholas glared at him.

"Okay, okay. Yes, I'm going to help. I almost died once because of this stupid bracelet. I'm not about to make it easy for the Siren to do it again."

"Good." Nicholas lightly punched Gates in the arm. When he instantly grimaced, he apologized.

"Sorry, man. Now, let's get back to work. Shine a light on the lock, please."

Gates reached into the bag he was holding and retrieved a penlight. He turned it on and aimed the beam just above the lock.

"You sure you don't want me to do that?"

Nicholas looked up. "Have you suddenly discovered how to pick a lock with one hand?"

Gates grimaced. "Sorry, I forgot. I'm nervous." His gaze darted behind them and to the left and right.

It took Nicholas several tries, but eventually, the back door opened. Dousing the light, Gates handed his friend the bag and followed him inside.

Several night-lights were plugged into the outlets as they walked through the kitchen and down the hallway, so they didn't need flashlights.

Nicholas turned to Gates and whispered, "Where did your contact tell us to go?"

His friend retrieved a piece of paper out of his pocket. He leaned against the wall for support. Gates beamed the light on the makeshift map and instructions by taking the flashlight out of his bag.

Suddenly, rapid beeping was heard throughout the first floor.

"He's got an alarm." Nicholas scanned the area for the keypad. Then, spotting it, he rushed to the front door. "What's the code to disarm it?"

"Hang on. I'm looking," Gates called out.

"We've got forty-five seconds left. Hurry it up."

Frantically, Nicholas was watching the time count down. "Gates," he called over his shoulder. "Ten seconds."

When his buddy didn't reply, he yelled, "Gates!"

"Five, two, six, one."

Punching the keypad, Nicholas entered the numbers and the disarm button. The beeping ceased, and the pad turned green. He blew a breath out in relief.

Gates came up behind Nicholas. "Man, I just aged about three years." He headed for the steps. "He keeps the valuables in a guest room safe."

Nicholas hurried up the stairs while Gates took his time. Once he'd made the second landing, he turned right and headed down the hallway.

"First door on the left," Gates called up the stairs.

Scanning the room with a penlight, Nicholas spotted a bronze statue on the desk.

"That should be the Greek Spartan King Leonidas," Gates called from the doorway.

"It is. Now what?"

"Rotate the arm with the spear forty-five degrees and then back to its original position. Behind that painting is a wall safe. Key in five, four, six, six. It spells lion."

Nicholas shook his head. "This guy isn't that original."

He did as Gates instructed, and the safe opened without incident. Nicholas grabbed the bracelet and ignored the cash, loose diamonds and other jewelry pieces. Next, he closed the safe and pushed the painting back in place.

"Let's get out of here," Nicholas remarked while placing the Bellasini in a small velvet box.

"You're not going anywhere," a male voice declared.

Nicholas and Gates turned around to find a man holding a pistol blocking their path.

He was tall and was wearing a double-breasted gray suit with a purple silk tie and black dress shoes. He looked like he was going out for a night on the town instead of standing there pointing a gun at them. He was graying at the temples, but everywhere else his hair was black. His face was mottled red with anger.

"Give me one reason I shouldn't kill you both where you stand."

Gates opened his mouth to speak, but Nicholas said, "The Siren."

The man was visibly shaken but didn't lower the gun. Instead, he moved across the room to stand behind his desk. He dropped into the chair heavily but kept the gun trained on Nicholas and Gates. He motioned for them to sit on the couch.

"What does she have to do with this?"

Nicholas shrugged. "Well, she wants the bracelet back that you stole and won't stop until she gets it."

The color drained from his face. "I didn't steal anything. I purchased that bracelet—"

"From the man that stole it from her," Nicholas replied. "Do you think she'll care that you have a receipt?"

"I don't believe you." He motioned toward Gates. "Don't tell me he works for the Siren?"

"No, I'm the guy who had the misfortune of standing next to her when she discovered her eighteenth-century Bellasini bracelet had been stolen," Gates chimed in. "But I was lucky. The guy who gave up your broker's name, not so much."

*"What?"* The man began to sweat. His gaze darted frantically between them.

"This isn't what I signed up for. I have a wife and kids." He reengaged the safety before setting the gun on the desk. "Take it and leave."

With Nicholas on his heels, Gates hurried on crutches as quickly as he could.

When they returned to the car, Nicholas started the engine but didn't immediately pull off. Instead, he leaned his head on the steering wheel.

Gates placed a hand on his shoulder. "Nico, are you okay?"

He ran a hand over his face. "That was close," he exclaimed. His voice shook with emotion. "We could've been killed, Gates."

"Tell me something I don't know. And for me, it's been twice!"


Hours later, Nicholas let himself into the loft-style condominium he shared with Sophia. Located near Canal Saint-Martin in the tenth arrondissement, it was in one of the hipper areas in Paris. Sophia had picked it because there were many artisanal boulangeries, or bakeries, coffee shops and fashion designer boutiques nearby.

He loved the exposed wood beams, cherrywood floors, open floor plan and floor-to-ceiling windows in every room.

Opening the door, Nicholas trudged inside, dragging his luggage behind him. After he closed and locked the door, he turned on the hall light to illuminate the way into the kitchen so he could get a glass of water.

He strolled into the dark living room. Groping at the wall, he found the light switch and flicked it on.

"Jeez," he yelled at the sight of a man sitting in a chair by the window. The glass he was holding crashed to the floor.

"Who are you? What are you doing in my apartment?" Nicholas said, overly loud.

"Waiting for you."

"I see that, but who are you? Did the Siren send you?"

Before the stranger could answer, Nicholas ran out of the room. Moments later, he returned with a butcher knife in his hand.

"Start talking," he said, brandishing the meat cleaver in front of him.

"I'm Andrew Riker. Your new guardian angel."

"My what?"

"I've been hired to protect you."

Andrew was about to stand, but Nicholas held the knife out and backed up. "Uh-uh. Not yet. By whom?"

"Your girlfriend, Sophia. She thinks you need safeguarding. Considering the company you've been keeping lately, she's not wrong."

Now that Nicholas was less rattled, he stepped around the broken glass and water and went to sit on the edge of the couch. He ran a shaky hand through his hair.

"I can't take too many more surprises," he muttered. "Start talking, and hurry to the part where I don't call the police or run for my life."

"Trust me. You wouldn't reach the phone—or the door."

Nicholas set the knife down on the coffee table and

stared at Andrew. "And that's supposed to help ease my mind?"

"Sophia knows everything, Nicholas. So now would be a good time to disclose how you got caught up with one of Europe's most notorious criminals."

"Look, I don't mean to be rude— Wait, why am I apologizing? You're the one breaking and entering. So why don't *you* start talking?"

Andrew stood up and began walking around the room. He picked up pictures and other decorative items as he went. "As I said, I was hired by your girlfriend because she found out that you got yourself kidnapped. She also knows that you've been working with the Siren to launder money through a joint account you opened in her name without her consent, which makes it illegal. Alexa King, currently protecting said girlfriend, has extensive information on your whereabouts concerning the Siren. We also know that you connected with a friend of yours, Gates Budreau, who dabbles in stolen goods. Sophia was recently kidnapped and extracted by Alexa's team, which I'm sure you knew by your facial expression. So we can conclude that she was taken to use as collateral to blackmail you into continuing to help the Siren. And by the looks of your buddy Gates, you've been much more helpful than he has. How am I doing so far?"

"On target," Nicholas replied grudgingly. He got up and went into the kitchen. Upon return, he carried a wastebasket, a roll of paper towels, and a small broom and dustpan. Kneeling, he began cleaning the mess.

"Gates asked me to do a favor and give a fake bracelet to a guy who purchased it for his wife," Nicholas explained while sweeping. "My job was to deliver it to the man and collect the payment while the original Bellasini bracelet was sold to a fence, or broker if you will, that Gates knew. But then he sold it to a collector."

"So the collector has it?"

Nicholas hedged. "Not exactly."

"Then what exactly? And I'd be truthful if I were you. Your life depends on my knowing all the facts."

He dumped the glass shards into the trash can. "Gates and I broke into his house to steal it. He caught us, but we convinced him we were working for the Siren and his life was in danger, so he gave it to us without a fuss."

Andrew nodded. "Anything else?"

"No, that about covers it."

"Nobody is safe until she gets that bracelet back."

"I know that. The Siren almost killed Gates over it, and I think she did kill a few of her men over losing it in the first place. Trust me, the last thing I want to do is keep this death trap, but I need to ensure that once she gets it, there are no more threats, kidnappings or retaliation against me, Sophia or Gates."

Andrew picked up his phone and dialed a number.

Nicholas glared at him. "What are you doing? I just came clean about the entire mess, and now is the ideal time you want to be making a phone call?"

"It's a perfect time," Andrew countered. "Sophia is well protected at Dragonfly, and I'm calling in a team to keep you and Gates safe while I go strike a deal with the Siren. Then we'll rendezvous with Alexa when I return."

"I don't think that's wise, dude. I don't know you that well, but you seem like a nice enough guy. I'd hate for you to do something that may get you killed."

"Thank you, Nicholas. I appreciate that, but this is what I do for a living, so relax."

With that, Andrew stepped away to make his phone call.

"Don't worry, man, relax," he mimicked Andrew's voice. "Yeah, I'm sure that's what the Siren's men said before they went headfirst over the Pearl Tower."

# Chapter 33

Andrew arrived in Lisbon without incident. A man was holding his name on a sign at Baggage Claim.

"I'm Andrew Riker," he announced as he walked up.

The man nodded. "Follow me."

His guide didn't bother with the pleasantries, which suited Andrew just fine. He didn't want to be here any more than the man wanted to be escorting him around Lisbon.

"Two necessary evils," Andrew said under his breath.

Once they were in the sedan and on their way, Andrew glanced at his watch. He was supposed to check in with Alexa in two hours. He wasn't looking forward to that conversation. Leaning against the plush leather seat, Andrew folded his arms across his chest and closed his eyes. He was tired, hungry and worried about his next conversation with Alexa. She would be livid.

She knew nothing about his plan to make a deal with the Siren. Andrew knew her reputation. She was deadly and wouldn't hesitate to dispose of anyone in her path. But he had a mission to complete, and there was no going back. Soon he'd tell Alexa of his plans, and then all hell would break loose. She'd be angry at him for keeping his operation from her, but it couldn't be helped. He'd sought out Randolph Livingston because of his resources. Andrew couldn't risk Alexa falling prey to the Siren's machinations. Most of them proved deadly, and if anything happened to Alexa…

Andrew stopped. He couldn't even finish his thought. She was too important to him to lose—end of story.

The driver didn't bother announcing that they'd arrived. Instead, he merely drove up the circular driveway and parked the car.

A man immediately stepped up and opened the door.

"Good evening, sir. Welcome to the Hotel Beleza."

Andrew got out of the car and buttoned his suit jacket. "Thank you."

The porter glanced at the trunk.

"Do you have any luggage, sir?"

"No, I don't. I'm just here for a meeting."

"Understood. If you step inside, a staff member can assist you."

Andrew stopped short when he reached the other side of the glass doors.

He could understand why the hotel was named "Beauty." The furnishings were decorated in warm tones of cream and gold. The furniture was cream with Tuscan brown wood for the arms and legs of the sofas and chairs and the tables throughout the reception area. The chandeliers were crystal, and the light bounced off the delicate gold chargers on the tables holding potted plants.

"Good evening, sir. How may I help you?"

"My name is Andrew Riker. I have a meeting with—"

"Of course, Mr. Riker. Please follow me."

The woman took him down a long hallway and through large French doors into a greenhouse. Andrew glanced around at the tropical plants.

He spotted a woman sitting on a stone bench. She was wearing a flowing kimono-style cardigan with a peacock feather design and form-fitting black pants. There was a small table next to her with a tea service and a tray of finger sandwiches and bite-size desserts. Siren was sipping tea when Andrew approached.

"Don't you just love teatime? It's so relaxing and civilized."

"Siren, I presume?"

"Yes." She set her cup down and observed him with mild interest. "What can I do for you, Mr. Riker? Do be seated. I don't like anyone standing over me."

He lowered himself in the chair next to her tea set. He waved away the proffered tea.

"It's what I can do for you that counts," he replied. He reached into his pocket, and out of nowhere, several men appeared with weapons drawn.

"Nice and slow, Mr. Riker. My men don't like sudden movements."

"So I see." Andrew retrieved his cell phone and flipped through several pages before handing it to the Siren.

"You arranged for this meeting to show me what?" she laughed. "A selfie?"

"In a manner of speaking. This picture was taken yesterday."

When she saw the image, the Siren's expression turned from amusement to menacing in seconds. "This is a dangerous game you're playing, Mr. Riker. I don't take kindly to anyone dangling my property over my head like a carrot. Especially someone I don't know."

Andrew retrieved his phone. "From what I've heard, you enjoy a good negotiation. So do I, provided it doesn't end in death."

The Siren tossed her head back and let out a boisterous laugh. "I like you, Riker. You have a sense of humor. That's an asset. Still, it takes extreme guts or stupidity to come here yourself."

He allowed himself a slight smirk. "Who says I'm alone?"

She nodded and then turned to her bodyguard. He retrieved a card from his pocket and handed it to Andrew.

"This is my address. I want my Bellasini in my hand no later than Friday."

"That's in three days."

"Not beyond you, I would think, considering you just showed me a picture of it." The Siren set her cup down and stood. "Don't keep me waiting, Mr. Riker. My patience is not inexhaustible."

Before Andrew could respond, she and her men swept past him and out of the door.

"Three days, huh." He needed to brief Alexa and then arrange to drop off the Siren's bracelet. A moment of discomfort washed over him as he anticipated her reaction to him seeking a known killer out to make a deal.

Andrew retrieved his cell phone from his pocket and made a call.

"It's me," he said, striding out the door and down the hall toward the lobby. "There's been a change in plans. Let the captain know that we're heading to Washington, DC." Ending the call, Andrew got back into the sedan and left.

The Siren observed Andrew's car drive away.

She tapped the headrest in front of her and the driver eased the black sedan out of its parking space and down the long driveway.

"I want someone monitoring Mr. Riker at all times," she told the man sitting next to her. "He's adorable, but I don't trust him. I want him watched 24/7. If he sneezes, I want to know about it. Is that clear?"

"Of course," her bodyguard replied. "I'll see to it personally."

The Siren settled against the buttery soft leather seat and gazed at the lights whizzing by her window. She suddenly looked much older than her forty-five years. Grasping at her head, she pulled the pearl Kanzashi hairpins from the tightly wound bun. Her red hair unraveled and cascaded down her shoulders. She tapped the elegant pin against her thigh. "Fair warning," she said almost as an afterthought. "I'm holding you responsible if anything goes wrong."

Her bodyguard swallowed loudly. "Understood."

Alexa strolled through the glass doors and into the lobby of the Salamander hotel in Washington, DC, and headed straight for Check-In. It was almost eight o'clock at night, and the reception area was buzzing with patrons. Oblivious to the comings and goings and the people chatting away in the elegantly furnished reception area, there was only one thing on Alexa's mind. Andrew.

She had missed him with an intensity that was overwhelming at times and brought her to a major decision. Talking to Andrew on the phone and sharing texts between missions wasn't enough. Tonight, Alexa would show Andrew that she was ready to take their relationship to the next level. She wanted him—all of him.

Alexa had spared no expense getting ready for their date night. She had spent most of the day at a spa getting pampered. There wasn't one inch of her body that hadn't been massaged, buffed and well-oiled. She had also treated herself to a manicure, pedicure, waxing and hairdo. Alexa was so relaxed, she had fallen asleep twice during her services.

"Hello, Miss King," one of the staff replied warmly. "Welcome back. I'll be with you in just a moment."

She waited patiently while the staff member finished up with a customer.

It was cold and overcast outside with a few indications that they might get some snow. Alexa took a few moments to remove her black leather gloves and loosen her black velvet wrap. Her excitement was practically bubbling over. Alexa's foot tapped an absent-minded tune on the marble floor while she waiting for Benny to finish helping a guest.

Benny finally glanced up to give Alexa his full attention. "Wow, you look amazing, Miss King! How can I be of service?"

Alexa smiled at the compliment. "Thank you, Benny. And it's nice to see you again."

"The pleasure is all mine, Miss King," he said warmly. Suddenly, he glanced around. "Are you on duty?"

"Not today," Alexa said with a grin. "I'm meeting my boyfriend here for dinner."

Benny's mouth dropped before he could catch himself. "Pardon me, Miss King, but did you say—"

"Yes, I did." Her smile was as bright as a solar flare as she provided Andrew's name.

Recovering from the shock, Benny checked for his room number and gave it to Alexa. "You know, in all the years I've known you, I've never heard you say that before?"

"Times change, Benny." She winked before heading for the elevator, her strappy black heels clicking on the floor as she walked.

On the ride up in the elevator, Alexa tried to quell her nervous energy. Now that she had decided to make love with Andrew, all the pent-up desire had her pulled as taut as a bowstring. She checked her pulse while waiting to arrive at his floor.

*You need to calm down*, she mused. *Even your heart rate is elevated.*

When she got there, she knocked twice and nervously shifted her weight from her left to right foot while she waited.

*Tonight, everything will change. No going back now, King. You've got this.*

Andrew opened the door. Alexa watched the happy smile he was wearing skid off his face. It was replaced with jaw-dropping surprise that made Alexa's insides warm with delight.

When she came inside and Andrew eased the black velvet wrap coat off her shoulders, he let out an audible gasp.

Alexa was wearing a wine velvet Bardot neckline dress. The off-the-shoulder, long-sleeve creation sinfully hugged her body from top to bottom and landed just below her knees. Andrew's gaze drifted lower, taking in her toned legs, and finally to the black crisscross-strap open-toed heels before trailing back up her body. Her hair was smoothed into a chignon bun at the nape of her neck and she wore long dangling gold earrings. Her makeup was minimal, except for the matte wine-colored lipstick.

When his heated gaze connected with hers, Alexa felt

like every nerve ending in her body had fired at the same time. She had to stifle a giggle when he almost dropped her coat to the floor when he took it off.

"Alexa...you are. Wow. Truly breathtaking," Andrew finally managed to get out.

When she leaned in to hug him, his cologne wafted into her nostrils. Closing her eyes, Alexa let herself enjoy the feel of being in his arms after so long apart.

"Thank you," she murmured against his ear. "You look amazing, too."

Andrew had chosen a black suit with a dark gray shirt, black tie and a black-and-gray silk pocket square.

They drifted apart from the hug just enough to kiss. The passionate embrace only stoked the tension circling around them.

Eventually, they moved apart so that Andrew could hang up Alexa's wrap. It gave Alexa time to glance around.

The opulent one-bedroom suite had beige walls and a sizable cream-colored sofa with seafoam-and-gold-patterned pillows. The carpet was also the same color scheme. The glass-and-gold coffee table across from a built-in entertainment unit held a flat-screen television. In the corner by the window were a wooden desk and a fabric chair in the same green color.

In the middle of the floor was an elegantly decorated table with long white taper candles, fresh flowers and covered dinner serving sets.

"I hope you don't mind dining in instead of going to a restaurant," Andrew said as he held out the chair for her and then turned on some soft music. "I found myself not wanting to share you tonight."

Alexa's face pinkened with the hint of a blush. "I'm glad you did. Everything is perfect, Drew."

The personal chef Andrew hired had prepared rack of lamb with an herb crust and plum sauce, along with herb-roasted potatoes and roasted asparagus.

They chatted while they ate, each content to enjoy the other's company.

"Ready for dessert?" he asked some time later when they were done.

Leaning back, Alexa rubbed her stomach. "I'm too full right now."

"I know the perfect thing to help you settle your meal." Andrew stood and helped Alexa up. He led her away from the table and drew her into his arms to dance.

"I'd forgotten how well we dance together," she replied as they moved in time to the lazy jazz tune drifting around the room.

"I haven't. I'll take any excuse I can to get you into my arms, Miss King."

Alexa closed her eyes and leaned her head on his shoulders. "All you have to do is ask, Mr. Riker."

"I've missed you, Lexi," Andrew said seriously. "So much."

"I've missed you, too, Andrew."

He spun her around and then dipped her. Andrew continued to lean over until he kissed her lips. "Have I mentioned how incredibly sexy you are?" he asked when he pulled her upright.

"I'd rather you show me, Drew."

Before he could respond, Alexa's hand drifted up between them and unbuttoned his suit jacket and eased it down his broad shoulders before tossing it on the chair. Next, she ran her hands across his chest and then up to his head to pull him down for another kiss before leading him over to the couch. When she guided him down, she straddled his lap.

"What are you doing?" he breathed against her lips as his hands came up to either side of her waist.

"Something we should've done a long time ago."

"Alexa," he said raggedly. The shred of control that Andrew was trying his best to exert was splintering by the minute. "I need to talk to you."

She began to unbutton his shirt. Next, she kissed a trail down his firm chest. She leaned forward and playfully bit his bottom lip. "It can wait until morning."

Andrew grasped Alexa's wrists to halt her progress before easing her off his lap.

"I'm afraid this can't. Alexa, I went to see the Siren."

# Chapter 34

"You what?"

A bucket of cold water couldn't have had a faster effect on squelching Alexa's libido.

Andrew repeated himself.

She smoothed her dress down. "I heard what you said. What I'm not clear on is what possessed you to do that?"

"The centuries-old gem bracelet stolen from the Siren was worth about sixty-three thousand dollars."

"That's a hefty price tag. But what does that have to do with us right now?"

"She kidnapped Sophia to use as an incentive for Nicholas to return it. Plus, a husband of one of Sophia's friends purchased a replica of the stolen piece. He bought it from Gates Budreau, a fence, or dealer in stolen goods, and friend of Nicholas. Gates talked him into delivering the fake to the man. Unfortunately, Nicholas didn't know about the original being stolen from the Siren until she had him kidnapped and brought to Torre de Pérolas."

"So, when did you find all this out?"

"After Sophia hired me to protect Nicholas, I insisted on full disclosure. So he told me everything, including him and his friend Gates breaking into the house of the guy that purchased the original."

"He did *what*?"

"Yeah. Luckily for them, Nicholas is quick on his toes and convinced the guy the Siren sent him. That was all he needed to hear, and he gave up the bracelet."

"So where is it now?"

"I have it."

Alexa frowned. "Why?"

"That's what I went to see her about. I struck a deal that

I'd give her the bracelet in exchange for her not coming after anyone else."

Andrew watched as Alexa's expression changed from avid interest to growing anger.

"You went to see the Siren without telling me about your plan first?"

"Yes."

"Andrew, why would you deliberately keep this from me? You know how dangerous she is—everyone knows— and yet you felt it was a good idea to negotiate with her or try to make deals with a known killer? The police have tried to get something to stick to the Siren for years, but she never directly gets her hands dirty. Instead, she uses her minions for all the scare tactics and shakedowns. Did you know they call her Lady Teflon?"

"That's exactly why I did it, Alexa. I wanted you as far away from the Siren as possible. This woman kidnaps, kills or has people beaten within an inch of their lives for the slightest provocation. I wasn't going to risk you getting on her radar."

"Oh, *you* weren't going to risk it?" Alexa snapped before jumping up from the couch. "How could you go behind my back? I deserved to know what you were planning. This affects my protectee, too."

"I had a call to make. Nicholas is under my protection, and I did what was necessary to keep him safe. Telling you beforehand had no upside."

Andrew regretted his word choice the second it left his lips. He closed his eyes and prepared himself for the retaliation, which was swift.

She sucked in a breath. Her eyes narrowed. "What did you just say to me?"

"Alexa, I—"

She held up her hand. "Uh-uh. Don't backpedal now, Drew. You said it, and you meant it. And for the record, I don't need you swooping in with your shiny red cape to save the day. I'm not some weakling who can't take care of herself."

"I never said that."

"I have a global company specializing in close protection and security," she continued as though he hadn't said anything. "Which qualifies me to fight my own battles—and those of my clients," she snapped.

Too angry to sit still, Andrew also bounded off the couch. They faced each other like it was a cage match.

"I'm aware of your credentials, Alexa. I'm the one who trained you, remember?"

"And you think that qualifies you to protect me when I don't need it?"

"No, but my being your boyfriend does. And before you try to disagree, you should know I stand by my decision. Nicholas and Gates are in danger every second they have that bracelet. I'm glad that Sophia had the foresight to ask me to protect him because at the rate those two were going, they'd eventually be found by the Siren's detail and killed. Sophia was captured once, Alexa. How long would it have been before she was retaken?"

Alexa was about to turn away, but he stopped her.

"Do you think I would stand by and risk that happening? If Sophia was in danger, I knew that would entail you putting yourself in harm's way to keep her safe—that wasn't a scenario I was willing to risk."

"I risk my life every day, Andrew. You know that. I don't interfere in your ops. You had no right injecting yourself into mine. When I need a guardian, I'll ask for one."

Agitated, Andrew paced the floor. "So, you're not going to try to see this from my side? You're going to ignore that I did what I had to because I care about you?"

"That doesn't give you the right to try to coddle me, Andrew."

"I will always protect you, Alexa, no matter what—and

that's with or without your permission. You do that for the people you love."

Alexa stopped for a moment. She was stunned at Andrew's declaration, but then she shook her head. "That's not love, Andrew. That's control. And if you think I'm giving anyone control over me, you're mistaken."

Andrew crossed his arms over his chest. "And there it is. I knew sooner or later that we'd get to the crux of the matter. This argument isn't about me keeping you in the dark about the Siren or your accusation that I'm trying to control you. It's about *your* need to control everything that happens in and around you because you're scared of feeling helpless."

Alexa recoiled as if she'd been struck. "That's not true."

"Isn't it?"

"No. It's about being in a relationship with someone you can communicate with and trust—someone that has your back."

"When have I not had your back, Alexa?" Andrew roared. "Everything I have done since we met was my attempt to protect and keep you safe. I had every intention of telling you about my meeting, and yes, I was dreading it because I knew you'd be upset, but I did it anyway. And before we made love," he added. "Because I never want anything standing between us."

"Really? Well, if that were the case," she shot back, "you would've told me about it before it happened, not after."

She brushed past him and went to the closet to get her coat.

"Where are you going?"

"Isn't it obvious? I'm leaving."

"Just like that? We haven't resolved anything, and you're just going to up and leave?"

"Yes, because if I stay, I'll say something that I can't take back."

"Alexa, if you head out that door, I can't guarantee I'll be here when you get back."

She wrapped her coat around her like a shield before she turned around. Their angry gazes connected from across the room.

"Goodbye, Andrew."

Storming out of his suite, Alexa was so angry that she was shaking. Once at the elevator lobby, she jammed her gloved finger on the down button and waited impatiently for it to arrive. She glanced over her shoulder a few times, but the corridor was empty. By the time she'd reached her car, she still hadn't calmed down.

Alexa drove straight from the hotel to her parents' house. When she entered the house, she found her parents in the family room playing cards.

Her mother glanced up in surprise. "Alexa? Hi, honey. What a wonderful surprise," Margot said. "Wow, you look beautiful! How'd your date with Andrew go?" She glanced at her watch. "Ended a bit early, didn't it?"

"Thanks, and yes, it did. Sorry to just pop in unannounced."

"Nonsense," her father replied. "This is your home, too, sweetheart. You know you're welcome anytime."

"Thanks." She plopped onto the couch, removed her heels and put her feet on the ottoman. "I didn't feel like going home."

Margot studied her daughter for a few moments before she said, "Alexa, what's wrong?"

"It's Andrew," she confessed, not bothering to deny there was a problem. "He and I just had a huge fight. Huge."

Her parents turned around in their chairs and gave their daughter their undivided attention.

"About what?" her father inquired.

Reaching for the unfinished bowl of chocolate-drizzled popcorn, she stopped.

"Hold that thought. I'm going to wash my hands." Alexa rushed from the room.

Jake turned to his wife in question.

"Don't ask me," she replied as if he'd spoken aloud.

"I guess we'll find out soon enough."

Alexa returned and resumed her seat. She picked up the bowl and dived into the chocolaty treat.

While she ate, she recapped her argument with Andrew. Then, when she was done, she turned to her parents.

"Well?"

"Well, what?" her mother countered.

"Was I wrong to get angry at his high-handedness?"

"Alexa, we're not getting into the middle of your disagreement with Andrew."

"Mom, I'm merely asking if you think I overreacted or if what I said was founded."

"I'm going to agree with your mother on this," Jake chimed in. "We'll leave you to work around your impasse with your boyfriend. But I will say that he has a point, honey."

Alexa stopped munching. "Dad?"

"Ever since the Great Falls park incident, you have been hypersensitive in a few areas."

"Your father is trying to say yes," her mother added. "You have a problem when you think you're not in control of a situation. I'm not saying I agree with how Andrew went about meeting with what's-her-name, but I agree with him wanting to keep you safe."

"I don't need him for that," she said grudgingly.

"Alexa, you are in a relationship now," Jake pointed out. "He cares about you. Andrew wanting to protect you is ingrained in him whether you want it to be or not. And the same for you. You'd protect him if the need arose, wouldn't you?"

"Dad, of course I would. But I don't need him keeping information from me."

"Of course you don't," he agreed. "And I agree with you on that. I'm merely pointing out that his motives didn't sound like he believed you incapable of protecting yourself."

She mulled over her parents' words while they returned to their game. Finally, when they were done and getting ready for bed, Alexa said, "Do you mind if I stay here tonight? I'm wiped out."

"Of course not." Margot went over to hug and kiss her daughter. "We'll see you in the morning."

"Good night, kiddo." Jake also did the same. "Turn everything off before you come up."

"Okay, Dad. Good night."

Alexa retrieved her bowl and resumed eating while she stared at the dwindling fire in the hearth. She was exhausted, and her mind was a jumble. Their fight was the first since becoming a couple, and it was a bad one. And considering that she had walked out on Andrew, possibly a game changer.

Pulling a throw blanket from the back of the couch, Alexa stretched out on the sofa and stared at the glowing embers in the fireplace. She pondered what Andrew and her parents had said about her need to control her surroundings. Her past was still tainting her view of the present. Deep down, Alexa knew they were right and that it was a problem she would have to acknowledge.

The fight with Andrew replayed in her mind's eye. The realization that she could lose him caused her stomach to ball up in knots and her heart to hammer in her chest. Alexa curled up into a ball. "My God, what have I done?"

# Chapter 35

"Sweetheart, wake up."

Feeling a gentle nudge on her shoulder, Alexa opened her eyes.

"Good morning, Lex," her mother replied, sitting on the coffee table adjacent to the sofa.

"What time is it?" Alexa murmured.

"It's a little after ten."

"Seriously? I can't believe I slept so long." She sat up and stretched. "Or that I didn't make it upstairs."

"Your dad made breakfast this morning. We saved you a plate."

Standing, Alexa folded up the blanket and laid it on the couch. "Thanks, Mom. I'm going to go up, shower and get dressed."

When she got upstairs, Alexa peered in the mirror in her bathroom. She wrinkled her face at her bloodshot and puffy eyes. "You look horrible," she said aloud.

Later, Alexa assessed the clothes she'd left in her closet. First, she retrieved a pair of jeans and a red wool turtleneck sweater. Next, she searched a few shoeboxes and found navy blue sneakers. Brushing her hair into a top bun, Alexa was almost done when her cell phone rang. Picking it up from her bed, she was disappointed that it was Dyan, not Andrew.

"Hey, Dyan. What's up?"

"What's wrong?" Her friend and employee sounded worried.

"Nothing," Alexa answered.

"Mmm, okay. I'm sorry to bother you on your day off, but Sophia is in an uproar. She spoke with Nicholas yesterday, and he was freaking out because he can't reach Andrew."

"What do you mean he can't reach him?"

"He said Andrew had an appointment and his team came in to guard Nicholas. Andrew was supposed to check in after the meeting, but that was yesterday, and there's still no word."

"He's here in DC. I met up with him yesterday, and we—"

"Fought?" Dyan asked.

Alexa sat on the edge of the bed. "Why would you say that?"

"Because you sound out of sorts."

"Yes, we did," she confessed. "And it was big."

"So where is he now?"

"I don't know." She got up and started throwing on clothes. "Andrew was at his hotel last night, and I haven't heard from him today. Hang on."

Alexa placed Dyan on hold and called Andrew's phone number. It rang several times before going to voice mail. Then, ending the call, she transferred back to Dyan.

"He's not answering, but his cell phone isn't turned off."

"Maybe he's in Portugal? Nico told Sophia about the Bellasini bracelet and Andrew's deal to return it to the Siren. The deadline was today."

"He wouldn't have left without saying goodbye," Alexa countered.

"Yeah, but you just said you had a huge fight. Maybe he did."

"Regardless of what happened, Andrew wouldn't do that. I'm going back to the hotel. In the meantime, I want his cell phone tracked and an update from his team on his flight plan."

"I'm on it," Dyan replied, and hung up.

Running down the stairs, Alexa went into the kitchen.

"I've got to go," she said. "Andrew missed a check-in with his team. He'd never do that, so I'm going to find him."

"I'll go with you," her father replied.

"No need, Dad, I'll be fine. I'll let you know if I need anything."

Margot hugged her daughter. "Be careful, Lex."

"Always, Mom."

The Salamander turned up nothing. Andrew had not checked out yet and no one had seen him leave that morning. One of the managers escorted Alexa to his room. There were no signs of a forced entry, and nothing seemed out of place. He was just gone.

Alexa went home. As she was parking, she received a call from Dyan.

"Hey, what do you have?"

"GPS shows that Andrew's cell phone is at your condo, Alexa."

She took a moment to lean against the steering wheel in relief. Andrew was safe and waiting for her at her place.

"Thanks for tracking him down, Dyan."

"My pleasure, Alexa. Can you—"

"Yes, I'll have him call Nicholas and his team," she agreed.

Ending the call, Alexa took the elevator upstairs. Turning the key in the lock, she realized that the bolt wasn't engaged. Opening the door, Alexa wasn't prepared for the scene inside.

Andrew was fighting for his life against three men. He was thrown into her entertainment center and crashed to the floor in a heap. Pictures and books that were on it followed him to the floor.

"Andrew!"

Alexa didn't think. She just reacted. Dropping her purse, she ran across the room and attacked the first man she reached.

Punching him in the gut, Alexa followed through with an uppercut. He stumbled but did not go down, so she grabbed a statue from her end table and whacked him. Then, she rushed to jump in front of Andrew, not bothering to watch the attacker go down.

While he struggled to his feet, Alexa bought him time by blocking a punch from the closest man. He brandished a Taser, but she knocked that out of his hand with a well-placed kick. She recovered and swept his legs out from under him before delivering an elbow strike to his mid-section.

Andrew hit his opponent in the nose, breaking it. The man screamed and dropped to his knees, blood gushing through his hands.

She turned to check on Andrew. "Are you okay?"

He wiped a trickle of blood from his mouth. "I've been better."

Before they could catch their breath, three additional men burst through Alexa's front door.

She didn't wait for them to get close to Andrew. Instead, she ran across the room and launched herself at the group. The first to recover, she delivered a blow to the carotid artery in one man's neck, rendering him unconscious. The second rushed past her. Before she could pursue him, another assailant grabbed her and shoved her into the wall and then the glass foyer table. It collapsed under her weight.

"Alexa!" she heard Andrew call out.

Breathing heavily, she scrambled to her feet. Two men held Andrew down. She went to move, but she was grabbed from behind. An arm snaked around her neck. While she struggled, she watched the third man rush up and stab Andrew.

"No!" she screamed as Andrew doubled over in a heap.

Alexa balled up her fist and hit the man holding her in the groin. Then, as he dropped to his knees, she delivered an uppercut to his jaw.

"Andrew," she yelled out, and ran to his side. She stopped halfway when she saw one of the men hold up a weapon.

She heard a muffled sound and then felt something pierce the skin on her neck.

Reaching up, Alexa retrieved a dart. She stared at it, but her vision grew blurry, and her steps faltered.

"No," she said in a voice that sounded foreign to her ears. Dropping to her knees, she struggled to move, but it was fruitless. Her body would not cooperate. The last thing Alexa saw was Andrew's still body sprawled out on her hardwood floor.

"Alexa? Lex, wake up!"

The darkness slowly receded. Her name was being called repeatedly, but it sounded to her like it was through a far-off tunnel.

"Is it raining?" she slurred.

Eventually, the haze cleared, and her parents and cousin, Zane, loomed overhead. Her face was wet to the touch. She glanced down and saw a washcloth in her mother's hand.

"Andrew?" Alexa bolted upright, her head spinning in protest of the sudden movement.

"Easy," her cousin warned. "Go slow, Alexa."

Zane helped Alexa to her feet. She weaved a few times as he lowered her on the couch.

"Drink this." Her father held a glass of water in front of her lips.

After taking several sips of the cool liquid, her throat felt better, but her body ached like she had been in a cage fight.

Gazing around the room, the events were beginning to return. Broken vases, a ruined entertainment center, glass everywhere, and several turned-over plants and pictures. Everywhere she looked relayed the remnants of the fight.

She checked her watch. Twelve hours had elapsed.

Alexa shook her head and instantly regretted it when pain grabbed a hold of her.

"That can't be right." She turned to her father.

"Dad, where's Andrew?"

Jake looked worried.

"He's not here, sweetheart. When we arrived, you were on the floor unconscious, and your apartment was empty."

Her worst nightmare realized, panic coursed through her, trying its best to incapacitate her, but Alexa tamped it down. She'd fall to pieces later. Andrew needed her now.

"They took him." She jumped to her feet but then swayed. Everyone reached out to steady her.

"I have to find him."

"Who's they? And you can't go anywhere just yet," her father reasoned.

Margot returned with a first aid kit she had found in Alexa's bathroom. Taking a Band-Aid and ointment out of the case, she bandaged her daughter's head.

"We need to take you to the hospital," her mother reasoned. "Who knows what those goons injected into you."

"She's not wrong," Zane replied while sweeping up debris and dumping it into the trash can he had retrieved from Alexa's kitchen while Jake assisted.

"There's no time," she said dismissively before turning to her father. "The Siren took him, and I'm going to get him back. But first, I need to go to Andrew's suite at the Salamander. I need the Bellasini. That's why he was taken."

"What?" Jake replied.

She got up. "I'll explain when I get back."

"No, you'll explain now, and we're all going with you," her mother countered.

"We don't have time," Alexa said tersely. "Plus, it will be dangerous, Mom. I'm not putting my family at risk."

"We're not asking," her father remarked.

"Fine," Alexa agreed. "Wait here."

She hurried up the stairs. When she returned, Alexa was wearing all-black tactical clothing with a backpack in her hand.

"Let's go."

While Jake drove, Alexa explained.

"Andrew has a centuries-old bracelet that was stolen from the Siren. A woman that is a criminal and killer. Sophia Porter's boyfriend, Nicholas, and his friend Gates were involved in its disappearance. Andrew promised to get it back in exchange for her leaving us all alone. Unfortunately, he didn't make the deadline, and now he's been taken for collateral."

When they arrived at the hotel, Benny escorted them to Andrew's room. Her family helped search.

"I found it," Margot exclaimed, coming out of the bedroom.

She held it up in the light. The sapphires, rubies and emeralds shone brilliantly.

Margot laid it against her skin. "Wow, this thing is something."

"Yes, and right now, it's the only thing keeping Andrew alive."

Alexa's phone rang. Not recognizing the number, she answered it anyway.

"Hello?"

"Hello, Alexa. I won't bother introducing myself. You have something I want, and I have something you want. I propose we make an exchange. Unless you don't want your boyfriend back?"

It took everything in her to remain calm. "Of course I want Andrew back—unharmed."

Her family stopped and zeroed in on the conversation.

"And I want my bracelet. So do we have a deal?"

"We do."

"And the girl, of course."

"I don't understand."

"Sure you do. Bring my bracelet and Miss Porter."

"I will do no such thing," Alexa said vehemently. "I'm not about to deliver my client to you."

"You will if you want to see Andrew again—alive, that is."

# Chapter 36

Terror ripped through Alexa, but she fought to remain calm.

"I'm doing what you asked. You wanted your bracelet, and I'm delivering it to you. Sophia has nothing to do with this."

"Oh, but she does, Miss King. She's the love of Nicholas Michaux's life and, therefore, essential to me. Besides, I have a bone to pick with Nico. He made me wait and caused me great inconvenience. So now, either bring the girl to me, or I start killing people, starting with your beloved parents, Jake and Margot. They have a lovely house, by the way. It's your call, Alexa."

Alexa's hand tightened on the cell phone. She glanced over at her father. "If you harm anyone I love," she whispered, "I promise I'll kill you."

"Aw, brave words. And while I appreciate your spunk, time is ticking, Miss King. You have the power to save everyone or kill them all. I don't care which you choose. I'm fine either way. I'm sure you'll be able to find the Pearl Tower. So don't keep me waiting."

"I want to speak with Andrew. I need to hear that he's still alive."

"Can't you just take my word for it?"

"No."

There was some shuffling on the Siren's line before she heard the one voice that mattered most.

"Hey, Lexi."

She closed her eyes and said a silent prayer. Andrew sounded tired, but it was still wonderful to hear his voice. "Drew," she breathed. "How are you?"

"Suffering from a minor knife wound, but I'll survive. Are you okay?"

She fought back tears. "I'm fine. Promise me that you'll keep yourself alive until I get there."

"No," he replied firmly. "Don't give her what she wants, Alexa. Stop worrying about me. I'll be fine."

There was a shuffle, and then she heard, "No, he won't unless you give me what I want. If you don't, your lover will die."

"He's injured and needs medical attention."

"You aren't in a position to demand anything."

"Yes, I am. I don't care how many threats you make. If anything happens to Andrew, the deal is off."

There was a long silence before the Siren said, "Fair enough. I suppose a dead hostage isn't much of an incentive, is it?"

She hung up before Alexa could respond.

Placing her phone back in her pocket, Alexa and her family rushed back to the car. Her father drove while Alexa gazed out the passenger window, struggling to pull herself together while she filled them in on the conversation.

"None of you can go home. It's not safe. She knows where you live and likely has her men watching the house." Tears flowed down her face, and her hands shook so badly that she crossed them.

"Don't worry about us," her father replied. "Getting Andrew back safely is the priority."

"I can't lose him," she said softly.

Jake squeezed her hand. "Everything will be okay, sweetheart."

"No, it won't. The last time Andrew and I were together, we fought, and I told him I didn't want to see him again. I didn't mean it," she cried. "I would give anything to take back what I said."

"Andrew knows that, sweetheart."

"How do you know, Dad?" she said tearfully.

"Because he knows your heart."

"Love is powerful and can heal all things," Margot replied from the back seat. She squeezed her daughter's shoulder. "It can survive even the most difficult of tests."

"I do love him," Alexa finally admitted. "I've wasted so much time being afraid, and now Andrew might die without knowing that."

"Alexa, you will save Andrew and defeat this crazy woman," Zane chimed in. "I know it."

She spun around. "How do you know?"

Zane flashed her a reassuring smile. "Because you're the best at what you do, Alexa. Trust that."

When they arrived at her condo, Alexa called her office to make arrangements for her team. Next, she phoned her friends Alejandro and Marena for help, along with Andrew's father, James, to bring him up to speed on the situation.

"I'll meet you in Lisbon," he stated.

There was no way that Alexa would try to talk James out of being involved in helping his son. So instead, she thanked him for the help and got to work.

Thirty minutes later, Jake pulled up at Ronald Reagan Washington National Airport. He retrieved her bags while Alexa said goodbye to her mother and cousin.

"Promise me that you'll go somewhere safe."

"They will," her cousin promised.

"Be careful, Alexa."

"I will, Mom."

Margot hugged her tight. "Okay. Then go get your man."

Alexa smiled and kissed her on the cheek. "That's the plan."

Zane enveloped her in a fierce hug. "I'm so proud of you. Now, go sweep the floor with this psychopath!"

"I will."

Jake was waiting behind them.

"You call me if you need anything, Lex," he said gruffly. "You hear me?"

Alexa went into his arms. "I will, Dad. I promise."

Taking her luggage, she waved goodbye to her family and headed to the jet. When she got on board, the flight attendant took her bags while Alexa spoke briefly to the captain. Then she trudged to her seat. However, she stopped short when she saw Dyan, her driver, Valerie, her assistant, Miranda, and Sophia waiting.

"What's going on? Why are you all here?"

"We're here to help," Dyan replied.

"You are helping by keeping Sophia safe," Alexa remarked sternly. She turned to her assistant. "Miranda, you should be at home resting."

"I'm fine, Alexa. And after all you've done for me there's no way I'm not helping, too."

"I heard about the Siren taking Andrew and her demands," Sophia chimed in. "I'm going with you."

"No, you're not," Alexa countered. "It's too dangerous to have you anywhere near her, Sophia. She wants to use you to make Nicholas suffer. I'm not giving you over to her—even to save Andrew. You're under my protection, which supersedes everything else."

"This is Andrew's life at stake, Alexa," Sophia countered.

"I'm aware, but I still won't risk your safety. He wouldn't want me to."

Sophia sat forward. "Well, it's not your call to make."

Alexa's eyebrows shot up. "The last time I checked, I'm still the CEO of Dragonfly. And my decision is final."

Sophia turned to Dyan and smiled. "Tell her."

"Alexa, Ruben canceled his contract. As a result, Sophia is no longer under Dragonfly's protection."

Alexa glared at Sophia. "What did you do?"

"I overheard you speaking with Dyan. That's how I learned the Siren demanded that you bring me, and you said no. I can't allow you to sacrifice the man you love for me. I've been horrible to you for years, Alexa. I've blamed you for things that weren't your fault. This is my chance to make amends for how I've treated you. You've lost a lot, too, and I won't be the cause of more heartbreak for you."

The captain announced that they had been cleared for departure. Seeing the resolute expressions of her staff and Sophia, Alexa shook her head and took a seat.

Exhaustion poured over her like rainwater, so Alexa took a quick nap before briefing her team on their operational plan. When she awoke, Dyan was on her computer, Sophia was watching something on her phone, and Miranda and Valerie were talking.

Realizing that she hadn't eaten all day, Alexa buzzed the flight attendant and requested some food.

Once she had slaked her hunger, she opened her laptop and got everyone's attention to go over the plan.

"We have three teams on the ground—Dragonfly's operatives, Andrew's men, and James and his officers. But I'll have operational control. While I'm meeting with the Siren, all teams will move in to surround the main house. James's men will cut the tower's main power and access to the backup generators while our team takes out their transportation. His men will move in and will be responsible for ensuring we retrieve Andrew and get back out safely."

"And what will I be doing?" Sophia inquired.

"Staying safe with the backup team."

"That's not going to work. You heard the Siren's demands. She wants you to deliver me as well, Alexa."

"Sophia—"

"Look, I've listened to your plan, and I think it's lacking one major thing."

Alexa looked up. "What's that?"

"Leverage."

"We have it. The Bellasini is what she wants most. We

keep that until everyone is out safely, and then I hand it over."

"That's not enough," Sophia persisted. "We need another carrot to dangle over her head, and that's where I can help."

"How?" Dyan queried.

"We hit her where it hurts—her wallet. Remember those accounts she forced Nicholas to open in his and my name so she could launder her money? Well, thanks to Nico, I've got access to them. We transfer those funds and use them as leverage to secure our safety."

Alexa shook her head and grinned. "Sophia, that's genius."

"Thank you." She beamed. "I'm sure her millions are worth more to her than that bracelet."

"Okay, ladies," Alexa said excitedly. "Let's go to work."

# Chapter 37

When they arrived at the Humberto Delgado Airport in Lisbon several hours later, Alexa felt secure that their plan would succeed. And thanks to Sophia, they had a wild card that the Siren would not anticipate.

A black Mercedes-Benz Sprinter van was waiting to escort them to their rental villa about forty minutes from the Siren's compound.

Their rental home was a majestic two-story casa of white stone with bright lights and mature trees and flowers. It was dark, and she was tired, so Alexa didn't pay too much attention to the exterior.

There were guards strategically placed outside. Several stepped up to retrieve their luggage when they left the van.

"Good evening, Miss King," a matronly woman said as they walked into the entryway. It was bright, with white walls and dark brown baseboards and doors. The tan and brown tiles were in a checkerboard pattern, and there was a grandfather clock and a table with two armchairs nearby. Tapestries and paintings were strategically placed around the space, as were statues, planters and mirrors.

The steps to the second floor looked centuries old, as did the wrought-iron railing.

"Welcome to Casa Encantada. My name is Senhora D'Sousa."

*"Olá,"* Alexa replied, and then switched to English. She introduced Sophia and her staff.

"Everything is in order. We have light refreshments in each bedroom, and every room has an en suite bathroom."

"Thank you, Senhora D'Sousa."

They followed the housekeeper upstairs. The older woman was short and shapely, and wore her salt-and-pepper hair pulled back into a chignon. She wore a navy blue dress with white trim and comfortable black shoes. She reminded Alexa of her aunt Ernestine.

Alexa walked in and glanced around the charming room. One of the men set her bags at the foot of the bed and left. Across the room was a sofa and coffee table with a food tray and a glass water bottle. Though exhausted, Alexa nibbled on some nuts and dried fruit and drank a small glass of water. Next, she took a quick shower. Then, not up to putting her clothes away, she only retrieved a pair of cotton pajamas and socks.

After dressing, Alexa climbed into the bed and turned off the light. She turned on her side and stared out the window. For the first time all day, Alexa was alone, and it was quiet. She took a moment to think about Andrew. Her heart ached at what he must be going through. Her newfound love expanded in her chest and fueled her desire to rescue him. She would do whatever it took and bring all her expertise and resources to bear to save the man she loved and to keep Sophia safe.

"Please hang in there, Drew. I'm coming," she murmured before falling asleep.

Andrew tried several times to find a comfortable position in which to sleep. His stab wound in his midsection was giving him a hard time. True to her word, the Siren had sent a doctor in to assess his injury. He was happy to hear that it wasn't fatal, but it required stitches.

He couldn't forgive himself for being so careless. But after his fight with Alexa, he hadn't slept well, tossing and turning all night before finally giving up on sleep. By daybreak, Andrew had decided to see Alexa and sort everything out. She had said goodbye, but it didn't occur to him for one minute that their relationship was in danger of being over.

He arrived at her condo, and when she didn't answer,

he turned to leave but heard a noise inside. Bracing the door, Andrew rotated the knob as quietly as he could and inched the door open.

Seeing two men moving around Alexa's apartment made him furious. He was then flooded with fear. Was she there? Was she hurt?

That thought prompted him to action. He barreled into Alexa's living room and began pounding on the intruders. Unfortunately, when a third man arrived, they were able to do him harm. When he looked up and saw Alexa rush into the mix, his first reaction was that he would kill her for being so reckless. The second was that he'd never seen her more beautiful. Watching her defend him made his heart swell with love and pride. Andrew had known before that he was in love with Alexa, but seeing her take on those men to keep him safe was his undoing. He fell even harder.

"Good night, my love," he whispered, and closed his eyes.

Alexa found James sitting in the dining room when she came down for breakfast the next day. She rushed right over and into his arms when she spotted him.

"I'm so glad you're here," she murmured against his chest.

"Where else would I be but here helping you bring JJ home?" he said, hugging her tightly.

"I'm sorry I couldn't stop them from taking Andrew."

"Uh-uh. None of that, Alexa. I know you did everything you could to defend him. So don't despair, kiddo. We are going to get him back. Our plan will work."

They were moving out that evening, so the entire team gathered to go over the plan until everyone was briefed and ready to go.

When Sophia saw Nicholas enter the room, she ran over and flung herself into his arms. He caught her and held her tight.

"Are you okay?" he whispered into her hair.

"Yes," Sophia confirmed. "I'm fine."

"I'm sorry," Nicholas confessed. "For all of it. When I heard you'd been taken…" He stopped and struggled to speak for a few seconds. "My entire world turned dark."

"I know," she agreed. "I'm sorry, too, Nico."

Nicholas leaned down and kissed Sophia with a passion that relayed his feelings as clear as if he'd spoken them aloud.

He searched her face. "Are you ready?"

"Yes," Sophia said with conviction. "Let's take her down."

Alexa's team moved out at two o'clock in the morning. Valerie drove one of the four black armored Mercedes-AMG G 63 SUVs that Alejandro Reyes supplied while the other teams were spread out between the other three and the Mercedes-Benz Sprinter vans. Everyone was dressed in black tactical gear with body armor, except Alexa.

"Are you okay?" she asked Sophia.

"Yes," she replied confidently. "I'm good."

A few moments later, she turned to Alexa. "But, if—"

"It won't," she replied, reading Sophia's mind. "You're going to be fine. We all are."

Per their usual procedure, the teams were dropped a mile off and continued the rest of the way on foot. All except Alexa's vehicle, which continued up to the house. Equipped with night-vision goggles, the groups splintered off when they reached the Siren's compound. Each team with a specific job to do.

Adjusting her communication device in her ear, Alexa said, "We've arrived. Bluebird and I are heading in."

"Roger that, Guardian. We're in position and awaiting your signal."

Valerie drove up to the door and stopped. Men immediately headed toward the car. Each took one side and swept it for explosives. Then, satisfied, they opened the back door.

"Watch yourself," Alexa warned Valerie.

"I will. You, too."

Opening the door, one of the Siren's men stepped aside to let Alexa and Sophia get out.

"Your driver can park around the—"

"She stays right where she is," Alexa said firmly. "I don't plan on being long."

He didn't reply but turned and headed to the house. Alexa and Sophia followed behind.

As they entered, they were patted down before being led to meet the Siren. Sophia was carrying a laptop bag that was searched as well. The man checked Alexa's pockets, but they only produced a penlight, lip balm, a key chain and the velvet bag holding the Siren's bracelet.

"They're clean," the man announced.

"This way," another replied.

Alexa took a mental note of every window, exit and person they passed.

They were led down the floating staircase into the Siren's dojo. She spotted the woman sitting across the room on a raised dais. Her red hair was braided into a single plait that rested on one shoulder. She was wearing black leather pants and a black top, and a red-and-black open-front cardigan that fell just above her ankles.

"You must be Alexa."

"Siren," Alexa replied.

"I see you brought the girl after all."

"Where's Andrew?"

The Siren waved to one of the men across the room, who left and returned with Andrew in tow. Alexa noted that he was disheveled and moved with difficulty because his hands were bound behind his back. By the thin line of his lips and gray pallor, Alexa suspected his injury was causing him pain.

He was given a chair to sit on between Alexa and the Siren.

"As you can see, I kept my end of the bargain. Now, where is my property?"

Alexa reached into her jacket and retrieved the velvet bag. She handed it to the closest man, who took it to his boss.

When she opened the pouch, her eyes lit up with excitement as she studied the bracelet. Then, satisfied, she nodded to one of her employees, who went over and cut the ties binding Andrew's hands.

Andrew sagged in relief and rubbed his wrists.

"Now, the girl."

"What about another trade, Siren?"

The older woman was intrigued. "I'm listening."

"Let Andrew and Sophia go in exchange for me."

"No," Andrew said, getting up. "You have what you wanted. Let Alexa and Sophia go and keep me."

Alexa shook her head. "Andrew and Sophia go."

"I have a counteroffer. How about I kill all of you and be done with it?"

"You could, but then you'd lose millions of newly laundered dollars—or did you forget that?"

The amused smile slid off the Siren's face like oil on a slick surface.

"Looks like you did forget." Alexa turned to Sophia and nodded.

Sophia walked over to a table, opened her laptop bag and retrieved her computer.

"Wait, what is she doing? Why wasn't she checked?" the Siren demanded.

"She was," one of her men replied. "She's not carrying any weapons."

Sophia logged in to her bank account and set up a transfer. Then logged in to the following account and repeated the action. Finally, she spun the PC around to face the Siren.

"If they don't leave, I hit this button, and your money goes poof."

The Siren's face remained calm. "Foolish girl, you can't press anything if you're dead."

"That's true, but if I don't text the branch manager an abort code in fifteen minutes, he will complete the transfer for me." Sophia smiled triumphantly. "What's it going to be, Siren?"

The Siren's expression turned furious. She let out a roar of anger, threw off her cardigan and charged at Sophia.

Alexa tapped her ear as she moved to intercept her foe. "Ten minutes," she whispered.

"Roger that," came the reply over her earpiece.

"Alexa," Andrew called out. He went to move, but one of the Siren's men grabbed his shoulder and forcefully shoved him into the seat, causing him to grimace in pain.

Placing herself in front of Sophia, Alexa evaded several of the Siren's hits, but one caught her square on the jaw, and she struggled to maintain her balance. When the Siren tried to sweep Alexa's legs out from under her, she nimbly avoided the move and countered with several body strikes, knocking the Siren to the ground.

Several of her men rushed to defend her, but she ordered them to stop.

"She's mine," the Siren announced, spitting out blood.

The two continued sparring, with neither gaining the advantage.

"She's tiring," Andrew called from across the room.

"Shut up," the man guarding him warned.

Andrew switched to German to instruct Alexa on a defensive move.

*"Danke,"* Alexa called out before implementing his suggestions.

She began hitting the Siren with combination moves that she couldn't defend.

Finally, realizing that Alexa was gaining the advantage in hand-to-hand combat, the Siren took it to the mat and tried to best Alexa with jujitsu. She tried a rear choke hold, but Alexa was trained on how to break it, and her response was automatic.

Tucking her head, Alexa grabbed the Siren's arm and pulled it down hard. Then, quickly, she wrapped her leg behind the Siren's calf, dropped her base, and spun around before pushing against her blocked leg. The Siren immediately lost balance and crashed to the floor. Alexa mounted her and delivered several blows.

Eventually, the Siren was able to push Alexa off and make it to the side wall. She retrieved a katana sword from its sheath.

Alexa yanked another of the ancient swords from the wall in the nick of time to defend herself against the Siren's attack.

Steel collided with steel as the two women fought. Each moved around the dojo mat with skilled precision as they engaged each other in battle. The Siren had more skill and thus the advantage in using the katana, but Alexa was calmer, providing her an edge.

Suddenly, a loud pop sounded, and the room went pitch-black.

"What's going on?" the Siren called out.

"I don't know, boss."

"Then go find out, you imbecile," she snapped.

Alexa silently dropped her sword and got low to the ground.

"Sophia?"

The younger woman flicked her miniature flashlight on and off once like Alexa instructed and remained quiet.

They heard a man moan, and then a loud thud.

"Andrew?" Alexa exclaimed, trying to determine the direction of the sound.

"I'm okay. One down," Andrew confirmed, breathing heavily. "Who knows how many more to go."

Suddenly, an arm snaked around Alexa's neck.

"I can play in the dark, too," the Siren whispered in Alexa's ear.

Bending over, Alexa flipped her and followed through with a hit to her solar plexus when she landed on the mat.

Gunshots rang out in the distance.

She retrieved her penlight from her pocket, turned it on and moved it in a sweeping motion around the room. "Andrew, Sophia, we've got to move."

"Okay," Andrew replied.

Alexa turned and flashed the light on the other side of the dojo.

"Sophia?"

"I'm here."

Seconds later, one of the men grabbed Sophia around the waist. Remaining calm, she fished her lipstick out of her pocket. Sophia twisted the barrel to the left and right before touching it to the man's arm around her neck.

He started shaking violently and then dropped to the floor.

Free, Sophia turned off the mini Taser, grabbed her bag and headed to the steps.

"Not so fast." The Siren slammed into Alexa, knocking her to the ground.

"Andrew, you two get out of here," she called out. "You'll have help."

As if on cue, the lights were restored, and James and his team rushed down the stairs.

The Siren used the distraction to pin Alexa to the ground. Then she retrieved a knife from her boot and slashed Alexa's arm. Next, she raised it to her face.

"I'm going to leave you with something you'll always remember," she threatened.

Grabbing the Siren's wrists, Alexa struggled to get the blade away from her face. When she was successful, Alexa placed her knee to her opponent's chest and launched the Siren over her head, giving herself time to get up.

Finding her sword, the Siren swung wide and would have seriously injured Alexa had she not jumped back.

Spotting her sword, Alexa dived to get it. When she got to her feet, she brandished it to keep the Siren at bay.

The clashing of steel against steel was deafening.

"Eileen, stop!"

The loud, deep voice boomed from across the room. Startled, the Siren whipped around. When she saw the man standing there, the color drained from her face, and her sword clattered to the floor.

"Dad?"

James was helping his son while his men disarmed the Siren's remaining bodyguards. When Andrew glanced up and saw who it was, he smiled.

"Good to see you again, Mr. Livingston."

"Likewise, Riker. Though I have to admit that you look terrible."

"Thank you," Andrew said tiredly.

"A member of your team contacted me with the coordinates. Thank you for that. You held up your end of our deal and found her. I'll do the same."

The Siren glanced at Andrew and then at her father. "What do you mean?"

Randolph regarded his daughter. "It's time we end this, Eileen."

Her face contorted with anger. "Stop calling me that," she said vehemently. "My name is Siren."

"You are Eileen Livingston, my daughter. And it's time you came home."

"I'm not going anywhere with you. And it's English. I'm using Mom's maiden name now," she spat. "And you can't just barge in here, throw your weight around and interfere with my plans. How'd you even find me?"

He didn't respond. Instead, Randolph touched her wrist. She yanked her arm away. "What are you doing?"

"That's your mother's bracelet. I gave it to her before she died."

The Siren jutted her chin out. "And she gave it to me. It's all I have left of her."

"That's not true," her father replied. "There are many things I have saved that belonged to her that now belong to you. But this—" he pointed to her hand "—was always your favorite, so I knew if it went missing, you'd move heaven and earth to get it back."

She backed up several paces. "You had it stolen?"

"Yes," Randolph replied. "It was the only way I could find you, to draw you out. I'm just sorry men had to die in your quest to get it back."

"You tricked me?" Her eyes grew bright with tears. She glared at Andrew. "You led him to me," she spat. "This is your fault." She tried to lunge at Andrew, but Alexa blocked her path.

"Don't try it," Alexa warned.

"Your reign of terror ends now, Eileen. You're coming with me, and I'll get you the help you need."

"No, I'm not. And stop calling me that. I'm a grown woman. If you think I'm going to give up my life of independence to be under your thumb again, you're mistaken, Father," she said as if the word were a curse. "I have a very lucrative business that I built from nothing. I worked hard to get where I am."

"No, you killed and intimidated people to get where you are. You're sick, and you need help," he said gently. "Please, let me help you."

The Siren continued to back up. "No." Her voice shook, and she looked confused. "You're just trying to trip me up. I ran away from that mausoleum for a reason, and I'm not returning."

Randolph signaled his men. The Siren spun around to look for her bodyguards, but they were gone. She ran to grab her sword, but they beat her to it.

"Don't touch me," she yelled when two men took her by the arms and ushered her up the stairs. "No, you can't do this. I'm the Siren. Do you hear me? I promise I'll kill every last one of you when I get the chance. I'm the Siren!"

The echoes of her screaming eventually faded away.

Randolph sank into a chair. He sighed loudly. "I'm sorry for all the trouble my daughter has caused. Unfortunately, she has a delusional disorder, just as her mother did. I took Eileen to the top mental health professionals. Her treatments worked for a while, but she refused to continue her sessions. Then, while I was on a business trip, Eileen got free of my staff and ran away."

His eyes were saturated with pain. "You can't imagine the helplessness of having a child run away and not being able to find them. I had my men searching everywhere, but my efforts were useless. By the time I heard about the Siren—" His voice was racked with grief. "I was too late to help my wife before she...died, but I have found a facility that can provide Eileen with the help she needs. One where I can visit her and help in the healing process."

"What about the people hurt or that died because of her?" Alexa asked.

"She isn't well enough to face prosecution, Miss King. And honestly, with my legal team, it's unlikely that she would. But this is my cross to bear, and I will do whatever it takes to ensure my daughter isn't a threat to anyone again."

Randolph got up and left with his men, looking decades older than when he first arrived.

Alexa held Andrew's hand. "It's over."

He squeezed it back. "Thanks to you."

"It was a group effort." She smiled and then grimaced at the cut on her lip. "Andrew, about the things I said—"

"Forgiven," he finished for her. "I went to your condo that morning to apologize and humbly ask you to reconsider leaving me. Alexa, I never meant for you to feel like I doubt how capable you are of protecting yourself, me or whomever you're hired to guard. You're my world, Alexa. You have been since you stepped into my life. And I will do anything to keep you safe from harm. It's who I am. I'm just sorry I went about it in a way that caused you to doubt my true intentions."

Alexa shook her head. "Forgiven. And you should know that I went back to the hotel that morning to tell you I was sorry for what I said. I'm truly grateful to you, Andrew, for how you've protected, cared about and supported my endeavors since we met. Because of your hard work, dedication and commitment, I found a career that I love and a passion for serving others in a way that keeps them safe."

"And *you* whole."

She smiled. "And me whole." She laced her fingers through his. "I'm not scared anymore. I know what we have is real. You were right. We can't live in a bubble worrying about losing those closest to us. I can finally let go of my past and direct that energy to my future."

He touched her cheek. "Our future," he corrected.

Alexa beamed with happiness. "Our future."

Andrew lowered his head and kissed her. Alexa's hands came up to rest on either side of his face. A few moments later, she pulled back.

"Do you know the first stop on our new journey?"

He grinned lasciviously. "Do tell."

"The hospital," she said lovingly.

Andrew chuckled and wrapped his arm around her waist.

"Lead the way, Miss King."

# Chapter 38

"Here, is this better?"

Alexa took a pillow from the couch and adjusted it behind Andrew's head.

"Much." He sighed happily. "You know, I don't think I ever told you how proud I am of you. You were willing to let me die to save Sophia. That shows that you take your job seriously."

She burst out laughing. "Well, I'm glad you approve. Though I had no intention of letting you die, Mr. Riker. In truth, I would've been devastated if something had happened to you."

"Because you realized you loved me?"

"Yes, after our fight and you were taken, it hit me square between my eyes that I loved you and didn't want to lose you."

Andrew touched her cheek. "You are never going to lose me, Lexi."

She settled next to him on the couch. "You can't promise that, Andrew. None of us is in control. Our lives could be over in the blink of an eye."

"True, but when you love someone, you give it your best shot and do what you can to keep each other safe."

She leaned in and kissed him. "I love you, too. But honestly, Drew, because of what we do for a living, sometimes it does worry me." She snuggled closer, careful not to lean on him too heavily.

They watched the fire blazing in the hearth in silence for a few minutes before Andrew said, "You know I'm not made of glass, right?"

"I know, but the doctor said it'll be another week before

you can get your stitches out. And until then, no strenuous activity—of any kind."

Andrew leaned over and kissed Alexa's lips, then a trail down her neck.

She immediately gravitated toward his touch. "You're not playing fair." Her words drifted out of her mouth like a soft caress.

"You know, there are a few things that I can think of that are not necessarily categorized as strenuous."

"No, sir," she laughed, pulling back. "You promised you'd be back to one hundred percent before the next group of trainees arrived. I love you, Andrew Riker, but those sparring sessions with overeager students can be a bit much."

"And I will," Andrew said, chuckling, before picking up her hand and kissing her palm. "And on that note, lunchtime is over. Back to work we go."

"Ugh," she protested. "I'd much rather be snuggling on the couch here with you."

"That prospect is just as exciting for me, but you know if we're late, Dad will come looking for us."

Alexa bolted off the sofa. "You've got a point. Let's go. Phalanx is calling."

They rode the ATV from the guest cabin back to the main building for their next class. Alexa enjoyed helping Andrew and his father with the training sessions. She had taken a leave of absence from fieldwork at Dragonfly to stay in Pagosa Springs for an extended period until Andrew was fully recovered. She was still acting CEO and conducted most of her business by video conference while Dyan handled meetings with new clients and Alexa's duties as the principal chief protection officer.

"There you two are," James said when they returned to the training room. "I thought I would have to send up a flare signal."

"You know Alexa wouldn't miss jujitsu training. She loves grappling with the students."

"I'd rather be grappling with you," she whispered in Andrew's ear.

His gaze could have scorched a block of ice.

"Anytime you want to try those nonstrenuous activities, just let me know."

She laughed and playfully pushed him away. Then, after taking off her coat, Alexa warmed up to prepare for their next class. When the students trickled in a few minutes later, Andrew took the lead, instructing the students on which grappling techniques they'd learn during the class.

While he explained, Alexa used a volunteer to execute the motions that Andrew relayed. Unfortunately, the student didn't understand the technique at one point, so Andrew stepped in to demonstrate.

"Be careful," Alexa warned.

"Always am." He winked.

As Andrew explained, he placed his hands on Alexa to show the trainees how their bodies should rotate in and out of a position. Next, he demonstrated how to flip an opponent using the attacker's body weight, not their own.

He flipped Alexa, and she landed on the mat.

"Sorry, my love," he said sweetly as she lay there staring up at the ceiling.

"No problem, my love," she responded with a saucy grin.

Rolling over, Alexa pushed herself up.

"You dropped something, Miss King," one of the students remarked.

"Oh?" Alexa was wearing a karate uniform called a gi, which didn't have pockets. "Thank you," she said, automatically looking down.

There was a black velvet ring box sitting on the mat. She stared at it for a few more seconds before gazing, bewildered, at Andrew.

"What in the world?" she said as she knelt to retrieve

the box. When she opened it, all the air left Alexa's lungs. She remained frozen in her spot, speechless as she stared at the square-cut diamond engagement ring with stair-step diamonds flanking the main one.

When she looked up, Andrew was down on one knee in front of her. Her hand covered her heart as she stared at him through unshed tears.

"Alexa Yvonne King, I have loved you since I carried you back after getting shot in the chest during training."

The group let out a collective gasp, each looking around worriedly.

"I had a bulletproof vest on," Alexa said, trying to ease the horrified students' minds.

"You are intelligent, caring, funny and sexy," he continued. "Plus, you truly make me the best version of myself. I would be elated to spend the rest of my life loving, working with and coming home to you. Will you do me the honor of becoming my wife?"

Alexa leaned forward. "James Andrew Riker II, I have admittedly been stubborn and have run from relationships, but you have shown me that love can be constant, and I don't have to fear it, nor does it have to end in sorrow or tragedy. Because of you, I know that love is patient, kind, understanding and long-lasting. Being vulnerable enough to give another person a chance to share your life is the greatest gift of all. I love you, Drew, and yes, I will marry you, and I can't wait to be your wife."

Beaming proudly, Andrew leaned over and kissed Alexa. She wrapped her arms around him and cried tears of joy as she returned the kiss. Everyone clapped as he placed the ring on the third finger of her left hand. Alexa peered at the brilliant diamond ring for several moments, in awe at the surprise proposal. Then she spotted her family standing off to the side. Alexa was so shocked that she yelped before rushing over to greet her parents, cousin, aunt and uncle. Next, James and Esther stepped up to offer their congratulations. James dismissed the class early so their families could return to the house and honor the newly engaged couple.

While they were celebrating, Alexa received a video call from Sophia. She and Nicholas wished her and Andrew congratulations.

"Thank you and Andrew for protecting us both," Nicholas stated. "And for keeping us, you know, from being dead."

Alexa's eyebrows rose. "Oh, you're welcome, Nico."

"You know, we worked so well together that anytime you and Andrew need operatives, Nico and I would be happy to lend a hand."

"Wow," Alexa said with genuine surprise. "If the need arises, we'll let you know."

"Cool. I have a special engagement gift for you, Alexa." Sophia grinned. "Just a moment."

She and Nicholas moved out of the way, and another woman moved into view.

Alexa was stupefied. "Oh my gosh. Shelley?"

"Yes," her old friend confirmed. "It's wonderful to see you, Alexa."

"Likewise," she said between tears. "I can't believe it's you. You look amazing," she cried.

"So do you. Sophia's told me so much about your life now. I'm so happy for you."

"Sophia has kept me in the loop, too. I'm glad you're living life to the fullest, Shelley."

They chatted for a few more minutes before Shelley had to go, but she promised to keep in touch.

"I'd love to as well," Alexa confirmed.

When they ended the call, Alexa found her fiancé and wrapped her arms around his middle. She told him about her video call with the Porters.

"Thank you," she said sincerely. "This was a perfect proposal, and I love you so much."

"I love you, too, soon-to-be Mrs. Riker."

"I love the sound of that."

\* \* \* \* \*

# *Romantic* Suspense

## Danger. Passion. Drama.

## Available Next Month

**Colton's Dangerous Cover**  Lisa Childs
**Peril In The Shallows**  Addison Fox

.............................................................................

**Operation Rafe's Redemption**  Justine Davis
**The Suspect Next Door**  Rachel Astor

.............................................................................

LOVE INSPIRED

**Alaskan Wilderness Rescue**  Sarah Varland
**Targeted For Elimination**  Jill Elizabeth Nelson
Larger Print

.............................................................................

LOVE INSPIRED

**Dangerous Texas Hideout**  Virgina Vaughan
**Wyoming Abduction Threat**  Elisabeth Rees
Larger Print

.............................................................................

LOVE INSPIRED

**Deadly Mountain Escape**  Mary Alford
**Silencing The Witness**  Laura Conaway
Larger Print

Keep reading for an excerpt of a new title
from the Romantic Suspense series,
CAVANAUGH JUSTICE: COLD CASE SQUAD
by Marie Ferrarella

# *Prologue*

*You never thought that I would ever amount to anything, did you, Aunt Lily?* the man asked sharply, his voice as taunting as he had once felt his aunt's had sounded. An ugly smile curved his mouth. *Well, I certainly fooled you, didn't I? The kid you always referred to as being such a big loser didn't turn out to be a loser after all, did he?*

Jon Murphy regarded the face of the woman in the picture on his desk.

He felt that the face was actually looking back at him. He could almost read her thoughts.

It was a big deal for him, keeping that framed photograph right there in front of him. There were times when he would have been a lot happier just hurling it, frame and all, across the room—if not into the garbage altogether.

But he knew that he needed the photograph. One, because he didn't want to answer a lot of questions about what had happened to it—people were incredibly nosy—and two, because it reminded him of his purpose and what he was doing here in the first place. Not in the classroom, but on earth.

His handsome face darkened as he thought about it. However, for once, he was at peace staring at the image of his late aunt.

For now.

For now because his appetite had been satisfied. But Jon Albert Murphy knew better than anyone that, at best, this was an extremely fleeting set of circumstances. His insatiable appetite to kill another woman would be back in full force before he could come to terms with it. It always ate away at him long before he was ready to eliminate the source of his anger.

A day lecturer, Murphy was sitting in his cubbyhole of an office—an insult to his honor as far as he was concerned—with the door closed. Even so, the lecturer was carrying on the discussion with the photograph entirely in his head. It wasn't the sort of "conversation" that he could risk having out loud, not when there was a chance that one of his students— or any student, really—could come walking into his office and overhear him.

For the most part, the students who attended Aurora Valley College were a rude bunch of wet-behind-the-ears kids, he thought angrily. Not at all like he had been at their age. He had learned early on, thanks to Aunt Lily, to keep to himself. And to never speak unless he was spoken to—and at times, not even then, because he might find himself the target of someone's unabashed wrath.

But then, the people who frequented the lecture hall where he spoke and the classroom where he taught hadn't been raised by his mother's aunt Lily. Aunt Lily who had used her razor-sharp tongue to create countless bleeding holes in his self-esteem from the very moment she had become his guardian.

Murphy remembered how stunned he had been when he discovered that his white trash mother had decided that she didn't want to be saddled with him any longer. That was when Aunt Lily had stepped up to take over.

At the time, he had been too naïve to understand why Aunt Lily had volunteered to do that. He had just thought that the woman was being kind to him. But he had learned all too quickly that that wasn't the case.

It had been his last innocent thought.

And then, for a moment, the lecturer smiled to himself. Murphy was more than willing to bet that, in the end, Aunt Lily wound up regretting the decision she had made to be his guardian. Things hadn't exactly turned out the way she had planned.

Murphy sighed, resigned, as he looked back at the paper he had half-heartedly been attempting to read.

These so-called "students" who attended Aurora Valley College, they were all a bunch of hopeless illiterates. Sometimes he couldn't help wondering why he bothered wasting his time with them.

But then, he thought, he knew exactly why he was doing this. Not to be dazzled by the magnitude of someone's brain. That was definitely not the reason why he had applied to Aurora Valley College for the position of lecturer in the English Department when it had come up.

He had come to the two-year college for an entirely different reason—a different agenda.

He had come here looking for another sort of gratification. One that Aurora Valley College had been able to provide him with.

*Several times over*, Murphy recalled with an eerie smile that would have unsettled anyone who looked at it.

Shifting, Murphy tried to make himself comfortable in the hand-me-down office chair he had inherited along with the desk. It was an impossible task as far as he was concerned. Another insult in his eyes.

The chair creaked as he leaned back in it and continued to read the incredibly dull paper. He could almost feel his eyes closing.

*Talk about boring*, he thought in disgust.

Murphy was surprised that he could read it and somehow still manage to remain awake. It was really a constant battle just to keep his eyes open.

Little by little, he forced himself to shift his mind

to the events he was anticipating happening later on this evening, after classes were over. Later this evening was when he was supposed to get together with Mrs. Lauren Dixon. The vivacious older blonde had asked him for help with her next paper. She had told him that she anticipated problems. Right.

As she made the request, the restaurant waitress had even blushed a little.

Like he didn't even know what was going on.

The corners of his mouth curved as he thought about meeting the woman in some little-frequented, off-campus location. Now all he had to do was decide if tonight was going to be the night when he made his move, or if he was going to put it off until some later date, anticipating the way it would feel.

Sometimes, he told himself, waiting for that final moment was half the fun.

Anticipation, Murphy thought as his pulse sped up and his smile widened, could be everything.

He finished reading the paper he was holding quickly, then decided to award it a giant C plus, far more than the execution was worth in his opinion. Who knew, he might want to cultivate some goodwill with this student at a later date as well.

No stone unturned, he decided with a wicked smile.